THE LIFE AND LETTERS

OF

LORD MACAULAY.

DA3
M3
T5
v. 2

THE LIFE AND LETTERS

OF

LORD MACAULAY

BY HIS NEPHEW

G. OTTO TREVELYAN

MEMBER OF PARLIAMENT FOR HAWICK DISTRICT OF BURGHS

IN TWO VOLUMES

VOL. II.

MAY 1960

NEW YORK

HARPER & BROTHERS, PUBLISHERS

FRANKLIN SQUARE

1876

62742

Entered according to Act of Congress, in the year 1875, by
HARPER & BROTHERS,
In the Office of the Librarian of Congress, at Washington.

CONTENTS.

CHAPTER VII.

1838-1839.

CHAPTER VIII.

1839-1841.

2675

CHAPTER IX.

1841–1844.

CHAPTER X.

1844–1847.

CHAPTER XI.

1847–1849.

CHAPTER XII.

1848–1852.

CHAPTER XIII.

1852–1856.

CHAPTER XIV.

1856–1858.

CHAPTER XV.

1859.

LIFE AND LETTERS

OF

LORD MACAULAY.

CHAPTER VII.

1838–1839.

THE *Lord Hungerford* justified her reputation of a bad sailer, and the homeward voyage was protracted into the sixth month. This unusual delay, combined with the knowledge that the ship had met with very rough weather after leaving the Cape, gave rise to a report that she had been lost, with all on board, and brought a succession of Whig politicians into the City to inquire at Lloyd's about the safety of her precious freight. But it was in the character of a son and brother, and not of a party orator, that Macaulay was most eagerly and anxiously expected. He had, indeed, been sorely missed.

"You can have no conception," writes one of his sisters, "of the change which has come over this household. It is as if the sun had deserted the earth. The chasm Tom's departure has made can never be supplied. He was so unlike any other being one ever sees, and his visits among us were a sort of refreshment which served not a little to enliven and cheer our monotonous way of life; but now day after day rises and sets without object or interest, so that sometimes I almost feel aweary of this world."

Things did not mend as time went on. With Zachary Macaulay, as had been the case with so many like him, the years which intervened between the time when his work was done and the time when he went to receive his wages were years of trouble, of sorrow, and even of gloom. Failing health; failing eye-sight; the sense of being helpless and useless, after an active and beneficent career; the consciousness of dependence upon others at an age when the moral disadvantages of poverty are felt even more keenly than youth feels its material discomforts—such were the clouds that darkened the close of a life which had never been without its trials. During the months that his children were on their homeward voyage his health was breaking fast; and before the middle of May he died, without having again seen their faces. Sir James Stephen, writing to Fanny Macaulay, says: "I know not how to grieve for the loss of your father, though it removes from this world one of the oldest, and, assuredly, one of the most excellent friends I have ever had. What rational man would not leap for joy at the offer of bearing all his burdens, severe as they were, if he could be assured of the same approving conscience, and of the same blessed reward? He was almost the last survivor of a noble brotherhood now reunited in affection and in employment. Mr. Wilberforce, Henry Thornton, Babington, my father, and other not less dear, though less conspicuous, companions of his many labors, have ere now greeted him as their associate in the world of spirits; and, above all, he has been welcomed by his Redeemer with 'Well done, good and faithful servant.'"

Zachary Macaulay's bust in Westminster Abbey bears on

its pedestal a beautiful inscription (which is, and probably will remain, his only biography), in which much more is told than he himself would wish to have been told about a man

WHO DURING FORTY SUCCESSIVE YEARS,
PARTAKING IN THE COUNSELS AND THE LABORS
WHICH, GUIDED BY FAVORING PROVIDENCE,
RESCUED AFRICA FROM THE WOES,
AND THE BRITISH EMPIRE FROM THE GUILT,
OF SLAVERY AND THE SLAVE-TRADE,
MEEKLY ENDURED THE TOIL, THE PRIVATION, AND THE REPROACH,
RESIGNING TO OTHERS THE PRAISE AND THE REWARD.

His tomb has for many years past been cut off from the body of the nave by an iron railing equally meaningless and unsightly; which withdraws from the eyes of his fellow-countrymen an epitaph at least as provocative to patriotism as those of the innumerable military and naval heroes of the seventeenth and eighteenth centuries, who fell in wars the very objects of which are for the most part forgotten, or remembered only to be regretted.

The first piece of business which Macaulay found waiting to be settled on his return to England was sufficiently disagreeable. As far back as July, 1835, he had reviewed Sir James Mackintosh's "History of the Revolution of 1688." This valuable fragment was edited by a Mr. Wallace, who accompanied it with a biographical sketch of his author, whom he treated throughout with an impertinence which had an air of inexcusable disloyalty; but which, in truth, was due to nothing worse than self-sufficiency, thrown into unpleasant relief by the most glaring bad taste. Macaulay, who from a boy had felt for Mackintosh that reverence which is

Dearer to true young hearts than their own praise,

fell upon the editor with a contemptuous vigor, of which some pretty distinct traces remain in the essay as it at present appears in the collected editions, where the following sentence may still be read: "It is plain that Thomas Burnet and his writings were never heard of by the gentleman who has been employed to edit this volume, and who, not content with de-

forming Sir James Mackintosh's text by such blunders, has
prefixed to it a bad memoir, has appended to it a bad continuation, and has thus succeeded in expanding the volume into
one of the thickest, and debasing it into one of the worst, that
we ever saw." What the first vehemence of Macaulay's indignation was may be estimated by the fact that this passage,
as it now stands, has been deprived of half its sting.

One extract from the article, in its original form, merits to
be reproduced here, because it explains, and in some degree
justifies, Macaulay's wrath, and in itself is well worth reading:

" He " (the editor) " affects, and, for aught we know, feels, something like
contempt for the celebrated man whose life he has undertaken to write,
and whom he was incompetent to serve in the capacity even of a correct-
or of the press. Our readers may form a notion of the spirit in which the
whole narrative is composed from expressions which occur at the beginning. This biographer tells us that Mackintosh, on occasion of taking his
medical degree at Edinburgh, 'not only put off the writing of his Thesis
to the last moment, but was an hour behind his time on the day of examination, and kept the Academic Senate waiting for him in full conclave.'
This irregularity, which no sensible professor would have thought deserving of more than a slight reprimand, is described by the biographer, after
a lapse of nearly half a century, as an incredible instance 'not so much of
indolence, as of gross negligence and bad taste.' But this is not all. Our
biographer has contrived to procure a copy of the Thesis, and has sat
down, with his 'As in præsenti' and his 'Propria quæ maribus' at his side,
to pick out blunders in a composition written by a youth of twenty-one
on the occasion alluded to. He finds one mistake, such a mistake as the
greatest scholar might commit when in haste, and as the veriest school-
boy would detect when at leisure. He glories over this precious discovery with all the exultation of a pedagogue. 'Deceived by the passive termination of the verb *defungor*, Mackintosh misuses it in a passive sense.'
He is not equally fortunate in his other discovery. '*Laude conspurcare*,'
whatever he may think, is not an improper phrase. Mackintosh meant to
say that there are men whose praise is a disgrace. No person, we are sure,
who has read this memoir, will doubt that there are men whose abuse is
an honor."

Mr. Wallace did not choose to rest quietly under a castiga-
tion which even Macaulay subsequently admitted to have been
in excess of his deserts.

3 Clarges Street, London, June 14th, 1838.

Dear Napier,—I did not need your letter to satisfy me of your kindness, and of the pleasure which my arrival would give you. I have returned with a small independence, but still an independence. All my tastes and wishes lead me to prefer literature to politics. When I say this to my friends here, some of them seem to think that I am out of my wits, and others that I am coquetting to raise my price. I, on the other hand, believe that I am wise, and know that I am sincere.

I shall be curious, when we meet, to see your correspondence with Wallace. Empson seemed to be a little uneasy lest the foolish man should give me trouble. I thought it impossible that he could be so absurd; and, as I have now been in London ten days without hearing of him, I am confirmed in my opinion. In any event, you need not be anxious. If it be absolutely necessary to meet him, I will. But I foresee no such necessity; and, as Junius says, I never will give a proof of my spirit at the expense of my understanding.

Ever yours most truly,　　　T. B. Macaulay.

London, August 14th, 1838.

Dear Napier,—Your old friend Wallace and I have been pretty near exchanging shots. However, all is accommodated, and, I think, quite unexceptionably. The man behaved much better to me than he did to you. Perhaps time has composed his feelings. He had, at all events, the advantage of being in good hands. He sent me by Tom Steele—a furious O'Connellite, but a gentleman, a man of honor, and, on this occasion at least, a man of temper—a challenge very properly worded. He accounted, handsomely enough, for the delay by saying that my long absence, and the recent loss in my family, prevented him from applying to me immediately on my return. I put the matter into Lord Strafford's hands. I had, to tell you the truth, no notion that a meeting could be avoided; for the man behaved so obstinately well that there was no possibility of taking Empson's advice, and sending for the police; and, though I was quite ready to disclaim all intention of giving personal offense, and to declare that, when I wrote the review, I was ignorant of Mr. Wallace's existence, I could not make any apology, or express the least regret, for having used strong language in defense of Mackintosh. Lord Strafford quite approved of my resolution. But he proposed a course which had never occurred to me; which at once removed all scruples on my side; and which, to my great surprise, Steele and Wallace adopted without a moment's hesitation. This was that Wallace should make a preliminary declaration that he meant, by his memoir, nothing disrespectful or unkind to Mackintosh, but the direct contrary; and that then I should declare that, in consequence of Mr. Wallace's declaration, I was ready to express my regret if I had used any language that could be deemed personally offensive. This way of settling the business appeared to both Lord Strafford and Rice perfectly honorable; and I was of the same mind; for certainly the language which I used could be justified only on the ground that Wallace had used Mackintosh ill; and when Wallace made a preliminary declaration that he intended nothing but kindness and honor to Mackintosh, I could not properly refuse to make some concession. I was much surprised that neither Steele nor Wallace objected to Lord Strafford's proposition; but, as they did not object, it was impossible for me to do so. In this way the matter was settled—much better settled than by refusing to admit Wallace to the privileges of a gentleman. I hope that you will be satisfied with the result. The kind anxiety which you have felt about me renders me very desirous to know that you approve of my conduct.

Yours ever,   T. B. MACAULAY.

3 Clarges Street, June 26th, 1838.

DEAR NAPIER,—I assure you that I would willingly, and even eagerly, undertake the subject which you propose, if I thought that I should serve you by doing so. But, depend upon it, you do not know what you are asking for. I have done my best to ascertain what I can and what I can not do. There are extensive classes of subjects which I think myself able to treat as few people can treat them. After this, you

can not suspect me of any affectation of modesty; and you
will therefore believe that I tell you what I sincerely think,
when I say that I am not successful in analyzing the effect of
works of genius. I have written several things on historical,
political, and moral questions, of which, on the fullest recon-
sideration, I am not ashamed, and by which I should be willing to be estimated; but I have never written a page of criticism on poetry, or the fine arts, which I would not burn if I
had the power. Hazlitt used to say of himself, "I am nothing
if not critical." The case with me is directly the reverse. I
have a strong and acute enjoyment of works of the imagination, but I have never habituated myself to dissect them. Perhaps I enjoy them the more keenly for that very reason. Such
books as Lessing's "Laocoön,"* such passages as the criticism
on "Hamlet" in "Wilhelm Meister," fill me with wonder and
despair. Now, a review of Lockhart's book ought to be a review of Sir Walter's literary performances. I enjoy many of
them — nobody, I believe, more keenly — but I am sure that
there are hundreds who will criticise them far better. Trust
to my knowledge of myself. I never in my life was more
certain of any thing than of what I tell you, and I am sure
that Lord Jeffrey will tell you exactly the same.

There are other objections of less weight, but not quite unimportant. Surely it would be desirable that some person
who knew Sir Walter, who had at least seen him and spoken
with him, should be charged with this article. Many people
are living who had a most intimate acquaintance with him.
I know no more of him than I know of Dryden or Addison,
and not a tenth part so much as I know of Swift, Cowper, or
Johnson. Then, again, I have not, from the little that I do
know of him, formed so high an opinion of his character as
most people seem to entertain, and as it would be expedient
for the *Edinburgh Review* to express. He seems to me to
have been most carefully, and successfully, on his guard against

---

* "I began Lessing's 'Laocoön,' and read forty or fifty pages: sometimes
dissenting, but always admiring and learning." — *Macaulay's Journal for
September 21st,* 1851.

the sins which most easily beset literary men. On that side he multiplied his precautions, and set double watch. Hardly any writer of note has been so free from the petty jealousies and morbid irritabilities of our caste. But I do not think that he kept himself equally pure from faults of a very different kind, from the faults of a man of the world. In politics, a bitter and unscrupulous partisan; profuse and ostentatious in expense; agitated by the hopes and fears of a gambler; perpetually sacrificing the perfection of his compositions, and the durability of his fame, to his eagerness for money; writing with the slovenly haste of Dryden, in order to satisfy wants which were not, like those of Dryden, caused by circumstances beyond his control, but which were produced by his extravagant waste or rapacious speculation; this is the way in which he appears to me. I am sorry for it, for I sincerely admire the greater part of his works; but I can not think him a high-minded man, or a man of very strict principle. Now these are opinions which, however softened, it would be highly unpopular to publish, particularly in a Scotch review.

But why can not you prevail on Lord Jeffrey to furnish you with this article? No man could do it half so well. He knew and loved Scott; and would perform the critical part of the work, which is much the most important, incomparably. I have said a good deal in the hope of convincing you that it is not without reason that I decline a task which I see that you wish me to undertake.

I am quite unsettled. Breakfasts every morning, dinners every evening, and calls all day, prevent me from making any regular exertion. My books are at the baggage warehouse. My book-cases are in the hands of the cabinet-maker. Whatever I write at present I must, as Bacon somewhere says, spin like a spider out of my own entrails, and I have hardly a minute in the week for such spinning. London is in a strange state of excitement. The western streets are in a constant ferment. The influx of foreigners and rustics has been prodigious, and the regular inhabitants are almost as idle and curious as the sojourners. Crowds assemble perpetually, nobody knows why, with a sort of vague expectation that there will be something to see; and, after staring at each other, disperse without seeing any thing. This will last till the Coronation is over. The only quiet haunts are the streets of the City. For my part, I am sick to death of the turmoil, and almost wish myself at Calcutta again, or becalmed on the equator. Ever yours most truly,　　　T. B. MACAULAY.

3 Clarges Street, London, July 20th, 1838.

DEAR NAPIER,—As to Brougham, I understand and feel for your embarrassments. I may perhaps refine too much; but I should say that this strange man, finding himself almost alone in the world, absolutely unconnected with either Whigs or Conservatives, and not having a single vote in either House of Parliament at his command except his own, is desirous to make the *Review* his organ. With this intention, unless I am greatly deceived, after having during several years contributed little or nothing of value, he has determined to exert himself as if he were a young writer struggling into note, and to make himself important to the work by his literary services. And he certainly has succeeded. His late articles, particularly the long one in the April number, have very high merit. They are, indeed, models of magazine writing as distinguished from other sorts of writing. They are not, I think, made for duration. Every thing about them is exaggerated, incorrect, sketchy. All the characters are either too black or too fair. The passions of the writer do not suffer him even to maintain the decent appearance of impartiality. And the style, though striking and animated, will not bear examination through a single paragraph. But the effect of the first perusal is great; and few people read an article in a review twice. A bold, dashing, scene-painting manner is that which always succeeds best in periodical writing; and I have no doubt that these lively and vigorous papers of Lord Brougham will be of more use to you than more highly finished compositions. His wish, I imagine, is to establish in this way such an ascendency as may enable him to drag the *Review* along with him to any party to which his furious passions may lead him; to the Radicals; to the Tories; to any set of men by whose help he may

be able to revenge himself on old friends, whose only crime
is that they could not help finding him to be an habitual and
incurable traitor. Hitherto your caution and firmness have
done wonders. Yet already he has begun to use the word
"Whig" as an epithet of reproach, exactly as it is used in the
lowest writings of the Tories, and of the extreme Radicals;
exactly as it is used in *Blackwood*, in *Fraser*, in *The Age*, in
Tait's Magazine. There are several instances in the article
on Lady Charlotte Bury. "The Whig notions of female propriety." "The Whig secret tribunal." I have no doubt that
the tone of his papers will become more and more hostile to
the Government; and that, in a short time, it will be necessary for you to take one of three courses, to every one of
which there are strong objections—to break with him; to admit his papers into the *Review*, while the rest of the *Review*
continues to be written in quite a different tone; or to yield
to his dictation, and to let him make the *Review* a mere tool
of his ambition and revenge.

As to Brougham's feelings toward myself, I know, and have
known for a long time, that he hates me. If during the last
ten years I have gained any reputation either in politics or in
letters—if I have had any success in life—it has been without
his help or countenance, and often in spite of his utmost exertions to keep me down. It is strange that he should be surprised at my not calling on him since my return. I did not
call on him when I went away. When he was chancellor,
and I was in office, I never once attended his levée. It would
be strange indeed if now, when he is squandering the remains
of his public character in an attempt to ruin the party of
which he was a member then, and of which I am a member
still, I should begin to pay court to him. For the sake of the
long intimacy which subsisted between him and my father,
and of the mutual good offices which passed between them, I
will not, unless I am compelled, make any public attack on
him. But this is really the only tie which restrains me; for
I neither love him nor fear him.

With regard to the Indian Penal Code, if you are satisfied
that Empson really wishes to review it on its own account,

and not merely out of kindness to me, I should not at all object to his doing so. The subject is one of immense importance. The work is of a kind too abstruse for common readers, and can be made known to them only through the medium of some popular exposition. There is another consideration which weighs much with me. The Press in India has fallen into the hands of the lower legal practitioners, who detest all law-reform; and their scurrility, though mere matter of derision to a person accustomed to the virulence of English factions, is more formidable than you can well conceive to the members of the civil service, who are quite unaccustomed to be dragged rudely before the public. It is, therefore, highly important that the members of the Indian Legislature, and of the Law Commission, should be supported against the clamorous abuse of the scribblers who surround them by seeing that their performances attract notice at home, and are judged with candor and discernment by writers of a far higher rank in literature than the Calcutta editors. For these reasons I should be glad to see an article on the Penal Code in the *Edinburgh Review*. But I must stipulate that my name may not be mentioned, and that every thing may be attributed to the Law Commission as a body. I am quite confident that Empson's own good taste, and regard for me, will lead him, if he should review the Code, to abstain most carefully from every thing that resembles puffing. His regard to truth and the public interest will, of course, lead him to combat our opinions freely wherever he thinks us wrong.

There is little chance that I shall see Scotland this year. In the autumn I shall probably set out for Rome, and return to London in the spring. As soon as I return, I shall seriously commence my "History." The first part (which, I think, will take up five octavo volumes) will extend from the Revolution to the commencement of Sir Robert Walpole's long administration; a period of three or four and thirty very eventful years. From the commencement of Walpole's administration to the commencement of the American war, events may be dispatched more concisely. From the commencement of the American war it will again become necessary to be copious.

These, at least, are my present notions. How far I shall bring the narrative down I have not determined. The death of George the Fourth would be the best halting-place. The "History" would then be an entire view of all the transactions which took place, between the Revolution which brought the Crown into harmony with the Parliament, and the Revolution which brought the Parliament into harmony with the nation. But there are great and obvious objections to contemporary history. To be sure, if I live to be seventy, the events of George the Fourth's reign will be to me then what the American war and the Coalition are to me now.

Whether I shall continue to reside in London seems to me very uncertain. I used to think that I liked London; but, in truth, I liked things which were in London, and which are gone. My family is scattered. I have no Parliamentary or official business to bind me to the capital. The business to which I propose to devote myself is almost incompatible with the distractions of a town life. I am sick of the monotonous succession of parties, and long for quiet and retirement. To quit politics for letters is, I believe, a wise choice. To cease to be a member of Parliament only to become a diner-out would be contemptible; and it is not easy for me to avoid becoming a mere diner-out if I reside here.

Ever yours,   T. B. M.

London, September 15th, 1838.

DEAR ELLIS,—On Monday I shall set off for Liverpool by the railroad, which will then be opened for the whole way. I shall remain there about a week. The chief object of my visit is to see my little nephew, the son of my sister Margaret. It is no visit of pleasure, though I hear every thing most hopeful and pleasing about the boy's talents and temper.* Indeed, it is not without a great effort that I force my-

---

* The boy died in 1847, having already shown as fair promise of remarkable ability and fine character as can be given at the age of thirteen. "I feel the calamity much," Macaulay wrote. "I had left the dear boy my library, little expecting that I should ever wear mourning for him."

self to go. But I will say no more on this subject, for I can
not command myself when I approach it.

Empson came to London yesterday night, with his lady in
high beauty and good humor. It is, you know, quite a pro-
verbial truth that wives never tolerate an intimacy between
their husbands and any old friends, except in two cases: the
one, when the old friend was, before the marriage, a friend of
both wife and husband; the other, when the friendship is of
later date than the marriage. I may hope to keep Empson's
friendship under the former exception, as I have kept yours
under the latter.

Empson brings a sad account of poor Napier: all sorts of
disquiet and trouble, with dreadful, wearing complaints which
give his friends the gravest cause for alarm. And, as if this
were not enough, Brougham is persecuting him with the utmost malignity. I did not think it possible for human nature, in an educated, civilized man—a man, too, of great intellect—to have become so depraved. He writes to Napier in
language of the most savage hatred, and of the most extravagant vaunting. The ministers, he says, have felt only his little finger. He will now put forth his red right hand. They
shall have no rest. As to me, he says that I shall rue my base-
ness in not calling on him. But it is against Empson that he
is most furious. He says that, in consequence of this new
marriage,* he will make it the chief object of his life to prevent Jeffrey from ever being Lord President of the Court of
Session. He thinks that there is some notion of making Empson editor of the *Review.* If that be done, he says, he will re-
linquish every other object in order to ruin the *Review.* He
will lay out his last sixpence in that enterprise. He will make
revenge on Empson the one business of the remaining years
of his life. Empson says that nothing so demoniacal was ever
written in the world. For my part, since he takes it into his
head to be angry, I am pleased that he goes on in such a way;
for he is much less formidable in such a state than he would
be if he kept his temper. I sent to Napier on Thursday a

---

* Mr. Empson had married the daughter of Lord Jeffrey.

long article on Temple. It is superficial; but on that account, among others, I shall be surprised if it does not take.

Hayter has painted me for his picture of the House of Commons. I can not judge of his performance. I can only say, as Charles the Second did on a similar occasion, "Odds fish! if I am like this, I am an ugly fellow."

Yours ever,   T. B. M.

In the middle of October Macaulay started for a tour in Italy. Just past middle life, with his mind already full, and his imagination still fresh and his health unbroken, it may be doubted whether any traveler had carried thither a keener expectation of enjoyment since Winckelmann for the first time crossed the Alps. A diary, from which extracts will be given in the course of this chapter, curiously illustrates the feelings with which he regarded the scenes around him. He viewed the works, both of man and of nature, with the eyes of an historian, and not of an artist. The leading features of a tract of country impressed themselves rapidly and indelibly on his observation; all its associations and traditions swept at once across his memory; and every line of good poetry which its fame or its beauty had inspired rose almost involuntarily to his lips. But, compared with the wealth of phrases on which he could draw at will when engaged on the description of human passions, catastrophes, and intrigues, his stock of epithets applicable to mountains, seas, and clouds was singularly scanty; and he had no ambition to enlarge it. When he had recorded the fact that the leaves were green, the sky blue, the plain rich, and the hills clothed with wood, he had said all he had to say, and there was an end of it. He had neither the taste nor the power for rivaling those novelists who have more colors in their vocabulary than ever Turner had on his palette; and who spend over the lingering phases of a single sunset as much ink as Richardson consumed in depicting the death of his villain or the ruin of his heroine. "I have always thought," said Lady Trevelyan, "that your uncle was incomparable in showing a town, or the place where any famous event occurred; but that he did not care for scenery, merely as scenery. He enjoyed the country, in his way. He liked sitting out on a lawn, and seeing grass and flowers around him. Occasionally a view made a great impression on him, such as the view down upon Susa, going over Mont Cenis; but I doubt whether any scene pleased his eye more than his own beloved Holly Lodge, or Mr. Thornton's garden at Battersea Rise. When we were recalling the delights of an excursion among the Surrey hills, or in the by-ways at the English lakes, he would be inclined to ask, 'What went ye out for to see?' Yet he readily took in the points of a landscape; and I remember being much struck by his description of the country before you reach Rome, which he gives in "Horatius." When I followed him over that ground many years after, I am sure that I marked the very turn in the road where the lines struck him:

> From where Cortona lifts to heaven
> Her diadem of towers;

and so on through 'reedy Thrasymene,' and all the other localities of the poem."

"*Chalons-sur-Saône, Tuesday, October 23d*, 1838.—The road from Autun is for some way more beautiful than any thing I had yet seen in France; or, indeed, in that style, anywhere else, except, perhaps, the ascent to the table-land of the Neilgherries. I traversed a winding pass, near two miles in length, running by the side of a murmuring brook, and between hills covered with forest. The landscape appeared in the richest coloring of October, under a sun like that of an English June. The earth was the earth of autumn, but the sky was the sky of summer. The foliage—dark-green, light-green, purple, red, and yellow—seen by the evening sun, produced the effect of the plumage of the finest Eastern birds. I walked up the pass exceedingly pleased. To enjoy scenery you should ramble amidst it; let the feelings to which it gives rise mingle with other thoughts; look around upon it in intervals of reading; and not go to it as one goes to see the lions fed at a fair. The beautiful is not to be stared at, but to be lived with. I have no pleasure from books which equals that of reading over for the hundredth time great productions which I almost know by heart; and it is just the same with scenery."

"*Lyons, Thursday, October 25th.*—My birthday. Thirty-eight years old. Thought of Job, Swift, and Antony. Dressed, and went down to the steamer. I was delighted by my first sight of the blue, rushing, healthful-looking Rhone. I thought, as I wandered along the quay, of the singular love and veneration which rivers excite in those who live on their banks; of the feeling of the Hindoos about the Ganges; of the Hebrews about the Jordan; of the Egyptians about the Nile; of the Romans,

Cuique fuit rerum promissa potentia Tibrin;

of the Germans about the Rhine. Is it that rivers have, in a greater degree than almost any other inanimate object, the appearance of animation, and something resembling character? They are sometimes slow and dark-looking; sometimes fierce and impetuous; sometimes bright, dancing, and almost flippant. The attachment of the French for the Rhone may be explained into a very natural sympathy. It is a vehement, rapid stream. It seems cheerful, and full of animal spirits, even to petulance. But this is all fanciful."

"*October 26th.*—On board the steamer for Avignon. Saw the famous junction of the two rivers, and thought of Lord Chatham's simile.* But his expression 'languid, though of no depth,' is hardly just to the Saône, however just it may be to the Duke of Newcastle. We went down at a noble rate. The day, which had been dank and foggy, became exceedingly beautiful. After we had left Valence the scenery grew wilder: the hills bare and rocky like the sides of Lethe water in Cumberland; the mountains of Dauphiné in the distance reminded me of the outline of Ceylon as I saw it from the sea; and, here and there, I could catch a glimpse of white peaks which I fancied to be the summits of the Alps. I chatted with the French gentlemen on board, and found them intelligent and polite. We talked of their roads and public works, and they complimented me on my knowledge of French history and geography. 'Ah, monsieur, vous avez beaucoup approfondi ces choses-là.' The evening was falling when we came to the Pont St. Esprit, a famous work of the monks, which pretends to no ornament, and needs none."

"*October 28th.*—The day began to break as we descended into Marseilles. It was Sunday; but the town seemed only so much the gayer. I looked hard for churches, but for a long time I saw none. At last I heard bells, and the noise guided me to a chapel, mean inside and mean outside, but crowded as Simeon's church used to be crowded at Cambridge. The mass was nearly over. I staid to the end, wondering that so many reasonable beings could come together to see a man bow, drink, bow again, wipe a

---

* "One fragment of this celebrated oration remains in a state of tolerable preservation. It is the comparison between the coalition of Fox and Newcastle, and the junction of the Rhone and the Saône. 'At Lyons,' said Pitt, 'I was taken to see the place where the two rivers meet; the one gentle, feeble, languid, and, though languid, yet of no depth; the other a boisterous and impetuous torrent. But, different as they are, they meet at last.'"—*Macaulay's Essay on Chatham.*

cup, wrap up a napkin, spread his arms, and gesticulate with his hands; and to hear a low muttering which they could not understand, interrupted by the occasional jingling of a bell. A fine steamer sails to-morrow for Leghorn. I am going to lock this hulking volume up, and I shall next open it in Tuscany."

"*Wednesday, October 31st.*—This was one of the most remarkable days of my life. After being detained, by the idle precautions which are habitual with these small absolute governments, for an hour on deck, that the passengers might be counted; for another hour in a dirty room, that the agent of the police might write down all our names; and for a third hour in another smoky den, while a custom-house officer opened razor-cases to see that they concealed no muslin, and turned over dictionaries to be sure that they contained no treason or blasphemy, I hurried on shore, and by seven in the morning I was in the streets of Genoa. Never had I been more struck and enchanted. There was nothing mean or small to break the charm, as one huge, massy, towering palace succeeded to another. True it is that none of these magnificent piles is a strikingly good architectural composition; but the general effect is majestic beyond description. When the King of Sardinia became sovereign of Genoa, he bought the house of the Durazzo family, and found himself at once lodged as nobly as a great prince need wish to be. What a city, where a king has only to go into the market to buy a Luxembourg, or a St. James's! Next to the palaces, or rather quite as much, I admired the churches. Outside they are poor and bad, but within they dazzled and pleased me more than I can express. It was the awakening of a new sense, the discovery of an unsuspected pleasure. I had drawn all my notions of classical interiors from the cold, white, and naked walls of such buildings as St. Paul's, or St. Genevieve's; but the first church-door that I opened at Genoa let me into another world. One harmonious glow pervaded the whole of the long Corinthian arcade from the entrance to the altar. In this way I passed the day, greatly excited and delighted."

With this, perhaps the only jingling sentence which he ever left unblotted, Macaulay closes the account of his first, but far from his last, visit to the queen of the Tyrrhenian sea. To the end of his days, when comparing, as he loved to compare, the claims of European cities to the prize of beauty, he would place at the head of the list the august names of Oxford, Edinburgh, and Genoa.

"*November 2d.*—I shall always have an interesting recollection of Pisa. There is something pleasing in the way in which all the monuments of Pisan greatness lie together, in a place not unlike the close of an English cathedral, surrounded with green turf; still kept in the most perfect preservation, and evidently matters of admiration and of pride to the whole population.   Pisa has always had a great hold on my mind: partly from its misfortunes; and partly, I believe, because my first notions about the Italian republics were derived from Sismondi, whom I read while at school: and Sismondi, who is, or fancies that he is, of Pisan descent, does all in his power to make the country of his ancestors an object of interest.   I like Pisa, too, for having been Ghibelline.   After the time of Frederick Barbarossa, my preference, as far as one can have preferences in so wretched a question, are all Ghibelline.

" As I approached Florence the day became brighter; and the country looked, not indeed strikingly beautiful, but very pleasing.   The sight of the olive-trees interested me much.   I had, indeed, seen what I was told were olive-trees, as I was whirled down the Rhône from Lyons to Avignon; but they might, for any thing I saw, have been willows or ash-trees. Now they stood, covered with berries, along the road for miles.   I looked at them with the same sort of feeling with which Washington Irving says that he heard the nightingale for the first time when he came to England, after having read descriptions of her in poets from his childhood. · I thought of the Hebrews, and their numerous images drawn from the olive; of the veneration in which the tree was held by the Athenians; of Lysias's speech; of the fine ode in the 'Œdipus at Colonus;' of Virgil and Lorenzo de' Medici.   Surely it is better to travel in mature years, with all these things in one's head, than to rush over the Continent while still a boy!"

"*Florence, November 3d.*—Up before eight, and read Boiardo at breakfast.   My rooms look into a court adorned with orange-trees and marble statues.   I never look at the statues without thinking of poor Mignon.

> Und Marmorbilder stehn und sehn mich an:
> Was hat man dir, du armes Kind, gethan?

I know no two lines in the world which I would sooner have written than those.   I went to a Gabinetto Litterario hard by, subscribed, and read the last English newspapers.   I crossed the river, and walked through some of the rooms in the Palazzo Pitti; greatly admiring a little painting, by Raphael, from Ezekiel, which was so fine that it almost reconciled me to seeing God the Father on canvas.

"Then to the Church of Santa Croce: an ugly, mean outside; and not much to admire in the architecture within, but consecrated by the dust of some of the greatest men that ever lived.   It was to me what a first visit to Westminster Abbey would be to an American.   The first tomb which caught my eye, as I entered, was that of Michael Angelo.   I was much moved, and still more so when, going forward, I saw the stately monument lately erected to Dante.   The figure of the poet seemed to me fine and finely placed, and the inscription very happy—his own words, the proclamation which resounds through the shades when Virgil returns,

> Onorate l'altissimo poeta.

The two allegorical figures were not much to my taste. It is particularly absurd to represent Poetry weeping for Dante. These weeping figures are all very well when a tomb is erected to a person lately dead; but when a group of sculpture is set up over a man who has been dead more than five hundred years, such lamentation is nonsensical. Who can help laughing at the thought of tears of regret shed because a man who was born in the time of our Henry the Third is not still alive? Yet I was very near shedding tears of a different kind as I looked at this magnificent monument, and thought of the sufferings of the great poet, and of his incomparable genius, and of all the pleasure which I have derived from him, and of his death in exile, and of the late justice of posterity. I believe that very few people have ever had their minds more thoroughly penetrated with the spirit of any great work than mine is with that of the 'Divine Comedy.' His execution I take to be far beyond that of any other artist who has operated on the imagination by means of words.

> O degli altri poeti onore e lume,
> Vagliami il lungo studio e 'l grande amore
> Che m' han fatto cercar lo tuo volume.[1]

I was proud to think that I had a right to apostrophize him thus. I went on, and next I came to the tomb of Alfieri, set up by his mistress, the Countess of Albany. I passed forward, and in another minute my foot was on the grave of Machiavel."

"*November 7th.*—While walking about the town, I picked up a little mass-book, and read for the first time in my life—strange, and almost disgraceful that it should be so—the service of the mass from beginning to end. It seemed to me inferior to our Communion Service in one most important point. The phraseology of Christianity has in Latin a barbarous air, being altogether later than the age of pure Latinity. But the English language has grown up in Christian times, and the whole vocabulary of Christianity is incorporated with it. The fine passage in the Communion Service, 'Therefore with angels, and archangels, and all the company of heaven,' is English of the best and most genuine description. But the answering passage in the mass, 'Laudant angeli, adorant dominationes, tremunt potestates, cœli cœlorumque virtutes ac beata seraphim,' would not

---

[1] Glory and light of all the tuneful train,
May it avail me that I long with zeal
Have sought thy volume, and with love immense
Have conn'd it o'er!

merely have appeared barbarous, but would have been utterly unintelligible—a mere gibberish—to every one of the great masters of the Latin tongue, Plautus, Cicero, Cæsar, and Catullus. I doubt whether even Claudian would have understood it. I intend to frequent the Romish worship till I come thoroughly to understand this ceremonial."

Florence, November 4th, 1838.

DEAR NAPIER,—I arrived here the day before yesterday in very good health, after a journey of three weeks from London. I find that it will be absolutely impossible for me to execute the plan of reviewing Panizzi's edition of Boiardo in time for your next number. I have not been able to read one-half of Boiardo's poem, and, in order to do what I propose, I must read Berni's *rifacimento* too, as well as Pulci's "Morgante;" and this, I fear, will be quite out of the question. The day is not long enough for what I want to do in it : and if I find this to be the case at Florence, I may be sure that at Rome I shall have still less leisure. However, it is my full intention to be in England in February, and on the day on which I reach London I will begin to work for you on Lord Clive.

I know little English news. I steal a quarter of an hour in the day from marbles and altar-pieces to read the *Times* and the *Morning Chronicle*. Lord Brougham, I have a notion, will often wish that he had left Lord Durham alone. Lord Durham will be in the House of Lords, with his pugnacious spirit, and with his high reputation among the Radicals. In oratorical abilities there is, of course, no comparison between the men ; but Lord Durham has quite talents enough to expose Lord Brougham, and has quite as much acrimony and a great deal more nerve than Lord Brougham himself. I should very much like to know what the general opinion about this matter is. My own suspicion is that the Tories in the House of Lords will lose reputation, though I do not imagine that the Government will gain any. As to Brougham, he has reached that happy point at which it is equally impossible for him to gain character and lose it.

Ever, dear Napier, yours most truly,

T. B. MACAULAY.

There was, indeed, very little reputation to be gained out of the business. No episode in our political history is more replete with warning to honest and public-spirited men, who, in seeking to serve their country, forget what is due to their own interests and their own security, than the story of Lord Durham. He accepted the governorship of Canada during a supreme crisis in the affairs of that colony. He carried with him thither the confidence of the great body of his fellow-countrymen — a confidence which he had conciliated by his earnest and courageous demeanor in the warfare of Parliament; by the knowledge that, when he undertook his present mission, he had stipulated for the largest responsibility and refused the smallest emolument; and, above all, by the appeal which, before leaving England, he made in the House of Lords to friends and foes alike. "I feel," he said, "that I can accomplish my task only by the cordial and energetic support— a support which I am sure I shall obtain—of my noble friends, the members of Her Majesty's Cabinet; by the co-operation of the Imperial Parliament; and, permit me to say, by the generous forbearance of the noble lords opposite, to whom I have always been politically opposed." From his political opponents, in the place of generous forbearance, he met with unremitting persecution; and, as for the character of the support which he obtained from those ministers who had themselves placed him in the forefront of the battle, it is more becoming to leave it for Tory historians to recount the tale. To Lord Brougham's treatment of his former colleague justice is done in the last sentence of Macaulay's letter. But Macaulay was mistaken in expecting that Lord Durham would call his enemies to account, and still less his friends. His heart was broken, but not estranged. His tongue, which had too seldom, perhaps, refrained from speaking out what was brave and true, could keep silence when silence was demanded by the claims of past alliances and the memory of old friendships. During the remnant of his life, Lord Durham continued to support the Whig Cabinet with all the loyalty and modesty of a young peer hopeful of an under-secretaryship, or grateful for having been selected to second the Address. But none the less had the blow gone home; and the Administration, which had so long been trembling and dying, was destined to survive by many months the most single-minded and high-natured among that company of statesmen who had wrought for our people the great deliverance of 1832.

"*Friday, November 9th.*—Went to Dante's 'bel San Giovanni,' and heard mass there. Then to another church, and heard another mass. I begin to follow the service as well as the body of the hearers, which is not saying much. I paid a third visit to Santa Croce, and noticed in the cloister a monument to a little baby, ' Il più bel bambino che mai fosse ;' not a very wise inscription for parents to put up, but it brought tears into my eyes. I thought of the little thing* who lies in the cemetery at Calcutta. I meditated some verses for my ballad of ' Romulus,'† but made only one stanza to my satisfaction. I finished Casti's ' Giuli Tre,' and have liked it less than I expected. The humor of the work consists in endless repetition. It is a very hazardous experiment to attempt to make fun out of that which is the great cause of yawning, perpetual harping on the same topic. Sir Walter Scott was very fond of this device for exciting laughter : as witness Lady Margaret, and his Sacred Majesty's disjune ; Claude Halcro, and Glorious John ; Sir Dugald Dalgetty, and the Marischal College of Aberdeen ; the Baillie, and his father, the deacon ; old Trapbois, and ' for a consideration.' It answered, perhaps once, for ten times that it failed."

"*Saturday, November 10th,* 1838.—A letter from Mr. Aubin, our chargé d'affaires here, to say that he has a confidential message for me, and asking when he might call. I was in bed. I sent word that I would call on him as soon as I had breakfasted. I had little doubt that the ministers wanted my help in Parliament. I went to him, and he delivered to me two letters—one from Lord Melbourne, and the other from Rice. They press me to become judge-advocate, and assure me that a seat in Parliament may be procured for me with little expense. Rice dwells much on the salary, which he says is £2500 a year. I thought it had been cut down; but he must know. He also talks of the other advantages connected with the place. The offer did not strike me as even tempting. The money I do not want. I have little, but I have enough. The Right Honorable before my name is a bauble which it would be far, very far indeed, beneath me to care about. The power is nothing. As an independent member of Parliament I should have infinitely greater power. Nay, as I am, I have far greater power. I can now write what I choose ; and what I write may produce considerable effect on the public mind. In office I must necessari-

---

* A little niece, who died in 1837, three months old.

† The poem which was published as " The Prophecy of Capys."

ly be under restraint. If, indeed, I had a cabinet office, I should be able to do something in support of my own views of government; but a man in office, and out of the Cabinet, is a mere slave. I have felt the bitterness of that slavery once. Though I hardly knew where to turn for a morsel of bread, my spirit rose against the intolerable thralldom. I was mutinous, and once actually resigned. I then went to India to get independence, and I have got it, and I will keep it. So I wrote to Lord Melbourne and Rice. I told them that I would cheerfully do any thing to serve them in Parliament; but that office, except, indeed, office of the highest rank, to which I have no pretensions, had not the smallest allurements for me; that the situation of a subordinate was unsuited to my temper; that I had tried it, that I had found it insupportable, and that I would never make the experiment again. I begged them not to imagine that I thought a place which Mackintosh had been anxious to obtain beneath me. Very far from it. I admitted it to be above the market price of my services; but it was below the fancy price which a peculiar turn of mind led me to put on my liberty and my studies. The only thing that would ever tempt me to give up my liberty and my studies was the power to effect great things; and of that power, as they well knew, no man had so little as a man in office out of the Cabinet.

"I never in my life took an important step with greater confidence in my own judgment, or with a firmer conviction that I was doing the best for my own happiness, honor, and usefulness. I have no relentings. If they take me at my word, and contrive to bring me into Parliament without office, I shall be, I think, in the most eligible of situations; but this I do not much expect."

On the 12th of November, Macaulay set out from Florence, by way of Cortona and Perugia.

"*Tuesday, November 13th.*—My journey lay over the field of Thrasymenus, and as soon as the sun rose, I read Livy's description of the scene, and wished that I had brought Polybius too. However, it mattered little, for I could see absolutely nothing. I was exactly in the situation of the consul, Flaminius—completely hid in the morning fog. I did not discern the lake till the road came quite close to it, and then my view extended only over a few yards of reedy mud and shallow water, so that I can truly say that I have seen precisely what the Roman army saw on that day. After some time we began to ascend, and came at last, with the help of oxen, to an eminence on which the sun shone bright. All the hill-tops round were perfectly clear, and the fog lay in the valley below like a lake winding among mountains. I then understood the immense advantage which Hannibal derived from keeping his divisions on the heights, where he could see them all, and where they could all see each other, while the Romans were stumbling and groping, without the possibility of concert, through the thick haze below. Toward evening I began to notice the white oxen of Clitumnus."

"*November* 14th.—Up and off by half-past four. The sun triumphed over the mist just as I reached Narni. The scenery was really glorious; far finer than that of Matlock or the Wye, in something of the same style. The pale line of the river which brawled below, though in itself not agreeable, was interesting from classical recollections. I thought how happily Virgil had touched the most striking and characteristic features of Italian landscape. As the day wore on, I saw the Tiber for the first time. I saw Mount Soracte, and, unlike Lord Byron, I loved the sight for Horace's sake. And so I came to Civita Castellana, where I determined to stop, though it was not much after two. I did not wish to enter Rome by night. I wanted to see the dome of St. Peter's from a distance, and to observe the city disclosing itself by degrees."

"*November* 15th.—On arriving this morning, I walked straight from the hotel door to St. Peter's. I was so much excited by the expectation of what I was to see, that I could notice nothing else. I was quite nervous. The colonnade in front is noble—very, very noble—yet it disappointed me, and would have done so had it been the portico of Paradise. In I went, and I was for a minute fairly stunned by the magnificence and harmony of the interior. I never in my life saw, and never, I suppose, shall again see, any thing so astonishingly beautiful. I really could have cried with pleasure. I rambled about for half an hour or more, paying little or no attention to details, but enjoying the effect of the sublime whole.

"In rambling back to the Piazza di Spagna I found myself before the portico of the Pantheon. I was as much struck and affected as if I had not known that there was such a building in Rome. There it was, the work of the age of Augustus; the work of men who lived with Cicero, and Cæsar, and Horace, and Virgil. What would they have said if they had seen it stuck all over with 'Invito Sacro,' and 'Indulgenza Perpetua?'"

"*November* 16th.—As soon as it cleared up, I hastened to St. Peter's again. There was one spot near which an Englishman could not help lingering for a few minutes. In one of the side aisles, a monument by Canova marks the burial-place of the latest princes of the House of Stuart; James the Third; Charles Edward; and Cardinal York, whom the last of the Jacobites affected to call Henry the Ninth. I then went toward the river, to the spot where the old Pons Sublicius stood, and looked about to see how my Horatius agreed with the topography. Pretty well: but his house must be on Mount Palatine; for he would never see Mount Cœlius from the spot where he fought.* Thence to the Capitol, and wandered

---

* But he saw on Palatinus
   The white porch of his home;
And he spake to the noble river
   That rolls by the walls of Rome.

through the gallery of paintings placed there by Benedict the Fourteenth, my favorite Pope."

"*November 22d.*—I went to see a famous relic of antiquity, lately discovered—the baker's tomb. This baker, and his wife, and the date of his baking performances, and the meaning of that mysterious word 'apparet,' are now the great subjects of discussion among the best circles of Rome. Strange city; once sovereign of the world, whose news now consists in the discovery of the buried tomb of a tradesman who has been dead at least fifteen hundred years! The question whether 'apparet' is the short for 'apparitoris' is to them what the Licinian Rogations and the Agrarian Laws were to their fathers; what the Catholic Bill and the Reform Bill have been to us. Yet, to indulge in a sort of reflection which I often fall into here, the day may come when London, then dwindled to the dimensions of the parish of St. Martin's, and supported in its decay by the expenditure of wealthy Patagonians and New Zealanders,* may have no more important questions to decide than the arrangement of 'Afflictions sore long time I bore' on the grave-stone of the wife of some baker in Houndsditch."

"*November 26th.*—At ten, Colyar† came, and we set out. The day would furnish matter for a volume. We went to the English College, and walked about the cloisters—interesting cloisters to an Englishman. There lie several of our native dignitaries who died at Rome before the Reformation. There lie, too, the bones of many Jacobites, honest martyrs to a worthless cause. We looked into the refectory, much like the halls of the small colleges at Cambridge in my time—that of Peterhouse, for example—and smelling strongly of yesterday's supper, which strengthened the resemblance. We found the principal, Dr. Wiseman, a young ecclesiastic full of health and vigor—much such a ruddy, strapping divine as I remember Whewell eighteen years ago—in purple vestments standing in the cloister. With him was Lord Clifford, in the uniform of a deputy-lieutenant of Devonshire, great from paying his court to Pope Gregory. He was extremely civil, and talked with gratitude of General Macaulay's kindness to him in Italy. Wiseman chimed in. Indeed, I hear my uncle's praises wherever I go. Lord Clifford is not at all like my notion of a

---

* It may be worth mention that the celebrated New Zealander appears at the end of the third paragraph of the essay on Von Ranke's "History of the Popes."

† Mr. Colyar was an English Catholic gentleman, residing in Rome, who was particularly well-informed with regard to every thing concerning the city, ancient and modern. He was in high favor with priests and prelates, and was, therefore, an invaluable acquaintance for English travelers, at whose disposal he was very ready to place both his knowledge and his influence.

Vol. II.—3

great Catholic peer of old family. I always imagine such a one proud
and stately, with the air of a man of rank, but not of fashion; such a personage as Mrs. Inchbald's Catholic lord in the 'Simple Story,' or as Sir
Walter's Lord Glenallan without the remorse. But Lord Clifford is all
quicksilver. He talked about the pope's reception of him and Lord
Shrewsbury. His holiness is in high health and spirits, and is a little
more merry than strict formalists approve. Lord Shrewsbury says that
he seems one moment to be a boy eager for play, and the next to be another Leo arresting the march of Attila. The poor King of Prussia, it
seems, is Attila. We went into Dr. Wiseman's apartments, which are
snugly furnished in the English style, and altogether are very like the
rooms of a senior Fellow of Trinity. After visiting the library, where I
had a sight of the identical copy of Fox's 'Book of Martyrs' in which Parsons made notes for his answer, I took leave of my countrymen with great
good-will.

"We then crossed the river, and turned into the Vatican. I had walked a hundred feet through the library without the faintest notion that I
was in it. No books, no shelves, were visible. All was light and brilliant; nothing but white and red and gold; blazing arabesques, and
paintings on ceiling and wall. And this was the Vatican Library; a
place which I used to think of with awe as a far sterner and darker Bodleian! The books and manuscripts are all in low wooden cases ranged
round the walls; and as these cases are painted in light colors, they har-
monize with the gay aspect of every thing around them, and might be
supposed to contain musical instruments, masquerade dresses, or china
for the dances and suppers for which the apartments seem to be meant.
They bore inscriptions, however, more suited to my notions of the place.

"Thence I went through the Museum, quite distracted by the multitude
and magnificence of the objects which it contained. The splendor of the
ancient marbles, the alabaster, the huge masses of porphyry, the granites
of various colors, made the whole seem like a fairy region. I wonder that
nobody in this moneyed and luxurious age attempts to open quarries like
those which supplied the ancients. The wealth of modern Europe is far
greater than that of the Roman Empire; and these things are highly valued, and bought at enormous prices. And yet we content ourselves with
digging for them in the ruins of this old city and its suburbs, and never
think of seeking them in the rocks from which the Romans extracted
them. Africa and Greece were the parts of the world which afforded the
most costly marbles; and perhaps, now that the French have settled in
Africa, and that a Bavarian prince reigns in Greece, some researches may
be made.

"I looked into the apartments where the works in mosaic are carried
on. A noble figure of Isaiah, by Raphael, had just been completed. We
ought to have a similar workshop connected with the National Gallery.

What a glorious vestibule to a palace might be made, with the cartoons in mosaic covering the walls! The best portraits of the great men of England, reproduced in the same material, beginning with Holbein's Wolsey and More, and coming down to Lawrence's Wellington and Canning, would be worthy decorations to the new Houses of Parliament. I should like to see the walls of St. Paul's incrusted with porphyry and verd-antique, and the ceiling and dome glittering with mosaics and gold.

"The Demosthenes is very noble. There can be no doubt about the face of Demosthenes. There are two busts of him in the Vatican, besides this statue. They are all exactly alike, being distinguished by the strong projection of the upper lip. The face is lean, wrinkled, and haggard; the expression singularly stern and intense. You see that he was no trifler, no jester, no voluptuary, but a man whose soul was devoured by ambition, and constantly on the stretch. The soft, sleek, plump, almost sleepy, though handsome, face of Æschines presents a remarkable contrast. I was much interested by the bust of Julius, with the head veiled. It is a most striking countenance, indeed. He looks like a man meant to be master of the world. The endless succession of these noble works bewildered me, and I went home almost exhausted with pleasurable excitement."

In a letter written during the latter half of December, Macaulay gives his impressions of the Papal Government at greater length than in his diary.

"Rome was full enough of English when I arrived, but now the crowd is insupportable. I avoid society as much as I can without being churlish; for it is boyish to come to Italy for the purpose of mixing with the set, and hearing the tattle, to which one is accustomed in Mayfair. The Government treats us very well. The pope winks at a Protestant chapel, and indulges us in a reading-room, where the *Times* and *Morning Chronicle* make their appearance twelve days after they are published in London. It is a pleasant city for an English traveler. He is not harassed or restrained. He lives as he likes, and reads what he likes, and suffers little from the vices of the Administration; but I can conceive nothing more insupportable than the situation of a layman who should be a subject of the pope. In this government there is no avenue to distinction for any but priests. Every office of importance, diplomatic, financial, and judicial, is held by the clergy. A prelate, armed with most formidable powers, superintends the police of the streets. The military department is directed by a commission, over which a cardinal presides. Some petty magistracy is the highest promotion to which a lawyer can look forward; and the greatest nobles of this singular State can expect nothing better than some place in the pope's household, which may entitle them to walk in procession on the great festivals. Imagine what England would be if all the members of Parliament, the ministers, the judges, the embassadors, the governors of colonies, the very commanders-in-chief and lords of the admiralty, were, without one exception, bishops or priests; and if the highest post open to the noblest, wealthiest, ablest, and most ambitious layman were a lordship of the bed-chamber! And yet this would not come up to the truth, for our clergy can marry; but here every man who takes a wife cuts himself off forever from all dignity and power, and puts himself into the same position as a Catholic in England before the Emancipation Bill. The Church is, therefore, filled with men who are led into it merely by ambition, and who, though they might have been useful and respectable as laymen, are hypocritical and immoral as churchmen; while, on the other hand, the State suffers greatly, for you may guess what sort of secretaries at war and chancellors of the exchequer are likely to be found among bishops and canons. Corruption infects all the public offices. Old women above, liars and cheats below—that is the Papal Administration. The States of the pope are, I suppose, the worst governed in the civilized world; and the imbecility of the police, the venality of the public servants, the desolation of the country, and the wretchedness of the people, force themselves on the observation of the most heedless traveler. It is hardly an exaggeration to say that the population seems to consist chiefly of foreigners, priests, and paupers. Indeed, whenever you meet a man who is neither in canonicals nor rags, you may bet two to one that he is an Englishman."

"*Tuesday, December 4th.*—I climbed the Janiculan Hill to the Convent of St. Onofrio, and went into the church. It contains only one object of interest—a stone in the pavement, with the words 'Hic jacet Torquatus Tassus.' He died in this convent, just before the day fixed for his coronation at the Capitol. I was not quite in such raptures as I have heard other people profess. Tasso is not one of my favorites, either as a man or a poet. There is too little of the fine frenzy in his verses, and too much in his life.

"I called on the American consul. He was very civil, and, *à la mode d'Amérique*, talked to me about my writings.* I turned the conversation

---

* An injury of this nature was still fresh in Macaulay's mind. Writing from Florence, he says: "I do not scamper about with a note-book in my hand, and a cicerone gabbling in my ear; but I go often, and stay long, at the places which interest me. I sit quietly an hour or two every morning in the finest churches, watching the ceremonial, and the demeanor of the congregation. I seldom pass less than an hour daily in the Tribune, where the Venus de' Medici stands, surrounded by other masterpieces in sculpture and painting. Yesterday, as I was looking at some superb portraits by Raphael and Titian, a Yankee clergyman introduced himself to me; told

instantly. No topic, I am glad to say, is less to my taste. I dined by myself, and read an execrably stupid novel called 'Tylney Hall.' Why do I read such stuff?"

"*Saturday, December 8th.*—No letters at the post-office, the reading-room shut, and the churches full. It is the feast of the Immaculate Conception of the Virgin Mary; a day held in prodigious honor by the Franciscans, who first, I believe, introduced this absurd notion, which even within the Catholic Church the Dominicans have always combated, and which the Council of Trent, if I remember Fra Paolo right, refused to pronounce orthodox. I spent much of the day over Smollett's 'History.' It is exceedingly bad: detestably so.* I can not think what had happened to him. His carelessness, partiality, passion, idle invective, gross ignorance of facts, and crude general theories, do not surprise me much. But the style, wherever he tries to be elevated, and wherever he attempts to draw a character, is perfectly nauseous; which I can not understand. He says of old Horace Walpole that he was an embassador without dignity, and a plenipotentiary without address. I declare I would rather have a hand cut off than publish such a precious antithesis."

"*Tuesday, December 18th.*—I staid at home till late, reading and meditating. I have altered some parts of 'Horatius' to my mind; and I have thought a good deal during the last few days about my 'History.' The great difficulty of a work of this kind is the beginning. How is it to be joined on to the preceding events? Where am I to commence it? I can not plunge, slap-dash, into the middle of events and characters. I can not, on the other hand, write a history of the whole reign of James the Second

---

me that he had heard who I was; that he begged to thank me for my writings in the name of his countrymen; that he had himself reprinted my paper on Bacon; that it had a great run in the States; and that my name was greatly respected there. I bowed, thanked him, and stole away; leaving the Grand Duke's pictures a great deal sooner than I had intended."

The same scene, with the same actors, was repeated on the next day beneath the frown of the awful duke who sits aloft in the chapel of the Medici, adjoining the Church of San Lorenzo; whither Macaulay had repaired " to snatch a mass, as one of Sir Walter's heroes says."

* Even Charles Lamb, who was far too chivalrous to leave a favorite author in the lurch, can find nothing to say in defense of Smollett's "History" except a delightful, but perfectly gratuitous, piece of impertinence to Hume. "Smollett they" (the Scotch) "have neither forgotten nor forgiven for his delineation of Rory and his companion upon their first introduction to our metropolis. Speak of Smollett as a great genius, and they will retort upon you Hume's 'History' compared with *his* Continuation of it. What if the historian had continued 'Humphry Clinker?'"

as a preface to the history of William the Third; and if I did, a history of Charles the Second would still be equally necessary, as a preface to that of the reign of James the Second. I sympathize with the poor man who began the war of Troy 'gemino ab ovo.' But, after much consideration, I think that I can manage, by the help of an introductory chapter or two, to glide imperceptibly into the full current of my narrative. I am more and more in love with the subject. I really think that posterity will not willingly let my book die.

"To St. Peter's again. This is becoming a daily visit."

Rome, December 19th, 1838.

Dear Lord Lansdowne,—I have received your kind letter, and thank you for it. I have now had ample time to reflect on the determination which I expressed to Lord Melbourne and Rice; and I am every day more and more satisfied that the course which I have taken is the best for myself, and the best also for the Government. If I thought it right to follow altogether my own inclinations, I should entirely avoid public life. But I feel that these are not times for flinching from the Whig banner. I feel that at this juncture no friend of toleration and of temperate liberty is justified in withholding his support from the ministers; and I think that, in the present unprecedented and inexplicable scarcity of Parliamentary talent among the young men of England, a little of that talent may be of as much service as far greater powers in times more fertile of eloquence. I would, therefore, make some sacrifice of ease, leisure, and money, in order to serve the Government in the House of Commons. But I do not think that public duty at all requires me to overcome the dislike which I feel for official life. On the contrary, my duty and inclination are here on one side. For I am certain that, as an independent member of Parliament, I should have far more weight than as judge-advocate. It is impossible for me to be ignorant of my position in the world, and of the misconstructions to which it exposes me. Entering Parliament as judge-advocate, I should be considered as a mere political adventurer. My speeches might be complimented as creditable rhetorical performances, but they would never produce the sort of effect which I have seen produced by very rude sentences stammered by such men as Lord Spencer and Lord Ebrington. If I enter Parliament as a placeman, nobody will believe, what nevertheless is the truth, that I am quite as independent, quite as indifferent to salary, as the Duke of Northumberland can be. As I have none of that authority which belongs to large fortune and high rank, it is absolutely necessary to my comfort, and will be greatly conducive to my usefulness, that I should have the authority which belongs to proved disinterestedness. I should also, as a member of Parliament not in office, have leisure for other pursuits, which I can not bear to think of quitting, and which you kindly say you do not wish me to quit. A life of literary repose would be most to my own taste. Of my literary repose I am, however, willing to sacrifice exactly as much as public duty requires me to sacrifice; but I will sacrifice no more; and by going into Parliament without office I both make a smaller personal sacrifice, and do more service to the public, than by taking office. I hope that you will think these reasons satisfactory; for you well know that, next to my own approbation, it would be my first wish to have yours.

I have been more delighted than I can express by Italy, and above all by Rome. I had no notion that an excitement so powerful and so agreeable, still untried by me, was to be found in the world. I quite agree with you in thinking that the first impression is the weakest; and that time, familiarity, and reflection, which destroy the charm of so many objects, heighten the attractions of this wonderful place. I hardly know whether I am more interested by the old Rome or by the new Rome—by the monuments of the extraordinary empire which has perished, or by the institutions of the still more extraordinary empire which, after all the shocks which it has sustained, is still full of life and of perverted energy. If there were not a single ruin, fine building, picture, or statue in Rome, I should think myself repaid for my journey by having seen the head-quarters of Catholicism, and learned something of the nature and effect of the strange Brahmanical government established in the Ecclesiastical State. Have you read Von Ranke's "History of the Papacy since the Reformation?" I have owed much of my pleasure here to what I learned from him.

Rome is full of English. We could furnish exceedingly respectable Houses of Lords and Commons. There are at present twice as many coroneted carriages in the Piazza di Spagna as in St. James's parish. Ever, my dear lord, yours most faithfully,   T. B. MACAULAY.

"*Saturday, December 22d.*—The Canadian insurrection seems to be entirely crushed. I fear that the victorious caste will not be satisfied without punishments so rigorous as would dishonor the English Government in the eyes of all Europe, and in our own eyes ten years hence. I wish that ministers would remember that the very people who bawl for wholesale executions now will be the first to abuse them for cruelty when this excitement is gone by. The Duke of Cumberland in Scotland did only what all England was clamoring for; but all England changed its mind, and the duke became unpopular for yielding to the cry which was set up in a moment of fear and resentment. As to hanging men by the hundred, it really is not to be thought of with patience. Ten or twelve examples well selected would be quite sufficient, together with the slaughter and burning which have already taken place. If the American prisoners are transported, or kept on the roads at hard labor, their punishment will do more good than a great wholesale execution. The savage language of some of the newspapers, both in Canada and London, makes me doubt whether we are so far beyond the detestable Carlists and Christinos of Spain as I had hoped.

"I read a good deal of Gibbon. He is grossly partial to the pagan persecutors; quite offensively so. His opinion of the Christian fathers is very little removed from mine; but his excuses for the tyranny of their oppressors give to his book the character which Porson describes.* He writes like a man who had received some personal injury from Christianity, and wished to be revenged on it and all its professors. I dined at home, and read some more of 'Pelham' in the evening. I know few things of the kind so good as the character of Lord Vincent."

---

* The passage alluded to occurs in the Preface to the "Letters to Archdeacon Travis," which Macaulay regarded as a work of scholarship second only to Bentley's "Phalaris." " His " (Gibbon's) " reflections are often just and profound. He pleads eloquently for the rights of mankind and the duty of toleration; nor does his humanity ever slumber unless when women are ravished or the Christians persecuted....... He often makes, when he can not readily find, an occasion to insult our religion; which he hates so cordially that he might seem to revenge some personal insult. Such is his eagerness in the cause, that he stoops to the most despicable pun, or to the most awkward perversion of language, for the pleasure of turning the Scriptures into ribaldry, or of calling Jesus an impostor."

Macaulay, who had not yet lost his taste for a show, took full advantage of his presence at Rome during the Christmas festivals. He pronounced the procession in St. Peter's to be the finest thing of the kind that he had ever seen; but it would be unfair on him to expose to general criticism his off-hand description of a pageant, which no written sentences, however carefully arranged and polished, could depict one-tenth as vividly as the colors in which Roberts loved to paint the swarming aisles of a stately cathedral. And yet, perhaps, not even Titian himself (although in a picture at the Louvre, according to Mr. Ruskin, he has put a whole library of dogmatic theology into the backs of a row of bishops) could find means to represent on canvas the sentiments which suggest themselves to the spectators of this, the most impressive of earthly ceremonies. "I was deeply moved," says Macaulay, "by reflecting on the immense antiquity of the papal dignity, which can certainly boast of a far longer clear, known, and uninterrupted succession than any dignity in the world; linking together, as it does, the two great ages of human civilization. Our modern feudal kings are mere upstarts compared with the successors in regular order, not, to be sure, of Peter, but of Sylvester and Leo the Great."

There was one person among the by-standers through whose brain thoughts of this nature were doubtless coursing even more rapidly than through Macaulay's own. "On Christmas-eve I found Gladstone in the throng; and I accosted him; as we had met, though we had never been introduced to each other. He received my advances with very great *empressement* indeed, and we had a good deal of pleasant talk."

"*December* 29*th.*—I went to Torlonia's to get money for my journey. What a curious effect it has to see a bank in a palace, among orange-trees, colonnades, marble statues, and all the signs of the most refined luxury! It carries me back to the days of the merchant-princes of Florence; when philosophers, poets, and painters crowded to the house of Cosmo de' Medici. I drew one hundred pounds' worth of scudi, and had to lug it through the streets in a huge canvas bag, muttering with strong feeling Pope's 'Blest paper credit.' I strolled through the whole of the vast collection of the Vatican with still increasing pleasure. The 'Communion of St. Jerome' seems to me finer and finer every time that I look at it; and the 'Transfiguration' has at last made a complete conquest of me. In spite of all the faults of the plan, I feel it to be the first picture in the world. Then to St. Peter's for the last time, and rambled about it quite sadly. I could not have believed that it would have pained me so much to part from stone and mortar."

"*January 1st,* 1839. — I shall not soon forget the three days which I passed between Rome and Naples. As I descended the hill of Velletri, the huge Pontine Marsh was spread out below like a sea. I soon got into it; and, thank God, soon got out of it. If the Government has not succeeded in making this swamp salubrious, at any rate measures have been taken for enabling people to stay in it as short a time as possible. The road is raised, dry, and well paved; as hard as a rock, and as straight as an arrow. It reminded me of the road in the 'Pilgrim's Progress,' running through the Slough of Despond, the quagmire in the Valley of the Shadow of Death, and the Enchanted Land. At the frontier the custom-house officer begged me to give him a place in my carriage to Mola. I refused, civilly, but firmly. I gave him three crowns not to plague me by searching my baggage, which indeed was protected by a *lascia passare.* He pocketed the three crowns, but looked very dark and sullen at my refusal to accept his company. Precious fellow, to think that a public functionary to whom a little silver is a bribe is fit society for an English gentleman!

"I had a beautiful view of the Bay of Gaeta, with Vesuvius at an immense distance. The whole country is most interesting historically. They pretend to point out on the road the exact spot where Cicero was murdered. I place little more faith in these localities than in the head of St. Andrew, or the spear of Longinus; but it is certain that hereabouts the event took place. The inn at Mola, in which I slept, is called the Villa di Cicerone. The chances are infinite that none of the ruins now extant belonged to Cicero; but it pleased me to think how many great Romans, when Rome was what England is now, loved to pass their occasional holidays on this beautiful coast. I traveled across the low country through which Horace's Liris flows; by the marshes of Minturnæ, where Marius hid himself from the vengeance of Sulla; over the field where Gonsalvo de Cordova gained the great victory of Garigliano. The plain of Capua seemed to retain all its old richness. Since I have been in Italy, I have often thought it very strange that the English have never introduced the olive into any of those vast regions which they have colonized. I do not believe that there is an olive-tree in all the United States, or in South Africa, or in Australasia.

"On my journey through the Pontine Marshes I finished Bulwer's 'Alice.' It affected me much, and in a way in which I have not been affected by novels these many years. Indeed, I generally avoid all novels which are said to have much pathos. The suffering which they produce is to me a very real suffering, and of that I have quite enough without them. I think of Bulwer, still, as I have always thought. He has considerable talent and eloquence; but he is fond of writing about what he only half understands, or understands not at all. His taste is bad; and bad from a cause which lies deep and is not to be removed—from want of soundness, manliness, and simplicity of mind. This work, though better than any thing of his that I have read, is far too long."

"*Thursday, January 3d.*—I must say that the accounts which I had heard of Naples are very incorrect. There is far less beggary than at Rome, and far more industry. Rome is a city of priests. It reminded me of the towns in Palestine which were set apart to be inhabited by the Levites. Trade and agriculture seem only to be tolerated as subsidiary to devotion. Men are allowed to work; because, unless somebody works, nobody can live; and, if nobody lives, nobody can pray. But as soon as you enter Naples you notice a striking contrast. It is the difference between Sunday and Monday. Here the business of civil life is evidently the great thing, and religion is the accessory. A poet might introduce Naples as Martha, and Rome as Mary. A Catholic may think Mary's the better employment; but, even a Catholic, much more a Protestant, would prefer the table of Martha. I must ask many questions about these matters. At present, my impressions are very favorable to Naples. It is the only place in Italy that has seemed to me to have the same sort of vitality which you find in all the great English ports and cities. Rome and Pisa are dead and gone; Florence is not dead, but sleepeth; while Naples overflows with life.

"I have a letter from Empson, who tells me that every body speaks handsomely about my refusal of the judge-advocateship. Holt Mackenzie praised the 'Code' highly at Rogers's the other day. I am glad of it. It is, however, a sort of work which must wait long for justice, as I well knew when I labored at it."

"*Naples, Sunday, January 6th.*—I climbed to the top of the hill to see Virgil's tomb. The tomb has no interest but what it derives from its name. I do not know the history of this ruin; but, if the tradition be an immemorial tradition—if nobody can fix any time when it originated—I should be inclined to think it authentic. Virgil was just the man whose burial-place was likely to be known to every generation which has lived since his death. There has been no period, from the Augustan age downward, when there were not readers of the 'Æneid' in Italy. The suspicious time with the religion of the Catholic Church is the early time. I suppose nobody doubts that the sepulchre now shown as that of Christ is the same with the sepulchre of Helena, or that the place now pointed out as the tomb of St. Paul is the same which was so considered in the days of Chrysostom. The local traditions of Christianity are clear enough during the last thirteen hundred or fourteen hundred years. It is during the first two or three centuries that the chain fails. Now, as to Virgil, there can be no doubt that his burial-place would have been as well known till the dissolution of the Western Empire as that of Shakspeare is now; and, even in the dark ages, there would always have been a certain number of people interested about his remains. I returned to my hotel, exceedingly tired with walking and climbing. I dined; had a pint of bottled porter, worth all the Falernian of these days; and finished the evening by my fireside over Theodore Hook's 'Jack Brag.' He is a clever, coarse, vulgar writer."

"*Friday, January 11th.*—When I woke it was snowing; so that I determined to give up Pæstum, for which I was rather sorry; when, at about eleven, it became fine and clear. But I was not quite well, and it is bitterly cold to a returned Indian. I staid by my fire and read Bulwer's 'Pompeii.' It has eloquence and talent, like all his books. It has also more learning than I expected; but it labors under the usual faults of all works in which it is attempted to give moderns a glimpse of ancient manners. After all, between us and them there is a great gulf, which no learning will enable a man to clear. Strength of imagination may empower him to create a world unlike our own; but the chances are a thousand to one that it is not the world which has passed away. Perhaps those act most wisely who, in treating poetically of ancient events, stick to general human nature, avoid gross blunders of costume, and trouble themselves about little more. All attempts to exhibit Romans talking slang, and jesting with each other, however clever, must be failures. There are a good many pretty obvious blots in Bulwer's book. Why, in the name of common sense, did Glaucus neglect to make himself a Roman citizen? He, a man of fortune and talents residing in Italy, intimate with Romans of distinction! Arbaces, too, is not a citizen. Rich, powerful, educated subjects of Rome, dwelling in a considerable Italian town, and highly acceptable in all societies there, yet not citizens! The thing was never heard of, I imagine. The Christianity of Bulwer's book is not to my taste. The Trinity; the Widow's son; the recollections of the preaching of St. Paul, spoil the classical effect of the story. I do not believe that Christianity had, at that time, made the very smallest impression on the educated classes in Italy; some Jews, of course, excepted. Bulwer brings down the Greek valor and free spirit to too late an age. He carries back the modern feelings of philanthropy to too early an age. His Greeks are made up of scraps of the Athenian republican, and scraps of the Parisian *philosophe;* neither of which suit with the smart, voluble, lying, cringing jack-of-all-trades that a Greek under the Flavian family would have been. It is very clever, nevertheless."

"*January 12th.*—This was the king's birthday. The court was attended by many foreigners. The king paid no attention to the English—not even to so great a man as the Duke of Buccleuch—but reserved his civil-ities for the Russians. Fool, to think that either the lion or the bear cares which side the hare takes in these disputes! In the evening, as I was sipping Marsala, and reading a novel called 'Crichton,' by the author of 'Rookwood,' and worse than 'Rookwood,' in came Verney to beg me to take a seat in his opera-box at the Teatro di San Carlo, which was to be illuminated in honor of the day. I care little for operas; but as this theatre is said to be the finest in Italy—indeed, in Europe—and as the occasion was a great one, I agreed. The royal family were below us, so that we did not see them; and I am sure that I would not give a carlino to see every Bourbon, living and dead, of the Spanish branch. The performance tired me to death, or rather to sleep; and I actually dozed for half an hour. Home, and read 'Gil Blas.' Charming. I am never tired of it."

Macaulay returned from Naples to Marseilles by a coasting steamer, which touched at Civita Vecchia, where—

"Goulburn came on board.* He was very civil and friendly. We chatted a good deal at dinner, and even got upon politics, and talked without the least acrimony on either side. Once I had him, and he felt it. He was abusing the election committees. 'You really think, then, Mr. Goulburn, that the decisions of the election committees are partial and unfair?' 'I do,' he said, 'most decidedly.' 'Well, then,' said I, 'I can not but think that it was rather hard to pass a vote of censure on O'Connell for saying so.' I never saw a man more completely at a nonplus. He quite colored —face, forehead, and all—and looked

'As I have seen him in the Capitol,
    Being crossed in conference with some senators.'

He had really nothing to say, except that he had given his opinion about election committees to me in private. I told him that I, of course, understood it so; and I was too generous and polite to press my victory. But, really, a vote of censure is a serious thing; and I do not conceive that any man is justified in voting for it, unless he thinks it deserved. There is little difference between a dishonest vote in an election committee and a dishonest vote in a question of censure. Both are judicial proceedings. The oath taken by members of a committee is merely a bugbear for old women, and men like old women. A wise and honest man has other guides than superstition to direct his conduct. I like Goulburn's conversation and manners. I had a prejudice against him which, like most prejudices conceived merely on the ground of political difference, yields

---

* Mr. Goulburn was subsequently chancellor of the exchequer in Sir Robert Peel's Government.

readily to a little personal intercourse. And this is a man whom I have disliked for years without knowing him, and who has probably disliked me with just as little reason! A lesson.

"I read Botta's 'History of the American War.' The book interested me, though he is not a writer to my taste. He is fair enough; and when he misrepresents, it is rather from ignorance than from partiality. But he is shallow, and his style is the most affected that can be imagined. I can better excuse his speeches, put into the mouths of his heroes, and his attempts to give a classical air to our English debates; his substitution of 'Signor Giorgio Grenville' for 'the right honorable gentleman,' and 'cari concittadini,' or 'venerabili senatori,' for 'Mr. Speaker.' But his efforts at naïveté move my disgust. The affectation of magnificence I can pardon, but the affectation of simplicity is loathsome; for magnificence may co-exist with affectation, but simplicity and affectation are in their natures opposite. Botta uses so many odd old words that even Italians require a glossary to read him; and he is particularly fond of imitating the infantine style which is so delightful in Boccaccio. He perpetually introduces into his narratives vulgar Florentine proverbs of the fourteenth century. He tells us that God, 'who does not stay till Saturday to pay wages,' took signal vengeance on the ravagers of Wyoming; and that they were repaid for their outrages 'with collier's measure.'"

"*Paris, February 2d,* 1839.—The sky was clear; though it was very cold, and the snow covered every thing. I resolved to go to Versailles. The palace is a huge heap of littleness. On the side toward Paris the contrast between the patches of red brick in the old part, and the attempt at classical magnificence in the later part, is simply revolting. Enormous as is the size of the Place des Armes, it looks paltry beyond description. The statues which used to stand at Paris on the bridge in front of the Chamber of Deputies are ranged round this court. Wretched, strutting things they were; heroes storming like captains of banditti blustering through a bad melodrama in a second-rate theatre. I had hoped never to have seen them again when I missed them on the bridge; and I fancied, more fool I, that the Government might have had the good taste to throw them into the Seine. In the middle of the court is an equestrian statue of Louis XIV. He showed his sense, at least, in putting himself where he could not see his own architectural performances. I was glad to walk through the Orangerie, and thence I went some little way into the gardens. The snow was several inches deep; but I saw enough to satisfy me that these famous grounds, in meanness and extravagance, surpassed my expectations; and my expectations were not moderate. The garden façade of the palace is certainly fine by contrast with the other front; but when the enormous means employed are compared with the effect, the disproportion is wonderful. This façade is about two thousand feet in length, and is elevated on a lofty terrace. It ought to be one of the most striking works of human power and art. I doubt whether there be anywhere any single architectural composition of equal extent. I do not believe that all the works of Pericles—nay, that even St. Peter's, colonnade and all—cost so much as was lavished on Versailles; and yet there are a dozen country houses of private individuals in England alone which have a greater air of majesty and splendor than this huge quarry. Castle Howard is immeasurably finer. I went inside, and was struck by the good sense — I would even say magnanimity — which the present king has shown in admitting all that does honor to the nation, without regard to personal or family considerations. The victories of Bonaparte furnish half the rooms. Even Charles the Tenth is fairly dealt with. Whatever titles he had to public respect—the African victories; Navarino; the Dauphin's exploits, such as they were, in Spain—all have a place here. The most interesting thing, however, in the whole palace is Louis the Fourteenth's bedroom, with its original furniture. I thought of all St. Simon's anecdotes about that room and bed."

CHAPTER VIII.

1839–1841.

Macaulay returns to London.—He meets Lord Brougham—Letters to Mr.
Napier and Mrs. Trevelyan. — Correspondence with Mr. Gladstone. —
Heated State of Politics.—The Hostility of the Peers to Lord Melbourne's
Government.—Macaulay's View of the Situation.—Verses by Praed.—
The Bed-chamber Question.—Macaulay is elected for Edinburgh.—De-
bate on the Ballot.—Macaulay becomes a Cabinet Minister.—The *Times*.
—Windsor Castle.—Vote of Want of Confidence.—The Chinese War.—
Irish Registration : Scene in the House of Commons.—Letters to Napier.
—Religious Difficulties in Scotland.—Lord Cardigan.—The Corn Laws.
—The Sugar Duties.—Defeat of the Ministry, and Dissolution of Parlia-
ment.—Macaulay is re-elected for Edinburgh.—His Love for Street-bal-
lads.—The Change of Government.

At the end of the first week in February, 1839, Macaulay
was again in London.

"*Friday, February 8th.*—I have been reading Lord Durham's Canadian
report, and think it exceedingly good and able. I learn, with great concern, that the business has involved Lord Glenelg's resignation. Poor fellow! I love him and feel for him.* I bought Gladstone's book: a capital
Shrove-tide cock to throw at. Almost too good a mark."

"*February 13th.*—I read, while walking, a good deal of Gladstone's book.
The Lord hath delivered him into our hand. I think I see my way to a
popular, and at the same time gentleman-like, critique. I called on the
Miss Berrys, who are very desirous to collect my articles. I gave them a
list, and procured some numbers for them at a book-seller's near Leicester
Square. Thence to Ellis, and repeated him ' Romulus,' the alterations in
' Horatius,' and the beginning of ' Virginia.' He was much pleased. We
walked away together to Lincoln's Inn Fields, and met Brougham : an awkward moment. But he greeted me just as if we had parted yesterday,
shook hands, got between us, and walked with us some way. He was in
extraordinary force, bodily and mental. He declared vehemently against

---

* See page 263 of vol. i.

the usage which Lord Glenelg has experienced, and said that it was a case for pistoling, an infamous league of eleven men to ruin one. It will be long enough before he takes to the remedy which he recommends to others. He talked well and bitterly of Lord Durham's report. It was, he said, a second-rate article for the *Edinburgh Review.* 'The matter came from a swindler; the style from a coxcomb; and the dictator furnished only six letters, D-U-R-H-A-M.' As we were walking, Allen the Quaker came by. Brougham hallooed to him, and began to urge him to get up the strongest opposition to Lord John Russell's education plan. I was glad when we parted. Home, and thought about Gladstone. In two or three days I shall have the whole in my head, and then my pen will go like fire."

3 Clarges Street, February 26th, 1839.

DEAR NAPIER,—I can now promise you an article in a week, or ten days at furthest. Of its length I can not speak with certainty. I should think it would fill about forty pages; but I find the subject grow on me. I think that I shall dispose completely of Gladstone's theory. I wish that I could see my way clearly to a good counter-theory; but I catch only glimpses here and there of what I take to be truth.

I am leading an easy life; not unwilling to engage in the Parliamentary battle if a fair opportunity should offer, but not in the smallest degree tormented by a desire for the House of Commons, and fully determined against office. I enjoyed Italy intensely; far more than I had expected. By-the-bye, I met Gladstone at Rome. We talked and walked together in St. Peter's during the best part of an afternoon. He is both a clever and an amiable man.

As to politics, the cloud has blown over; the sea has gone down; the barometer is rising. The session is proceeding through what was expected to be its most troubled stage in the same quiet way in which it generally advances through the dog-days toward its close. Every thing and every body is languid, and even Brougham seems to be somewhat mitigated. I met him in Lincoln's Inn Fields, the other day, when I was walking with Ellis. He greeted me as if we had breakfasted together that morning, and went on to declaim against every body with even more than his usual parts, and with all his usual rashness and flightiness. Ever yours,

T. B. MACAULAY.

London, March 20th, 1839.

DEAREST HANNAH,—I have passed some very melancholy days since I wrote last. On Sunday afternoon I left Ellis tolerably cheerful. His wife's disorder was abating. The next day, when I went to him, I found the house shut up. I meant only to have asked after him; but he would see me. He gave way to very violent emotion; but he soon collected himself, and talked to me about her for hours. "I was so proud of her," he said. "I loved so much to show her to any body that I valued. And now, what good will it do me to be a judge or to make ten thousand a year? I shall not have her to go home to with the good news." I could not speak, for I know what that feeling is as well as he. He talked much of the sources of happiness that were left to him—his children, his relations and hers, and my friendship. He ought, he said, to be very grateful that I had not died in India, but was at home to comfort him. Comfort him I could not, except by hearing him talk of her with tears in my eyes. I staid till late. Yesterday I went again, and passed most of the day with him, and I shall go to him again to-day; for he says, and I see, that my company does him good. I would with pleasure give one of my fingers to get him back his wife, which is more than most widowers would give to get back their own.

I have had my proofs from Napier. He magnifies the article prodigiously. In a letter to Empson he calls it exquisite and admirable, and to me he writes that it is the finest piece of logic that ever was printed. I do not think it so; but I do think that I have disposed of all Gladstone's theories unanswerably; and there is not a line of the paper with which even so strict a judge as Sir Robert Inglis or my uncle Babington could quarrel at as at all indecorous. How is my dear little girl? Is she old enough to take care of a canary bird or two. From her tenderness for the little fish, I think I may venture to trust her with live animals.

I have this instant a note from Lord Lansdowne, who was in the chair of *the* Club* yesterday night, to say that I am

---

* The Club, as it was invariably called (for its members would not stoop

unanimously elected. Poor Ellis's loss had quite put it out of my head. Ever yours, T. B. M.

On the 10th of April Macaulay received a letter from Mr. Gladstone, who in generous terms acknowledged the courtesy, and, with some reservations, the fairness of his article. "I have been favored," Mr. Gladstone wrote, "with a copy of the forthcoming number of the *Edinburgh Review;* and I perhaps too much presume upon the bare acquaintance with you, of which alone I can boast, in thus unceremoniously assuming you to be the author of the article entitled 'Church and State,' and in offering you my very warm and cordial thanks for the manner in which you have treated both the work, and the author on whom you deigned to bestow your attention. In whatever you write, you can hardly hope for the privilege of most anonymous productions, a real concealment; but, if it had been possible not to recognize you, I should have questioned your authorship in this particular case, because the candor and single-mindedness which it exhibits are, in one who has long been connected in the most distinguished manner with political party, so rare as to be almost incredible...... In these lacerating times one clings to every thing of personal kindness in the past, to husband it for tho future; and, if you will allow me, I shall earnestly desire to carry with me such a recollection of your mode of dealing with a subject upon which the attainment of truth, we shall agree, so materially depends upon the temper in which the search for it is instituted and conducted."

How much this letter pleased Macaulay is indicated by the

---

to identify it by any distinctive title) was the club of Johnson, Gibbon, Burke, Goldsmith, Garrick, and Reynolds. Under the date April 9th, 1839, the following entry occurs in Macaulay's diary: "I went to the Thatched House, and was well pleased to meet the Club for the first time. We had Lord Holland in the chair, the Bishop of London, Lord Mahon, Phillips the painter, Milman, Elphinstone, Sir Charles Grey, and Hudson Gurney. I was amused, in turning over the records of the Club, to come upon poor Bozzy's signature, evidently affixed when he was too drunk to guide his pen."

fact of his having kept it unburned; a compliment which, except in this single instance, he never paid to any of his correspondents. "I have very seldom," he writes in reply to Mr. Gladstone, "been more gratified than by the very kind note which I have just received from you. Your book itself, and every thing that I heard about you, though almost all my information came — to the honor, I must say, of our troubled times—from people very strongly opposed to you in politics, led me to regard you with respect and good-will, and I am truly glad that I have succeeded in marking those feelings. I was half afraid, when I read myself over again in print, that the button, as is too common in controversial fencing even between friends, had once or twice come off the foil."

The emphatic allusions which both these letters contain to the prevailing bitterness and injustice of party feeling may well sound strangely to us, who have already for two sessions been living in that atmosphere of good temper and good manners which pervades the House of Commons whenever the Conservatives are contented and the Liberals despondent. It was a different matter in 1839. The closing years of the Whig Administration were one long political crisis, with all the disagreeable and discreditable accompaniments from which no political crisis is free. Public animosity and personal virulence had risen to a higher, or, at any rate, to a more sustained temperature than had ever been reached since the period when, amidst threats of impeachment and accusations of treason, perfidy, and corruption, Sir Robert Walpole was tottering to his fall.

Lord Melbourne's Cabinet had rendered immense services to the country, and the greatest of those services was the fact of its own existence. In November, 1834, the king, of his own will and pleasure, had imposed a Tory government on a House of Commons which contained a large Whig majority. The fierce onslaught upon that government, so gallantly and skillfully led by Lord John Russell, while it presented (as it could not fail to present) a superficial appearance of factious self-seeking, was in truth a struggle fought to establish, once and forever, the most vital of all constitutional principles.

Not a vote nor a speech was thrown away, of all that were directed against Sir Robert's Peel's first ministry. It was worth
any expenditure of time and breath and energy to vindicate
the right of the country to choose its rulers for itself, instead
of accepting those who might be imposed upon it from above.
The story of the session of 1835 reads strangely to us who
have been born, and hope to grow old, within the reign of the
monarch who, by a long course of loyal acquiescence in the declared wishes of her people, has brought about what is nothing less than another Great Revolution, all the more beneficent because it has been gradual and silent. We can not,
without an effort of the imagination, understand the indignation and disquietude of the Whig leaders, when they saw William the Fourth recurring to those maxims of personal government which his father had effectually practiced, and after
which his brother had feebly and fitfully hankered. To get
Peel out was in their eyes the whole duty of public men; a
duty which they strenuously and successfully accomplished.
But, in pursuing their end with an audacity and determination
which those who had not divined the real bearings of the situation mistook for want of scruple, they made hosts of new
enemies, and imbittered all their old ones. They aroused
against themselves the furies of resentment, alarm, and distrust, which attended them relentlessly until they in their turn
succumbed. The passions heated during the debates of 1835
were cooled only in the deluge which overwhelmed the Whigs
at the general election of 1841.

The Peers gave them no chance from the first. Those who
have joined in the idle jubilation over the impotence and
helplessness of the House of Lords, with which, in our own
day, triumphant partisans celebrated the downfall of the Irish
Church and the abolition of purchase in the army, would do
well to study the history of the decline and fall of Lord Melbourne's Administration. There they would learn how sub-
stantial, and how formidable, is the power of Conservative
statesmen who, surveying the field of action from the secure
stronghold of an assembly devoted to their interests, can discern through all the dust and clamor of a popular movement

the exact strength and attitude of the hostile forces. An Upper Chamber which will accept from ministers whom it detests no measure that has not behind it an irresistible mass of excited public opinion, has, sooner or later, the fate of those ministers in its hands. For, on the one hand, the friction generated by the process of forcing a bill through a reluctant House of Lords annoys and scandalizes a nation which soon grows tired of having a revolution once a twelvemonth; and, on the other hand, the inability of a cabinet to conduct through both Houses that continuous flow of legislation which the ever-changing necessities of a country like ours demand, alienates those among its more ardent supporters who take little account of its difficulties, and see only that it is unable to turn its bills into acts.

Never was the game of obstruction played more ably, and to better purpose, than during the three sessions which preceded, and the three which followed, the accession of Queen Victoria. "Lord Cadogan," Macaulay writes, "talked to me well of the exceedingly difficult situation of the ministers in the Lords. They have against them Brougham, the first speaker of the age; the duke, with the highest character of any public man of the age; Lyndhurst, Aberdeen, Ellenborough, and others, every one of whom is an overmatch for our best orator. And this superiority in debate is backed by a still greater superiority in number." These advantages, in point of votes and talents, were utilized to the utmost by consummate parliamentary strategy. The struggle was fought out over the destination of a sum of money expected to accrue from the improved management of Church property in Ireland. The Whigs proposed to appropriate this money to the education of the people at large, without distinction of religious persuasion; while the Opposition insisted on leaving it at the disposal of the Church, to be used exclusively for Church purposes. It was an admirable battle-ground for the Conservatives. The most exalted motives of piety and patriotism, the blindest prejudices of race and creed, were alike arrayed behind the impregnable defenses which guarded the position so adroitly selected by the Tory leaders. In the fourth

year of the contest the ministers yielded, with a disastrous
effect upon their own influence and reputation, from which
they never recovered. But the victory had been dearly
bought. In exchange for the reversion of a paltry hundred
thousand pounds, the Irish Establishment had bartered away
what remained to it of the public confidence and esteem.
The next sacrifice which it was called upon to make was of a
very different magnitude; and it was fated to read by the
light of a bitter experience the story of the Sibylline books
—that fable the invention of which is in itself sufficient to
stamp the Romans as a constitutional people.

Macaulay's letters from Calcutta prove with what profound
uneasiness he watched the course of public affairs at home. A
looker-on, who shares the passions of the combatants, is seldom inclined to underrate the gravity of the situation, or the
drastic nature of the remedies that are required. "I am quite
certain," so he writes to Mr. Ellis, "that in a few years the
House of Lords must go after Old Sarum and Gatton. What
is now passing is mere skirmishing and manœuvring between
two general actions. It seems to be of little consequence to
the final result how these small operations turn out. When
the grand battle comes to be fought, I have no doubt about
the event." At length his sense of coming evil grew so keen,
that he took the step of addressing to Lord Lansdowne a carefully reasoned letter, a state paper in all but the form; urging the imminent perils that threatened a constitution in
which a reformed House of Commons found itself face to face
with an unreformed House of Lords; and setting forth in detail a scheme for reconstructing the Upper Chamber on an
elective basis. Macaulay's notions were not at all to his old
friend's taste; and, after a single interchange of opinions, the
subject never re-appeared in their correspondence.

On the tactics pursued by Peel and Lyndhurst, Macaulay
expressed the sentiments of a Whig politician in the language of a student of history. "Your English politics," he
writes from India during the first week of 1838, "are in a
singular state. The elections appear to have left the two
parties still almost exactly equal in Parliamentary strength.

There seems to be a tendency in the public mind to moderation : but there seems also to be a most pernicious disposition
to mix up religion with politics. For my own part, I can conceive nothing more dangerous to the interests of religion than
the new Conservative device of representing a reforming spirit as synonymous with an infidel spirit. For a short time the
Tories may gain something by giving to civil abuses the sanctity of religion ; but religion will very soon begin to contract
the unpopularity which belongs to civil abuses. There will
be, I am satisfied, a violent reaction ; and ten years hence
Christianity will be as unpopular a topic on the hustings as
the duty of seeking the Lord would have been at the time
of the Restoration. The world is governed by associations.
That which is always appealed to as a defense for every grievance will soon be considered as a grievance itself. No cry
which deprives the people of valuable servants, and raises job-
bers and oppressors to power, will long continue to be a popular cry."

There is something almost pathetic in this unbounded and
unshaken faith in the virtues of a political party. The praise
which in a confidential letter a man bestows upon his contemporaries is pretty sure to be sincere ; and when Macaulay
described Lord Melbourne's Administration as a breakwater
which stemmed the advancing tide of Tory jobbery, no one
who knew him, or who knows his writings, can doubt that he
believed what he said. And yet it required not a little courage to represent the Whigs of 1838 as deaf to the claims of
private interests and family connections. So widespread and
so deeply rooted was the conviction that the ministers gave
more thought to placing their dependents than to governing
the country, that their best actions were beginning to be mis-
construed by their oldest friends. The invaluable series of
investigations, by royal commissions, into all that concerned
the moral, social, and religious welfare of the people, which
was conducted under Lord Melbourne's auspices, presented itself to all his opponents, and some of his allies, in the light of
a gigantic machinery devised by the people in power with the
express purpose of providing for briefless sons and nephews.

Sydney Smith, whose appetite for reform was very soon sati-
ated when the era of reform had once fairly set in, declared in
a burst of humorous consternation that the whole earth was
in commission, and that mankind had been saved from the
Flood only to be delivered over to barristers of six years'
standing. The *onus probandi*, he declared, rested with any
one who said that he was not a commissioner; and the only
doubt which a man felt on seeing a Whig whom he had never
met before was, not whether he was a commissioner or no, but
what the department of human life might be into which he
had been appointed to inquire.

That which was fussiness and nepotism in the eyes of an
original founder of the *Edinburgh Review*, to a contributor
to the *Morning Post* seemed little better than recklessness
and rapacity. It was about this period that Praed assailed
the ministry in some of the most incisive couplets which a
political satirist has ever penned.*

> Sure none should better know how sweet
> The tenure of official seat
> Than one who every session buys
> At such high rate the gaudy prize;
> One who for this so long has borne
> The scowl of universal scorn;
> Has seen distrust in every look;
> Has heard in every voice rebuke;
> Exulting yet, as home he goes
> From sneering friends and pitying foes,
> That, shun him, loathe him, if they will,
> He keeps the seals and salary still.
>   And, truth to say, it must be pleasant
> To be a minister at present:
> To make believe to guide the realm
> Without a hand upon the helm,
> And wonder what with such a crew
> A pilot e'er should find to do;

* The little poem from which these lines are taken has hitherto remained unpublished, with the exception of the concluding appeal to the
young queen—a passage which is marked by an elevation of tone unusual
in Praed's political effusions.

> To hold what people are content
> To fancy is the government,
> And touch extremely little of it
> Except the credit and the profit;
> When Follett presses, Sugden poses,
> To bid gay Stanley* count the noses,
> And leave the Cabinet's defense
> To Bulwer's wit and Blewitt's sense;
> To hear demands of explanation
> On India, Belgium, trade, taxation,
> And answer that perhaps they'll try
> To give an answer by-and-by;
> To save the Church and serve the Crown
> By letting others pull them down;
> To promise, pause, prepare, postpone,
> And end by letting things alone;
> In short, to earn the people's pay
> By doing nothing every day;
> These tasks, these joys, the Fates assign
> To well-placed Whigs in Thirty-nine.

A greater man than Praed or Sydney Smith has traced an indelible record of the impression produced upon himself, and others like him, by the events of that melancholy epoch. Carlyle had shared to the full in the ardor and enthusiasm which hailed the passing of the Great Reform Bill; and he now had rather more than his share of the disappointment and the gloom, which, after seven years' experience of a Reformed House of Commons, led by the Whigs, and thwarted by the Peers, had begun to settle down upon the minds of all who loved their country better than their party. In more than one of his volumes he has told us the story of a "young ardent soul, looking with hope and joy into a world infinitely beautiful to him, though overhung with falsities and foul cobwebs, which were to be swept away amidst heroic joy, and enthusiasm of victory and battle;" and of the discouragement that eclipsed these gallant anticipations, when one session after

---

* The late Lord Stanley, of Alderley, was Treasury whip to the Melbourne Administration. The traditions of the lobby still point to his tenure of office as the culminating epoch in the art of Parliamentary management.

another was spent on getting, "with endless jargoning, debating, motioning, and counter-motioning, a settlement effected between the Honorable Mr. This and the Honorable Mr. That as to their respective pretensions to ride the high horse." The time had arrived when to the passion and energy of 1832 had succeeded the unedifying spectacle of "hungry Greek throttling down hungry Greek on the floor of St. Stephen's, until the loser cried, 'Hold! The place is thine.' "

The responsibility for the continuance of this sterile and ignoble political ferment, which for some years had lain at the door of the House of Lords, began to be shared by the Whig Government soon after Macaulay's return from India. From that time forward Lord Melbourne and his brother-ministers could not have failed to perceive, by those signs which are so familiar to veteran politicians, that their popularity was waning; and that, with their popularity, their power for good was disappearing fast. When their measures were mangled and curtailed in the Commons, and quashed in the Peers— when one election after another told the same tale of general dissatisfaction and distrust—it became incumbent on them to show themselves at least as ready to surrender office as, in 1835, they had been resolute in seizing it. The hour had arrived when statesmen should have caught eagerly at the first opportunity of proving that our unwritten constitution provides a key to that problem on the right solution of which the prosperity, and even the existence, of a free community depends—the problem how rulers, who have for a time lost the favor and confidence of the governed, may for a time be removed from power, without impairing the force and the authority of the Executive Government. Unfortunately there were considerations, honorable in themselves, which deterred the Cabinet from that wise and dignified course; and the month of May, 1839, saw the leaders of the great party, which had marched into office across the steps of a throne, standing feebly at bay behind the petticoats of their wives and sisters. Whether the part which they played was forced upon them by circumstances, or whether it was not, their example was disastrous in its effect upon English public life. Our standard of ministerial duty was lower from that day forth; until, in June, 1866, it was raised to a higher point than ever by the refusal of Earl Russell and his colleagues to remain in power, after they had found themselves unable to carry in its integrity the measure of Reform which they had promised to the nation.

As soon as the Whigs had made up their minds to solve the Bed-chamber difficulty by resuming office, they were, naturally enough, anxious to bring within the walls of the House of Commons all the ability and eloquence of their party. Times were coming when they were likely to find occasion for as much oratory as they could muster. Toward the end of May the elevation to the peerage of Mr. Abercromby, the Speaker, left a seat at Edinburgh vacant. The ministers did all that could be done in London to get Macaulay accepted as the Liberal candidate, and the constituency gave a willing response. He introduced himself to the electors in a speech that in point of style came up to their expectations, and with the substance of which they were very well contented. He conciliated the Radicals by pledging himself to the ballot; the reminiscences of Lord Melville's despotism were still too fresh in Scotch memories to make it worth while for the Tories even to talk of contesting the representation of the Scotch capital; and the Whigs would have been monsters of ingratitude if they had not declared to a man in favor of one who was a Whig with the same intensity of conviction that Montrose had been a Royalist, or Carnot a Jacobin. "I look with pride," said Macaulay, "on all that the Whigs have done for the cause of human freedom and of human happiness. I see them now hard pressed, struggling with difficulties, but still fighting the good fight. At their head I see men who have inherited the spirit and the virtues, as well as the blood, of old champions and martyrs of freedom. To those men I propose to attach myself. While one shred of the old banner is flying, by that banner will I, at least, be found. Whether in or out of Parliament—whether speaking with that authority which must always belong to the representative of this great and enlightened community, or expressing the humble sentiments of a

private citizen—I will to the last maintain inviolate my fidel-
ity to principles which, though they may be borne down for a
time by senseless clamor, are yet strong with the strength, and
immortal with the immortality, of truth; and which, however
they may be misunderstood or misrepresented by contemporaries, will assuredly find justice from a better age." Such
fervor will provoke a smile from those who survey the field
of politics with the serene complacency of the literary critic,
more readily than from statesmen who have learned the value
of party loyalty by frequent and painful experience of its opposite.

The first speech which Macaulay made after his re-appear-
ance in Parliament was on Mr. Grote's motion for leave to introduce the Ballot Bill. That annual question (to which the
philosophical reasoning and the classical erudition of its champion had long ere this ceased to impart any charm more attractive than respectability), in 1839 had recovered a certain
flavor of novelty from the fact that Lord Melbourne's Cabinet,
at its wits' end for something that might make it popular, had
agreed that the more advanced among the ministers might be
at liberty to vote as they pleased. The propriety of this course
was, naturally enough, challenged by their opponents. Macaulay had an admirable opportunity of giving the House,
which was eager to hear him, a characteristic touch of his
quality, as he poured forth a torrent of historical instances to
prove that governments which had regard for their own sta-
bility, or for the consciences of their individual members, always had recognized, and always must recognize, the necessity of dealing liberally with open questions. "I rejoice," he
said, "to see that we are returning to the wise, the honest,
the moderate maxims which prevailed in this House in the
time of our fathers. If two men are brought up together
from their childhood; if they follow the same studies, mix in
the same society, and exercise a mutual influence in forming
each other's minds, a perfect agreement between them on political subjects can not even then be expected. But governments are constructed in such a manner that forty or fifty gentlemen, some of whom have never seen each other's faces till

they are united officially, or have been in hot opposition to each other all the rest of their lives, are brought all at once into intimate connection. Among such men unanimity would be an absolute miracle. 'Talk of divided houses!' said Lord Chatham. 'Why there never was an instance of a united Cabinet! When were the minds of twelve men ever cast in one and the same mold? Within the memory of many persons now living the rule was this, that all questions whatever were open questions in a Cabinet, except those which came under two classes—measures brought forward by the Government as a government, which all the members of the Government were, of course, expected to support; and motions brought forward with the purpose of casting a censure, express or implied, on the Government, or any department of it, which all the members of the Government were, of course, expected to oppose. Let honorable gentlemen," said Macaulay, warming to his theme, " run their minds over the history of Mr. Pitt's administration :" and honorable gentlemen were reminded, or, not impossibly, informed, how, on Parliamentary Reform, Mr. Pitt and Mr. Dundas had voted against Lord Mulgrave and Lord Grenville; and how, on the question of the slave-trade, Mr. Dundas and Lord Thurlow had voted against Lord Grenville and Mr. Pitt; and so on through the law of libel, and the impeachment of Warren Hastings, and the dropping of the impeachment of Warren Hastings, until the names of Mr. Pitt's Cabinet had been presented to the view of honorable gentlemen in every possible variation, and every conceivable combination. " And was this the effect of any extraordinary weakness on the part of the statesman who was then prime minister? No. Mr. Pitt was a man whom even his enemies acknowledged to possess a brave and commanding spirit. And was the effect of his policy to enfeeble his administration, to daunt his adherents, to render them unable to withstand the attacks of the Opposition? On the contrary, never did a ministry present a firmer or more serried front; nor is there the slightest doubt but that their strength was increased in consequence of their giving each member more individual liberty."

Sir Robert Peel, after expressing in handsome and even chivalrous terms his satisfaction at finding himself once more confronted by so redoubtable an antagonist, proceeded to reply with a feeble and partial argument, set off by a fine quotation from Burke. To this day there remains unanswered Macaulay's protest against the cruelty of needlessly placing men in a position where they must be false either to their personal convictions or to a factitious theory of ministerial obligation—a protest which has still greater force when directed against the extravagant impolicy of bringing the immense weight and authority of the Treasury bench to influence the vote upon an abstract motion, which can have no possible value, except in so far as it affords a genuine and unbiased indication of Parliamentary opinion.

London, July 4th, 1839.

DEAR NAPIER,—I am sorry that you had set your heart on a paper from me. I was really not aware that you expected one, or I would have written earlier to tell you that it would be quite impossible for me to do any thing of the kind at present. I mean to give you a life of Clive for October. The subject is a grand one, and admits of decorations and illustrations innumerable.

I meant to have spoken on the Education question; but the ministers pushed up Vernon Smith just as I was going to rise, and I had no other opportunity till Goulburn sat down, having thoroughly wearied the House. Five hundred people were coughing and calling for the question; and, though some of our friends wanted me to try my fortune, I was too prudent. A second speech is a critical matter; and it is always hazardous to address an impatient audience after midnight.

I do not like to write for you on Education, or on other pending political questions. I have two fears—one that I may commit myself, the other that I may unseat myself. I shall keep to history, general literature, and the merely speculative part of politics, in what I write for the *Review*.

Ever yours,   T. B. M.

Edinburgh, September 2d, 1839.

DEAR NAPIER,—I shall work on Clive as hard as I can, and make the paper as short as I can; but I am afraid that I can not positively pledge myself either as to time or as to length. I rather think, however, that the article will take.

I shall do my best to be in London again on the 18th. God knows what these ministerial changes may produce. Office was never, within my memory, so little attractive, and therefore, I fear, I can not, as a man of spirit, flinch, if it is offered to me. Ever yours,   T. B. MACAULAY.

London, September 20th, 1839.

DEAR NAPIER,—I reached town early this morning; having, principally on your account, shortened my stay at Paris, and crossed to Ramsgate in such weather that the mails could not get into the harbor at Dover. I hoped to have five or six days of uninterrupted work, in which I might finish my paper for the *Review*. But I found waiting for me—this is strictly confidential—a letter from Lord Melbourne with an offer of the Secretaryship at War, and a seat in the Cabinet. I shall be a good deal occupied, as you may suppose, by conferences and correspondence during some time; but I assure you that every spare minute shall be employed in your. service. I shall hope to be able, at all events, to send you the article by the 30th. I will write the native names as clearly as I can, and trust to your care without a proof.

My historical plans must for the present be suspended;* but I see no reason to doubt that I shall be able to do as much as ever for the *Review*. Again, remember, silence is the word. Yours ever,   T. B. M.

Macaulay accepted the Secretaryship at War without any show of reluctance; but he did not attain to this great elevation without incurring the penalties of success. A man who,

---

* "*Friday, March 9th.*—I began my 'History' with a sketch of the early revolutions of England. Pretty well; but a little too stately and rhetorical."—*Macaulay's Journal for* 1839.

having begun life without rank, fortune, or private interest, finds himself inside the Cabinet and the Privy Council before his fortieth birthday, must expect that the world will not be left in ignorance of any thing that can be said against him. The *Times*, which had been faithful to Sir Robert Peel through every turn of fortune, grafted on to its public quarrel with the Whig Government a personal grudge against the new minister. That grudge was vented in language that curiously marks the change which, between that day and this, has come over the tone of English journalism. For weeks together, even in its leading articles, the great newspaper could find no other appellation for the great man than that of " Mr. Babble-tongue Macaulay." When, in company with Sheil, he was sworn of the Privy Council, the disgust of the *Times* could only be expressed by ejaculations which even then were unusual in political controversy. " These men Privy Councilors! These men petted at Windsor Castle! Faugh! Why, they are hardly fit to fill up the vacancies that have occurred by the lamented death of her majesty's two favorite monkeys."

It so happened that, at this very moment, Macaulay got into a scrape which enabled his detractors to transfer their abuse from the general to the particular. When it became his duty to announce to his constituents that he had taken office, he was careless enough to date his address from Windsor Castle. The *Times* rose, or rather sunk, to the occasion; but it would be an ungracious act to dignify the ephemeral scurrility of some envious scribbler by reproducing it under the name of that famous journal, which, for a generation back, has seldom allowed a week to pass without an admiring reference to Macaulay's writings, or a respectful appeal to his authority.

Many months elapsed before the new Secretary at War heard the last of Windsor Castle. That unlucky slip of the pen afforded matter for comment and banter, in Parliament, on the hustings, and through every corner of the daily and weekly press. It has obtained a chance of longer life than it deserves by reason of a passing allusion in the published works of Thackeray.* In later years the great novelist appears to have felt undue contrition for what was, after all, a very innocent, and not ill-natured, touch of satire. In his generous and affecting notice of Macaulay's death he writes: "It always seemed to me that ample means, and recognized rank, were Macaulay's as of right. Years ago there was a wretched outcry raised because Mr. Macaulay dated a letter from Windsor Castle, where he was staying. Immortal gods! Was this man not a fit guest for any palace in the world, or a fit companion for any man or woman in it? I dare say, after Austerlitz, the old court officials and footmen sneered at Napoleon for dating from Schönbrunn. But that miserable Windsor Castle outcry is an echo out of fast-retreating old-world remembrances. The place of such a natural chief was among the first of the land; and that country is best, according to our British notion at least, where the man of eminence has the best chance of investing his genius and intellect."

Macaulay took his promotion quietly, and paid little or no heed to the hard words which it brought him. He kept his happiness in his own hands, and never would permit it to depend upon the good-will or the forbearance of others. His biographer has no occasion to indite those woful passages in which the sufferings of misunderstood genius are commended to the indignant commiseration of posterity. In December, 1839, he writes to Mr. Napier: "You think a great deal too much about the *Times*. What does it signify whether they

---

* "Time was when the author's trade was considered a very mean one, which a gentleman of family could not take up but as an amateur. This absurdity is pretty well worn out now, and I do humbly hope and pray for the day when the other shall likewise disappear. If there be any nobleman with a talent that way, why, why don't we see him among R.A.'s?

501 The School-master (sketch taken abroad)......................	Brum, Henry, Lord, R.A., F.R.S., S.A. of the National Institute of France.
502 View of the Artist's residence at Windsor......................	Maconkey, Right Honorable T. B.
503 Murder of the Babes in the Tower.	Bustle, Lord J. Pill, Right Honorable Sir Robert.
504 A Little Agitation................	O'Carroll, Daniel, M.R.I.A.

Fancy, I say, such names as these figuring in the Catalogue of the Academy!"

abuse me or not? There is nothing at all discouraging in their violence. It is so far from being a means or a proof of strength, that it is both a cause and a symptom of weakness." This is the only instance throughout his entire journals and correspondence in which Macaulay even refers to a series of invectives extending over many months, and of a nature most unusual in the columns of a leading newspaper, when the subject of attack is a man of acknowledged eminence and blameless character.

He was just now less disposed than ever to trouble himself about the justice or injustice of the treatment which he met with from the outside world. An event had occurred, most unexpectedly, which opened to him a long and secure prospect of domestic happiness. At the end of the year 1839, his brother-in-law, Mr. Trevelyan, was appointed to the Assistant-secretaryship of the Treasury — one of the few posts in the English civil service which could fully compensate a man of energy and public spirit for renouncing the intensely interesting work, and the rare opportunities of distinction, presented by an Indian career. "This event," writes Lady Trevelyan, "of course made England our home during your uncle's life. He could never afterward speak of it without emotion. Throughout the autumn of 1839, his misery at the prospect of our return to India was the most painful and hourly trial; and when the joy and relief came upon us it restored the spring and flow of his spirits. He took a house in Great George Street, and insisted on our all living together; and a most happy year 1840 was."

Like other happy years, it was a busy year too. Macaulay, who had completely laid aside his "History" for the present, devoted his powers to his official work. He conducted the business of his department in Parliament with the unobtrusive assiduity and the unvaried courtesy by which a prudent minister may do so much to shorten discussion and to deprecate opposition. And, indeed, the spirit of the age was such that he had every chance of an easy life. The House of Commons of 1840 spent upon the army very little of its own time, or of the nation's money. The paucity and insignificance of the questions which it fell to Macaulay's lot to master might well rouse the envy of a secretary of state for war in these troubled days of alternate military reorganization and reaction. He passed his estimates, which were of an amount to make a modern reformer's mouth water, after a short grumble from Hume, and a single division, in which that implacable economist took with him into the lobby hardly as many adherents as the Government asked for millions. Mr. Charles Macaulay, who at this time was his brother's private secretary, is the authority for an anecdote which is worth recording. He remembers being under the gallery with Sulivan, the Assistant-secretary of War, and with the estimate clerk of the War Office, when Macaulay was submitting to the House his first army estimate. In the course of his speech he made a statement to which the estimate clerk demurred. " That is a mistake," said the clerk. " No, it isn't," said Sulivan, " for a hundred pounds! I never knew him make a blunder in any thing which he had once got up;" and it turned out that Sulivan was right.

On the 14th of March, 1840, Macaulay writes to Mr. Ellis: " I have got through my estimates with flying colors; made a long speech of figures and details without hesitation or mistake of any sort; stood catechising on all sorts of questions; and got six millions of public money in the course of an hour or two. I rather like the sort of work, and I have some aptitude for it. I find business pretty nearly enough to occupy all my time; and if I have a few minutes to myself, I spend them with my sister and niece; so that, except while I am dressing and undressing, I get no reading at all. I do not know but that it is as well for me to live thus for a time. I became too mere a bookworm in India, and on my voyage home. Exercise, they say, assists digestion; and it may be that some months of hard official and Parliamentary work may make my studies more nourishing."

But Macaulay's course in Parliament was not all plain-sailing when he ventured from the smooth waters of the War Office into the broken seas of general politics. The session of 1840 had hardly commenced, when Sir John Yarde Buller

moved a resolution professing want of confidence in the ministry — a motion which the Tories supported with all their
strength both of vote and lung.   For the first, and, as he himself willingly confessed, for the last, time in his life Macaulay
did not get a fair hearing.   On the second night of the debate, Sir James Graham, speaking with the acrimony which
men of a certain character affect when they are attacking old
allies, by a powerful invective, spiced with allusions to the
Windsor Castle address, had goaded the Opposition ranks
into a fit of somewhat insolent animosity.   When Macaulay
rose to reply, the indications of that animosity were so mani-
fest that he had almost to commence his remarks with an appeal for tolerance.   "I trust," he said, "that the first cabinet
minister who, when the question is, whether the Government
be or be not worthy of confidence, offers himself in debate,
will find some portion of that generosity and good feeling
which once distinguished English gentlemen."   The words
"first cabinet minister" were no sooner out of his mouth
than the honorable gentlemen opposite, choosing willfully to
misconstrue those words as if he were putting forward an absurd claim to the leading place in the Cabinet, burst forth
into a storm of ironical cheering which would have gone far
to disconcert O'Connell.   Macaulay (who, to speak his best,
required the sympathy, or, at any rate, the indulgence, of his
audience) said all that he had to say, but said it without spirit
or spontaneity; and did not succeed in maintaining the enthusiasm either of himself or his hearers at the rather high-
pitched level of the only one of his Parliamentary efforts
which could in any sense be described as a failure.*

Some days afterward he met Sir James Graham in the
park, who expressed a hope that nothing which appeared

---

* In 1853, Macaulay was correcting his speeches for publication. On the
28th of July of that year he writes in his journal: "I worked hard, but
without much heart; for it was that unfortunate speech on Buller's motion in 1840; one of the few unlucky things in a lucky life. I can not
conceive why it failed. It is far superior to many of my speeches which
have succeeded. But, as old Demosthenes said, the power of oratory is as
much in the ear as in the tongue."

rude or offensive had escaped his lips. " Not at all," said
Macaulay. " Only I think that your speech would have been
still more worthy of you if you had not adopted the worn-
out newspaper jests about my Windsor letter." On the 7th
of April, Sir James himself brought forward a vote of censure on the Government for having led the country into war
with China; and Macaulay, who again followed him in the
debate, achieved a brilliant and undoubted success in an oration crowned by a noble tribute to the majesty of the British
flag—quite incomparable as an example of that sort of rhetoric which goes straight to the heart of a British House of
Commons.* When they met again, Sir James said to him:
" In our last encounter none but polished weapons were used
on both sides; and I am afraid that public opinion rather in-
clines to the belief that you had the best of it." "As to the
polished weapons," said Macaulay, " my temptations are not
so misleading as yours. You never wrote a Windsor letter."
His adversaries paid him a high compliment when they were
reduced to make so much of a charge, which was the gravest

---

* " I was much touched, and so, I dare say, were many other gentlemen,
by a passage in one of Captain Elliot's dispatches. I mean that passage
in which he describes his arrival at the factory in the moment of extreme
danger. As soon as he landed he was surrounded by his countrymen, all
in an agony of distress and despair. The first thing which he did was to
order the British flag to be brought from his boat and planted in the balcony. The sight immediately revived the hearts of those who had a minute before given themselves up for lost. It was natural that they should
look up with hope and confidence to that victorious flag. For it reminded
them that they belonged to a country unaccustomed to defeat, to submis-
sion, or to shame; to a country which had exacted such reparation for the
wrongs of her children as had made the ears of all who heard it to tingle;
to a country which made the Dey of Algiers humble himself to the dust before her insulted consul; to a country which had avenged the victims of
the Black Hole on the field of Plassey; to a country which had not degenerated since the great Protector vowed that he would make the name of
Englishman as much respected as ever had been the name of Roman citizen. They knew that, surrounded as they were by enemies, and sepa-
rated by great oceans and continents from all help, not a hair of their
heads would be harmed with impunity."

that malice itself ever brought against him in his character of a public man.

Throughout the sessions of 1840 and 1841, a series of confused and angry discussions took place over a multitude of bills dealing with the registration of voters in Ireland; which were brought forward from every quarter of the House, and with every possible diversity of view. In these debates Macaulay gave marked proof of having profited by the severe legal training which was not the least valuable and enduring reward of his Indian labors. Holding his own against Sugden in technical argument, he enforced his points with his customary wealth of language and illustration, much of which unfortunately perished between his lips and the reporters' gallery. "Almost every clause of this bill which is designed for keeping out the wrongful, acts just as effectually against the rightful, claimant. Let me suppose the case of a man of great wealth, and of imperious, obstinate, and arbitrary temper; one of those men who think much of the rights of property, and little of its duties. Let me suppose that man willing to spend six or seven thousand a year in securing the command of a county—an ambition, as every one knows, not impossible even in England. I will not mention any recent transaction; nor do I wish to mix up personalities with this serious debate; but no one is ignorant how a certain man now dead, provoked by the opposition he received in a certain town, vowed that he would make the grass grow in its streets, and how that vow was kept. Another great person ejected four hundred voters in one shire, and entered two hundred and twenty-five civil actions. Such a man could easily command an Irish county. It would only be a picture the less in his gallery, or an antique gem the less in his collection."

The conflict was not always carried on with such scrupulous abstinence from personalities.

"*Thursday, June* 11*th.*—I went from the Office to the House, which was engaged upon Stanley's Irish Registration Bill. The night was very stormy. I have never seen such unseemly demeanor, or heard such scurrilous language, in Parliament. Lord Norreys was whistling, and making all sorts of noises. Lord Maidstone was so ill-mannered that I hope he was drunk. At last, after much grossly indecent conduct, at which Lord Eliot expressed his disgust to me, a furious outbreak took place. O'Connell was so rudely interrupted that he used the expression 'beastly bellowings.' Then rose such an uproar as no O. P. mob at Covent Garden Theatre, no crowd of Chartists in front of a hustings, ever equaled. Men on both sides stood up, shook their fists, and bawled at the top of their voices. Freshfield, who was in the chair, was strangely out of his element. Indeed, he knew his business so little that, when first he had to put a question, he fancied himself at Exeter Hall, or The Crown and Anchor, and said: 'As many as are of that opinion please to signify the same by holding up their hands.' He was quite unable to keep the smallest order when the storm came. O'Connell raged like a mad bull; and our people—I for one —while regretting and condemning his violence, thought it much extenuated by the provocation. Charles Buller spoke with talent, as he always does; and with earnestness, dignity, and propriety, which he scarcely ever does. A short and most amusing scene passed between O'Connell and Lord Maidstone, which in the tumult escaped the observation of many, but which I watched carefully. 'If,' said Lord Maidstone, 'the word beastly is retracted, I shall be satisfied. If not, I shall not be satisfied.' 'I do not care whether the noble lord is satisfied or not.' 'I wish you would give me satisfaction.' 'I advise the noble lord to carry his liquor meekly.' At last the tumult ended from absolute physical weariness. It was past one, and the steady bellowers of the Opposition had been howling from six o'clock with little interruption. I went home with a headache, and not in high spirits. But how different my frame of mind from what it was two years ago! How profoundly domestic happiness has altered my whole way of looking at life! I have my share of the anxieties and vexations of ambition, but it is only a secondary passion now."

November, 1839.

DEAR NAPIER,—I send back the paper on Clive. Remember to let me have a revise. I have altered the last sentence, so as to make it clearer and more harmonious; but I can not consent to leave out the well-earned compliment* to my dear old friend, Lord William Bentinck, of whom Victor Jacquemont said, as truly as wittily, that he was William Penn on the throne of the Mogul, and at the head of two hundred thousand soldiers. Ever yours,　　　　T. B. MACAULAY.

---

* "To the warrior, history will assign a place in the same rank with Lucullus and Trajan. Nor will she deny to the reformer a share of that veneration with which France cherishes the memory of Turgot, and with which the latest generations of Hindoos will contemplate the statue of Lord William Bentinck."

Lord William Bentinck, since his return from India, had taken an active, and sometimes even a turbid, part in politics as member for Glasgow. Those who will turn to the last words of the "Essay on Lord Clive" will understand Mr. Napier's uneasiness at the notion of placing on so conspicuous a literary pedestal the effigy of one who, for the time, had come to be regarded as the radical representative of a large Scotch constituency is apt to be regarded during a period of Conservative reaction.

London, October 14th, 1840.

DEAR NAPIER,—I am glad that you are satisfied.* I dare say that there will be plenty of abuse; but about that I have long ceased to care one straw.

I have two plans, indeed three, in my head. Two might, I think, be executed for the next number. Gladstone advertises another book about the Church. That subject belongs to me; particularly as he will very probably say something concerning my former article.

Leigh Hunt has brought out an edition of Congreve, Wycherley, and Farquhar. I see it in the windows of the book-sellers' shops, but I have not looked at it. I know their plays, and the literary history of their time, well enough to make an amusing paper. Collier's controversy with Congreve on the subject of the drama deserves to be better known than it is; and there is plenty of amusing and curious anecdote about Wycherley. If you will tell Longman to send me the book, I will see whether I can give you a short, lively article on it.

My third plan can not yet be executed. It is to review Capefigue's history of the Consulate and Empire of Napoleon. A character both of the man and of the government such as the subject deserves has not yet, in my opinion, appeared. But there are still two volumes of Capefigue's book to come, if not more; and, though he writes with wonderful rapidity, he can hardly bring them out till the beginning of next year.

Ever yours,　　　　　　　　　　T. B. MACAULAY.

---

* This refers to the article on Von Ranke's "History of the Popes."

London, October 29th, 1840.

DEAR NAPIER,—I have received Hunt's book, and shall take it down with me to Southampton, whither I hope to be able to make a short trip. I shall give it well to Hunt about Jeremy Collier, to whom he is scandalously unjust. I think Jeremy one of the greatest public benefactors in our history.

Poor Lord Holland! It is vain to lament. A whole generation is gone to the grave with him. While he lived, all the great orators and statesmen of the last generation were living too. What a store of historical information he has carried away! But his kindness, generosity, and openness of heart were more valuable than even his fine accomplishments. I loved him dearly. Ever yours truly,   T. B. MACAULAY.

London, November 13th, 1840.

DEAR NAPIER,—Yesterday evening I received Gladstone's book, and read it. I do not think that it would be wise to review it. I observed in it very little that had any reference to politics, and very little indeed that might not be consistently said by a supporter of the Voluntary system. It is, in truth, a theological treatise; and I have no mind to engage in a controversy about the nature of the sacraments, the operation of holy orders, the visibility of the Church, and such points of learning; except when they are connected, as in his former work they were connected, with questions of government. I have no disposition to split hairs about the spiritual reception of the body and blood of Christ in the eucharist, or about baptismal regeneration. I shall try to give you a paper on a very different subject—Wycherley, and the other good-for-nothing fellows whose indecorous wit Leigh Hunt has edited.

I see that a life of Warren Hastings is just coming out. I mark it for mine. I will try to make as interesting an article, though I fear not so flashy, as that on Clive.

The state of things at Edinburgh has greatly vexed me. Craig advises me not to, go down, at least for some time. But, if I do not go soon, I shall not be able to go at all this year. What do you think about the matter?

Ever yours,   T. B. MACAULAY.

There was, indeed, little to tempt him northward. All Scotland was in a ferment between two great controversies; and the waves of religious passion, still surging with the excitement of the Church Extension agitation, already felt the first gusts of the rising storm which was soon to rage over the more momentous question of patronage. Lord Melbourne and his colleagues were ignorant of the strength and meaning either of the one movement or the other. Incapable of leading the opinion of the country, they meddled from time to time only to make discords more pronounced, and difficulties more insoluble, than ever. The nation was split up into ill-defined, but not, on that account, less hostile, camps. On the platform and at the polling-booth—in the pulpit, the press, the presbyteries, and the law courts—churchmen were arrayed against dissenters, and against each other. The strife was one whose issues could never be finally determined, except in accordance with principles which Paisley weavers and Perth-shire shepherds were beginning to understand much more clearly than ever did her majesty's ministers. It was the general opinion of Macaulay's friends at Edinburgh that he would do well to avoid exposing himself to the blows which were sure to fall about the head of a Parliamentary representative at a time when his constituents were engaged in such fierce cross-fighting. He certainly consulted his comfort, and possibly his political interests, when he decided on refraining from an interference which would have offended most parties and satisfied none.

London, December 8th, 1840.

DEAR NAPIER,—I shall work at my article on Hunt whenever I have a leisure hour, and shall try to make it amusing to lovers of literary gossip.

I will not plague you with arguments about the Eastern question. My own opinion has long been made up. Unless England meant to permit a virtual partition of the Ottoman Empire between France and Russia, she had no choice but to act as she has acted. Had the treaty of July not been signed, Nicholas would have been really master of Constantinople, and Thiers of Alexandria. The treaty once made, I never would have consented to flinch from it, whatever had been the danger. I am satisfied that the war party in France is insatiable and unappeasable; that concessions would only have strengthened and emboldened it; and that, after stooping to the lowest humiliations, we should soon have had to fight without allies, and at every disadvantage. The policy which has been followed I believe to be not only a just and honorable, but eminently a pacific policy. Whether the peace of the world will long be preserved I do not pretend to say; but I firmly hold that the best chance of preserving it was to make the treaty of July, and, having made it, to execute it resolutely. For my own part, I will tell you plainly that if the course of events had driven Palmerston to resign, I would have resigned with him, though I had stood alone. Look at what the late ministers of Louis Philippe have avowed with respect to the Balearic Islands. Were such designs ever proclaimed before, except in a crew of pirates or a den of robbers? Look at Barrot's speeches about England. Is it for the sake of such friendships as this that our country is to abdicate her rank, and sink into a dependency? I like war quite as little as Sir William Molesworth or Mr. Fonblanque. It is foolish and wicked to bellow for war merely for war's sake, like the rump of the Mountain at Paris. I would never make offensive war. I would never offer to any other power a provocation which might be a fair ground for war. But I never would abstain from doing what I had clear right to do because a neighbor chooses to threaten me with an unjust war; first, because I believe that such a policy would, in the end, inevitably produce war; and, secondly, because I think war, though a very great evil, by no means so great an evil as subjugation and national humiliation.

In the present case, I think the course taken by the Government unexceptionable. If Guizot prevails—that is to say, if reason, justice, and public law prevail—we shall have no war. If the writers of the *National* and the singers of the "Marseillaise" prevail, we can have no peace. At whatever cost, at whatever risk, these banditti must be put down; or they will put down all commerce, civilization, order, and the independence of nations.

Of course, what I write to you is confidential: not that I should hesitate to proclaim the substance of what I have said on the hustings, or in the House of Commons; but because I do not measure my words in pouring myself out to a friend. But I have run on too long, and should have done better to have given the last half-hour to Wycherley.

Ever yours, T. B. MACAULAY.

London, January 11th, 1841.

DEAR NAPIER,—As to my paper on the dramatists, if you are content, so am I. I set less value on it than on any thing I have written since I was a boy.

I have hardly opened Gleig's book on Warren Hastings, and I can not yet judge whether I can review it before it is complete. I am not quite sure that so vast a subject may not bear two articles. The scene of the first would lie principally in India. The Rohilla War, the disputes of Hastings and his Council, the character of Francis, the death of Nuncomar, the rise of the empire of Hyder, the seizure of Benares, and many other interesting matters, would furnish out such a paper. In the second, the scene would be changed to Westminster. There we should have the Coalition; the India Bill; the impeachment; the characters of all the noted men of that time, from Burke, who managed the prosecution of Hastings, down to the wretched Tony Pasquin, who first defended and then libeled him. I hardly know a story so interesting, and of such various interest. And the central figure is in the highest degree striking and majestic. I think Hastings, though far from faultless, one of the greatest men that England ever produced. He had pre-eminent talents for government, and great literary talents too; fine taste, a princely spirit, and heroic equanimity in the midst of adversity and danger. He was a man for whom nature had done much of what the Stoic philosophy pretended, and only pretended, to do for its disciples. "Mens æqua in arduis" is the inscription under his picture in the Government House at Calcutta, and never was there a more appropriate motto. This story has never been told as well as it deserves. Mill's account of Hasting's administration is indeed very able—the ablest part, in my judgment, of his work—but it is dry. As to Gleig, unless he has greatly improved since he wrote Sir Thomas Munro's life, he will make very little of his subject. I am not so vain as to think that I can do it full justice; but the success of my paper on Clive has emboldened me, and I have the advantage of being in hourly intercourse with Trevelyan, who is thoroughly well acquainted with the languages, manners, and diplomacy of the Indian courts. Ever yours,   T. B. MACAULAY.

London, April 26th, 1841.

DEAR NAPIER,—I have arranged with Leigh Hunt for a paper on the Colmans, which will be ready for the July number. He has written some very pretty lines on the queen, who has been very kind to him, both by sending him money and by countenancing his play. It has occurred to me that if poor Southey dies (and his best friends must now pray for his death), Leigh Hunt might very fitly have the laurel, if that absurd fashion is to be kept up; or, at all events, the pension and the sack.

I wish that you could move Rogers to write a short character of Lord Holland for us. Nobody knew his house so well; and Rogers is no mean artist in prose.*

As to Lord Cardigan, he has deserved some abuse; he has had ten times as much as he deserved; and, as I do not choose to say a word more than I think just against him, I come in for a share. You may easily suppose that it troubles me very little. Ever yours,   T. B. MACAULAY.

During the session of 1841, Macaulay, as Secretary at War, had very little to do in the House of Commons except to defend Lord Cardigan; but that in itself was quite sufficient occupation for one minister. Mr. Kinglake, who enjoyed large, and even overabundant, opportunities for studying his lord-

---

* In a letter of May 4th, 1841, Macaulay writes: "Lady Holland is so earnest with me to review her husband's 'Protests in the House of Lords' that I hardly know what to do. I can not refuse her."

ship, has described his character in a passage almost too well
known for quotation: "Having no personal ascendency, and
no habitual consideration for the feelings of others, he was
not, of course, at all qualified to exert easy rule over English
gentlemen. There surely was cruelty in the idea of placing
human beings under the military control of an officer at once
so arbitrary and so narrow; but the notion of such a man having been able to purchase for himself a right to hold Englishmen in military subjection is, to my mind, revolting." Lord
Cardigan bought himself up from cornet to lieutenant-colonel
in the course of seven years; and by an expenditure, it is said,
of four times as many thousand pounds. So open-handed a
dealer had, of course, the pick of the market. He selected a
fine cavalry regiment, which he proceeded to drag through a
slough of scandal, favoritism, petty tyranny, and intrigue, into
that glare of notoriety which to men of honor is even more
painful than the misery which a commanding officer of Lord
Cardigan's type has such unbounded power of inflicting upon
his subordinates. Within the space of a single twelvemonth,
one of his captains was cashiered for writing him a challenge;
he sent a coarse and insulting verbal message to another, and
then punished him with prolonged arrest, because he respectfully refused to shake hands with the officer who had been
employed to convey the affront; he fought a duel with a lieutenant who had left the corps, and shot him through the body;
and he flogged a soldier on Sunday, between the services, on
the very spot where, half an hour before, the man's comrades
had been mustered for public worship. The Secretary at War
had to put the best face he could on these ugly stories. When
it was proposed to remove Lord Cardigan from the command
of his regiment, Macaulay took refuge in a position which he
justly regarded as impregnable: "Honorable gentlemen should
beware how they take advantage of the unpopularity of an
individual to introduce a precedent which, if once established,
would lead to the most fatal effects to the whole of our military system, and work a great injustice to all officers in her
majesty's service. What is the case with officers in the army?
They buy their commissions at a high price, the interest of

which would be very nearly equal to the pay they receive; they devote the best years of their lives to the service, and are liable to be sent to the most unhealthy parts of the globe, where their health, and sometimes their lives, fall a sacrifice. Is it to be expected that men of spirit and honor will consent to enter this service, if they have not, at least, some degree of security for the permanence of their situations?"—in other words, if they are not allowed to do as they will with their own.

Meanwhile the political crisis was approaching its agony. The Whig Government was now in such a plight that it could neither stand with decency nor fall with grace. Their great measure of the year, the Irish Registration Bill, narrowly escaped the perils of a second reading, and was ingloriously wrecked in committee. Their last year's deficit, of something under one million, had this year grown to something over two; and they could no longer rely upon the wave of popular favor to tide them over their troubles. All the enthusiasm for progress which still survived had been absorbed into the ranks of those fiery reformers who were urging the crusade against the Corn Laws under the guidance of leaders who sat elsewhere than on the Treasury bench, or did not sit in Parliament at all. As far back as 1839, Macaulay was writing in his diary: "The cry for free trade in corn seems to be very formidable. The *Times* has joined in it. I was quite sure that it would be so. If the ministers play their game well, they may now either triumph completely, or retire with honor. They have excellent cards, if they know how to use them." Dire necessity had gradually brought even the most timid members of the Cabinet to acquiesce in these heroic sentiments, and the Whigs at length made up their minds to come before the country in the character of Free-traders. In a letter to Mr. Napier, on the 30th day of April, 1841, Macaulay says: "All the chances of our party depend on to-night. We shall play double or quits. I do not know what to expect; and as far as I am concerned, I rather hope for a defeat. I pine for liberty and ease, freedom of speech, and freedom of pen. I have all that I want; a small competence, domestic happiness, good health and spirits. If at forty I can get from under this yoke, I shall not easily be induced to bear it again." So wrote the Secretary at War in the morning; and at four o'clock in the afternoon of the same day Lord John Russell gave notice that on the 31st of May he should move that the House resolve itself into a committee to consider the acts relating to the trade in corn.

But it was too late to make a change of front in the face of the greatest Parliamentary captain of the age, and of a whole phalanx of statesmen who were undoubtedly superior to the ministers in debate, and who were generally believed to be far abler as administrators. A great deal was to happen between the 30th of April and the 31st of May. One main feature in the budget was a proposal to reduce the duty on foreign sugar; a serious blow to the privilege which the free labor of our own colonies enjoyed, as against the slave labor of the Spanish plantations. Lord Sandon moved an amendment, skillfully framed to catch the votes of Abolitionist members of the Liberal party, and the question was discussed through eight live-long nights, with infinite repetition of argument and dreariness of detail. Mr. Gladstone, who had early learned that habit of high-toned courtesy which is the surest presage of future greatness, introduced into the last sentences of a fine speech an allusion that pleased no one so much as him against whom it was directed. "There is a another name," said he, " strangely associated with the plan of the ministry. I can only speak from tradition of the struggle for the abolition of slavery; but, if I have not been misinformed, there was engaged in it a man who was the unseen ally of Mr. Wilberforce, and the pillar of his strength; a man of profound benevolence, of acute understanding, of indefatigable industry, and of that self-denying temper which is content to work in secret, to forego the recompense of present fame, and to seek for its reward beyond the grave. The name of that man was Zachary Macaulay, and his son is a member of the existing Cabinet."

In the early morning of the 19th of May, Lord Sandon's amendment was carried by thirty-six votes; and on the mor-

row the House was crammed inside and out, in the confident
expectation of such an announcement as generally follows
upon a crushing ministerial defeat. Neither the friends of
the Government nor its enemies could believe their ears,
when the chancellor of the exchequer, with the self-possess-
ed air of a minister who has a working majority and a financier who has an available surplus, gave notice that he should
bring forward the usual sugar duties in Committee of Ways
and Means; and, before the audience could recover its breath,
Lord John Russell followed him with a motion that this
House, on its rising, do adjourn to Monday. The Earl of
Darlington, in a single sentence of contemptuous astonishment, asked on what day the noble lord proposed to take the
question of the Corn Laws. When that day had been ascer-
tained to be the 4th of June, the subject dropped at once;
and an unhappy member began upon the grievances of the
Royal Marines, amidst the buzz of conversation, expressive of
gratified or disappointed curiosity, with which, after a thrill-
ing episode, the House relieves its own nerves, and tortures
those of the wretch whose ambition or ill-luck has exposed
him to the most formidable ordeal which can be inflicted on
a public speaker.

But the matter was not to end thus. The 4th of June,
instead of being the first day of the debate on the Corn Laws,
was the fifth and last of an obstinate and dubious conflict
waged over a direct vote of want of confidence; which was
proposed by the Conservative leader in a quiet and carefully reasoned speech, admirably worthy of the occasion, and of
himself. Macaulay, who had shown signs of immense interest while Sir Robert was unfolding his budget of historical
parallels and ruling cases, replied on the same night with an
ample roll of the instances in which Lord Sunderland, and
Mr. Pitt, and Lord Liverpool had accepted defeat without resorting either to resignation or dissolution. But all the prec-
edents in the journals of Parliament, though collected by
Hallam and set forth by Canning, would have failed to prove
that the country had any interest whatsoever in the continued
existence of a ministry which had long been powerless, and

was rapidly becoming discredited. When Sir James Graham rose, there was a break in that tone of mutual forbearance which the principal speakers on either side had hitherto maintained. The honorable baronet could not resist the temptation of indulging himself in an invective which, as he proceeded toward his peroration, degenerated into a strain of downright ribaldry ;* but the Government was already too far gone to profit by the mistakes or the excesses of its adversaries ; and the Opposition triumphed by one vote, in a House fuller by twenty than that which, ten years before, had carried the second reading of the Reform Bill by exactly the same majority.

Within three weeks Parliament was dissolved, and the ministers went to the country on the question of a fixed duty on foreign wheat. There could be but one issue to a general election which followed upon such a session, and but one fate in store for a party whose leaders were fain to have recourse to so feeble and perfunctory a cry. Lord Melbourne and his colleagues had touched the Corn Laws too late, and too timidly, for their reputation, and too soon for the public opinion of the constituencies. They sent their supporters on what was indeed a forlorn-hope, when, as a sort of political after-thought, they bid them attack the most powerful interest in the nation. North of Trent the Whigs held their ground ; but throughout the southern districts of England they were smitten hip and thigh, from Lincoln to St. Ives. The adherents of the Government had to surrender something of their pre-

---

* "I can not address the people of this country in the language of the quotation used by the noble lord,

'O passi graviora ;'

for never was a country cursed with a worse, a more reckless, or a more dangerous government. The noble lord, the Secretary for Ireland, talks of 'lubricity ;' but, thank God, we have at last pinned you to something out of which you can not wriggle ; and, as we have the melancholy satisfaction to know that there is an end to all things, so I can now say with the noble lord :

'Dabit Deus his quoque finem ;

thank God we have at last got rid of such a government as this.'"

dominance in the boroughs, while those who sat for the counties were turned out by shoals. There were whole shires which sent back their writs inscribed with an unbroken tale of Protectionists. All the ten Essex members were Conservatives, in town and country alike; and so were all the twelve members for Shropshire. Before the Irish returns had come to hand, it was already evident that the ministerial loss would be equivalent to a hundred votes on a stand and fall division. The Whigs had experienced no equally grave reverse since, in 1784, Pitt scattered to the winds the Coalition majority; and no such other was destined again to befall them,

> Until a day more dark and drear,
> And a more memorable year,

should, after the lapse of a generation, deliver over to misfortune and defeat

> A mightier host and haughtier name.

Scotland, as usual, was not affected by the contagion of reaction. Indeed, the troubles of candidates to the north of the Border proceeded rather from the progressive than the retrogressive tendencies of the electors. Macaulay was returned unopposed, in company with Mr. William Gibson Craig; though he had been threatened with a contest by the more ardent members of that famous party in the Scotch Church which, within two years from that time, was to give such a proof as history will not forget of its willingness to sacrifice, for conscience' sake,* things far more precious even than the honor of sending to St. Stephen's an eloquent and distinguished representative.

To Miss F. Macaulay.

Edinburgh, June 28th, 1841.

DEAREST FANNY,—We have had a meeting—a little stormy when church matters were touched on, but perfectly cordial on

---

* The disruption of the Scotch Church took place on the 18th of May, 1843.

other points. I took the bull by the horns, and have reason to believe that I was right, both in principle and in policy. A Non-intrusion opposition has been talked of. My language at the meeting displeased the violent churchmen, and they were at one time minded even to coalesce with the Tories against me. The leading Non-intrusionists, however, have had a conference with me; and though we do not exactly agree, they own that they shall get more from me than from a Tory. I do not think that there is now any serious risk of a contest, and there is none at all of a defeat; but in the mean time I am surrounded by the din of a sort of controversy which is most distasteful to me. "Yes, Mr. Macaulay; that is all very well for a statesman. But what becomes of the headship of our Lord Jesus Christ?" And I can not answer a constituent quite as bluntly as I should answer any one else who might reason after such a fashion.

Ever yours,   T. B. M.

London, July 12th, 1841.

DEAR ELLIS,—I can not send you "Virginius," for I have not a copy by me at present, and have not time to make one. When you return I hope to have finished another ballad, on the Lake Regillus. I have no doubt that the author of the original ballad had Homer in his eye. The battle of the Lake Regillus is a purely Homeric battle. I am confident that the ballad-maker has heard of the fight over the body of Patroclus. We will talk more about this. I may, perhaps, publish a small volume next spring. I am encouraged by the approbation of all who have seen the little pieces. I find the unlearned quite as well satisfied as the learned.

I have taken a very comfortable suite of chambers in The Albany; and I hope to lead during some years a sort of life peculiarly suited to my taste—college life at the West End of London. I have an entrance-hall, two sitting-rooms, a bedroom, a kitchen, cellars, and two rooms for servants—all for ninety guineas a year; and this in a situation which no younger son of a duke need be ashamed to put on his card. We shall have, I hope, some very pleasant breakfasts there, to say nothing of dinners. My own housekeeper will do very well for a few plain dishes, and The Clarendon is within a hundred yards.

I own that I am quite delighted with our prospects. A strong opposition is the very thing that I wanted. I shall be heartily glad if it lasts till I can finish a "History of England, from the Revolution to the Accession of the House of Hanover." Then I shall be willing to go in again for a few years. It seems clear that we shall be just about three hundred. This is what I have always supposed. I got through very triumphantly at Edinburgh, and very cheap. I believe I can say what no other man in the kingdom can say. I have been four times returned to Parliament by cities of more than a hundred and forty thousand inhabitants; and all those four elections together have not cost me five hundred pounds.

Your ballads are delightful. I like that of Ips,* Gips, and

---

* Ips, Gips, and Johnson were three Northumbrian butchers, who, when riding from market, heard a cry for help, and came upon a woman who had been reduced to the distressful plight in which ladies were so often discovered by knights errant.

Then Johnson, being a valiant man, a man of courage bold,
He took his coat from off his back to keep her from the cold.

As they rode over Northumberland, as hard as they could ride,
She put her fingers in her ears, and dismally she cried.

Then up there start ten swaggering blades, with weapons in their hands,
And riding up to Johnson they bid him for to stand.

"It's I'll not stand," says Ipson: "then no, indeed, not I."
"Nor I'll not stand," says Gipson: "I'll sooner live than die."
"Then I will stand," says Johnson: "I'll stand the while I can.
I never yet was daunted, nor afraid of any man."

Johnson thereupon drew his sword, and had disposed of eight out of his ten assailants, when he was stabbed from behind by the woman, and died, upbraiding her with having killed

The finest butcher that ever the sun shone on.

It is not so easy to identify "Napoleon" among a sheaf of ballads entitled "The Island of St. Helena," "Maria Louisa's Lamentation," and "Young Napoleon, or the Bunch of Roses;" though from internal evidence there is reason to believe that the song in question was "Napoleon's Farewell to Paris," which commences with an apostrophe so gorgeous as to suggest the

Johnson best. "Napoleon" is excellent, but hardly equal to
the "Donkey wot wouldn't go." Ever yours,

T. B. MACAULAY.

Macaulay's predilection for the Muse of the street has already furnished more than one anecdote to the newspapers.
It is, indeed, one of the few personal facts about him which
up to this time have taken hold of the public imagination.
He bought every half-penny song on which he could lay his
hands; if only it was decent, and a genuine, undoubted poem
of the people. He has left a scrap-book containing about
eighty ballads; for the most part vigorous and picturesque
enough, however defective they may be in rhyme and grammar; printed on flimsy, discolored paper, and headed with
coarsely executed vignettes, seldom bearing even the most remote reference to the subject which they are supposed to illustrate. Among the gems of his collection he counted "Plato, a favorite song," commencing with a series of questions in
which it certainly is not easy to detect traces of the literary
style employed by the great dialectician:

> Says Plato, "Why should man be vain,
>   Since bounteous Heaven has made him great?
> Why look with insolent disdain
>   On those not decked with pomp or state?"

It is not too much to say that Macaulay knew the locality,
and, at this period of his life, the stock in trade, of every
book-stall in London. "After office hours," says his brother
Charles, "his principal relaxation was rambling about with
me in the back lanes of the City. It was then that he began
to talk of his idea of restoring to poetry the legends of which
poetry had been robbed by history; and it was in these walks

---

idea that the great Emperor's curious popularity with our troubadours of
the curbstone is of Irish origin.

> Farewell, ye splendid citadel, Metropolis, called Paris,
>   Where Phœbus every morning shoots refulgent beams;
> Where Flora's bright Aurora advancing from the Orient
>   With radiant light illumines the pure shining streams.

that I heard for the first time from his lips the "Lays of Rome," which were not published until some time afterward. In fact, I heard them in the making. I never saw the hidden mechanism of his mind so clearly as in the course of these walks. He was very fond of discussing psychological and ethical questions; and sometimes, but more rarely, would lift the veil behind which he habitually kept his religious opinions."

On the 19th of August Parliament met to give effect to the verdict of the polling-booths. An amendment on the address, half as long as the address itself, the gist of which lay in a respectful representation to her majesty that her present advisers did not possess the confidence of the country, was moved simultaneously in both Houses. It was carried on the first night of the debate by a majority of seventy-two in the Lords, and on the fourth night by a majority of ninety-one in the Commons. Macaulay, of course, voted with his colleagues; but he did not raise his voice to deprecate a consummation which on public grounds he could not desire to see postponed, and which, as far as his private inclinations were concerned, he had for some time past anticipated with unfeigned and all but unmixed delight.

London, July 27th, 1841.

DEAR NAPIER,—I am truly glad that you are satisfied. I do not know what Brougham means by objecting to what I have said of the first Lord Holland. I will engage to find chapter and verse for it all. Lady Holland told me that she could hardly conceive where I got so correct a notion of him.

I am not at all disappointed by the elections. They have, indeed, gone very nearly as I expected. Perhaps I counted on seven or eight votes more; and even these we may get on petition. I can truly say that I have not, for many years, been so happy as I am at present. Before I went to India, I had no prospect in the event of a change of government, except that of living by my pen, and seeing my sisters governesses. In India I was an exile. When I came back, I was for a time at liberty; but I had before me the prospect of parting in a few months, probably forever, with my dearest sister and her children. That misery was removed; but I found myself in office, a member of a government wretchedly weak, and struggling for existence. Now I am free. I am independent. I am in Parliament, as honorably seated as man can be. My family is comfortably off. I have leisure for literature, yet I am not reduced to the necessity of writing for money. If I had to choose a lot from all that there are in human life, I am not sure that I should prefer any to that which has fallen to me. I am sincerely and thoroughly contented. Ever yours,   T. B. MACAULAY.

CHAPTER IX.

1841-1844.

Macaulay settles in The Albany.—Letters to Mr. Napier.—Warren Hastings, and "The Vicar of Wakefield."—Leigh Hunt.—Macaulay's Doubts about the Wisdom of publishing his Essays.—Lord Palmerston as a Writer.—The "Lays of Rome."—Handsome Conduct of Professor Wilson.—Republication of the Essays.—Miss Aikin's "Life of Addison."—Macaulay in Opposition.—The Copyright Question.—Recall of Lord Ellenborough.—Macaulay as a Public Speaker: Opinions of the Reporters' Gallery.—Tour on the Loire.—Letters to Mr. Napier.—Payment of the Irish Roman Catholic Clergy.—Barère.

THE change of government was any thing but a misfortune to Macaulay. He lost nothing but an income which he could well do without, and the value of which he was ere long to replace many times over by his pen; and he gained his time, his liberty, the power of speaking what he thought, writing when he would, and living as he chose. The plan of life which he selected was one eminently suited to the bent of his tastes and the nature of his avocations. Toward the end of the year 1840, Mr. and Mrs. Trevelyan removed to Clapham; and on their departure, Macaulay broke up his establishment in Great George Street, and quartered himself in a commodious set of rooms on a second floor in The Albany; that luxurious cloister, whose inviolable tranquillity affords so agreeable a relief from the roar and flood of the Piccadilly traffic. His chambers, every corner of which was library, were comfortably, though not very brightly, furnished. The ornaments were few, but choice: half a dozen fine Italian engravings from his favorite great masters; a handsome French clock, provided with a singularly melodious set of chimes, the gift of his friend and publisher, Mr. Thomas Longman; and the well-known bronze statuettes of Voltaire and Rousseau (neither of them heroes of his own),* which had been presented to him by Lady Holland as a remembrance of her husband.

The first use which Macaulay made of his freedom was in the capacity of a reviewer. Mr. Gleig, who had served with distinction during the last years of the great French war as a regimental officer, after having been five times wounded in action, had carried his merit into the Church, and his campaigning experiences into military literature. The author of one book which is good, and of several which are not amiss, he flew at too high game when he undertook to compile the "Memoirs of Warren Hastings." In January, 1841, Macau-

---

* Macaulay says in a letter to Lord Stanhope : "I have not made up my mind about John, Duke of Bedford. Hot-headed he certainly was. That is a quality which lies on the surface of a character, and about which there can be no mistake. Whether a man is cold-hearted, or not, is a much more difficult question. Strong emotions may be hid by a stoical deportment. Kind and caressing manners may conceal an unfeeling disposition. Romilly, whose sensibility was morbidly strong, and who died a martyr to it, was by many thought to be incapable of affection. Rousseau, who was always soaking people's waistcoats with his tears, betrayed and slandered all his benefactors in turn, and sent his children to the Enfans Trouvés."

Macaulay's sentiments with regard to Voltaire are pretty fully expressed in his essay on Frederic the Great. In 1853 he visited Ferney. "The cabinet where Voltaire used to write looked, not toward Mont Blanc, of which he might have had a noble view, but toward a terrace and a grove of trees. Perhaps he wished to spare his eyes. He used to complain that the snow hurt them. I was glad to have seen a place about which I had read and dreamed so much ; a place which, eighty years ago, was regarded with the deepest interest all over Europe, and visited by pilgrims of the highest rank and greatest genius. I suppose that no private house ever received such a number of illustrious guests during the same time as were entertained in Ferney between 1768 and 1778. I thought of Marmontel, and his 'ombre chevalier;' of La Harpe, and his quarrel with the Patriarch ; of Madame de Genlis, and of all the tattle which fills 'Grimm's Correspondence.' Lord Lansdowne was much pleased. Ellis less so. He is no Voltairian ; nor am I, exactly ; but I take a great interest in the literary history of the last century." In his diary of the 28th of December, 1850, he writes, "Read the 'Physiology of Monkeys,' and Collins's account of Voltaire—as mischievous a monkey as any of them."

lay, who was then still at the War Office, wrote to the editor of the *Edinburgh Review* in these terms : " I think the new ' Life of Hastings' the worst book that I ever saw. I should be inclined to treat it mercilessly, were it not that the writer, though I never saw him, is, as an army chaplain, in some sense placed officially under me; and I think that there would be something like tyranny and insolence in pouring contempt on a person who has a situation from which I could, for aught I know, have him dismissed, and in which I certainly could make him very uneasy. It would be far too Crokerish a proceeding for me to strike a man who would find some difficulty in retaliating. I shall therefore speak of him much less sharply than he deserves; unless, indeed, we should be out, which is not improbable. In that case I should, of course, be quite at liberty."

Unfortunately for Mr. Gleig, the Whigs were relegated to private life in time to set Macaulay at liberty to make certain strictures; which, indeed, he was under an absolute obligation to make if there was any meaning in the motto of the *Edinburgh Review.** The first two paragraphs of the " Essay on Warren Hastings " originally ran as follows:

"This book seems to have been manufactured in pursuance of a contract, by which the representatives of Warren Hastings, on the one part, bound themselves to furnish papers, and Mr. Gleig, on the other part, bound himself to furnish praise. It is but just to say that the covenants on both sides have been most faithfully kept; and the result is before us in the form of three big bad volumes, full of undigested correspondence and undiscerning panegyric.

"If it were worth while to examine this performance in detail, we could easily make a long article by merely pointing out inaccurate statements, inelegant expressions, and immoral doctrines. But it would be idle to waste criticism on a book-maker; and, whatever credit Mr. Gleig may have justly earned by former works, it is as a book-maker, and nothing more, that he now comes before us. More eminent men than Mr. Gleig have written nearly as ill as he, when they have stooped to similar drudgery. It would be unjust to estimate Goldsmith by ' The Vicar of Wakefield,' or Scott by the ' Life of Napoleon.' Mr. Gleig is neither a Goldsmith nor a Scott; but it would be unjust to deny that he is capable of some-

---

* " Judex damnatur cum nocens absolvitur."

thing better than these 'Memoirs.' It would also, we hope and believe, be unjust to charge any Christian minister with the guilt of deliberately maintaining some of the propositions which we find in this book. It is not too much to say that Mr. Gleig has written several passages which bear the same relation to 'The Prince' of Machiavelli that 'The Prince' of Machiavelli bears to 'The Whole Duty of Man,' and which would excite admiration in a den of robbers, or on board of a schooner of pirates. But we are willing to attribute these offenses to haste, to thoughtlessness, and to that disease of the understanding which may be called the *furor biographicus*, and which is to writers of lives what the goître is to an Alpine shepherd, or dirt-eating to a negro slave."

If this passage was unduly harsh, the punishment which overtook its author was instant and terrible. It is difficult to conceive any calamity which Macaulay would regard with greater consternation than that, in the opening sentences of an article which was sure to be read by every body who read any thing, he should pose before the world for three mortal months in the character of a critic who thought "The Vicar of Wakefield" a bad book.

Albany, London, October 26th, 1841.

DEAR NAPIER,—I write chiefly to point out, what I dare say you have already observed, the absurd blunder in the first page of my article. I have not, I am sorry to say, the consolation of being able to blame either you or the printers: for it must have been a slip of my own pen. I have put "The Vicar of Wakefield" instead of the "History of Greece." Pray be so kind as to correct this in the errata of the next number. I am, indeed, so much vexed by it that I could wish that the correction were made a little more prominent than usual, and introduced with two or three words of preface. But this I leave absolutely to your taste and judgment.

Ever yours truly,   T. B. MACAULAY.

Albany, London, October 30th, 1841.

DEAR NAPIER,—I have received your letter, and am truly glad to find that you are satisfied with the effect of my article. As to the pecuniary part of the matter, I am satisfied, and more than satisfied. Indeed, as you well know, money has never been my chief object in writing. It was not so even when I was very poor; and at present I consider myself as one of the richest men of my acquaintance; for I can well afford to spend a thousand a year, and I can enjoy every comfort on eight hundred. I own, however, that your supply comes agreeably enough to assist me in furnishing my rooms, which I have made, unless I am mistaken, into a very pleasant student's cell.

And now a few words about Leigh Hunt. He wrote to me yesterday in great distress, and inclosed a letter which he had received from you, and which had much agitated him. In truth, he misunderstood you; and you had used an expression which was open to some little misconstruction. You told him that you should be glad to have a "gentleman-like" article from him, and Hunt took this for a reflection on his birth. He implored me to tell him candidly whether he had given you any offense, and to advise him as to his course. I replied that he had utterly misunderstood you; that I was sure you meant merely a literary criticism; that your taste in composition was more severe than his, more indeed than mine; that you were less tolerant than myself of little mannerisms springing from peculiarities of temper and training; that his style seemed to you too colloquial; that I myself thought that he was in danger of excess in that direction; and that, when you received a letter from him promising a very "chatty" article, I was not surprised that you should caution him against his besetting sin. I said that I was sure that you wished him well, and would be glad of his assistance; but that he could not expect a person in your situation to pick his words very nicely; that you had during many years superintended great literary undertakings; that you had been under the necessity of collecting contributions from great numbers of writers, and that you were responsible to the public for the whole. Your credit was so deeply concerned that you must be allowed to speak plainly. I knew that you had spoken to men of the first consideration quite as plainly as to him. I knew that you had refused to insert passages written by so great a man as Lord Brougham. I knew that you had not scrupled to hack and hew articles on foreign politics which had been concocted in the hotels of embassadors, and had received the *imprimatur* of secretaries of state. I said that, therefore, he must, as a man of sense, suffer you to tell him what you might think, whether rightly or wrongly, to be the faults of his style. As to the sense which he had put on one or two of your expressions, I took it on myself, as your friend, to affirm that he had mistaken their meaning, and that you would never have used those words if you had foreseen that they would have been so understood. Between ourselves, the word "gentleman-like" was used in rather a harsh way.* Now I have told you what has passed between him and me; and I leave you to act as you think fit. I am sure that you will act properly and humanely. But I must add that I think you are too hard on his article.

As to "The Vicar of Wakefield," the correction must be deferred, I think, till the appearance of the next number. I am utterly unable to conceive how I can have committed such a blunder, and failed to notice it in the proofs.

Ever yours,   T. B. Macaulay.

Albany, London, November 5th, 1841.

Dear Napier,—Leigh Hunt has sent me a most generous and amiable letter which he has received from you. He seems much touched by it, and more than satisfied, as he ought to be.

I have at last begun my historical labors; I can hardly say with how much interest and delight. I really do not think that there is in our literature so great a void as that which I am trying to supply. English history, from 1688 to the French Revolution, is, even to educated people, almost a *terra incognita*. I will venture to say that it is quite an even chance whether even such a man as Empson, or Senior, can repeat accurately the names of the prime ministers of that time in order. The materials for an amusing narrative are

---

* It is worth notice that "gentleman-like" is the precise epithet which Macaulay applied to his own article on Gladstone's "Church and State." See page 48.

immense. I shall not be satisfied unless I produce something which shall for a few days supersede the last fashionable novel on the tables of young ladies.

I should be very much obliged to you to tell me what are the best sources of information about the Scotch Revolution in 1688, the campaign of Dundee, the massacre of Glencoe, and the Darien scheme. I mean to visit the scenes of all the principal events both in Great Britain and Ireland, and also on the Continent. Would it be worth my while to pass a fortnight in one of the Edinburgh libraries next summer? Or do you imagine that the necessary information is to be got at the British Museum?

By-the-bye, a lively picture of the state of the Kirk is indispensable. Ever yours, T. B. MACAULAY.

Albany, London, December 1st, 1841.

DEAR NAPIER,—You do not seem to like what I suggested about Henry the Fifth.* Nor do I, on full consideration. What do you say to an article on Frederic the Great? Tom Campbell is bringing out a book about his majesty.

Now that I am seriously engaged in an extensive work, which will probably be the chief employment of the years of health and vigor which remain to me, it is necessary that I should choose my subjects for reviews with some reference to that work. I should not choose to write an article on some point which I should have to treat again as a historian; for, if I did, I should be in danger of repeating myself. I assure you that I a little grudge you Westminster Hall, in the paper on Hastings. On the other hand, there are many characters and events which will occupy little or no space in my "History," yet with which, in the course of my historical researches, I shall necessarily become familiar. There can not be a better instance than Frederic the Great. His personal character,

---

* Macaulay had written on the 10th of November: "If Longman will send me Mr. Tyler's book on Henry the Fifth, I will see whether I can not, with the help of Froissart and Monstrelet, furnish a spirited sketch of that short and most brilliant life."

manners, studies, literary associates; his quarrel with Voltaire, his friendship for Maupertuis, and his own unhappy *métromanie* will be very slightly, if at all, alluded to in a "History of England."* Yet in order to write the "History of England," it will be necessary to turn over all the memoirs, and all the writings, of Frederic, connected with us, as he was, in a most important war. In this way my reviews would benefit by my historical researches, and yet would not forestall my "History," or materially impede its progress. I should not like to engage in any researches altogether alien from what is now my main object. Still less should I like to tell the same story over and over again, which I must do if I were to write on such a subject as the "Vernon Correspondence," or Trevor's "History of William the Third." Ever yours,

T. B. MACAULAY.

In January, 1842, Macaulay writes to Mr. Napier: "As to Frederic, I do not see that I can deal with him well under seventy pages. I shall try to give a life of him after the manner of Plutarch. That, I think, is my forte. The paper on Clive took greatly. That on Hastings, though in my own opinion by no means equal to that on Clive, has been even more successful. I ought to produce something much better than either of those articles with so excellent a subject as Frederic. Keep the last place for me if you can. I greatly regret my never having seen Berlin and Potsdam."

Albany, London, April 18th, 1842.

MY DEAR NAPIER,—I am much obliged to you for your criticisms on my article on Frederic. My copy of the *Review* I have lent, and can not therefore refer to it. I have, however, thought over what you say, and should be disposed to admit part of it to be just. But I have several distinctions and limitations to suggest.

---

* At this period of his career Macaulay still purposed, and hoped, to write the history of England "down to a time which is within the memory of men still living."

The charge to which I am most sensible is that of interlarding my sentences with French terms. I will not positively affirm that no such expression may have dropped from my pen, in writing hurriedly on a subject so very French. It is, however, a practice to which I am extremely averse, and into which I could fall only by inadvertence. I do not really know to what you allude; for as to the words "Abbé" and "Parc-aux-Cerfs," which I recollect, those surely are not open to objection. I remember that I carried my love of English in one or two places almost to the length of affectation. For example, I called the "Place des Victoires" the "Place of Victories;" and the "Fermier Général" D'Etioles a "publican." I will look over the article again, when I get it into my hands, and try to discover to what you allude.

The other charge, I confess, does not appear to me to be equally serious. I certainly should not, in regular history, use some of the phrases which you censure. But I do not consider a review of this sort as regular history, and I really think that, from the highest and most unquestionable authority, I could vindicate my practice. Take Addison, the model of pure and graceful writing. In his *Spectators* I find "wench," "baggage," "queer old put," "prig," "fearing that they should smoke the Knight." All these expressions I met this morning, in turning over two or three of his papers at breakfast. I would no more use the word "bore" or "awkward squad" in a composition meant to be uniformly serious and earnest, than Addison would in a state paper have called Louis an "old put," or have described Shrewsbury and Argyle as "smoking" the design to bring in the Pretender. But I did not mean my article to be uniformly serious and earnest. If you judge of it as you would judge of a regular history, your censure ought to go very much deeper than it does, and to be directed against the substance as well as against the diction. The tone of many passages, nay, of whole pages, would justly be called flippant in a regular history. But I conceive that this sort of composition has its own character and its own laws. I do not claim the honor of having invented it; that praise belongs to Southey; but I may say that I have in some points improved upon his design. The manner of these little historical essays bears, I think, the same analogy to the manner of Tacitus or Gibbon which the manner of Ariosto bears to the manner of Tasso, or the manner of Shakspeare's historical plays to the manner of Sophocles. Ariosto, when he is grave and pathetic, is as grave and pathetic as Tasso; but he often takes a light, fleeting tone which suits him admirably, but which in Tasso would be quite out of place. The despair of Constance in Shakspeare is as lofty as that of Œdipus in Sophocles; but the levities of the bastard Faulconbridge would be utterly out of place in Sophocles. Yet we feel that they are not out of place in Shakspeare.

So with these historical articles. Where the subject requires it, they may rise, if the author can manage it, to the highest altitudes of Thucydides. Then, again, they may without impropriety sink to the levity and colloquial ease of Horace Walpole's Letters. This is my theory. Whether I have succeeded in the execution is quite another question. You will, however, perceive that I am in no danger of taking similar liberties in my "History." I do, indeed, greatly disapprove of those notions which some writers have of the dignity of history. For fear of alluding to the vulgar concerns of private life, they take no notice of the circumstances which deeply affect the happiness of nations. But I never thought of denying that the language of history ought to preserve a certain dignity. I would, however, no more attempt to preserve that dignity in a paper like this on Frederic than I would exclude from such a poem as "Don Juan" slang terms, because such terms would be out of place in "Paradise Lost," or Hudibrastic rhymes, because such rhymes would be shocking in Pope's "Iliad."

As to the particular criticisms which you have made, I willingly submit my judgment to yours, though I think that I could say something on the other side. The first rule of all writing—that rule to which every other is subordinate—is that the words used by the writer shall be such as most fully and precisely convey his meaning to the great body of his readers. All considerations about the purity and dignity of style ought to bend to this consideration. To write what is not understood in its whole force for fear of using some word which was unknown to Swift or Dryden would be, I think, as absurd as to build an observatory like that at Oxford, from which it is impossible to observe, only for the purpose of exactly preserving the proportions of the Temple of the Winds at Athens. That a word which is appropriate to a particular idea, which every body, high and low, uses to express that idea, and which expresses that idea with a completeness which is not equaled by any other single word, and scarcely by any circumlocution, should be banished from writing, seems to be a mere throwing-away of power. Such a word as "talented" it is proper to avoid: first, because it is not wanted; secondly, because you never hear it from those who speak very good English. But the word "shirk" as applied to military duty is a word which every body uses; which is the word, and the only word, for the thing; which in every regiment and in every ship belonging to our country is employed ten times a day; which the Duke of Wellington, or Admiral Stopford, would use in reprimanding an officer. To interdict it, therefore, in what is meant to be familiar, and almost jocose, narrative seems to me rather rigid.

But I will not go on. I will only repeat that I am truly grateful for your advice, and that if you will, on future occasions, mark with an asterisk any words in my proof-sheets which you think open to objection, I will try to meet your wishes, though it may sometimes be at the expense of my own. Ever yours most truly,   T. B. MACAULAY.

Albany, London, April 25th, 1842.

DEAR NAPIER,—Thank you for your letter. We shall have no disputes about diction. The English language is not so poor but that I may very well find in it the means of contenting both you and myself.

I have no objection to try Madame D'Arblay for the October number. I have only one scruple—that some months ago Leigh Hunt told me that he thought of proposing that subject to you, and I approved of his doing so. Now, I should have no scruple in taking a subject out of Brougham's hands, because he can take care of himself, if he thinks himself ill-used. But I would not do any thing that could hurt the feelings of a man whose spirit seems to be quite broken by adversity, and who lies under some obligations to me.

By-the-way, a word on a subject which I should be much obliged to you to consider, and advise me upon. I find that the American publishers have thought it worth while to put forth two, if not three, editions of my reviews; and I receive letters from them saying that the sale is considerable. I have heard that several people here have ordered them from America. Others have cut them out of old numbers of the *Edinburgh Review*, and have bound them up in volumes. Now, I know that these pieces are full of faults, and that their popularity has been very far beyond their merit; but, if they are to be republished, it would be better that they should be republished under the eye of the author, and with his corrections, than that they should retain all the blemishes inseparable from hasty writing and hasty printing. Longman proposed something of the kind to me three years ago; but at that time the American publication had not taken place, which makes a great difference. Give me your counsel on the subject. Ever yours truly,   T. B. MACAULAY.

Albany, London, June 24th, 1842.

DEAR NAPIER,—I have thought a good deal about republishing my articles, and have made up my mind not to do so. It is rather provoking, to be sure, to learn that a third edition is coming out in America, and to meet constantly with smuggled copies. It is still more provoking to see trash, of which I am perfectly guiltless, inserted among my writings. But, on the whole, I think it best that things should remain as they are. The public judges, and ought to judge, indulgently of periodical works. They are not expected to be highly finished. Their natural life is only six weeks. Sometimes their writer is at a distance from the books to which he wants to refer. Sometimes he is forced to hurry through his task in order to catch the post. He may blunder; he may contradict himself; he may break off in the middle of a story; he may give an immoderate extension to one part of his subject, and dismiss an equally important part in a few words. All this is readily forgiven if there be a certain spirit and vivacity in his style. But, as soon as he republishes, he challenges a comparison with all the most symmetrical and polished of human compositions. A painter who has a picture in the exhibition of the Royal Academy would act very unwisely if he took it down and carried it over to the National Gallery. Where it now hangs, surrounded by a crowd of daubs which are only once seen and then forgotten, it may pass for a fine piece. He is a fool if he places it side by side with the masterpieces of Titian and Claude. My reviews are generally thought to be better written, and they certainly live longer, than the reviews of most other people; and this ought to content me. The moment I come forward to demand a higher rank, I must expect to be judged by a higher standard. Fonblanque may serve for a beacon. His leading articles in the *Examiner* were extolled to the skies, while they were considered merely as leading articles; for they were in style and manner incomparably superior to any thing in the *Courier*, or *Globe*, or *Standard;* nay, to any thing in the *Times.* People said that it was a pity that such admirable compositions should perish; so Fonblanque determined to republish them in a book. He never considered that in that form they would be compared not with the rant and twaddle of the daily and weekly press, but with Burke's pamphlets, with Pascal's letters, with Addison's *Spectators* and *Freeholders.* They would not stand this new test a moment. I shall profit by the warning. What the Yankees may do I can not help; but I will not found my pretensions to the rank of a classic on my reviews. I will remain, according to the excellent precept in the Gospel, at the lower end of the table, where I am constantly accosted with "Friend, go up higher," and not push my way to the top at the risk of being compelled with shame to take the lowest room. If I live twelve or fifteen years, I may perhaps produce something which I may not be afraid to exhibit side by side with the performance of the old masters.

Ever yours truly,   T. B. MACAULAY.

Albany, London, July 14th, 1842.

DEAR NAPIER,—As to the next number, I must beg you to excuse me. I am exceedingly desirous to get on with my "History," which is really in a fair train. I must go down into Somersetshire and Devonshire to see the scene of Monmouth's campaign, and to follow the line of William's march from Torquay. I have also another plan of no great importance, but one which will occupy me during some days. You are acquainted, no doubt, with Perizonius's theory about the early Roman history—a theory which Niebuhr revived, and which Arnold has adopted as fully established. I have myself not the smallest doubt of its truth. It is, that the stories of the birth of Romulus and Remus, the fight of the Horatii and Curatii, and all the other romantic tales which fill the first three or four books of Livy, came from the lost ballads of the early Romans. I amused myself in India with trying to restore some of these long-perished poems. Arnold saw two of them,* and wrote to me in such terms of eulogy that I have been induced to correct and complete them. There are four of them, and I think that, though they are but trifles, they may pass for scholar-like and not inelegant trifles. I must prefix short prefaces to them, and I think of publishing them next November in a small volume. I fear, therefore, that just at present I can be of no use to you. Nor, indeed, should I find it easy to select a subject. "Romilly's Life" is a little stale. Lord Cornwallis is not an attractive subject. Clive and Hastings were great men, and their history is full of great events. Cornwallis was a respectable specimen of mediocrity. His wars were not brilliantly successful; fiscal reforms were his principal measures; and to interest English readers in questions of Indian finance is quite impossible.

---

* Dr. Arnold never saw the "Lays" in print. Just a month previous to the date of this letter Macaulay wrote to his sister Fanny: "But poor Arnold! I am deeply grieved for him and for the public. It is really a great calamity, and will be felt as such by hundreds of families. There was no such school: and from the character of the trustees, who almost all are strong, and even bitter, Tories, I fear that the place is likely to be filled by somebody of very different spirit."

I am a little startled by the very careless way in which the review on duelling has been executed. In the historical part there are really as many errors as assertions. Look at page 439. Ossory never called out Clarendon. The peer whom he called out, on the Irish Cattle Bill, was Buckingham. The provocation was Buckingham's remark that whoever opposed the bill had an Irish interest, or an Irish understanding. It is Clarendon who tells the whole story. Then, as to the scuffle between Buckingham and a free-trading Lord Dorchester in the lobby, the scuffle was not in the lobby, but at a conference in the Painted Chamber; nor had it any thing to do with free trade; for at a conference all the Lords are on one side. It was the effect of an old quarrel, and of an accidental jostling for seats. Then, a few lines lower, it is said that Lady Shrewsbury dissipated all her son's estate, which is certainly not true; for soon after he came of age he raised forty thousand pounds by mortgage, which at the then rate of interest he never could have done unless he had a good estate. Then, in the next page, it is said that Mohun murdered rather than killed the Duke of Hamilton—a gross blunder. Those who thought that the duke was murdered always attributed the murder not to Mohun, but to Mohun's second, Macartney. The fight between the two principals was universally allowed to be perfectly fair. Nor did Steele rebuke Thornhill for killing Dering, but, on the contrary, did his best to put Thornhill's conduct in the most amiable light, and to throw the whole blame on the bad usages of society. I do not know that there ever was a greater number of mistakes as to matters of fact in so short a space. I have read only those two pages of the article. If it is all of a piece, it is a prodigy indeed.

Let me beg that you will not mention the little literary scheme which I have confided to you. I should be very sorry that it were known till the time of publication arrives.

Ever yours truly,   T. B. MACAULAY.

Albany, London, July 20th, 1842.

DEAR NAPIER,—I do not like to disappoint you; and I really would try to send you something, if I could think of a subject that would suit me. My objections to taking Romilly's "Life" are numerous. One of them is that I was not acquainted with him, and never heard him speak, except for a few minutes when I was a child. A stranger who writes a description of a person whom hundreds still living knew intimately, is almost certain to make mistakes; and, even if he makes no absolute mistake, his portrait is not likely to be thought a striking resemblance by those who knew the original. It is like making a bust from a description. The best sculptor must disappoint those who knew the real face. I felt this even about Lord Holland; and nothing but Lady Holland's request would have overcome my unwillingness to say any thing about his Parliamentary speaking, which I had never heard. I had, however, known him familiarly in private; but Romilly I never saw except in the House of Commons.

You do not quite apprehend the nature of my plan about the old Roman ballads; but the explanation will come fast enough. I wish from my soul that I had written a volume of my "History." I have not written half a volume; nor do I consider what I have done as more than rough-hewn.

I hear with some concern that Dickens is going to publish a most curious book against the Yankees. I am told that all the Fearons, Trollopes, Marryats, and Martineaus together have not given them half so much offense as he will give. This may be a more serious affair than the destruction of the *Caroline*, or the mutiny in the *Creole*.*

Ever yours,   T. B. Macaulay.

In a subsequent letter Macaulay says: "I wish Dickens's book to be kept for me. I have never written a word on that subject, and I have a great deal in my head. Of course, I shall be courteous to Dickens, whom I know, and whom I

---

* The *Caroline* was an American steamboat, which had been employed to convey arms and stores to the Canadian insurgents. A party of loyalists seized the vessel, and sent her down the Falls of Niagara. The *Creole* difficulty arose from the mutiny of a ship-load of Virginian slaves, who, in an evil hour for their owner, bethought themselves that they were something better than a cargo of cattle.

think both a man of genius and a good-hearted man, in spite
of some faults of taste."

Mr. Napier was very anxious to turn the enforced leisure
of the Whig leaders to some account by getting an article for
his October number from the Foreign Secretary of the late
Administration. In August, 1842, Macaulay writes: "I had a
short talk about the *Edinburgh Review* with Palmerston, just
before he left London. I told him, what is quite true, that
there were some public men of high distinction whom I would
never counsel to write, both with a view to the interests of
the *Review*, and to their own; but that he was in no danger
of losing by his writings any part of the credit which he had
acquired by speech and action. I was quite sincere in this,
for he writes excellently." Lord Palmerston, after thinking
the matter over, sent Macaulay a letter promising to think it
over a little more; and stating, in his free, pleasant style, the
difficulties which made him hesitate about acceding to the proposal. "If one has any good hits to make about the present
state of foreign affairs, one feels disposed to reserve them for
the House of Commons; while, in order to do justice to the
British Government, it might now and then be necessary to
say things about some foreign governments which would not
come altogether well from any body who had been, and might
be thought likely again at some future time to be, concerned in
the management of affairs. Perhaps you will say that the last
consideration need not restrain the pen of any of us, according
to present appearances."

Albany, London, August 22d, 1842.

Dear Ellis,—For the ballads many thanks. Some of them
are capital.

I have been wishing for your advice. My little volume is
nearly finished, and I must talk the prefaces over with you
fully. I have made some alterations which I think improvements, and, in particular, have shortened the "Battle of Regillus" by near thirty lines without, I think, omitting any important circumstance.

It is odd that we never, in talking over this subject, remembered that in all probability the old Roman lays were in the

Saturnian metre; and it is still more odd that my ballads should, by mere accident, be very like the Saturnian metre; quite as like, indeed, as suits the genius of our language. The Saturnian metre is acatalectic dimeter iambic, followed by three trochees. A pure Saturnian line is preserved by some grammarian :

Dabunt malum Metelli Nævio poetæ.

Now, oddly enough, every tetrastich, and almost every distich, of my ballads opens with an acatalectic dimeter iambic line.

Lars Porsena of Clusium

is precisely the same with

Dabunt malum Metelli.

I have not kept the trochees, which really would be very unpleasing to an English ear. Yet there are some verses which the omission of a single syllable would convert into pure Saturnian metre; as,

In Alba's lake no fisher
(His) nets to-day is flinging.

Is not this an odd coincidence?

The only pure Saturnian line that I have been able to call to mind in all English poetry is in the nursery song—

The queen was in her parlor
Eating bread and honey.

Let me know when you come to town. I shall be here. Fix a day for dining with me next week—the sooner after your arrival, the better. I must give you one good boring about these verses before I deliver them over to the printer's devils.

Have you read Lord Londonderry's "Travels?" I hear that they contain the following pious expressions of resignation to the divine will: "Here I learned that Almighty God, for reasons best known to himself, had been pleased to burn down my house in the county of Durham." Is not the mixture of vexation with respect admirable? Ever yours,   T. B. M.

In a later letter to Mr. Ellis, Macaulay says: "Your objection to the lines

> 'By heaven,' he said, ' yon rebels
> Stand manfully at bay,'

is quite sound.   I also think the word 'rebels' objectionable, as raising certain modern notions about allegiance, divine right, Tower Hill, and the Irish Croppies, which are not at all to the purpose.   What do you say to this couplet?

> Quoth he, ' The she-wolf's litter
> Stand savagely at bay.'

'Litter' is used by our best writers as governing the plural number."

Albany, September 29th, 1842.

DEAR ELLIS,—Many thanks for the sheets.   I am much obliged to Adolphus for the trouble which he has taken. Some of his criticisms are quite sound.   I admit that the line about bringing Lucrece to shame is very bad, and the worse for coming over so often.*   I will try to mend it.   I admit, also, that the inventory of spoils in the last poem is, as he says, too long.   I will see what can be done with it.   He is not, I think, in the right about "the true client smile."   "The true client smile" is not exactly in the style of our old ballads; but it would be dangerous to make these old ballads models, in all points, for satirical poems which are supposed to have been produced in a great strife between two parties, crowded together within the walls of a republican city.   And yet even in an old English ballad I should not be surprised to find a usurer described as having the "righte Jew grinne."

I am more obliged to Adolphus than I can express for his interest in these trifles.   As to you, I need say nothing.   But pray be easy.   I am so, and shall be so.   Every book settles

---

* It is evident from this letter that the line

> "That brought Lucrece to shame"

originally stood wherever the line

> "That wrought the deed of shame"

stands now.

its own place. I never did, and never will, directly or indirectly, take any step for the purpose of obtaining praise or deprecating censure. Longman came to ask what I wished him to do before the volume appeared. I told him that I stipulated for nothing but that there should be no puffing of any sort. I have told Napier that I ask it, as a personal favor, that my name and writings may never be mentioned in the *Edinburgh Review*. I shall certainly leave this volume as the ostrich leaves her eggs in the sand. **T. B. MACAULAY.**

Albany, October 19th, 1842.

DEAR NAPIER,—This morning I received Dickens's book. I have now read it. It is impossible for me to review it; nor do I think that you would wish me to do so. I can not praise it, and I will not cut it up. I can not praise it, though it contains a few lively dialogues and descriptions; for it seems to me to be, on the whole, a failure. It is written like the worst parts of "Humphrey's Clock." What is meant to be easy and sprightly is vulgar and flippant, as in the first two pages. What is meant to be fine is a great deal too fine for me, as the description of the Fall of Niagara. A reader who wants an amusing account of the United States had better go to Mrs. Trollope, coarse and malignant as she is. A reader who wants information about American politics, manners, and literature had better go even to so poor a creature as Buckingham. In short, I pronounce the book, in spite of some gleams of genius, at once frivolous and dull.

Therefore I will not praise it. Neither will I attack it; first, because I have eaten salt with Dickens; secondly, because he is a good man, and a man of real talent; thirdly, because he hates slavery as heartily as I do; and, fourthly, because I wish to see him enrolled in our blue-and-yellow corps, where he may do excellent service as a skirmisher and sharpshooter. Ever yours truly, **T. B. MACAULAY.**

My little volume will be out, I think, in the course of the week. But all that I leave to Longman, except that I have positively stipulated that there shall be no puffing.

The sails of the little craft could dispense with an artificial breeze. Launched without any noise of trumpets, it went bravely down the wind of popular favor. Among the first to discern its merits was Macaulay's ancient adversary, Professor Wilson, of Edinburgh, who greeted it in *Blackwood's Magazine* with a pæan of hearty, unqualified panegyric; which was uttered with all the more zest because the veteran gladiator of the press recognized an opportunity for depreciating, by comparison with Macaulay, the reigning verse-writers of the day.

"What! poetry from Macaulay? Ay, and why not? The House hushes itself to hear him, even though Stanley is the cry! If he be not the first of critics (spare our blushes), who is? Name the Young Poet who could have written 'The Armada.' The Young Poets all want fire; Macaulay is full of fire. The Young Poets are somewhat weakly; he is strong. The Young Poets are rather ignorant; his knowledge is great. The Young Poets mumble books; he devours them. The Young Poets dally with their subject; he strikes its heart. The Young Poets are still their own heroes; he sees but the chiefs he celebrates. The Young Poets weave dreams with shadows transitory as clouds without substance; he builds realities lasting as rocks. The Young Poets steal from all and sundry, and deny their thefts; he robs in the face of day. Whom? Homer."

Again and again, in the course of his article, Christopher North indulges himself in outbursts of joyous admiration, which he had doubtless repressed, more or less consciously, ever since the time when, "twenty years ago, like a burnished fly in pride of May, Macaulay bounced through the open windows of *Knight's Quarterly Magazine*." He instructs his readers that a war-song is not to be skimmed through once, and then laid aside like a pamphlet on the Corn Laws.

"Why, Sir Walter kept reciting his favorite ballads almost every day for forty years, and with the same fire about his eyes, till even they grew dim at last. Sir Walter would have rejoiced in Horatius as if he had been a doughty Douglas.

Now, by our sire Quirinus,
It was a goodly sight
To see the thirty standards
Swept down the tide of flight.

That is the way of doing business! A cut-and-thrust style, without any flourish. Scott's style when his blood was up, and the first words came like a vanguard impatient for battle."

The description of Virginia's death is pronounced by the reviewer to be "the only passage in which Mr. Macaulay has sought to stir up pathetic emotion. Has he succeeded? We hesitate not to say that he has, to our heart's desire. This effect has been wrought simply by letting the course of the great natural affections flow on, obedient to the promptings of a sound, manly heart." Slight as it is, this bit of criticism shows genuine perspicacity. Frequent allusions in Macaulay's journals leave no doubt that in these lines he intended to embody his feelings toward his little niece Margaret, now Lady Holland, to whom then, as always, he was deeply and tenderly attached.

By making such cordial amends to an author whom in old days he had unjustly disparaged, Professor Wilson did credit to his own sincerity; but the public approbation needed no prompter, either then or thereafter. Eighteen thousand of the "Lays of Ancient Rome" were sold in ten years; forty thousand in twenty years; and, by June, 1875, upward of a hundred thousand copies had passed into the hands of readers. But it is a work of superfluity to measure by statistics the success of poems every line of which is, and long has been, too hackneyed for quotation.

Albany, London, November 16th, 1842.

DEAR NAPIER,—On my return from a short tour, I found your letter on my table. I am glad that you like my "Lays," and the more glad because I know that, from good-will to me, you must have been anxious about their fate. I do not wonder at your misgivings. I should have felt similar misgivings if I had learned that any person, however distinguished by talents and knowledge, whom I knew as a writer only by prose works, was about to publish a volume of poetry. Had I seen advertised a poem by Mackintosh, by Dugald Stewart, or even by Burke, I should have augured nothing but failure; and I am far from putting myself on a level even with the least of the three. So much the better for me. Where people look for no merit, a little merit goes a long way; and, without the smallest affectation of modesty, I confess that the success of my little book has far exceeded its just claims. I shall be in no hurry to repeat the experiment; for I am well aware that a second attempt would be made under much less favorable circumstances. A far more severe test would now be applied to my verses. I shall, therefore, like a wise gamester, leave off while I am a winner, and not cry Double or Quits.

As to poor Leigh Hunt, I wish that I could say, with you, that I heard nothing from him. I have a letter from him on my table asking me to lend him money, and lamenting that my verses want the true poetical aroma which breathes from Spenser's "Faery Queen." I am much pleased with him for having the spirit to tell me, in a begging letter, how little he likes my poetry. If he had praised me, knowing his poetical creed as I do, I should have felt certain that his praises were insincere. Ever yours,   T. B. Macaulay.

Albany, London, December 3d, 1842.

Dear Napier,—Longman has earnestly pressed me to consent to the republication of some of my reviews. The plan is one of which, as you know, I had thought; and which, on full consideration, I had rejected. But there are new circumstances in the case. The American edition is coming over by wholesale.* To keep out the American copies by legal measures, and yet to refuse to publish an edition here, would be an odious course, and in the very spirit of the dog in the manger. I am, therefore, strongly inclined to accede to Longman's proposition. And if the thing is to be done, the sooner the better.

I am about to put forth a second edition of my Roman "Lays." They have had great success. By-the-bye, Wilson, whom I never saw but at your table, has behaved very handsomely about them. I am not in the habit of returning thanks for favorable criticism; for, as Johnson says in his "Life of Lyttelton," such thanks must be paid either for flattery or for

---

* In a subsequent letter Macaulay writes: "The question is now merely this—whether Longman and I, or Carey & Hart, of Philadelphia, shall have the supplying of the English market with these papers. The American copies are coming over by scores, and measures are being taken for bringing them over by hundreds."

justice. But when a strong political opponent bestows fervent praise on a work which he might easily depreciate by means of sly sneer and cold commendations, and which he might, if he chose, pass by in utter silence, he ought, I think, to be told that his courtesy and good feeling are justly appreciated. I should be really obliged to you if, when you have an opportunity, you will let Professor Wilson know that his conduct has affected me as generous conduct affects men not ungenerous. Ever yours,   T. B. MACAULAY.

Macaulay spent the first weeks of 1843 in preparing for the republication of his "Essays." "I find from many quarters," he writes to Mr. Longman on the 25th of January, "that it is thought that the article on Southey's edition of Bunyan ought to be in the collection. It is a favorite with the Dissenters." And again: "Pray omit all mention of my Prefatory Notice. It will be very short and simple, and ought by no means to be announced beforehand as if it were any thing elaborate and important." The world was not slow to welcome, and, having welcomed, was not in a hurry to shelve, a book so unwillingly and unostentatiously presented to its notice. Upward of a hundred and twenty thousand copies have been sold in the United Kingdom alone by a single publisher. Considerably over a hundred and thirty thousand copies of separate essays have been printed in the series known by the name of The Traveler's Library. And it is no passing, or even waning, popularity which these figures represent. Between the years 1843 and 1853 the yearly sales by Messrs. Longman of the collected editions averaged 1230 copies; between 1853 and 1864 they rose to an average of 4700; and since 1864 more than six thousand copies have, one year with another, been disposed of annually. The publishers of the United States are still pouring forth reprints by many thousands at a time; and in British India, and on the Continent of Europe, these productions, which their author classed as ephemeral, are so greedily read and so constantly reproduced, that, taking the world as a whole, there is probably never a moment when they are out of the hands of the compositor. The market for them in their native country is so steady, and apparently so inexhaustible, that it perceptibly falls and rises with the general prosperity of the nation; and it is hardly too much to assert that the demand for Macaulay varies with the demand for coal. The astonishing success of this celebrated book must be regarded as something of far higher consequence than a mere literary or commercial triumph. It is no insignificant feat to have awakened in hundreds of thousands of minds the taste for letters and the yearning for knowledge; and to have shown by example that, in the interests of its own fame, genius can never be so well employed as on the careful and earnest treatment of serious themes.

Albany, London, January 18th, 1843.

DEAR NAPIER,—Another paper from me is at present out of the question. One in half a year is the very utmost of which I can hold out any hopes. I ought to give my whole leisure to my "History;" and I fear that if I suffer myself to be diverted from that design as I have done, I shall, like poor Mackintosh, leave behind me the character of a man who would have done something, if he had concentrated his powers, instead of frittering them away. I do assure you that if it were not on your account, I should have already given up writing for the *Review* at all. There are people who can carry on twenty works at a time. Southey would write the "History of Brazil" before breakfast, an ode after breakfast, then the "History of the Peninsular War" till dinner, and an article for the *Quarterly Review* in the evening. But I am of a different temper. I never write to please myself until my subject has for the time driven every other out of my head. When I turn from one work to another, a great deal of time is lost in the mere transition. I must not go on dawdling and reproaching myself all my life.

Ever yours,   T. B. MACAULAY.

Albany, London, April 19th, 1843.

DEAR NAPIER,—You may count on an article from me on Miss Aikin's "Life of Addison." Longman sent me the sheets as they were printed. I own that I am greatly disappointed. There are, to be sure, some charming letters by Addison which have never yet been published ; but Miss Aikin's narrative is dull, shallow, and inaccurate. Either she has fallen off greatly since she wrote her former works, or I have become much more acute since I read them. By-the-bye, I have an odd story to tell you. I was vexed at observing, in a very hasty perusal of the sheets, a great number of blunders, any of which singly was discreditable, and all of which united were certain to be fatal to the book. To give a few specimens, the lady called Evelyn "Sir John Evelyn ;" transferred Christ Church from Oxford to Cambridge ; confounded Robert Earl of Sunderland, James the Second's minister, with his son, Charles Earl of Sunderland, George the First's minister; confounded Charles Montague, Earl of Halifax, with George Savile, Marquis of Halifax ; called the Marquis of Hertford "Earl of Hertford," and so forth. I pointed the grossest blunders out to Longman, and advised him to point them out to her without mentioning me. He did so. The poor woman could not deny that my remarks were just ; but she railed most bitterly both at the publishers, and at the Mr. Nobody, who had had the insolence to find any blemish in her writings. At first she suspected Sedgwick. She now knows that she was wrong in that conjecture, but I do not think that she has detected me. This, you will say, is but a bad return to me for going out of my way to save her book from utter ruin. I am glad to learn that, with all her anger, she has had the sense to cancel some sheets in consequence of Mr. Nobody's criticisms.

My collected reviews have succeeded well. Longman tells me that he must set about a second edition. In spite, however, of the applause and of the profit, neither of which I despise, I am sorry that it had become necessary to republish these papers. There are few of them which I read with satisfaction. Those few, however, are generally the latest, and this is a consolatory circumstance. The most hostile critic must admit, I think, that I have improved greatly as a writer. The third volume seems to me worth two of the second, and the second worth ten of the first.

Jeffrey is at work on his collection. It will be delightful, no doubt; but to me it will not have the charm of novelty; for I have read and re-read his old articles till I know them by heart. Ever yours,   T. B. MACAULAY.

Albany, June 15th, 1843.

DEAR NAPIER,—I mistrust my own judgment of what I write so much, that I shall not be at all surprised if both you and the public think my paper on Addison a failure ; but I own that I am partial to it. It is now more than half finished. I have some researches to make before I proceed; but I have all the rest in my head, and shall write very rapidly. I fear that I can not contract my matter into less than seventy pages. You will not, I think, be inclined to stint me.

I am truly vexed to find Miss Aikin's book so very bad that it is impossible for us, with due regard to our own character, to praise it. All that I can do is to speak civilly of her writings generally, and to express regret that she should have been nodding. I have found, I will venture to say, not less than forty gross blunders as to matters of fact in the first volume. Of these I may, perhaps, point out eight or ten as courteously as the case will bear. Yet it goes much against my feelings to censure any woman, even with the greatest lenity. My taste and Croker's are by no means the same. I shall not again undertake to review any lady's book till I know how it is executed. Ever yours,   T. B. MACAULAY.

Albany, London, July 22d, 1843.

DEAR NAPIER,—I hear generally favorable opinions about my article. I am much pleased with one thing. You may remember how confidently I asserted that "little Dicky" in the "Old Whig" was the nickname of some comic actor.*

---

* "One calumny, which has been often repeated, and never yet contradicted, it is our duty to expose. It is asserted, in the 'Biographia Britannica,' that Addison designated Steele as 'little Dicky.' This assertion was repeated by Johnson, who had never seen the 'Old Whig,' and was therefore excusable. It has also been repeated by Miss Aikin, who has seen the 'Old Whig,' and for whom therefore there is less excuse. Now, it is true that the words 'little Dicky' occur in the 'Old Whig' and that Steele's name

Several people thought that I risked too much in assuming this so strongly on mere internal evidence. I have now, by an odd accident, found out who the actor was. An old prompter of Drury Lane Theatre, named Chetwood, published in 1749 a small volume, containing an account of all the famous performers whom he remembered, arranged in alphabetical order. This little volume I picked up yesterday, for sixpence, at a book-stall in Holborn; and the first name on which I opened was that of Henry Norris, a favorite comedian, who was nicknamed Dicky, because he first obtained celebrity by acting the part of Dicky in the "Trip to the Jubilee." It is added that his figure was very diminutive. He was, it seems, in the height of his popularity at the very time when the "Old Whig" was written. You will, I think, agree with me that

was Richard. It is equally true that the words 'little Isaac' occur in the 'Duenna,' and that Newton's name was Isaac. But we confidently affirm that Addison's little Dicky had no more to do with Steele than Sheridan's little Isaac with Newton. If we apply the words 'little Dicky' to Steele, we deprive a very lively and ingenious passage not only of all its wit, but of all its meaning. Little Dicky was evidently the nickname of some comic actor who played the usurer Gomez, then a most popular part, in Dryden's 'Spanish Friar.'"

This passage occurs in Macaulay's article on Miss Aikin's "Life and Writings of Addison," as it originally appeared in July, 1843. There is a marked difference of form between this and all his previous contributions to the *Edinburgh Review*. The text of the article on Addison is, with few and slight variations, the text of the collected edition; while all that relates to Miss Aikin is relegated to the foot-notes. Thus in the note on page 239 we read: "Miss Aikin says that the *Guardian* was launched in November, 1713. It was launched in March, 1713, and was given over in the following September." And in the note on page 247: "Miss Aikin has been most unfortunate in her account of this Rebellion. We will notice only two errors, which occur in one page. She says that the Rebellion was undertaken in favor of James the Second, who had been fourteen years dead, and that it was headed by Charles Edward, who was not born."

Macaulay was now no longer able to conceal from himself the fact that, whether he liked it or not, his "Essays" would live; and he accordingly took pains to separate the part of his work which was of permanent literary value from those passing strictures upon his author which as a reviewer he was bound to make, in order to save himself the trouble of subsequent revision and expurgation.

this is decisive. I am a little vain of my sagacity, which I really think would have dubbed me a "vir clarissimus" if it had been shown on a point of Greek or Latin learning; but I am still more pleased that the vindication of Addison from an unjust charge, which has been universally believed since the publication of the "Lives of the Poets," should thus be complete. Should you have any objection to inserting a short note at the end of the next number? Ten lines would suffice; and the matter is really interesting to all lovers of literary history.

As to politics, the ministers are in a most unenviable situation; and, as far as I can see, all the chances are against them. The immense name of the duke, though now only a "magni nominis umbra," is of great service to them. His assertion, unsupported by reasons, saved Lord Ellenborough. His declaration that sufficient precautions had been taken against an outbreak in Ireland has done wonders to calm the public mind. Nobody can safely venture to speak in Parliament with bitterness or contempt of any measure which he chooses to cover with his authority. But he is seventy-four, and, in constitution, more than seventy-four. His death will be a terrible blow to these people. I see no reason to believe that the Irish agitation will subside of itself, or that the death of O'Connell would quiet it. On the contrary, I much fear that his death would be the signal for an explosion. The aspect of foreign politics is gloomy. The finances are in disorder. Trade is in distress. Legislation stands still. The Tories are broken up into three or more factions, which hate each other more than they hate the Whigs—the faction which stands by Peel, the faction which is represented by Vivian and the *Morning Post*, and the faction of Smythe and Cochrane. I should not be surprised if, before the end of the next session, the ministry were to fall from mere rottenness.

Ever yours,   T. B. MACAULAY.

Macaulay was right in thinking that the Government was rotten, and Lord Palmerston* in believing that it was safe.

---

* See page 106.

Sir Robert Peel was not the first minister, and perhaps he is not destined to be the last, who has been chained down to office by the passive weight of an immense but discontented majority. Unable to retire in favor of his opponents, and compelled to disgust his supporters at every turn, he had still before him three more years of public usefulness and personal mortification. One, at any rate, among his former antagonists did much to further his measures, and little or nothing to aggravate his difficulties. The course which Macaulay pursued between the years 1841 and 1846 deserves to be studied as a model of the conduct which becomes a statesman in opposition. In following that course he had a rare advantage. The continuous and absorbing labors of his " History " filled his mind and occupied his leisure, and relieved him from the craving for occupation and excitement that lies at the root of half the errors to which politicians out of office are prone—errors which the popular judgment most unfairly attributes to lack of patriotism, or excess of gall. In the set party fights that from time to time took place, he spoke seldom, and did not speak his best; but when subjects came to the front on which his knowledge was great, and his opinion strongly marked, he interfered with decisive and notable effect.

It has been said of Macaulay, with reference to this period of his political career, that no member ever produced so much effect upon the proceedings of Parliament who spent so many hours in the Library and so few in the House. Never has any public man, unendowed with the authority of a minister, so easily molded so important a piece of legislation into a shape which so accurately accorded with his own views, as did Macaulay the Copyright Act of 1842. In 1814, the term during which the right of printing a book was to continue private property had been fixed at twenty-eight years from the date of publication. The shortness of this term had always been regarded as a grievance by authors and by publishers, and was beginning to be so regarded by the world at large. " The family of Sir Walter Scott," says Miss Martineau in her "History of England," " stripped by his great losses, might be supposed to have an honorable provision in his splendid array of

works, which the world was still buying as eagerly as ever:
but the copyright of "Waverley" was about to expire; and
there was no one who could not see the injustice of trans-
ferring to the public a property so evidently sacred as
theirs."

An arrangement which bore hardly upon the children of
the great Scotchman, whose writings had been popular and
profitable from the first, was nothing less than cruel in the
case of authors who, after fighting a life-long battle against
the insensibility of their countrymen, had ended by creating
a taste for their own works. Wordsworth's poetry was at
length being freely bought by a generation which he himself
had educated to enjoy it; but, as things then stood, his death
would at once rob his heirs of all share in the produce of the
"Sonnets" and the "Ode to Immortality," and would leave
them to console themselves as they best might with the copyright of the "Prelude." Southey (firmly possessed, as he
was, with the notion that posterity would set the highest value
upon those among his productions which living men were
the least disposed to purchase) had given it to be understood
that, in the existing state of the law, he should undertake no
more works of research like the "History of Brazil," and no
more epic poems on the scale of "Madoc" and "Roderick."
But there was nothing which so effectually stirred the sympa-
thies of men in power, and persuaded their reason, as a petition presented to the House of Commons by "Thomas Carlyle, a writer of books;" which began by humbly showing
"That your petitioner has written certain books, being incited
thereto by certain innocent and laudable considerations;" which
proceeded to urge "that this his labor has found hitherto, in
money or money's worth, small recompense or none: that he
is by no means sure of its ever finding recompense: but thinks
that, if so, it will be at a distant time, when he, the laborer, will
probably no longer be in need of money, and those dear to
him will still be in need of it;" and which ended by a prayer
to the House to forbid "extraneous persons, entirely uncon-
cerned in this adventure of his, to steal from him his small
winnings, for a space of sixty years at the shortest. After

sixty years, unless your honorable House provide otherwise, they may begin to steal."

In the session of 1841 Sergeant Talfourd brought in a measure, devised with the object of extending the term of copyright in a book to sixty years, reckoned from the death of the author. Macaulay, speaking with wonderful force of argument and brilliancy of illustration, induced a thin House to reject the bill by a few votes. Talfourd, in the bitterness of his soul, exclaimed that Literature's own familiar friend, in whom she trusted, and who had eaten of her bread, had lifted up his heel against her. A writer of eminence has since echoed the complaint; but none can refuse a tribute of respect to a man who, on high grounds of public expediency, thought himself bound to employ all that he possessed of energy and ability on the task of preventing himself from being placed in a position to found a fortune, which, by the year 1919, might well have ranked among the largest funded estates in the country.

Admonished, but not deterred, by Sergeant Talfourd's reverse, Lord Mahon next year took up the cause of his brother authors, and introduced a bill in which he proposed to carry out the objectionable principle, but to carry it less far than his predecessor. Lord Mahon was for giving protection for five-and-twenty years, reckoned from the date of death; and his scheme was regarded with favor, until Macaulay came forward with a counter-scheme, giving protection for forty-two years, reckoned from the date of publication. He unfolded his plan in a speech, terse, elegant, and vigorous; as amusing as an essay of Elia, and as convincing as a proof of Euclid.*

---

* "But this is not all. My noble friend's plan is not merely to institute a lottery in which some writers will draw prizes and some will draw blanks. His lottery is so contrived that, in the vast majority of cases, the blanks will fall to the best books, and the prizes to books of inferior merit.

"Take Shakspeare. My noble friend gives a longer protection than I should give to 'Love's Labor's Lost,' and 'Pericles, Prince of Tyre ;' but he gives a shorter protection than I should give to 'Othello' and 'Macbeth.'

"Take Milton. Milton died in 1674. The copyrights of Milton's great works would, according to my noble friend's plan, expire in 1699. 'Comus'

When he resumed his seat, Sir Robert Peel walked across the floor, and assured him that the last twenty minutes had rad-

---

appeared in 1634, the 'Paradise Lost' in 1668. To 'Comus,' then, my noble friend would give sixty-five years of copyright, and to 'Paradise Lost' only thirty-one years. Is that reasonable? 'Comus' is a noble poem; but who would rank it with the 'Paradise Lost?' My plan would give forty-two years both to the 'Paradise Lost' and to 'Comus.'

"Let us pass on from Milton to Dryden. My noble friend would give more than sixty years of copyright to Dryden's worst works; to the encomiastic verses on Oliver Cromwell, to the 'Wild Gallant,' to the 'Rival Ladies,' to other wretched pieces as bad as any thing written by Flecknoe or Settle: but for 'Theodore and Honoria,' for 'Tancred and Sigismunda,' for 'Cimon and Iphigenia,' for 'Palamon and Arcite,' for 'Alexander's Feast,' my noble friend thinks a copyright of twenty-eight years sufficient. Of all Pope's works, that to which my noble friend would give the largest measure of protection is the volume of 'Pastorals,' remarkable only as the production of a boy. Johnson's first work was a translation of a book of travels in Abyssinia, published in 1735. It was so poorly executed that in his later years he did not like to hear it mentioned. Boswell once picked up a copy of it, and told his friend that he had done so. 'Do not talk about it,' said Johnson: 'it is a thing to be forgotten.' To this performance my noble friend would give protection, during the enormous term of seventy-five years. To the 'Lives of the Poets' he would give protection during about thirty years.......

"I have, I think, shown from literary history that the effect of my noble friend's plan would be to give crude and imperfect works a great advantage over the highest productions of genius. What I recommend is that the certain term, reckoned from the date of publication, shall be forty-two years instead of twenty-eight years. In this arrangement there is no uncertainty, no inequality. The advantage which I propose to give will be the same to every book. No work will have so long a copyright as my noble friend gives to some books, or so short a copyright as he gives to others. No copyright will last ninety years. No copyright will end in twenty-eight years. To every book published in the last seventeen years of a writer's life I give a longer term of copyright than my noble friend gives; and I am confident that no person versed in literary history will deny this: that in general the most valuable works of an author are published in the last seventeen years of his life. To 'Lear,' to 'Macbeth,' to 'Othello,' to the 'Faery Queen,' to the 'Paradise Lost,' to Bacon's 'Novum Organum' and 'De Augmentis,' to Locke's 'Essay on the Human Understanding,' to Clarendon's 'History,' to Hume's 'History,' to Gibbon's 'History,' to Smith's 'Wealth of Nations,' to Addison's *Spectators*, to almost all the great works of Burke, to 'Clarissa' and 'Sir Charles Grandison,' to 'Jo-

ically altered his own views on the law of copyright. One member after another confessed to an entire change of mind; and, on a question which had nothing to do with party, each change of mind brought a vote with it. The bill was remodeled on the principle of calculating the duration of copyright from the date of publication, and the term of forty-two years was adopted by a large majority. Some slight modifications were made in Macaulay's proposal; but he enjoyed the satisfaction of having framed according to his mind a statute which may fairly be described as the charter of his craft, and of having added to Hansard what are by common consent allowed to be among its most readable pages.

There was another matter, of more striking dimensions in the eyes of his contemporaries, on which, by taking an independent course and persevering in it manfully, Macaulay brought round to his own opinion first his party, and ultimately the country. The Afghan war had come to a close in the autumn of 1842. The Tories claimed for Lord Ellenborough the glory of having saved India; while the Opposition held that he had with difficulty been induced to refrain from throwing obstacles in the way of its being saved by others. Most Whigs believed, and one Whig was ready on all fit occasions to maintain that his lordship had done nothing to deserve national admiration in the past, and a great deal to arouse the gravest apprehensions for the future. Macaulay had persuaded himself, and was now bent on persuading others, that, as long as Lord Ellenborough continued governor-general, the peace of our Eastern empire was not worth six months' purchase.

Albany, February, 1843.

DEAR ELLIS,—I never thought that I should live to sympa-

---

seph Andrews,' 'Tom Jones,' and 'Amelia,' and, with the single exception of 'Waverley,' to all the novels of Sir Walter Scott, I give a longer term of copyright than my noble friend gives. Can he match that list? Does not that list contain what England has produced greatest in many various ways—poetry, philosophy, history, eloquence, wit, skillful portraiture of life and manners? I confidently, therefore, call on the committee to take my plan in preference to the plan of my noble friend."

thize with Brougham's abuse of the Whigs; but I must own that we deserve it all. I suppose that you have heard of the stupid and disgraceful course which our leaders have resolved to take. I really can not speak or write of it with patience. They are going to vote thanks to Ellenborough, in direct opposition to their opinion, and with an unanswerable case against him in their hands, only that they may save Auckland from recrimination. They will not save him, however. Cowardice is a mighty poor defense against malice. And to sacrifice the whole weight and respectability of our party to the feelings of one man is—but the thing is too bad to talk about. I can not avert the disgrace of our party, but I do not choose to share it. I shall therefore go to Clapham quietly, and leave those who have cooked this dirt-pie for us to eat it. I did not think that any political matter would have excited me so much as this has done. I fought a very hard battle, but had nobody except Lord Minto and Lord Clanricarde to stand by me. I could easily get up a mutiny among our rank and file, if I chose; but an internal dissension is the single calamity from which the Whigs are at present exempt. I will not add it to all their other plagues. Ever yours,

T. B. MACAULAY.

On the 20th of February the House of Commons was called upon to express its gratitude to the governor-general; and a debate ensued, in which the speeches from the front Opposition bench were as good as could be made by statesmen who had assumed an attitude such that they could not very well avoid being either insincere or ungracious. The vote of thanks was unanimously passed; and, within three weeks' time, the Whigs were, almost to a man, engaged in hot support of a motion of Mr. Vernon Smith involving a direct and crushing censure on Lord Ellenborough. Lord Stanley (making, as he was well able, the most of the opportunity) took very good care that there should be no mistake about the consistency of men who, between the opening of the session and the Easter holidays, had thanked a public officer for his "ability and judgment," and had done their best to stigmatize him

as guilty of conduct "unwise, indecorous, and reprehensible."
Happily, Macaulay's conscience was clear; and his speech, in
so far as the reader's pleasure is a test of excellence, will bear
comparison with any thing that still remains of those orations
against Warren Hastings, in which the great men of a former
generation contested with each other the crown of eloquence.

The division went as divisions go, in the most good-natured of all national assemblies, when the whole strength of a
powerful government is exerted to protect a reputation. On
the 14th of March the Duke of Wellington wrote to Lord
Ellenborough: "Nothing could have been more satisfactory
than the debate in the House of Lords, and I am told it
was equally so in the Commons." The duke's informant
could not have seen far below the surface. Macaulay's measured and sustained denunciation of Lord Ellenborough's perilous levity had not fallen on inattentive ears. He had made,
or at any rate had implied, a prophecy. "Who can say what
new freak we may hear of by the next mail? I am quite confident that neither the Court of Directors nor her majesty's
ministers can look forward to the arrival of that mail without uneasiness." He had given a piece of advice. "I can not
sit down without addressing myself to those Directors of the
East India Company who are present. I exhort them to
consider the heavy responsibility which rests on them. They
have the power to recall Lord Ellenborough; and I trust that
they will not hesitate to exercise that power." The prophecy
came true, and the advice was adopted to the letter. Before
another twelvemonth had elapsed, Lord Ellenborough was in
a worse scrape than ever. This time Macaulay resolved to
take the matter in hand himself. He had a notice of motion
on the books of the House, and his speech was already in his
head, when, on the 26th of April, 1844, Sir Robert Peel announced that her majesty's government had received a communication from the Court of Directors "stating that they
had exercised the power which the law gives them to recall at
their will and pleasure the Governor-general of India."

Macaulay's reputation and authority in Parliament owed
nothing to the outward graces of the orator. On this head

the recollections of the reporters' gallery (which have been
as gratefully accepted as they were kindly offered) are unanimous and precise. Mr. Clifford, of *The Times*, says: " His action—the little that he used—was rather ungainly. His voice
was full and loud; but it had not the light and shade, or the
modulation, found in practiced speakers. His speeches were
most carefully prepared, and were repeated without the loss
or omission of a single word."

This last observation deserves a few sentences of comment.
Macaulay spoke frequently enough on the spur of the moment, and some excellent judges were of opinion that on
these occasions his style gained more in animation than it lost
in ornament. Even when he rose in his place to take part in
a discussion which had been long foreseen, he had no notes in
his hand and no manuscript in his pocket. If a debate was
in prospect, he would turn the subject over while he paced
his chamber or tramped along the streets. Each thought, as
it rose in his mind, embodied itself in phrases, and clothed itself in an appropriate drapery of images, instances, and quotations; and when, in the course of his speech, the thought recurred, all the words which gave it point and beauty spontaneously recurred with it.

" He used scarcely any action," says a gentleman on the
staff of *The Standard*. " He would turn round on his heel,
and lean slightly on the table; but there was nothing like
demonstrative or dramatic action. He spoke with great rapidity; and there was very little inflection in the voice,
which, however, in itself was not unmusical. It was somewhat monotonous, and seldom rose or fell. The cadences
were of small range. He spoke with very great fluency, and
very little emphasis. It was the matter and the language,
rather than the manner, that took the audience captive."

Mr. Downing, of *The Daily News*, writes: " It was quite
evident that Macaulay had not learned the art of speaking
from the platform, the pulpit, the forum, or any of the usual
modes of obtaining a fluent diction. He was at once too robust and too recondite for these methods of introduction to
the oratorical art. In all probability it was that fullness of

mind, which broke out in many departments, that constituted him a born orator. Vehemence of thought, vehemence of language, vehemence of manner, were his chief characteristics. The listener might almost fancy he heard ideas and words gurgling in the speaker's throat for priority of utterance. There was nothing graduated or undulating about him. He plunged at once into the heart of the matter, and continued his loud resounding pace from beginning to end, without halt or pause. This vehemence and volume made Macaulay the terror of the reporters; and when he engaged in a subject outside their ordinary experience, they were fairly nonplused by the display of names, and dates, and titles. He was not a long-winded speaker. In fact, his earnestness was so great that it would have failed under a very long effort. He had the faculty, possessed by every great orator, of compressing a great deal in a short space."

A fourth witness, after confirming the testimony of his colleagues, concludes with the remark: "Macaulay was wonderfully telling in the House of Commons. Every sentence was perfectly devoured by the listeners."

As soon as the session of 1843 ended, Macaulay started for a trip up and down the Loire. Steaming from Orleans to Nantes, and back again from Nantes to Angers, he indulged to the full his liking for river travel and river scenery, and his passion for old cities which had been the theatre of memorable events. His letters to his sister abundantly prove that he could have spoken off a very passable historical hand-book for Central France, without having trained himself for the feat by a course of special reading. His catalogue of the successive occupants of Chambord is marvelously accurate and complete, from Francis the First and his Italian architects, to the time when "the royalists got up a subscription to purchase it for the Duke of Berri's posthumous son, whom they still call Henry the Fifth. The project was not popular, but, by dint of bullying, and telling all who objected that they would be marked men as long as they lived, a sufficient sum was extorted." There are touches that mark the historian in his description of the Castle of Blois, when he speaks of "the chimney at which Henry, Duke of Guise, sat down for the last time to warm himself," and " the observatory of Catherine de' Medici, designed rather for astrological than for astronomical observations ;" but, taken as a whole, the letters have too much of the tourist's journal about them to bear printing in their integrity.

"Paris, August 21st, 1843.

"DEAREST HANNAH,—What people travel for is a mystery. I have never during the last forty-eight hours had any wish so strong as to be at home again. To be sure, those forty-eight hours have hardly been a fair specimen of a traveler's life. They have been filled with little miseries, such as made Mr. Testy roar, and Mr. Sensitive sigh. I could very well add a chapter to the 'Miseries of Human Life.' For example :

"Groan 1. The Brighton railway; in a slow train; a carriage crowded as full as it would hold; a sick lady smelling of ether; a healthy gentleman smelling of brandy; the thermometer at 102° in the shade, and I not in the shade, but exposed to the full glare of the sun from noon till half after two, the effect of which is that my white trousers have been scorched into a pair of very serviceable nankeens.

"Groan 2—and for this Fanny is answerable, who made me believe that the New Steyne Hotel at Brighton was a good one. A coffee-room ingeniously contrived on the principle of an oven, the windows not made to open ; a dinner on yesterday's pease-soup and the day before yesterday's cutlets; not an ounce of ice ; and all beverages—wine, water, and beer—in exactly the state of the Church of Laodicea.

"Groan 3. My passage to Dieppe. We had not got out of sight of the Beachy Head lights when it began to rain hard. I was therefore driven into the cabin, and compelled to endure the spectacle, and to hear the unutterable groans and gasps, of fifty sea-sick people. I went out when the rain ceased ; but every thing on deck was soaked. It was impossible to sit, so that I walked up and down the vessel all night. The wind was in our faces, and the clear gray dawn was visible before we entered the harbor of Dieppe. Our baggage was to be examined at seven ; so that it was too late to go to bed, and yet too early to find any shop open, or any thing stirring. All our bags and boxes were in the custody of the authorities, and I had to pace sulkily about the pier for a long time, without even the solace of a book.

"Groan 4. The custom-house. I never had a dispute with custom-house officers before, having found that honesty answered in England, France, and Belgium, and corruption in Italy. But the officer at Dieppe, finding among my baggage some cotton stockings which had not been yet worn, threatened to confiscate them, and exacted more than they were worth—between thirteen and fourteen francs—by way of duty. I had just bought these unlucky stockings to do honor to our country in the eyes of foreigners; being unwilling that the washer-women of Paris and Orleans should see an English member of Parliament's stockings either in holes or darned. See what the fruits of patriotism are!

"Groan 5. Mine inn at Dieppe. I need not describe it, for it was the very same at which we stopped for a night in 1840, and at which you eat of a gigot as memorable as Sam Johnson's shoulder of mutton.* I did not discover where I was till too late. I had a cup of coffee worse than I thought any French cook could make for a wager. In the bedroom, where I dressed, there was a sort of soap which I had half a mind to bring away, that men of science might analyze it. It would be, I should think, an excellent substitute for Spanish flies in a blister. I shaved with it, and the consequence is that I look as if I had that complaint which our mother held in such horror. If I used such cosmetics often, I should be forced to beg Queen Victoria to touch me.

"The cathedral, which was my chief object at Chartres, rather disappointed me; not that it is not a fine church; but I had heard it described as one of the most magnificent in Europe. Now, I have seen finer Gothic churches in England, France, and Belgium. It wants vastness; and its admirers make the matter worse by proving to you that it is a great deal larger than it looks, and by assuring you that the proportions are so exquisite as to produce the effect of littleness. I have heard the same cant canted about a much finer building — St. Peter's. But, surely, it is impossible to say a more severe thing of an architect than that he has a knack of building edifices five hundred feet long, which look as if they were only three hundred feet long. If size be an element of the sublime in architecture—and this, I imagine, every body's feelings will prove then a great architect ought to aim, not at making buildings look smaller than they are, but at making them look larger than they are. If there be any proportions which have the effect of making St. Paul's look larger than St. Peter's, those are good proportions. To say that an artist is so skillful that he makes buildings which are really large look small, is as absurd as it would be to say that a novelist has such skill in narration as to make amusing stories dull, or to say that a controversialist has such skill in argument, that strong reasons, when he states them, seem to be weak ones."

"September 1st, 1843.—I performed my journey to Bourges comfortably enough, in the coupé of the diligence. There was a prodigious noise all

---

* In the review on Croker, Macaulay calls it a leg of mutton. As a matter of fact, Boswell does not specify whether it was a leg or a shoulder. Whatever the joint may have been, Dr. Johnson immortalized it in these words, "It is as bad as bad can be—it is ill-fed, ill-killed, ill-kept, and ill-dressed."

night of people talking in English on the roof. At Vierzon, I found that this noise proceeded from seven English laborers, good-looking fellows enough, who were engaged to work on a line of railroad, and were just going to quit the coach. I asked them about their state and prospects, told them that I hoped they would let a countryman treat them to breakfast, and gave them a napoleon for that purpose. They were really so pleased and grateful for being noticed in that way that I was almost too strongly moved by their thanks. Just before we started, one of them, a very intelligent man and a sort of spokesman, came to the window, and asked me with great earnestness to tell them my name, which I did. 'Ah, sir, we have all heard of you. You have always been a good friend to the country at home; and it will be a great satisfaction to us all to know this.' He told me, to my comfort, that they did very well—being, as he said, sober men; that the wages were good; and that they were well treated, and had no quarrels with their French fellow-laborers.

"I could not, after this, conceal my name from a very civil, good-natured Frenchman who traveled in the coupé with me, and with whom I had already had some conversation. He insisted on doing the honors of Bourges to me, and has really been officiously kind and obliging. Indeed, in this city I have found nothing but courtesy worthy of Louis the Fourteenth's time. Queer old-fashioned country gentlemen of long descent, who recovered part of their estates on their return from emigration, abound in the neighborhood. They have hotels in Bourges, where they often pass the winter, instead of going up to Paris. The manners of the place are most ceremonious. Hats come off at every word. If you ask your way, a gentleman insists on escorting you. Did you ever read 'Georges Dandin?' If not, read it before you sleep. There you will see how Molière has portrayed the old-fashioned provincial gentry. I could fancy that many Messieurs and Mesdames de Sotenville were to be found at Bourges."

"*September 6th.*—I know nothing about politics except what I glean from French newspapers in the coffee-houses. The people here seem to be in very ill-humor about the queen's visit; and I think it, I must own, an ill-judged step. Propriety requires that a guest, a sovereign, and a woman should be received by Louis Philippe with something of chivalrous homage, and with an air of deference. To stand punctiliously on his quality in intercourse with a young lady would be uncourteous, and almost insulting. But the French have taken it strongly into their heads that their Government is acting a servile part toward England, and they are therefore disposed to consider every act of hospitality and gallantry on the part of the king as a national humiliation. I see that the journals are crying out that France is forever degraded because the band of a French regiment played 'God Save the Queen' when her majesty landed. I fear that Louis Philippe can not possibly behave on this occasion so as at once to gratify his guest and his subjects. They are the most unreasonable people which

exists; that is the truth; and they will never be wiser until they have
had another lesson like that of 1815."

"*September 9th*, 1843.—It was just four in the morning when I reached
Angers; but I found a café open, made a tolerable breakfast, and before
five was on board a steamer for Tours. It was a lovely day. The banks
were seen to every advantage, and, without possessing beauty of the highest class, presented an endless succession of pretty and cheerful landscapes.
With the scenery, and a book, I was in no want of company. A Frenchman, however, began to talk to me, and proved a sensible and well-bred
man. He had been in England, and, when ill, had been kindly treated by
the people among whom he found himself. He always, therefore, he said,
made a point of paying attention to Englishmen. I could not help telling
him that he might easily get himself into a scrape with some swindler, or
worse, if he carried his kindness to our nation too far. 'Sans doute,' said
he, 'il faut distinguer;' and then he paid me the highest compliment that
ever was paid me in my life; for he said that nobody who knew the world
could fail to perceive that I was what the English call a gentleman, 'homme
comme il faut.' That you may fully appreciate the value of this compliment, I must tell you that, having traveled all the preceding night, I had
a beard of two days' growth, that my hair was unbrushed, my linen of yesterday, my coat like a miller's, and my waistcoat, which had been white
when I left Nantes, in a state which filled me with self-abhorrence. Nor
had he the least notion who I was; for I gave no hint, and my name was
not on my baggage. I shall therefore henceforward consider myself as a
person of singularly noble look and demeanor.

"Will you let me recommend you a novel? Try 'Sœur Anne,' by Paul
de Kock. It is not improper, and the comic parts are really delightful. I
have laughed over them till I cried. There are tragic parts which I skip-
ped for fear of crying in another sense."

Albany, London, November 25th, 1843.

DEAR NAPIER,—Many thanks for your excellent letter. I
have considered it fully, and I am convinced that by visiting
Edinburgh at present I should do unmixed harm.

The question respecting the Catholic clergy is precisely in
that state in which a discussion at a public meeting can do no
good, and may do great mischief. It is in a state requiring
the most painful attention of the ablest heads; nor is it by
any means certain that any attention, or any ability, will produce a satisfactory solution of the problem.

My own view is this: I do not on principle object to the
paying of the Irish Catholic priests. I regret that such a step

was not taken in 1829. I would, even now, gladly support any well-digested plan which might be likely to succeed. But I fear that the difficulties are insurmountable. Against such a measure there are all the zealots of the High Church, and all the zealots of the Low Church; the Bishop of Exeter, and Hugh Macneile; Oxford, and Exeter Hall; all the champions of the voluntary system; all the English Dissenters; all Scotland; all Ireland, both Orangemen and Papists. If you add together the mass which opposed the late Government on the Education question, the mass which opposed Sir James Graham's Education clauses last year,* and the mass which is crying out for repeal in Ireland, you get something like a notion of the force which will be arrayed against a bill for paying the Irish Catholic clergy.

What have you on the other side? You have the statesmen, both Tory and Whig; but no combination of statesmen is a match for a general combination of fools. And, even among the statesmen, there is by no means perfect concord. The Tory statesmen are for paying the Catholic priests, but not for touching one farthing of the revenue of the Protestant Church. The Liberal statesmen (I for one, if I may lay claim to the name) would transfer a large part of the Irish Church revenues from the Protestants to the Catholics. For such a measure I should think it my duty to vote, though I were certain my vote would cost me my seat in Parliament. Whether I would vote for a measure which, leaving the Protestant Church of Ireland untouched, should add more than half a million to our public burdens for the maintenance of the popish priesthood is another question. I am not ashamed to say that I have not quite made up my mind, and that I should be glad, before I made it up, to hear the opinions of others.

As things stand, I do not believe that Sir Robert or Lord John, or even Sir Robert and Lord John united, could induce one third part of the members of the House of Commons to

---

* In 1843, Sir James Graham, speaking for the Government, proposed a scheme for educating the population of our great towns, which was defeated by the opposition of the Non-conformists.

vote for any plan whatever, of which the object should be the direct payment of the Irish Catholic priests. Thinking thus, I have turned my mind to the best indirect ways of effecting this object, and I have some notions which may possibly bear fruit. I shall probably take an opportunity of submitting them to the House of Commons. Now, I can conceive nothing more inexpedient than that, with these views, I should at the present moment go down to Edinburgh. If I did, I should certainly take the bull by the horns. I should positively refuse to give any promise. I should declare that I was not, on principle, opposed to the payment of Catholic priests; and I should reserve my judgment as to any particular mode of payment till the details were before me. The effect would be a violent explosion of public feeling. Other towns would follow the example of Edinburgh. Petitions would pour in by thousands as soon as Parliament had assembled; and the difficulties with which we have to deal, and which are great enough as it is, would be doubled.

I do not, however, think that the *Edinburgh Review* ought to be under the same restraint under which a Whig cabinet is necessarily placed. The *Review* has not to take the queen's pleasure, to count votes in the Houses, or to keep powerful supporters in good humor. It should expound and defend the Whig theory of government; a theory from which we are forced sometimes to depart in practice. There can be no objection to Senior's arguing in the strongest manner for the paying of the Catholic priests. I should think it very injudicious to lay down the rule that the Whig *Review* should never plead for any reforms except such as a Whig ministry could prudently propose to the Legislature.

I have a plan in my head which I hope you will not dislike. I think of reviewing the "Memoirs" of Barère. I really am persuaded that I could make something of that subject.

  Ever yours,   T. B. MACAULAY.

       Albany, London, December 13th, 1843.

DEAR NAPIER,—You shall have my paper on Barère before Parliament meets. I never took to writing any thing with

more hearty good-will. If I can, I will make the old villain
shake, even in his grave. Some of the lies in which I have
detected him are such as you, with all your experience in literary matters, will find it difficult to believe without actual
inspection of the authorities.*

What do you hear of Jeffrey's book?† My own general
impression is that the selection is ill made, and that a certain
want of finish, which in a periodical work is readily excused,
and has sometimes even the effect of a grace, is rather too
perceptible in many passages. On the other hand, the variety and versatility of Jeffrey's mind seem to me more extraordinary than ever. I think that there are few things in
the four volumes which one or two other men could not have
done as well; but I do not think that any one man except
Jeffrey—nay, that any three men—could have produced such
diversified excellence. When I compare him with Sydney
and myself, I feel, with humility perfectly sincere, that his
range is immeasurably wider than ours. And this is only as
a writer; but he is not only a writer, he has been a great advocate, and he is a great judge. Take him all in all, I think
him more nearly a universal genius than any man of our
time; certainly far more nearly than Brougham, much as
Brougham affects the character. Brougham does one thing
well, two or three things indifferently, and a hundred things
detestably. His Parliamentary speaking is admirable, his forensic speaking poor, his writings, at the very best, second-rate.
As to his hydrostatics, his political philosophy, his equity judg-
ments, his translations from the Greek, they are really below
contempt. Jeffrey, on the other hand, has tried nothing in
which he has not succeeded, except Parliamentary speaking;
and there he obtained what to any other man would have

---

* " As soon as he ceases to write trifles, he begins to write lies; and such
lies! A man who has never been within the tropics does not know what a
thunder-storm means; a man who has never looked on Niagara has but a
faint idea of a cataract; and he who has not read Barère's 'Memoirs,' may
be said not to know what it is to lie."—*Macaulay's Article on Barère.*

† Lord Jeffrey's contribution to the *Edinburgh Review.*

been great success, and disappointed his hearers only because their expectations were extravagant. Ever yours,

T. B. MACAULAY.

Albany, London, April 10th, 1844.

DEAR NAPIER,—I am glad that you like my article. It does not please me now, by any means, as much as it did while I was writing it. It is shade, unrelieved by a gleam of light.* This is the fault of the subject rather than of the painter; but it takes away from the effect of the portrait. And thus, to the many reasons which all honest men have for hating Barère I may add a reason personal to myself, that the excess of his rascality has spoiled my paper on him.

Ever yours, T. B. MACAULAY.

---

* "Whatsoever things are false, whatsoever things are dishonest, whatsoever things are unjust, whatsoever things are impure, whatsoever things are hateful, whatsoever things are of evil report, if there be any vice, and if there be any infamy, all these things were blended in Barère."

CHAPTER X.

1844–1847.

Letters to Mr. Napier.—Macaulay modifies his Design for an Article on
Burke and his Times into a Sketch of Lord Chatham's Later Years.—
Tour in Holland.—Scene off Dordrecht.—Macaulay on the Irish Church.
—Maynooth. — The Ministerial Crisis of December, 1845: Letters to
Lady Trevelyan.—Letter to Mr. Macfarlan.   Fall of Sir Robert Peel.—
Macaulay becomes Paymaster-general.—His Re-election at Edinburgh.
—His Position in the House of Commons.—General Election of 1847.—
Macaulay's Defeat at Edinburgh.

Albany, London, August 14th, 1844.

DEAR NAPIER,—I have been working hard for you during
the last week, and have covered many sheets of foolscap; and
now I find that I have taken a subject altogether unmanageable.* There is no want of materials. On the contrary, facts
and thoughts, both interesting and new, are abundant. But this
very abundance bewilders me. The stage is too small for the
actors; the canvas is too narrow for the multitude of figures.
It is absolutely necessary that I should change my whole plan.
I will try to write for you, not a history of England during
the earlier part of George the Third's reign, but an account

---

* The unmanageable subject was a review of Burke's life and writings.
"I should wish," Macaulay writes, "to say a good deal about the ministerial revolutions of the early part of George the Third's reign; about the
characters of Bute, Mansfield, Chatham, Townshend, George Grenville, and
many others; about Wilkes's and Churchill's lampoons, and so forth. I
should wish, also, to go into a critical examination of the 'Essay on the
Sublime and Beautiful,' and to throw out some hints on the subject which
have long been rolling up and down in my mind. But this would be
enough for a long article; and, when this is done, we have only brought
Burke to the threshold of the House of Commons. The American War,
the Coalition, the Impeachment of Hastings, the French Revolution, still
remain."

of the last years of Lord Chatham's life. I promised, or half promised, this ten years ago, at the end of my review of Thackeray's book. Most of what I have written will come in very well. The fourth volume of the Chatham correspondence has not, I think, been reviewed. It will furnish a heading for the article. Ever yours truly,   T. B. MACAULAY.

A week later Macaulay writes : " The article on Chatham goes on swimmingly. A great part of the information which I have is still in manuscript—Horace Walpole's " Memoirs of George the Third's Reign," which were transcribed for Mackintosh; and the first Lord Holland's diary, which Lady Holland permitted me to read. I mean to be with you on Saturday, the 31st. I would gladly stay with you till the Tuesday ; but I shall not be quite my own master. It is certainly more agreeable to represent such a place as Paisley, or Wolverhampton, than such a place as Edinburgh. Hallam or Everett can enjoy the society and curiosities of your fine city ; but I am the one person to whom all those things are interdicted."

Shortly before Macaulay's arrival in India, a civilian, employed as Resident at a native court, came under the suspicion of having made use of his position to enrich himself by illicit means. Bills came to hand through Persia, drawn in his favor for great sums of money on the East India Company itself. The Court of Directors naturally took the alarm, and sent a hint to the governor-general, who wrote to the officer in question inviting him to clear his character before a commission of inquiry. But the bird had already flown. The late Resident was well on his way to Europe ; and his answer to Lord William Bentinck, in which the offer of an investigation was civilly but most positively declined, was actually addressed from the Sandheads at the mouth of the Hooghly. The following letters will sufficiently indicate the aspect under which the transaction presented itself to Macaulay. His behavior on this occasion may seem unnecessarily harsh to that section of society which, in its dealings with gilded rogues, takes very good care not to err on the side of intolerance ; but most readers will think the better of him because, when he found himself in questionable company, he obeyed the instinct which prompted him to stand on his dignity as an honest man.

Rotterdam, October 9th, 1844.

DEAR HANNAH,—After a very pleasant day at Antwerp, I started at seven yesterday morning by the steamer for Rotterdam. I had an odd conversation on board, and one which, I think, will amuse both you and Trevelyan. As we passed Dordrecht, one of the passengers, an Englishman, said that he had never seen any thing like it. Parts of it reminded me of some parts of Cape Town, and I said so. An elderly gentleman immediately laid hold of me. "You have been at the Cape, sir?" "Yes, sir." "Perhaps you have been in India?" "Yes, sir." "My dear, here is a gentleman who has been in India." So I became an object of attention to an ill-looking, vulgar woman, who appeared to be the wife of my questioner; and to his daughter, a pretty girl enough, but by no means lady-like. "And how did you like India? Is it not the most delightful place in the world?" "It is well enough," I said, "for a place of exile." "Exile!" says the lady. "I think people are exiled when they come away from India." "I have never," said the old gentleman, "had a day's good health since I left India." A little chat followed about mangoes and mango-fish, punkas and palanquins, white ants and cockroaches. I maintained, as I generally do on such occasions, that all the fruits of the tropics are not worth a pottle of Covent Garden strawberries, and that a lodging up three pairs of stairs in London is better than a palace in a compound at Chowringhee. My gentleman was vehement in asserting that India was the only country to live in. "I went there," he said, "at sixteen, in 1800, and staid till 1830, when I was superannuated. If the Company had not chosen to superannuate me, I should have been there still. I should like to end my days there." I could not conceive what he meant by being superannuated at a time when he could have been only forty-six years old, and consequently younger than most of the field-officers in the Indian army, and than half the senior merchants in the Civil Service; but I was too polite to interrogate him.

That was a politeness, however, of which he had no notion.
"How long," he asked, "were you in India?" "Between
four and five years." "A clergyman, I suppose?" Whether
he drew this inference from the sanctity of my looks, or from
my olive-colored coat and shawl waistcoat, I do not pretend
to guess; but I answered that I had not the honor to belong to so sacred a profession. "A mercantile gentleman, no
doubt?" "No." Then his curiosity got the better of all the
laws of good-breeding, and he went straight to the point.
"May I ask, sir, to whom I have the honor of talking?" I
told him. "Oh, sir," said he, "you must often have heard of
me. I am Mr. ——. I was long at Lucknow." "Heard of
you!" thought I. "Yes; and a pretty account I have heard
of you!" I should have at once turned on my heel and walked away, if his daughter had not been close to us; and, scoun-
drel as he is, I could not affront him in her presence. I merely said, with the coldest tone and look, "Certainly I have
heard of Mr. ——." He went on, "You are related, I think,
to a Civil servant who made a stir about Sir Edward Colebrooke." It was just on my lips to say, "Yes. It was by
my brother-in-law's means that Sir Edward was *superannuated;*" but I commanded myself, and merely said that I
was nearly related to Mr. Trevelyan; and I then called to the
steward, and pretended to be very anxious to settle with him
about some coffee that I had taken. While he was changing
me a gold William, I got away from the old villain, went to
the other end of the poop, took out my book, and avoided
looking toward him during the rest of the passage. And yet
I could not help thinking a little better of him for what had
happened, for it reminded me of what poor Macnaghten once
said to me at Ootacamund: "—— has certain excuses which
Colebrooke and others have not had; for he is really so great
a fool that he can hardly be called a responsible agent." I
certainly never knew such an instance of folly as that to which
I had just been witness. Had he been a man of common
sense, he would have avoided all allusion to India; or, at any
rate, would have talked about India only to people who were
likely to be unacquainted with his history. He must have

known that I was Secretary to the Board of Control when that Board expressed its entire concurrence in the measures taken by the Company against him. Ever yours,

T. B. M.

Four days later, Macaulay writes from Amsterdam : "I have been pestered by those ——s all the way from Rotterdam hither, and shall probably be pestered by them the whole way back. We are always in the same inns; we always go to museums at the same hour; and we have been as near as possible to traveling in the same diligence. I resolutely turn away from the old rogue, and pretend not to see him. He perfectly comprehends my meaning, and looks as if he were in the pillory. But it is not pleasant to have such scenes daily in the presence of his wife and daughter."

During 1844 and 1845 Macaulay pretty frequently addressed the House of Commons. He earned the gratitude of the Unitarians by his successful vindication of their disputed title to their own chapels and cemeteries. By his condemnation of theological tests at Scotch universities, and his adventurous assault upon the Church of Ireland, he appealed to the confidence of those Edinburgh dissenters whose favor he for some time past had been most undeservedly losing. It is hard to conceive how United Presbyterians, and Free Churchmen fresh from the Disruption, could have found it in their hearts to quarrel with a representative who was able to compose, and willing to utter, such a declaration as this: "I am not speaking in anger, or with any wish to excite anger in others; I am not speaking with rhetorical exaggeration; I am calmly and deliberately expressing, in the most appropriate terms, an opinion which I formed many years ago, which all my observations and reflections have confirmed, and which I am prepared to support by reasons, when I say that, of all the institutions of the civilized world, the Established Church of Ireland seems to me the most absurd."

When Sir James Graham was called to account for opening Mazzini's envelopes, Macaulay attacked that unlucky statesman in a speech, which, in writing to a correspondent, he men-

tions as having fallen "like a shell in a powder-magazine."
He likewise was active and prominent in the controversy that
raged over the measure by which the question of Maynooth
College was sent to an uneasy sleep of five-and-twenty years.
The passage in which he drew a contrast, glowing with life
and color, between the squalor of the Irish seminary and the
wealth of the colleges at Cambridge and Oxford, will rank
higher than any other sample of his oratory in the estimation
of school-boys; and especially of such school-boys as are looking forward longingly to the material comforts of a university career.* But men who are acquainted with those temptations and anxieties which underlie the glitter of Parliamentary success will give their preference to the closing sentences
—sentences more honorable to him who spoke them than the
most finished and famous among all his perorations. " Yes,
sir, to this bill, and to every bill which shall seem to me likely
to promote the real union of Great Britain and Ireland, I will
give my support, regardless of obloquy, regardless of the risk
which I may run of losing my seat in Parliament. For such
obloquy I have learned to consider as true glory; and as to
my seat, I am determined that it never shall be held by an ig-
nominious tenure; and I am sure that it can never be lost in
a more honorable cause." These words were not the idle
flourish of an adroit speaker, certain of impunity, and eager

---

* "When I think of the spacious and stately mansions of the heads of
houses, of the commodious chambers of the fellows and scholars, of the re-
fectories, the combination rooms, the bowling-greens, the stabling, of the
state and luxury of the great feast-days, of the piles of old plate on the
tables, of the savory steam of the kitchens, of the multitude of geese and
capons which turn at once on the spits, of the oceans of excellent ale in the
butteries; and when I remember from whom all this splendor and plenty
are derived; when I remember what was the faith of Edward the Third and
of Henry the Sixth, of Margaret of Anjou and Margaret of Richmond, of William of Wykeham and William of Waynefleet, of Archbishop Chicheley and
Cardinal Wolsey; when I remember what we have taken from the Roman
Catholics—King's College, New College, Christ Church, my own Trinity;
and when I look at the miserable Dotheboys Hall which we have given
them in exchange, I feel, I must own, less proud than I could wish of being a Protestant and a Cambridge man."— *Page* 366 *of Macaulay's Speeches.*

only for the cheer which is the unfailing reward of a cheap affectation of courage and disinterestedness. They were given forth in grave earnest, and dictated by an expectation of impending trouble which the event was not slow to justify.

In September, 1853, when Macaulay, much against his will, was preparing his speeches for publication, he notes in his diary : "After breakfast I wrote out the closing passages of Maynooth. How white poor Peel looked while I was speaking! I remember the effect of the words, ' There you sit—.' I have a letter from my Dutch translator. He is startled by the severity of some of my speeches, and no wonder. He knows nothing of the conflict of parties."

Peel might well look white beneath the flood of unanswerable taunts which was poured forth by his terrible ally. Even in his utmost need, it was a heavy price to pay for the support of Macaulay and his party. "There is too much ground for the reproaches of those who, having, in spite of a bitter experience, a second time trusted the right honorable baronet, now find themselves a second time deluded. It has been too much his practice, when in opposition, to make use of passions with which he has not the slightest sympathy, and of prejudices which he regards with a profound contempt. As soon as he is in power a change takes place. The instruments which have done his work are flung aside; the ladder by which he has climbed is kicked down. . . . . Can we wonder that the eager, honest, hot-headed Protestants, who raised you to power in the confident hope that you would curtail the privileges of the Roman Catholics, should stare and grumble when you propose to give public money to the Roman Catholics? Can we wonder that from one end of the country to the other every thing should be ferment and uproar ; that petitions should, night after night, whiten all our benches like a snow-storm? Can we wonder that the people out-of-doors should be exasperated by seeing the very men who, when we were in office, voted against the old grant to Maynooth, now pushed and pulled into the House by your whippers-in to vote for an increased grant? The natural consequences follow. All those fierce spirits whom you hallooed on to harass us now turn round and begin to worry you. The Orangeman raises his war-whoop; Exeter Hall sets up its bray; Mr. Macneile shudders to see more costly cheer than ever provided for the priests of Baal at the table of the queen; and the Protestant operatives of Dublin call for impeachments in exceedingly bad English. But what did you expect? Did you think, when, to serve your turn, you called the devil up, that it was as easy to lay him as to raise him? Did you think, when you went on, session after session, thwarting and reviling those whom you knew to be in the right, and flattering all the worst passions of those whom you knew to be in the wrong, that the day of reckoning would never come? It has come. There you sit, doing penance for the disingenuousness of years."

Between the House of Commons and his "History," Macaulay had no time to spare for writing articles. Early in 1845 a rumor had found its way into the newspapers, to the effect that he had discontinued his connection with the *Edinburgh Review*. He at once assured Mr. Napier that the rumor in question had not been set on foot by himself; but in the same letter he announced his resolution to employ himself exclusively upon his "History," until the first portion of it was completed. "If I had not taken that resolution, my "History" would have perished in embryo, like poor Mackintosh's. As soon as I have finished my first two volumes I shall be happy to assist you again; but when that will be it is difficult to say.* Parliamentary business, at present, prevents me from writing a line. I am preparing for Lord John's debate on sugar, and for Joseph Hume's debate on India; and it is one of my infirmities—an infirmity, I grieve to say, quite incurable—that I can not correctly and heartily apply my mind to several subjects together. When an approaching debate is in my head, it is to no purpose that I sit down at my desk to write history, and I soon get up again in disgust."

London, December 11th, 1845.

DEAR HANNAH,—I am detained for a few minutes at Ellis's

---

* Macaulay never again wrote for the *Edinburgh Review*.

chambers with nothing to do. I will therefore employ my
leisure in writing to you on a sheet of paper meant for some
plea or replication. Yesterday morning I learned that the
ministers had gone down to the Isle of Wight for the purpose
of resigning, and that Lord John had been sent for. This
morning all the world knows it. There are many reports;
but my belief is that the Duke of Wellington, after having
consented to support Peel, was alarmed by the symptoms of
opposition among the Lords of the Tory party, and retracted.
How this is we shall probably soon learn. In the mean time,
London is in confusion. The politicians run from club to
club picking up and circulating rumors, and nobody knows
exactly what to expect. All discerning men, among whom I
rank myself, are anxious and melancholy. What is to befall
the country? Will Lord John attempt to form a government? Can such a government abolish the corn duties?
Can it stand three months with the present House of Commons? Would even a dissolution give the Whigs a working
majority in the Commons? And, even if we had such a majority in the Commons, what could we do with the Lords?
Are we to swamp them, as Lord Grey's ministry proposed to
do? Have we sufficient support in the country to try so extreme a measure? Are we to go on, as Lord Melbourne's
ministry did—unable to carry our own bills, and content with
holding the executive functions, and distributing the loaves
and fishes? Or are we, after an unsuccessful attempt to settle the Corn question, to go out? If so, do we not leave the
question in a worse position than at present? Or are Peel
and Lord John to unite in one government? How are personal pretensions to be adjusted in such an arrangement?
How are questions of foreign policy, and of Irish policy, to
be settled? How can Aberdeen and Palmerston pull together? How can Lord John himself bear to sit in the same Cabinet with Graham? And, supposing all these difficulties got
over, is it clear that even a coalition between Peel and the
Whigs could carry the repeal of the Corn Law through the
Lords? What, then, remains, except an Ultra-Tory administration composed of such men as the Dukes of Buckingham

and Richmond? Yet how can such an administration look in the face an opposition which will contain every statesman and orator in the House of Commons? What, too, will be the effect produced out-of-doors by such an administration? What is there that may not be apprehended if we should have a year of severe distress, and if the manufacturers should impute all their sufferings to the selfish tyranny and rapacity of the ministers of the crown? It is difficult, I think, to conceive a darker prospect than that which lies before us. Yet I have a great confidence in the sense, virtue, and self-command of the nation; and I therefore hope that we shall get out of this miserable situation, as we have got out of other situations not less miserable.

I have spent some hours in carefully considering my own position, and determining on my own course. I have at last made up my mind; and I send you the result of my deliberations.

If, which is not absolutely impossible, though improbable, Peel should still try to patch up a Conservative administration, and should, as the head of that administration, propose the repeal of the Corn Laws, my course is clear. I must support him with all the energy that I have, till the question is carried. Then I am free to oppose him. If an Ultra-Tory ministry should be framed, my course is equally clear. I must oppose them with every faculty that God has given me.

If Lord John should undertake to form a Whig ministry, and should ask for my assistance, I can not in honor refuse it. But I shall distinctly tell him, and tell my colleagues and constituents, that I will not again go through what I went through in Lord Melbourne's administration. I am determined never again to be one of a government which can not carry the measures which it thinks essential. I am satisfied that the great error of Lord Melbourne's government was, that they did not resign as soon as they found that they could not pass the Appropriation Clause. They would have gone out with flying colors, had they gone out then. This was while I was in India. When I came back, I found the Liberal ministry in a thoroughly false position; but I did not think it right to separate myself from them. Now the case is different. Our hands are free. Our path is still clear before us; and I never will be a party to any step which may bring us into that false position again. I will therefore, supposing that Lord John applies to me, accept office on this express condition—that if we find that we can not carry the total repeal of the Corn Laws, we will forthwith resign; or, at all events, that I shall be at liberty forthwith to resign. I am quite sure that this is the right course; and I am equally sure that, if I take it, I shall be out of office at Easter.

There remains another possible case. What if Lord John and Peel should coalesce, and should offer me a place in their Cabinet? I have fully made up my mind to refuse it. I should not at all blame them for coalescing. I am willing, as an independent member, to support them as far as I can; and, as respects the question of the Corn Laws, to support them with all my heart and soul. But, after the language which I have held respecting Peel, and which I am less than ever disposed to retract, I feel that I can not, without a loss of personal dignity, and without exposing myself to suspicions and insinuations which would be insupportable to me, hold any situation under him. The circumstance that my fortune, though amply sufficient for my wants, is small when compared with the fortunes of all the other Cabinet ministers of our time, makes it fit that I should avoid with punctilious care every thing which the multitude may attribute to sordid motives. There are other reasons, which do not apply to Lord John, to Lord Lansdowne, to Palmerston, to Baring, to Labouchere, and to Grey; but which would prevent me from holding office in such an arrangement. My opinions about the Irish Church are stronger than those of my friends, and have recently been expressed in a manner which has excited attention. The question of the ballot would also be an insuperable obstacle. I have spoken and voted for it; I will not vote against it for a place; and I am certain that Peel will never consent to let it be an open question. This is an objection which does not apply to Lord John, and to others whom I have named, for they always opposed the ballot. My full resolution therefore is, if a coalition ministry should be formed, to support it, but not to be a member of it.

I hope that you will not be dissatisfied with this long exposition of my views and intentions. I must now make haste home, to dress for dinner at Milman's, and for the Westminster Play. Ever yours,   T. B. M.

                                    Albany, December 13th, 1845.

DEAR HANNAH,—I am glad that you sympathize with me, and approve of my intentions. I should have written yesterday; but I was detained till after post-time at a consultation of Whigs, which Lord John had summoned. We were only five — Lord John, Lord Cottenham, Clarendon, Palmerston, and myself. This morning we met again at eleven, and were joined by Baring, by Lord Lansdowne, and by the Duke of Bedford. The posture of affairs is this: Lord John has not consented to form a ministry. He has only told the queen that he would consult his friends and see what could be done. We are all most unwilling to take office, and so is he. I have never seen his natural audacity of spirit so much tempered by discretion, and by a sense of responsibility, as on this occasion. The question of the Corn Laws throws all other questions into the shade. Yet even if that question were out of the way, there would be matters enough to perplex us. Ireland, we fear, is on the brink of something like a servile war—the effect, not of Repeal agitation, but of the severe distress endured by the peasantry. Foreign politics look dark. An augmentation of the army will be necessary. Pretty legacies to leave to a ministry which will be in a minority in both Houses! I have no doubt that there is not a single man among us who would not at once refuse to enlist, if he could do so with a clear conscience. Nevertheless, our opinion is that, if we have a reasonable hope of being able to settle the all-important question of the Corn Laws in a satisfactory way, we ought, at whatever sacrifice of quiet and comfort, to take office, though only for a few weeks. But can we entertain such a hope? That is the point; and till we are satisfied about it we can

not positively accept or refuse. A few days must pass before
we are able to decide.

It is clear that we can not win the battle with our own un-
assisted strength. If we win it at all, it must be by the help
of Peel, Graham, and their friends. Peel has not seen Lord
John; but he left with the queen a memorandum, containing
a promise to support a corn bill founded on the principles of
Lord John's famous letter to the electors of London.* Graham has had both a correspondence and a personal conference
with Lord John and with Lord Lansdowne, and has given similar assurances. But we all feel that this is too vague, and
that we may still be left in the lurch. Lord John has asked
for a sketch of Peel's own plan. This we can not get. In
fact, strange as it seems, the plan was never drawn up in a
distinct form, or submitted to the late Cabinet in detail. As
soon as the general nature of it was stated, the opposition became so strong that nothing was said as to minor points. We
have therefore determined on the following course: All our
friends who are likely to be Cabinet ministers are summoned
to London, and will, with scarcely an exception, be here in a
day or two. We shall then resolve on the heads of a Corn
Law, such as we think that we can with honor introduce.
When this is done, we shall send it to Peel and Graham, and
demand categorically whether they will cordially support such
a bill, ay or no. If they refuse, or use vague language, we
shall at once decline to form a government. If they pledge
themselves to stand by us, we must undertake the task.

This is a very strange, indeed an unprecedented, course.
But the situation is unprecedented. We are not coming into
office as conquerors, leading a majority in Parliament, and
driving out our predecessors. Our predecessors at a most
critical moment throw up the reins in confusion and despair,
while they have a strong majority in both Houses, and implore us, who are a minority, to extricate the country from its

---

* "The imposition of any duty at present, without a provision for its
extinction within a short period, would but prolong a contest already sufficiently fruitful of animosity and discontent." Such was the cardinal sentence of Lord John Russell's celebrated letter.

troubles. We are therefore entitled, if we consent, to demand their honest support as a right, not to supplicate it as a favor. My hope is that Peel will not accede to our terms, and that we shall be set at liberty. He will then be forced to go on with a ministry patched up as well as he can patch it up. In the mean time, nothing can be more public-spirited or disinterested than the feelings of all our friends who have yet been consulted. This is a good sign.

If I do come in, I shall take a carriage by the month from Newman, and remain at the Albany for some weeks. I have no doubt that we shall all be out by Easter in any event. If we should remain longer, I must, of course, take a house; but nobody can expect that I should be provided with a house at a day's notice. Ever yours,   T. B. M.

Albany, December 19th, 1845.

DEAR HANNAH,—It is an odd thing to see a ministry making. I never witnessed the process before. Lord John has been all day in his inner library. His antechamber has been filled with comers and goers, some talking in knots, some writing notes at tables. Every five minutes somebody is called into the inner room. As the people who have been closeted come out, the cry of the whole body of expectants is, "What are you?" I was summoned almost as soon as I arrived, and found Lord Auckland and Lord Clarendon sitting with Lord John. After some talk about other matters, Lord John told me that he had been trying to ascertain my wishes, and that he found that I wanted leisure and quiet more than salary and business. Labouchere had told him this. He therefore offered me the Pay Office, one of the three places which, as I have often told you, I should prefer. I at once accepted it. The tenure by which I shall hold it is so precarious that it matters little what its advantages may be; but I shall have two thousand a year for the trouble of signing my name. I must indeed attend Parliament more closely than I have of late done; but my mornings will be as much my own as if I were out of office. If I give to my 'History' the time which I used to pass in transacting business when I was Secretary at War, I shall get on nearly as fast as when I was in opposition. Some other arrangements promise to be less satisfactory. Palmerston will hear of nothing but the Foreign Office, and Lord Grey therefore declines taking any place. I hope that Lord John will give one of the secretary-ships of state to George Grey. It would be a great eleva-tion; but I am sure that it is the right thing to do. I have told Grey that I look to him as our future leader in the Com-mons, and that no pretensions of mine shall ever interfere with this. Labouchere feels exactly as I do. Labouchere and Baring are at least as good men of business as Grey; and I may say without vanity that I have made speeches which were out of the reach of any of the three. But, taking the talent for business and the talent for speaking together, Grey is undoubtedly the best qualified among us for the lead; and we are perfectly sensible of this. Indeed, I may say that I do not believe that there was ever a set of public men who had less jealousy of each other, or who formed a more correct estimate of themselves, than the younger members of this Cabinet. Ever yours,   T. B. M.

Albany, London, December 20th, 1845.

DEAR HANNAH,—All is over. Late at night, just as I was undressing, a knock was given at the door of my chambers. A messenger had come from Lord John with a short note. The quarrel between Lord Grey and Lord Palmerston had made it impossible to form a ministry. I went to bed and slept sound. In the morning I went to the corner of Belgrave Square, which is now the great place for political news, and found that Lord John had gone to Windsor to resign his trust into the queen's hands.

I have no disposition to complain of the loss of office. On the contrary, my escape from the slavery of a place-man is my only consolation.* But I feel that we are in an ignomin-

---

* " On the whole," Macaulay wrote to Mr. Ellis, " I am inclined to think that what has happened will do more good than harm. Perhaps the pleasure with which I have this morning looked round my chambers and

ious position as a party. After agreeing on the principles of our measure, after agreeing that our public duty required us to take office, we have now thrown the game up, not on account of any new matter affecting the national interests, but solely because we are, as the French say, *mauvais coucheurs*, and can not adjust ourselves to accommodate each other. I do not blame Lord John; but Lord Grey and Lord Palmerston are both at fault. I think Lord Grey, highly as I esteem his integrity and ability, chiefly responsible for the unfortunate situation in which we are now placed; but I suspect that Palmerston will be made the scape-goat. He is no favorite with the public. A large portion of our own friends think him a dangerous minister. By the whole continental and American press he has been represented as the very Genius of War and Discord. People will now say that, when every other place was within his reach; when he might have had the Home Office, the Colonies, the Admiralty, a peerage —in short, his own terms—he declared that unless he was allowed to be where he was generally considered as a firebrand he would blow up his party, at a crisis when the fate of his party involved the fate of his country. I suspect that a great storm of public indignation will burst upon him, and that he will sink under it. In the mean time, what is to happen?

I have had an anxious time since you were away; but I can truly say that I have done nothing through all these troubles which I should be ashamed to hear proclaimed at Charing Cross, or which I would not do again. Ever yours,

T. B. M.

Macaulay's readiness to brave publicity was soon put to a most unpleasant test. Mr. Macfarlan, a constituent who was much in his confidence, had transmitted to him for presentation a memorial to the queen praying for the removal of all

---

resumed my 'History' has something to do in making me thus cheerful. Let me advise you to put forth a little tract, after the fashion of the seventeenth century, entitled 'A Secret History of some Late Passages, as they were communicated by a Person of Honor to T. F. E., a Gentleman of the Inner Temple.'"

restriction on the importation of corn. Macaulay replied by
a letter which commenced as follows: " You will have heard
the termination of our attempt to form a government. All
our plans were frustrated by Lord Grey. I hope that the
public interests will not suffer. Sir Robert Peel must now
undertake the settlement of the question. It is certain that
he can settle it. It is by no means certain that we could have
done so: for we shall to a man support him ; and a large proportion of those who are now in office would have refused to
support us. On my own share in these transactions I reflect
with unmixed satisfaction. From the first, I told Lord John
that I stipulated for one thing only—total and immediate repeal of the Corn Laws; that my objections to gradual abolition
were insurmountable, but that, if he declared for total and immediate repeal, I would be, as to all other matters, absolutely
in his hands; that I would take any office or no office, just as
it suited him best; and that he should never be disturbed by
any personal pretensions or jealousies on my part. If every
body else had acted thus, there would now have been a Liberal
ministry. However, as I said, perhaps it is the best as it is."

It unfortunately happened that Mr. Macfarlan, forgetting
both prudence and propriety in his eagerness to seize so good
an opportunity of establishing his member's character as an
uncompromising free-trader, thought the letter much too good
to be kept to himself. It accordingly appeared in the columns
of *The Scotsman*, and was copied into all the newspapers of the
country, to the heartfelt, and, as his diaries prove, the life-long,
regret of Macaulay. He was deeply pained at being paraded
before the world as the critic of an old friend and colleague.*

* " *May* 17*th*, 1850.—Macfarlan called; a man who did me a great injury; but he meant no harm, and I have long forgiven him; though to the
end of my life I shall occasionally feel twinges of a very painful sort at
the recollection."
And again: " *July* 4*th*, 1851.—I staid at home all the morning, and wrote
not amiss. Macfarlan called. What harm that man did me! What misery for a time he caused me! In my happy life that was one of the calamities which cut deep. There is still a scar." So keenly did Macaulay feel
the only circumstance which ever threw a momentary doubt upon the loyalty of his friendship.

Bowood, January 4th, 1846.

My dear Napier,—I am, as ever, grateful for your kindness. Of course you were perfectly right in supposing that I was altogether taken by surprise when I saw my letter to Macfarlan in print. I do not think that I was ever more astonished or vexed. However, it is very little my way to brood over what is done and can not be helped.

I am not surprised that many should blame me; and yet I can not admit that I was much to blame. I was writing to an active, friendly constituent who had during some years been in almost constant communication with me. We had corresponded about Edinburgh intrigues, about the Free Church, about Maynooth; and I had always written with openness, and had never found any reason to complain of indiscretion. After all, I wrote only what every body at Brooks's, and at the Reform Club, was saying from morning to night. I will venture to affirm that if the post-bags of the last fortnight were rummaged, it would appear that Lord John, Lord Morpeth, Lord Grey himself—in fact, every body concerned in the late negotiations—has written letters quite as unfit for the public eye as mine. However, I well know that the world always judges by the event; and I must be content to be well abused till some new occurrence puts Macfarlan's prank out of people's heads.

I should be much obliged to you, whenever an opportunity offers, to say from me that I am surprised and indignant at the unauthorized publication of a private letter unguardedly written; but that, whatever I have written, guardedly or unguardedly, is the truth by which I am prepared to stand.

Ever yours truly,　　　　T. B. Macaulay.

Albany, London, January 10th, 1846.

Dear Napier,—Thanks for all your kindness. I am sorry to be the cause of so much trouble to my friends. I have received a penitent letter from Macfarlan, offering to do any thing in his power.

The business is very disagreeable, but might have been worse. To say of a man that he has talents and virtue, but wants judgment and temper, is no very deadly outrage. I declare that I should not have scrupled to put this unlucky sentence,* with a little softening, into the *Edinburgh Review.* For example: "We can not but regret that a nobleman, whose talents and virtue we fully acknowledge, should have formed so high an estimate of his own pretensions, and should be so unwilling to make any concession to the opinions of others, that it is not easy to act in concert with him." There is nothing here which I would not say in the House of Commons.

I do not know whether it is worth while to mention the following circumstance: Macfarlan, soon after he got this unlucky letter, wrote to tell me that he thought the publication of it would be of use to me. I instantly wrote to beg that he would not think of such a thing, and gave as my reason the great esteem and admiration which, in spite of recent events, I felt for Lord Grey. Whether any good use can be made of this fact I do not know. I am very unwilling to be on bad terms with a man whom I greatly respect and value. I rely implicitly on your discretion. Ever yours truly,

T. B. MACAULAY.

At this period of his life Macaulay was still a hard hitter; but he timed his blows with due regard for the public interests. In January, 1845, he writes to Mr. Napier: "Many thanks for your kind expressions about the last session. I have certainly been heard with great favor by the House whenever I have spoken. As to the course which I have taken, I feel no misgivings. Many honest men think that there ought to be no retrospect in politics. I am firmly convinced that they are in error, and that much better measures than any which we owe to Peel would be very dearly purchased by the utter ruin of all public virtue, which must be the consequence of such immoral lenity."

So much for Maynooth, and for the past. With regard to

* The sentence which referred to "personal pretensions" and "jealousies."

the future, and the Corn Laws, he says: "As to any remarks which I may make on Peel's gross inconsistency, they must wait till his bill is out of all danger. On the Maynooth question he ran no risk of a defeat, and therefore I had no scruple about attacking him. But to hit him hard while he is fighting the land-owners would be a very different thing. It will be all that he can do to win the battle with the best help that we can give him. A time will come for looking back. At present our business is to get the country safe through a very serious and doubtful emergency."

But no aid from his opponents, however loyally rendered, could keep Sir Robert Peel in office when once that emergency was at an end. On the 26th of June, 1846, the Corn Law Bill passed the Peers; and, before the night was over, the Government had received its *coup de grâce* in the Commons. Lord John Russell was again commanded to form an administration. Macaulay obtained the post which he preferred, as the least likely to interfere with his historical labors; and, as Paymaster-general of the Army, he went down to Scotland to ask for re-election. On the 9th of July he wrote to Mrs. Trevelyan from the Royal Hotel: "I reached Edinburgh last night, and found the city in a storm. The Dissenters and Free Churchmen have got up an opposition on the old ground of Maynooth, and have sent for Sir Culling Eardley Smith. He is to be here this evening. Comically enough, we shall be at the same inn; but the landlord, waiters, chamber-maid, and boots are all with me. I have no doubt about the result. We had to-day a great meeting of electors. The lord provost presided. Near three thousand well-dressed people, chiefly voters, were present. I spoke for an hour—as well, they tell me, as I ever spoke in my life, and certainly with considerable effect. There was immense cheering, mingled with a little hissing. A show of hands was called for. I had a perfect forest, and the other side not fifty. I am exceedingly well, and in high spirits. I had become somewhat effeminate in literary repose and leisure. You would not know me again, now that my blood is up. I am such as when, twelve years ago, I fought the battle with Sadler at

Leeds." This ardor for the fray augured badly for Sir Culling Eardley. He proved no match for Macaulay, who outtalked him on the hustings; beat him by two to one at the poll; and returned to the Albany in triumph, none the worse for his exhilarating though rather expensive contest.

We are told by Gibbon, in the most delightful of autobiographies, that he never found his mind more vigorous, nor his composition more happy, than in "the winter hurry of society and Parliament." The historian of the Roman empire found a gentle stimulus and a salutary distraction in the discharge of his functions as Commissioner of Trade and Plantations, and in the debates on Burke's measures of economical reform. In like manner, the routine of the Pay Office, and the obligations of the Treasury bench in the House of Commons, were of benefit to Macaulay while he was engaged upon Monmouth's invasion, and the Revolution of 1688. The new paymaster-general discovered his duties to be even less burdensome than he had been given to suppose. An occasional board day at Chelsea, passed in checking off lists of names and signing grants of pension, made very moderate demands upon his time and energy; and in Parliament his brother members treated him with a respectful indulgence on which he very seldom trespassed. He only spoke five times in all during the sessions of 1846 and 1847; but whenever, and on whatever subject, he opened his lips, the columns of Hansard are thickly studded with compliments paid to him either in retrospect or by anticipation. His intention to take part in a discussion was, as it were, advertised beforehand by the misgivings of the speakers who differed from him. When the Ten Hours' Bill was under consideration, one of its most resolute opponents, fearing the effect which would be produced upon the House by a dissertation from Macaulay in favor of the principle of the Factory Acts, humorously deprecated the wrath of "his right honorable friend, under whose withering eloquence he would, there was little doubt, be very speedily extinguished."* On another occasion he was unexpected-

---

* On the 8th of October, 1853, Macaulay says, with the frankness of a man

ly called upon his feet to account for a letter, in which he had
expressed an opinion about the propriety of granting a pardon to the leaders of the Welsh Chartists.   When the House
had heard his explanation (into which he contrived to bring
an allusion to Judge Jeffreys and the Bloody Assize—a reminiscence, in all probability, of his morning's study), Mr. Disraeli gracefully enough expressed the general sentiment of
the audience: "It is always, to me at least, and I believe to
the House, so agreeable to listen to the right honorable gentleman under any circumstances, that we must have been all

---

who is speaking about his own performances without the fear of being
overheard: "I worked at the Factory speech, but did little.   I like the
speech amazingly.   I rather think that it is my very best."

At all events, it has proved a mine of wealth to those who, since Macaulay's day, have argued for extending the Factory Acts.   He made an effective use of the analogy of the Sunday in order to defend the principle
of regulating the hours of labor by law.   "Man, man is the great instru-
ment that produces wealth.   The natural difference between Campania
and Spitzbergen is trifling when compared with the difference between a
country inhabited by men full of bodily and mental vigor, and a country
inhabited by men sunk in bodily and mental decrepitude.   Therefore it is
that we are not poorer but richer, because we have, through many ages,
rested from our labor one day in seven.   That day is not lost.   While industry is suspended, while the plow lies in the furrow, while the Exchange
is silent, while no smoke ascends from the factory, a process is going on
quite as important to the wealth of nations as any process which is performed on more busy days.   Man, the machine of machines, the machine
compared with which all the contrivances of the Watts and the Ark-
wrights are worthless, is repairing and winding up, so that he returns to
his labors on the Monday with clearer intellect, with livelier spirits, with
renewed corporal vigor.   Never will I believe that what makes a population stronger, and healthier, and wiser, and better, can ultimately make it
poorer.   You try to frighten us by telling us that, in some German factories
the young work seventeen hours in the twenty-four; that they work so
hard that among thousands there is not one who grows to such a stature
that he can be admitted into the army; and you ask whether, if we pass
this bill, we can possibly hold our own against such competition as this.
Sir, I laugh at the thought of such competition.   If ever we are forced to
yield the foremost place among commercial nations, we shall yield it, not
to a race of degenerate dwarfs, but to some people pre-eminently vigorous
in body and in mind."

gratified to-night that he has found it necessary to vindicate his celebrated epistle."

In October, 1846, Macaulay writes to one of his sisters: "I have received the most disgusting letter, by many degrees, that I ever read in my life from old Mrs. ——. I can convey to you no idea of it but by transcribing it, and it is too long to transcribe. However, I will give you the opening: 'My dear Friend,—Many years have passed away since my revered husband and your excellent father walked together as Christian friends, and since I derived the sweetest comfort and pleasure from a close friendship with both your blessed parents.' After a great deal more about various revered and blessed people, she comes to the real object of her epistle, which is to ask for three livings and a bishopric. I have been accustomed to unreasonable and importunate suitors; but I protest that this old hag's impudence fairly took away my breath. In order to recommend her brats still more, she assures me that one of them has been curate to that blessed man, Mr. Close. She is so moderate as to say that for her son James she will accept, nay, very thankfully accept, even a living of five hundred a year. Another proof of her moderation is that, before she asks for a bishopric, she has the grace to say, 'I am now going to be very bold.' Really the comedy of actual life is beyond all comedy."

The repugnance which this deluge of unctuous importunity aroused in Macaulay's breast was not aggravated by any prepossession in favor of doctrines the opposite of evangelical. This is clearly proved, if proof be wanting, by the last sentence of a letter bearing upon what was perhaps the most important piece of business which it fell to him to transact as paymaster-general of the army.

Dear Ellis,—I have at this moment the disposal of a tolerable piece of patronage, the chaplainship of Chelsea Hospital; light duty, a nice house, coal, candles, and three hundred pounds a year. It would be an exceedingly pleasant situation for a literary man. But he must also be a man of piety and feeling; for, the hospital being full of old battered soldiers, the duty, though by no means onerous, consists chiefly in attending sick-beds, and I would not for any consideration assign such a duty to a person who would hurry through it in a perfunctory manner. Is there any among the junior fellows of Trinity who would suit? I do not want a politician; and nothing shall induce me to take a Puseyite.

Yours very truly,   T. B. M.

In Parliament, in society, and in literary and political circles throughout the country, Macaulay already enjoyed that general respect and good-will which attach themselves to a man who has done great things, and from whom something still greater is expected. But there was one city in the kingdom where he had ceased to be popular, and, unfortunately, that city was Edinburgh. The causes of his unpopularity were in part external and temporary, and in part can be detected only after an attentive review of his personal character.

In the year 1847 the disruption of the Scotch Church was already an accomplished and accepted fact; but that momentous crisis had left bitter feelings behind it. Our leading public men had displayed an indifference to the tendencies of religious opinion in Scotland, and a scandalous ignorance of her religious affairs, which had alienated from Whigs and Englishmen the confidence and attachment of the population north of Tweed. Macaulay, the most eminent Whig, and far the most eminent Englishman, who then sat for a Scotch constituency, was made the scape-goat for the sins of all his colleagues. He might have averted his fate by subservience, or mitigated it by prudence; but the necessity of taking a side about Maynooth obliged him to announce his views on the question of religious endowments, and his nature did not allow him to soften down those views by the use of dainty and ambiguous phraseology. He wished all the world to know that, however much the people whom he represented might regard ecclesiastical matters from the stand-point of the Church, he regarded them, and would always continue to regard them, exclusively from the stand-point of the State.

Radicalism, again, then as always, was stronger in Scotland

than in any other portion of the United Kingdom, and stronger in Edinburgh than in any other town of Scotland; for in Edinburgh the internal differences of the Liberal party were intensified by local circumstances. "Twenty years ago," writes a former supporter of Macaulay, "there was among us a great deal of what in Oxford is called Town and Gown. The Parliament-house, literature, and the university made the Gown. The tradesmen, as a class, maintained that the high Whigs, though calling themselves the friends of the people, were exclusive and overbearing; and there was some truth in this. The Whigs were always under terror of being coupled with Cobbett, Hunt, and their kind." Macaulay had his full share of this feeling. In May, 1842, when the People's Charter was presented to Parliament, he spoke, with an emphasis which nothing but sincere conviction could supply, against Mr. Thomas Duncombe's motion that the petitioners should be heard at the bar of the House. "Sir," he said, "I can not conscientiously assent to the motion. And yet I must admit that the honorable member for Finsbury has framed it with considerable skill. He has done his best to obtain the support of all those timid and interested politicians who think much more about the security of their seats than about the security of their country. It would be very convenient to me to give a silent vote with him. I should then have it in my power to say to the Chartists of Edinburgh, 'When your petition was before the House, I was on your side: I was for giving you a full hearing.' I should at the same time be able to assure my Conservative constituents that I never had supported, and never would support, the Charter. But, sir, though this course would be very convenient, it is one which my sense of duty will not suffer me to take." In a letter to Mr. Napier, dated the 10th of August, 1844, he writes: "I must put off my journey northward for a week. One of my reasons for this postponement (but let it rest between ourselves) is that on Wednesday, the 21st, Hume is to lay the first stone of a monument to the Republicans who were transported by Pitt and Dundas. Now, though I by no means approve of the severity with which those people were treated, I do not admire their proceedings, nor should I choose to attend the ceremony. But, if I arrived just before it, I should certainly be expected by a portion of my constituents either to attend or explain the reasons of my absence, and thus we should have another disagreeable controversy."

But Macaulay might have been as much of a Whig and an Erastian as he chose, if he had had in his composition more of the man of the world, and less of the man of the study. There was a perceptible want of lightness of touch in his method of doing the ordinary business which falls to the lot of a member of Parliament. "The truth is," wrote Lord Cockburn in July, 1846, "that Macaulay, with all his admitted knowledge, talent, eloquence, and worth, is not popular. He cares more for his 'History' than for the jobs of his constituents, and answers letters irregularly, and with a brevity deemed contemptuous ; and, above all other defects, he suffers severely from the vice of overtalking, and consequently of underlistening. A deputation goes to London to enlighten their representative. They are full of their own matter, and their chairman has a statement bottled and ripe, which he is anxious to draw and decant; but, instead of being listened to, they no sooner enter the audience-chamber than they find themselves all superseded by the restless ability of their eloquent member, who, besides mistaking speaking for hearing, has the indelicate candor not even to profess being struck by the importance of the affair."

Macaulay had exalted, and, as some would hold, overstrained ideas of the attitude which a representative should adopt in his pecuniary relations with the electors who have sent him to Parliament. Although one of the most generous of men, who knew no delight like giving, and who indulged himself in that respect with an indiscriminate and incautious facility which was at times little short of blameworthy, he was willing, when Edinburgh was in question, to be called stingy if he could only make it clear to his own conscience that he was not tampering with corruption.

London, July 14th, 1841.

My dear Mr. Black,—I am much gratified by what you

say about the race-cup. I had already written to Craig to say that I should not subscribe, and I am glad that my determination meets your approbation. In the first place, I am not clear that the object is a good one. In the next place, I am clear that, by giving money for such an object in obedience to such a summons, I should completely change the whole character of my connection with Edinburgh. It has been usual enough for rich families to keep a hold on corrupt boroughs by defraying the expense of public amusements. Sometimes it is a ball, sometimes a regatta. The Derby family used to support the Preston races. The members for Beverley, I believe, find a bull for their constituents to bait. But these were not the conditions on which I undertook to represent Edinburgh. In return for your generous confidence, I offer Parliamentary service, and nothing else. I am, indeed, most willing to contribute the little that I can spare to your most useful public charities. But even this I do not consider as matter of contract. Nor should I think it proper that the Town Council should call on me to contribute even to an hospital or a school. But the call that is now made is one so objectionable that, I must plainly say, I would rather take the Chiltern Hundreds than comply with it.

I should feel this if I were a rich man. But I am not rich. I have the means of living very comfortably, according to my notions, and I shall still be able to spare something for the common objects of our party, and something for the distressed. But I have nothing to waste on gayeties which can at best only be considered harmless. If our friends want a member who will find them in public diversions, they can be at no loss. I know twenty people who, if you will elect them to Parliament, will gladly treat you to a race and a race-ball once a month. But I shall not be very easily induced to believe that Edinburgh is disposed to select her representatives on such a principle. Ever yours truly,

T. B. MACAULAY.

Macaulay was so free from some faults to which literary men are proverbially inclined, that many of those who had claims upon his time and services were too apt to forget that, after all, he possessed the literary temperament. In the heyday of youth he relished the bustle of crowds, and could find amusement in the company of strangers; but as years went forward—as his spirits lost their edge and his health its spring —he was ever more and more disposed to recoil from publicity. Insatiable of labor, he regarded the near approach, and still more the distant prospect, of worry with an exaggerated disquietude which in his case was a premonitory symptom of the disease that was to kill him. Perpetually overworked by his "History" (and there is no overwork like that of a task which has grown to be dearer to a man than life itself), he no longer had the nerve required to face the social efforts, and to undergo the minute and unceasing observation to which he was, or fancied himself to be, exposed when on a visit to the city which he represented. "If the people of Edinburgh," he wrote to Mr. Napier, "were not my constituents, there is no place in the island where I should like so much to pass a few weeks; but our relation imposes both such constant exertion and such constant reserve, that a trip thither is neither pleasant nor prudent." And again: "I hope to be at Edinburgh on August the 19th or 20th. At so dead a time of the year I should think that it might be possible for me to escape speeches and meetings, particularly as I mean to go quietly, and without sending notice to any of our political managers. It is really very hard that I can not visit your city as any other gentleman and man of letters can do. My intention is to stay about a fortnight, and I should like to go out to you from Edinburgh on Saturday, the 20th, and to return on the Monday. I wish to avoid passing a Sunday in the good town; for to whatever church I go, I shall give offense to somebody."

Whatever may have been the origin and the extent of Macaulay's shortcomings as representative of Edinburgh, there were men at hand who were anxious, and very well able to turn them to their own account. But the injuries which he forgave I am forbidden to resent. No drop of ink from this pen shall resuscitate the memory of the intrigues that preceded and brought about the catastrophe of 1847; a catastrophe which was the outcome of jealousies which have long been dead, and the stepping-stone of ambitions which have ere this been gratified. But justice demands that on one point a protest should be made. There are some still alive who have persuaded themselves into the belief that they opposed Macaulay because he was not sound on the Corn Laws—and this in the teeth of the facts that from the year 1843 onward he was a consistent and hearty supporter of the uncompromising resolution annually brought forward by Mr. Charles Villiers; and that (as his letter to Mr. Macfarlan made only too notorious), at the crowning moment of the free-trade controversy, he statedly and resolutely refused to lend his assistance in forming any ministry which did not pledge itself to the total and immediate removal of the duty upon corn.* If such an early and signal repentance as this—(and I will not enter into the question whether or not his previous conduct had been such as called for repentance)—was ineffectual to clear him in the eyes of his constituents, then indeed the authority of an elector over his representative would be a tyranny which no man of right feeling would desire to exercise, and no man of honor could be expected to endure.

When Parliament was dissolved in the summer of 1847, all the various elements of discontent, political, ecclesiastical, and personal alike, mustered round the standard that was raised by Sir Culling Eardley's former committee, "which," says Lord Cockburn, "contained Established Churchmen and wild Voluntaries, intense Tories and declamatory Radicals, who agreed in nothing except in holding their peculiar religion as the Scriptural, and therefore the only safe, criterion of fitness for public duty. These men would have preferred Blackadder to Marlborough for the command of an army." "The struggle," says Hugh Miller, "is exciting the deepest interest, and, as the beginning of a decided movement on the part of Christians of various denominations to send men of avowed Christian principle to Parliament, may lead to great results." The common sense of the Scotch people brought this movement, such as it

---

* See page 152 of this volume.

was, to a speedy close; and it led to no greater result than
that of inflicting a transient scandal upon the sacred name of
religion, and giving Macaulay the leisure which he required in
order to put the finishing touch to the first two volumes of his
" History."

The leaders of the agitation judged it necessary to select a
stronger candidate than Sir Culling Eardley, and their choice
fell upon Mr. Charles Cowan, a son of one of the most respected citizens of Edinburgh, and himself a man of high private character, though not very conversant with public affairs.
The gentleman who introduced Mr. Cowan to the electors at
his first public meeting recommended him on the express
ground that " Christian men ought to send Christian men to
represent them." But when people inspired by these exemplary motives had once begun to move, others whose views
were of a more temporal and mundane complexion were not
behindhand in following their example. A deputation of
spirit-dealers waited upon Macaulay to urge the propriety of
altering the excise duties in the interest of their trade. They
failed to convince him; and he told them plainly that he
would do nothing for them, and most probably should do
something against them. The immediate consequence of this
unsatisfactory interview was the appearance of a fourth candidate, in the person of a Mr. Blackburn, who was described by
his own proposer as one who " came forward for the excise
trader, which showed that his heart was with the people," or
at any rate with that section of the people whose politics consisted in dislike to the whisky duty.

The contest was short, but sharp. For ten days the city
was white with broadsides, and the narrow courts off the High
Street rang with the dismal strains of innumerable ballad-
singers. The opposition was nominally directed against both
the sitting members; but from the first it was evident that all
the scurrility was meant exclusively for Macaulay. He came
scathless even out of that ordeal. The vague charge of being too much of an essayist and too little of a politician was
the worst that either saint or sinner could find to say of him.
The burden of half the election-songs was to the effect that

he had written poetry, and that one who knew so much about Ancient Rome could not possibly be the man for Modern Athens. The day of nomination was the 29th of July. The space in front of the hustings had been packed by the advocates of cheap whisky. Professor Aytoun, who stooped to second Mr. Blackburn, was applauded to his heart's content, while Macaulay was treated with a brutality the details of which are painful to read, and would be worse than useless to record. The polling took place on the morrow. A considerable number of the Tories, instead of plumping for Blackburn, or dividing their favors with the sitting members (who were both of them moderate Whigs and supporters of the Establishment), thought fit to give their second votes to Mr. Cowan, an avowed Voluntaryist in Church matters, and the accepted champion of the Radical party. "I waited with Mr. Macaulay," says Mr. Adam Black, "in a room of the Merchants' Hall, to receive at every hour the numbers who had polled in all the districts. At ten o'clock we were confounded to find that he was 150 below Cowan, but still had faint hopes that the next hour might turn the scale. The next hour came, and a darker prospect. At twelve o'clock he was 340 below Cowan. It was obvious now that the field was lost; but we were left from hour to hour under the torture of a sinking poll, till at four o'clock it stood thus: Cowan, 2063; Craig, 1854; Macaulay, 1477; Blackburn, 980."

Edinburgh, July 30th, 1847.

DEAREST HANNAH,—I hope that you will not be much vexed; for I am not vexed, but as cheerful as ever I was in my life. I have been completely beaten. The poll has not closed; but there is no chance that I shall retrieve the lost ground. Radicals, Tories, Dissenters, Voluntaries, Free Churchmen, spirit drinkers who are angry because I will not pledge myself to repeal all taxes on whisky, and great numbers of persons who are jealous of my chief supporters here, and think that the patronage of Edinburgh has been too exclusively distributed among a clique, have united to bear me down. I will make no hasty resolutions; but every thing seems to indicate that I ought to take this opportunity of retiring from public life. Ever yours,　　　　　　　　　　　　　　T. B. M.

Edinburgh, July 30th, 1847.

DEAR ELLIS,—I am beaten, but not at all the less happy for being so. I think that having once been manumitted, after the old fashion, by a slap in the face, I shall not take to bondage again. But there is time to consider that matter.

Ever yours,　　　　　　　　　　　　　T. B. MACAULAY.

That same night, while the town was still alive with jubilation over a triumph that soon lost its gloss even in the eyes of those who won it, Macaulay, in the grateful silence of his chamber, was weaving his perturbed thoughts into those exquisite lines which tell within the compass of a score of stanzas the essential secret of the life whose outward aspect these volumes have endeavored to portray.

> The day of tumult, strife, defeat, was o'er.
>   Worn out with toil, and noise, and scorn, and spleen,
> I slumbered, and in slumber saw once more
>   A room in an old mansion, long unseen.
>
> That room, methought, was curtained from the light ;
>   Yet through the curtains shone the moon's cold ray
> Full on a cradle, where, in linen white,
>   Sleeping life's first soft sleep, an infant lay.
>
> 　　*　　　*　　　*　　　*　　　*　　　*
>
> And lo! the fairy queens who rule our birth
>   Drew nigh to speak the new-born baby's doom :
> With noiseless step, which left no trace on earth,
>   From gloom they came, and vanished into gloom.
>
> Not deigning on the boy a glance to cast,
>   Swept careless by the gorgeous Queen of Gain.
> More scornful still, the Queen of Fashion passed,
>   With mincing gait and sneer of cold disdain.
>
> The Queen of Power tossed high her jeweled head,
>   And o'er her shoulder threw a wrathful frown.
> The Queen of Pleasure on the pillow shed
>   Scarce one stray rose-leaf from her fragrant crown.

Still fay in long procession followed fay;
   And still the little couch remained unblest:
But, when those wayward sprites had passed away,
   Came One, the last, the mightiest, and the best.

Oh! glorious lady, with the eyes of light,
   And laurels clustering round thy lofty brow,
Who by the cradle's side didst watch that night,
   Warbling a sweet strange music, who wast thou?

"Yes, darling; let them go," so ran the strain:
   "Yes; let them go—gain, fashion, pleasure, power,
And all the busy elves to whose domain
   Belongs the nether sphere, the fleeting hour.

"Without one envious sigh, one anxious scheme,
   The nether sphere, the fleeting hour resign.
Mine is the world of thought, the world of dream,
   Mine all the past, and all the future mine.
   *   *   *   *   *   *
"Of the fair brotherhood who share my grace,
   I, from thy natal day, pronounce thee free;
And, if for some I keep a nobler place,
   I keep for none a happier than for thee.

"There are who, while to vulgar eyes they seem
   Of all my bounties largely to partake,
Of me as of some rival's handmaid deem,
   And court me but for gain's, power's, fashion's sake.

"To such, though deep their lore, though wide their fame,
   Shall my great mysteries be all unknown:
But thou, through good and evil, praise and blame,
   Wilt not thou love me for myself alone?

"Yes; thou wilt love me with exceeding love;
   And I will tenfold all that love repay:
Still smiling, though the tender may reprove;
   Still faithful, though the trusted may betray.
   *   *   *   *   *   *
"In the dark hour of shame, I deigned to stand
   Before the frowning peers at Bacon's side;
On a far shore I smoothed with tender hand,
   Through months of pain, the sleepless bed of Hyde.

"I brought the wise and brave of ancient days
  To cheer the cell where Raleigh pined alone.
I lighted Milton's darkness with the blaze
  Of the bright ranks that guard the eternal throne.

"And even so, my child, it is my pleasure
  That thou not then alone shouldst feel me nigh,
When in domestic bliss and studious leisure
  Thy weeks uncounted come, uncounted fly.
        *   *   *   *   *   *
"No; when on restless night dawns cheerless morrow,
  When weary soul and wasting body pine,
Thine am I still, in danger, sickness, sorrow,
  In conflict, obloquy, want, exile, thine;

"Thine where on mountain waves the snow-birds scream,
  Where more than Thule's winter barbs the breeze,
Where scarce, through lowering clouds, one sickly gleam
  Lights the drear May-day of Antarctic seas;

"Thine when around thy litter's track all day
  White sand-hills shall reflect the blinding glare;
Thine when, through forests breathing death, thy way
  All night shall wind by many a tiger's lair;

"Thine most, when friends turn pale, when traitors fly,
  When, hard beset, thy spirit, justly proud,
For truth, peace, freedom, mercy, dares defy
  A sullen priesthood and a raving crowd.

"Amidst the din of all things fell and vile,
  Hate's yell, and envy's hiss, and folly's bray,
Remember me; and with an unforced smile
  See riches, baubles, flatterers, pass away.

"Yes, they will pass away, nor deem it strange;
  They come and go, as comes and goes the sea:
And let them come and go; thou, through all change,
  Fix thy firm gaze on virtue and on me."

CHAPTER XI.

1847–1849.

AFTER a few nights of sound sleep, and a few days of quiet
among his books, Macaulay had recovered both from the fa-
tigues of the contest and the vexation of the defeat. On the
6th of August, 1847, he writes to his sister Fanny: " I am
here in solitude, reading and working with great satisfaction
to myself. My table is covered with letters of condolence,
and with invitations from half the places which have not yet
chosen members. I have been asked to stand for Ayr, for
Wigton, and for Oxfordshire. At Wigton and in Oxfordshire
I was actually put in nomination without my permission, and
my supporters were with difficulty prevented from going to
the poll. From *The Sheffield Iris*, which was sent me to-day,
I see that a party wishes to put me up for the West Riding.
Craig tells me that there is a violent reaction at Edinburgh,
and that those who voted against me are very generally
ashamed of themselves, and wish to have me back again. I
did not know how great a politician I was till my Edinburgh

friends chose to dismiss me from politics. I never can leave public life with more dignity and grace than at present."

Such consolations as private life had to offer, Macaulay possessed in abundance. He enjoyed the pleasures of society in their most delightful shape; for he was one of a circle of eminent and gifted men who were the warm friends of himself and of each other. How brilliantly these men talked is already a matter of tradition. No report of their conversation has been published, and in all probability none exists. Scattered and meagre notices in the leaves of private diaries form the sole surviving record of many an Attic night and still more agreeable morning. Happily, Lord Carlisle's journal has preserved for us (as may be seen in the extracts which follow) at least the names of those with whom Macaulay lived, the houses which he frequented, and some few of the topics which he discussed. That journal proves, by many an affectionate and admiring expression, how highly my uncle was esteemed by one whose approbation and regard were never lightly given.*

"*June 27th*, 1843.—I breakfasted with Hallam, John Russell, Macaulay, Everett, Van de Weyer, Mr. Hamilton, U. S., and Mahon. Never were such torrents of good talk as burst and sputtered over from Macaulay and Hallam. A great deal about Latin and Greek inscriptions. They think the first unrivaled for that purpose; so free from articles and particles.

---

* Macaulay's acquaintance with the Howard family was of old standing, as may be gathered from a passage in a letter of the year 1833. This exceedingly droll production is too thickly strewn with personal allusions to admit of its being published, except in a fragmentary condition, which would be unjust to the writer, and not very interesting to the reader.

"I dined at Holland House yesterday.

DRAMATIS PERSONÆ.

Lord Holland	A fine old gentleman, very gouty and good-natured.
Earl Grey	Prime minister; a proud and majestic, yet polite and affable person.
The Rev. Sydney Smith	A holy and venerable ecclesiastic, director of the consciences of the above-named lords.

*   *   *   *   *   *   *   *

Lady Dover	A charming woman, like all the Howards of Carlisle."

Hallam read some wondrous extracts from the "Lives of the Saints,"* now being edited by Newman. Macaulay repeated, after the Yankees were gone, an egregious extract from a Natchez repudiation paper, making out our Saviour to be the first great repudiator when he overthrew the seats of the money-changers."

"*March 4th*, 1848.—Macaulay says that they" [the Parisian republicans] "are refuting the doctrines of political economy in the way a man would refute the doctrine of gravitation by jumping off the Monument."

"*January 6th*, 1849.—Finished Macaulay's two volumes. How admirable they are—full of generous impulse, judicial impartiality, wide research, deep thought, picturesque description, and sustained eloquence! Was history ever better written? Guizot† praises Macaulay. He says that he has truly hit the ruling passion of William the Third—his hatred for Louis the Fourteenth.

"*February 12th*.—Breakfasted with Macaulay. There were Van de Weyer, Hallam, Charles Austin, Panizzi, Colonel Mure, and Dicky Milnes; but he went to Yorkshire after the first cup. The conversation ranged the world: art, ancient and modern; the Greek tragedians; characters of the orators, how Philip and Alexander probably felt toward them as we do toward a scurrilous newspaper editor. It is a refreshing break in commonplace life. I staid till past twelve. His rooms at the top of the Albany are very liveable and studious-looking."

"*May 25th*.—Breakfasted with Rogers. It was a beautiful morning, and his house, view, and garden looked lovely. It was extremely pleasant. Mahon tried to defend Clarendon, but was put down by Hallam and Macaulay. Macaulay was very severe on Cranmer. Then we all quoted a good deal; Macaulay (as I had heard him before) four very fine lines from

---

* About this period Macaulay writes to Mr. Napier: "Newman announces an English Hagiology in numbers, which is to contain the lives of such blessed saints as Thomas à Becket and Dunstan. I should not dislike to be the Avvocato del Diavolo on such an occasion." And again: "I hear much of the miracles of the third and fourth centuries by Newman. I think that I could treat that subject without giving scandal to any rational person, and I should like it much. The times require a Middleton."

† Guizot was then a refugee in England. Shortly before this date, Macaulay writes to his sister Selina: "I left a card with Guizot, but did not ask to see him. I purposely avoided meeting him on Friday at Lord Holland's. The truth is, that I like and esteem the man, but I think the policy of the minister both at home and abroad detestable. At home it was all corruption, and abroad all treachery. I could not hold to him the language of entire respect and complacency without a violation of truth; and, in his present circumstances, I could not bear to show the least disapprobation."

the "Tristia," as being so contrary to their usual whining tone, and of even
a Miltonic loftiness of sentiment: ·

> En ego, quum patriâ caream, vobisque, domoque;
> Raptaque sint, adimi quæ potuere, mihi;
> Ingenio tamen ipse meo comitorque, fruorque.
> Cæsar in hoc potuit juris habere nihil.

I think we must have rather shot beyond Rogers sometimes."

"*October 11th.*—[Dinner at Lord Carlisle's.] The evening went off very
cozily and pleasantly, as must almost always happen with Macaulay. He
was rather paradoxical, as is apt to be his manner, and almost his only social fault. The greatest marvel about him is the quantity of trash he remembers. He went off at score with Lord Thurlow's poetry."

"*March 5th,* 1850.—Dined at the Club. Dr. Holland in the chair. Lord
Lansdowne, Bishop of London, Lord Mahon, Macaulay, Milman, Van de
Weyer, I, David Dundas, Lord Harry Vane, Stafford O'Brien. The bishop
talked of the wit of Rowland Hill. One day his chapel, with a thinner attendance than usual, suddenly filled during a shower of rain. He said: 'I
have often heard of religion being used as a cloak, but never before as an
umbrella.' In his later life he used to come to his chapel in a carriage.
He got an anonymous letter rebuking him for this, because it was not the
way his heavenly Master traveled. He read the letter from the pulpit,
said it was quite true, and that if the writer would come to the vestry afterward with a saddle and bridle he would ride him home. They talked a
good deal of French authors. The 'Tartuffe' was thought Molière's best
play; then the 'Misanthrope.' Macaulay prefers 'L'Avare.' We recited
Johnson's beautiful epitaphs on Philips and Levinge. Macaulay's flow
never ceased once during the four hours, but it is never overbearing."

"*March 23d.*—Breakfast with Macaulay. On being challenged, he repeated the names of the owners of the several carriages that went to Clarissa's funeral. We chiefly talked of Junius, and the irresistible proofs for
Sir Philip Francis."*

"*May 9th.*—Breakfast with Macaulay. We talked of Thiers and Lamartine as historians; Thiers not having any moral principle; Lamartine a
great artist, but without the least care for truth. They were just passing
to the Jesuits and Pascal when I thought it right (and I must claim some
merit in this) to go to the Ascension morning service at St. James's. After I went, the conversation got upon moral obligations, and was so eagerly

---

* Two days previously Macaulay and Carlyle had met at Lord Ashburton's house. It was, perhaps, on this occasion that Carlyle was wofully
bored by the irresistible proofs for Sir Philip Francis. "As if it could matter the value of a brass farthing to any living human being who was the
author of Junius!"

carried on by Hallam, Whewell, and Macaulay, though without the slightest loss of temper, that not one sentence could any of them finish. "

"*November* 11*th.* — Breakfasted with Macaulay, Charles Greville, Hobhouse, Sir R. Murchison, and Charles (Howard). The talk was even more than usually agreeable and interesting, and it got on very high themes. Macaulay argued very forcibly against Hobhouse and Charles Greville for the difference between the evidence of Christ's miracles and of the truth of transubstantiation. To put them on a level, Lazarus ought to have remained inanimate, colorless, and decomposing in the grave, while we should be called upon to believe that he had at the word of Christ become alive. He does not consider the doctrine of the Trinity opposed to reason. He was rather less opposed to the No Popery cry, so rife at present, than I might have expected. He* thinks the nonsense of people may be advan-

---

* Four days after this breakfast Macaulay wrote to his sister Fanny: "If I told you all that I think about these disputes, I should write a volume. The Pope hates the English nation and government. He meant, I am convinced, to insult and annoy the queen and her ministers. His whole conduct in Ireland has evidently been directed to that end. Nevertheless, the reasons popularly urged against this bull seem to me absurd. We always knew that the Pope claimed spiritual jurisdiction, and I do not see that he now claims temporal jurisdiction. I could wish that Lord John had written more guardedly; and that, I plainly see, is the wish of some of his colleagues, and probably, by this time, is also his own. He has got much applause in England: but, when he was writing, he should have remembered that he had to govern several millions of Roman Catholics in Ireland; that to govern them at all is no easy task; and that any thing which looks like an affront to their religion is certain to call forth very dangerous passions. In the mean time, these things keep London all alive. Yesterday the ballad-singers were entertaining a great crowd under my windows with bawling:

'Now all the old women are crying for fear
The Pope is a-coming: oh dear! oh dear!'

The wall of Burlington Gardens is covered with 'No Popery,' 'No Wafer Gods.' I can not help enjoying the rage and terror of the Puseyites, who are utterly prostrated by this outbreak of popular feeling."

And again, some days later, he says: "A deputation of my parish, St. James's, came to me yesterday to ask me to move a resolution at a public meeting. I refused, took their resolutions in my hand, and criticised them in such a way as, for the time at least, converted the delegates. They told me, at parting, that the whole should be recast; that intolerant sentiments should be expunged; and that, instead of calling for laws to punish avowed Roman Catholics, the parish would express its dislike of the concealed Roman Catholics who hold benefices in the Established Church."

tageously made use of to set them against the real mischief of popish interference."

"*May* 13*th*.—Dined at the Club. Bishop of Oxford, Dean of St. Paul's, Whewell, Macaulay, Lord Overstone, Dr. Holland, Sir J. Staunton, George Lewis. A good company, and it was most agreeable. They were very droll about Sir John Sinclair—his writing to Pitt that it was very desirable that the President of the Scotch Agricultural Society" [which office he then held] "should be a peer. Pitt answered that he quite agreed with him; accepted his resignation, and appointed Lord Somerville. The bishop said he remembered his complaining of it at his father's, at Kensington Gore; it had been 'such a willful misunderstanding.' Macaulay said that there are in his works two distinctions, the one the most complete, the other the most incomplete, that he remembers. The first is : 'There are two kinds of sleep : one with your night-cap, and the other without it.' The second : ' There are three kinds of bread : white bread, brown bread, and rolls.' At the end the bishop and I fought a mesmeric and electro-biological battle against the scornful opposition of all the rest."*

" *May* 15*th*.—Breakfasted with the Bishop of Oxford. It was remarkably pleasant; a little on derivations.† As an instance of unlucky quotation I gave Lord Fitzwilliam's, when calling on the Dissenters to join the Established Clergy in subscribing for the rebuilding of York Minster,

> Flectere si nequeo superos Acheronta movebo.

Van de Weyer remarked on the English horror of false quantities, which Macaulay defended justly on the plea that no one is bound to quote. No one resents the Duke of Wellington, in the theatre at Oxford, having called it Carŏlus, after being corrected for saying Jacŏbus. It was the duke's advice to Sir George Murray, when he said he never should be able to get on with speaking in the Commons, ' Say what you have to say, don't quote Latin, and sit down.' "

" *May* 27*th*.—Dined at the Club. The talk ran for some time on whether the north or south of different countries had contributed most to their literature. I remained on with Macaulay and Milman. The first gave a list of six poets, whom he places above all others, in the order of his preference : Shakspeare, Homer, Dante, Æschylus, Milton, Sophocles. Milman, on the whole, acquiesced. I fought some battle for Virgil coming before

---

* Macaulay's account of the evening is : "Pleasant party at the Club : but we got a little too disputatious at last about mesmerism and clairvoyance. It is difficult to discuss such matters without using language which seems to reflect on the understanding of those who believe what you think absurd. However, we kept within tolerable bounds."

† Lord Carlisle elsewhere says : "The conversation rather etymological, as perhaps it is too apt to be in this society."

Sophocles: but 'What,' said Macaulay, 'did Virgil ever write like the Philoctetes?' He would place Lucretius and Ariosto before him. He thinks the first part of 'Henry the Fourth' Shakspeare's best comic play; then the second part; then 'Twelfth Night:' but Shakspeare's plays are not to be classed into Tragedy and Comedy. It was the object of the Elizabethan drama, the highest form of composition he can conceive, to represent life as it is."

"*February 14th*, 1852.—Dined at Mrs. Drummond's. Trevelyans, Strutts, Fords, Merivales, Macaulay. It was very pleasant. Macaulay and Mrs. Strutt both own to the feeling Doctor Johnson had, of thinking one's self bound sometimes to touch a particular rail or post, and to tread always in the middle of the paving-stone. I certainly have had this very strongly. Macaulay wished that he could spend a day of every century in London since the Romans; though of the two he would rather spend a day in it eighteen hundred years hence, than eighteen hundred years ago, as he can less easily conceive it. We agreed there can never have been thirty years in which all mechanical improvements have made so much progress as in the last thirty; but he looks on printing as a greater discovery than steam, but not near so rapid in its obvious results. He told us of two letters he had received from America: one from a Mr. Crump, offering him five hundred dollars if he could introduce the name of Crump into his 'History:' another from a Young Men's Philosophical Society in New York, beginning, 'Possibly our fame has not pinioned the Atlantic.' "

"*May 4th.*—Dined with the Club. Very pleasant, though select. Something led to my reminding Lord Aberdeen that we both put 'Macbeth' the first of Shakspeare's great plays. Lord Lansdowne quite concurred. Macaulay thinks it may be a little owing to our recollections of Mrs. Siddons. He is much inclined to rank them thus: 'Othello,' 'Lear,' 'Macbeth,' 'Hamlet.'"*

"*November 29th.*—Breakfasted with Macaulay. He thinks that, though the last eight books of 'Paradise Lost' contain incomparable beauties, Milton's fame would have stood higher if only the first four had been preserved. He would then have been placed above Homer."

---

* In the course of the next month there was a breakfast at the Bishop of Oxford's. "Extremely agreeable," writes Lord Carlisle, "and would have been still more so, but there was a tendency to talk very loud, and all at once." On this occasion Macaulay told a story about one of the French prophets of the seventeeth century, who came into the Court of Queen's Bench and announced that the Holy Ghost had sent him to command Lord Holt to enter a *nolle prosequi.* "If," said Lord Holt, "the Holy Ghost had wanted a *nolle prosequi,* he would have bid you apply to the attorney-general. The Holy Ghost knows that I can not enter a *nolle prosequi.* But there is one thing which I can do. I can lay a lying knave by the heels;" and thereupon he committed him to prison.

There is nothing very attractive in a memorandum which baldly chronicles the fact that on a certain day, five-and-twenty years ago, Hallam and Milman and Macaulay undertook to classify in order of excellence the Greek tragedians or the Elizabethan dramatists. But it must be remembered that every one of these entries represents an hour of glowing declamation and sparkling repartee, interspersed with choice passages from the writer whose merits were in question, recited as poetry is recited by men who learn without effort and admire without affectation. "When I praise an author," Macaulay used to say, "I love to give a sample of his wares." That sample was sometimes only too favorable. He had so quick an eye for literary effect — so grateful was he to any book which had pleased him even for a moment — that he would pick out from such a book, and retain forever in his memory, what was perhaps the single telling anecdote or well-turned couplet which could be discovered in its pages.* A pointed story, extracted from some trumpery memoir of the last century, and retold in his own words—a purple patch from some third-rate sermon or political treatise, woven into the glittering fabric of his talk with that art which in his case was a second nature — have often and often tempted his younger hearers into toiling through volume after volume of prosy or flippant trash, in which a good paragraph was as rare as a silver spoon in a dust-heap.

Whatever fault might be found with Macaulay's gestures as an orator, his appearance and bearing in conversation were singularly effective. Sitting bolt upright, his hands resting on the arms of his chair or folded over the handle of his walk-

---

* "My father," says Sara Coleridge, "had a way of seizing upon the one bright thing out of long tracts of dull and tedious matter. I remember a great campanula which grew in a wood at Keswick. Two or three such I found in my native vale during the course of my flower-seeking days. As well might we present one of these as a sample of the blue-bells of bonny Cumberland, or the one or two oxslips which may be found among a multitude of cowslips in a Somersetshire meadow, as specimens of the flower-hood of the field—as give these extracts for proof of what the writer was generally wont to produce."

ing-stick; knitting his great eyebrows if the subject was one which had to be thought out as he went along, or brightening from the forehead downward when a burst of humor was coming; his massive features and honest glance suited well with the manly, sagacious sentiments which he set forth in his pleasant, sonorous voice, and in his racy and admirably intelligible language. To get at his meaning, people had never the need to think twice, and they certainly had seldom the time. And with all his ardor, and all his strength and energy of conviction, he was so truly considerate toward others, so delicately courteous with the courtesy which is of the essence, and not only in the manner! However eager had been the debate, and however prolonged the sitting, no one in the company ever had personal reasons for wishing a word of his unsaid, or a look or a tone recalled. His good things were never long in the making. During the Caffre war, at a time when we were getting rather the worst of it, he opened the street-door for a walk down Westbourne Terrace. "The blacks are flying," said his companion. "I wish they were in South Africa," was the instant reply. His quotations were always ready, and never off the mark. On a Sunday afternoon, when the family were engaged in discussing a new curate, one of the children, with true Clapham instinct, asked whether the reverend gentleman had ever received a testimonial. "I am glad, my boy," said Macaulay, "that you would not muzzle the ox that treadeth out the corn." Sometimes he would recast his thoughts, and give them over again in the shape of an epigram. "You call me a Liberal," he said; "but I don't know that in these days I deserve the name. I am opposed to the abolition of standing armies. I am opposed to the abrogation of capital punishment. I am opposed to the destruction of the National Church. In short, I am in favor of war, hanging, and Church establishments."

He was always willing to accept a friendly challenge to a feat of memory. One day, in the board-room of the British Museum, Sir David Dundas saw him hand to Lord Aberdeen a sheet of foolscap covered with writing arranged in three parallel columns down each of the four pages. This document, of which the ink was still wet, proved to be a full list of the senior wranglers at Cambridge, with their dates and colleges, for the hundred years during which the names of senior wranglers had been recorded in the University Calendar. On another occasion, Sir David asked, "Macaulay, do you know your popes?" "No," was the answer; "I always get wrong among the innocents." "But can you say your Archbishops of Canterbury?" "Any fool," said Macaulay, "could say his Archbishops of Canterbury backward;" and he went off at score, drawing breath only once in order to remark on the oddity of there having been both an Archbishop Sancroft and an Archbishop Bancroft, until Sir David stopped him at Cranmer.*

Macaulay could seldom be tempted to step outside his own immediate circle of friends and relations. His distaste for the chance society of a London drawing-room increased as years went on. Like Casaubon of old, he was well aware that a man can not live with the idlers, and with the Muses too. "He was peculiarly susceptible," says Lady Trevelyan, "of the feeling of ennui when in company. He really hated staying out, even in the best and most agreeable houses. It was with an effort that he even dined out, and few of those who met him, and enjoyed his animated conversation, could guess how much rather he would have remained at home, and how much difficulty I had to force him to accept invitations and prevent his growing a recluse. But, though he was very easily bored in general society, I think he never felt ennui when he was alone, or when he was with those he loved. Many people are very fond of children, but he was the only person I ever knew who never tired of being with them. Often has he come to our house, at Clapham or in Westbourne Terrace, directly after breakfast, and, finding me out, has dawdled away the whole morning with the children; and then, after sitting

---

* Macaulay was proud of his good memory, and had little sympathy with people who affected to have a bad one. In a note on the margin of one of his books he reflects upon this not uncommon form of self-depreciation, "They appear to reason thus: The more memory, the less invention."

with me at lunch, has taken Margaret a long walk through the City which lasted the whole afternoon. Such days are always noted in his journals as especially happy."

It is impossible to exaggerate the pleasure which Macaulay took in children, or the delight which he gave them. He was, beyond all comparison, the best of playfellows; unrivaled in the invention of games, and never wearied of repeating them. He had an inexhaustible repertory of small dramas for the benefit of his nieces, in which he sustained an endless variety of parts with a skill that, at any rate, was sufficient for his audience. An old friend of the family writes to my sister, Lady Holland: "I well remember that there was one never-failing game of building up a den with newspapers behind the sofa, and of enacting robbers and tigers; you shrieking with terror, but always fascinated, and begging him to begin again: and there was a daily recurring observation from him that, after all, children were the only true poets."

Whenever he was at a distance from his little companions, he consoled himself and them by the exchange of long and frequent letters. The earliest in date of those which he wrote in prose begins as follows:

September 15th, 1842.

MY DEAR BABA,*—Thank you for your very pretty letter. I am always glad to make my little girl happy, and nothing pleases me so much as to see that she likes books. For, when she is as old as I am, she will find that they are better than all the tarts, and cakes, and toys, and plays, and sights in the world. If any body would make me the greatest king that ever lived, with palaces, and gardens, and fine dinners, and wine, and coaches, and beautiful clothes, and hundreds of servants, on condition that I would not read books, I would not be a king. I would rather be a poor man in a garret with plenty of books, than a king who did not love reading—

Five years later on he writes: "I must begin sooner or

---

* Baba was a pet name for his niece Margaret, derived from the Indian nursery.

later to call you 'Margaret;' and I am always making good
resolutions to do so, and then breaking them. But I will pro-
crastinate no longer.

> Procrastination is the thief of time,

says Dr. Young. He also says,

> Be wise to-day. 'Tis madness to defer,

and,

> Next day the fatal precedent will plead.

That is to say, if I do not take care, I shall go on calling my
darling 'Baba' till she is as old as her mamma, and has a doz-
en Babas of her own. Therefore I will be wise to-day and
call her 'Margaret.' I should very much like to see you and
Aunt Fanny at Broadstairs: but I fear, I fear, that it can not
be. Your aunt asks me to shirk the Chelsea Board. I am
staying in England chiefly, in order to attend it. When Parliament is not sitting, my duty there is all that I do for two
thousand four hundred pounds a year. We must have some
conscience.

"Michaelmas will, I hope, find us all at Clapham over a noble goose. Do you remember the beautiful Puseyite hymn
on Michaelmas-day? It is a great favorite with all the Trac-
tarians. You and Alice should learn it. It begins:

> Though Quakers scowl, though Baptists howl,
> 　Though Plymouth Brethren rage,
> We Churchmen gay will wallow to-day
> 　In apple-sauce, onions, and sage.

> Ply knife and fork, and draw the cork,
> 　And have the bottle handy:
> For each slice of goose will introduce
> 　A thimbleful of brandy.

Is it not good? I wonder who the author can be. Not Newman, I think. It is above him. Perhaps it is Bishop Wilberforce."

The following letter is in a graver tone, as befits the correspondent of a young lady who has only two years of the
school-room still before her:

October 14th, 1851.

DEAR MARGARET,—Tell me how you like Schiller's "Mary Stuart." It is not one of my favorite pieces. I should put it fourth among his plays. I arrange them thus: "Wallenstein," "William Tell," "Don Carlos," "Mary Stuart," the "Maid of Orleans." At a great interval comes the "Bride of Messina;" and then, at another great interval, "Fieschi." "Cabal and Love" I never could get through. "The Robbers" is a mere school-boy rant, below serious criticism, but not without indications of mental vigor which required to be disciplined by much thought and study. But though I do not put "Mary Stuart" very high among Schiller's works, I think the Fotheringay scenes in the fifth act equal to any thing that he ever wrote—indeed, equal to any thing dramatic that has been produced in Europe since Shakspeare. I hope that you will feel the wonderful truth and beauty of that part of the play.

I can not agree with you in admiring "Sintram." There is an age at which we are disposed to think that whatever is odd and extravagant is great. At that age we are liable to be taken in by such orators as Irving, such painters as Fuseli, such plays as "The Robbers," such romances as "Sintram." A better time comes, when we would give all Fuseli's hobgoblins for one of Reynolds's little children, and all Sintram's dialogues with Death and the Devil for one speech of Mrs. Norris or Miss Bates. Tell me, however, as of course you will, quite truly what you think of "Sintram."

I saw a description of myself yesterday in a New York paper. The writer says that I am a stout man, with hazel eyes; that I always walk with an umbrella; that I sometimes bang the umbrella against the ground; that I often dine in the coffee-room of the Trafalgar on fish; that once he saw me break a decanter there, but that I did not appear to be at all ashamed of my awkwardness, but called for my bill as coolly as if nothing had happened. I have no recollection of such an occurrence; but, if it did take place, I do not think that it would have deprived me of my self-possession. This is fame. This is the advantage of making a figure in the world.

This has been the last week of the Great Exhibition. It makes me quite sad to think of our many, many happy walks there. To-morrow I shall go to the final ceremony, and try to hear the Bishop of London's thanksgiving, in which I shall very cordially join. This will long be remembered as a singularly happy year, of peace, plenty, good feeling, innocent pleasure, national glory of the best and purest sort.

I have bespoken a Schiller for you. It is in the binder's hands, and will be ready, I hope, before your return.

　　　　Ever yours,　　　　　　　　　　　　T. B. MACAULAY.

His poetical, no less than his epistolary, style was carefully adapted to the age and understanding of those whom he was addressing. Some of his pieces of verse are almost perfect specimens of the nursery lyric. From five to ten stanzas in length, and with each word carefully formed in capitals, most comforting to the eyes of a student who is not very sure of his small letters, they are real children's poems, and they profess to be nothing more. They contain none of those strokes of satire, and allusions to the topics and personages of the day, by which the authors of what is now called juvenile literature so often attempt to prove that they are fit for something better than the task on which they are engaged. But this very absence of pretension, which is the special merit of these trifles, renders them unworthy of a place in a book intended for grown-up readers. There are, however, few little people between three and five years old who would not care to hear how

> There once was a nice little girl,
> 　With a nice little rosy face.
> She always said "Our Father,"
> 　And she always said her grace:

and how, as the reward of her good behavior,

> They brought the browned potatoes,
> 　And minced veal, nice and hot,
> And such a good bread-pudding,
> 　All smoking from the pot!

And there are still fewer who would be indifferent to the fate
which befell the two boys who talked in church, when

> The beadle got a good big stick,
>   Thicker than uncle's thumb.
> Oh, what a fright those boys were in
>   To see the beadle come!

> And they were turned out of the church,
>   And they were soundly beat :
> And both those wicked, naughty boys
>   Went bawling down the street.

All his rhymes, whether written or improvised, he put down
to the credit of "The Judicious Poet." The gravity with
which he maintained the innocent delusion was too much for
children, who more than half believed in the existence of a
writer for whose collected works they searched the library in
vain; though their faith was from time to time shaken by the
almost miraculous applicability of a quotation to the most unexpected circumstances of the moment. St. Valentine's Day
brought Macaulay's nieces a yearly offering of rhyme, until
he thought them too old to care for verses which he himself
pronounced to be on a level with the bellman's, but which are
certainly as good, and probably as sincere, as nine-tenths of the
pastoral poetry that has been written during the last two centuries. In 1847 the annual effusion ran as follows:

> And canst thou spurn a kneeling bard,
>   Mine own, mine only Valentine ?
> The heart of beauty still is hard,
>   But ne'er was heart so hard as thine.
> Each year a shepherd sings thy praise,
>   And sings it in no vulgar strain ;
> Each year a shepherd ends his days,
>   A victim to thy cold disdain.

> In forty-five, relentless maid,
>   For thee melodious Strephon died ;
> For thee was gentle Thyrsis laid,
>   In forty-six, by Strephon's side.

The swain who to thy footstool bears,
 Next spring, the tribute of his verses,
Will tell thee that poor Damon shares
 The grave of Strephon and of Thyrsis.

Then will the whole Arcadian choir
 Their sweetest songster's fate bemoan,
Hang o'er his tomb his crook and lyre,
 And carve this ditty on the stone:
"Stop, passenger. Here Damon lies,
 Beloved of all the tuneful nine;
The third who perished by the eyes
 Of one too-charming Valentine."

THE BROKEN-HEARTED DAMON.

The longest and the most elaborate of these little compositions was addressed to the daughter of Earl Stanhope, now
the Countess Beauchamp. The allusion to the statue of Mr.
Pitt in Hanover Square is one of the happiest touches that
can be found in Macaulay's writings.

Good-morrow, gentle child, and then
Again good-morrow, and again,
Good-morrow following still good-morrow,
Without one cloud of strife or sorrow.
And when the god to whom we pay
In jest our homages to-day
Shall come to claim, no more in jest,
His rightful empire o'er thy breast,
Benignant may his aspect be,
His yoke the truest liberty:
And if a tear his power confess,
Be it a tear of happiness!
It shall be so. The Muse displays
The future to her votary's gaze.
Prophetic rage my bosom swells.
I taste the cake! I hear the bells!
From Conduit Street the close array
Of chariots barricades the way
To where I see, with outstretched hand,
Majestic, thy great kinsman stand,
And half unbend his brow of pride,
As welcoming so fair a bride.

The feelings with which Macaulay regarded children were near akin to those of the great writer to whom we owe the death of little Paul, and the meeting between the school-boy and his mother in the eighth chapter of " David Copperfield." " Have you seen the first number of Dombey ?" he writes. " There is not much in it; but there is one passage which made me cry as if my heart would break. It is the description of a little girl who has lost an affectionate mother, and is unkindly treated by every body. Images of that sort always overpower me, even when the artist is less skillful than Dickens." In truth, Macaulay's extreme sensibility to all which appealed to the sentiment of pity, whether in art or in nature, was nothing short of a positive inconvenience to him.* He was so moved by the visible representation of distressing scenes that he went most unwillingly to the theatre, for which during his Cambridge days he had entertained a passionate though passing fondness.† I remember well how, during the performance of " Masks and Faces," the sorrows of the broken-down author and his starving family in their Grub Street garret entirely destroyed the pleasure which he otherwise would have taken in Mrs. Stirling's admirable acting. And he was hardly less easily affected to tears by that which was sublime and stirring in literature, than by that which was melancholy and pathetic. In August, 1851, he writes from Malvern to his niece Margaret: " I finished the ' Iliad ' to-day. I had not read it through since the end of 1837, when I was at Calcutta, and when you often called me away from my studies to show you pictures and to feed the crows. I never admired the old fellow so much, or was so strongly moved by

---

* "*April 17th*, 1858.—In the *Times* of this morning there was an account of a suicide of a poor girl which quite broke my heart. I can not get it out of my thoughts, or help crying when I think of it."

† I recollect hearing Macaulay describe the wonder and delight with which, during a long vacation spent at the university, he saw his first play acted by a strolling company in the Barnwell Theatre. " Did you, then, never go to the play as a boy ?" asked some one who was present. " No," said he; " after the straitest sect of our religion I was bred a Pharisee."

him. What a privilege genius like his enjoys! I could not
tear myself away. I read the last five books at a stretch during my walk to-day, and was at last forced to turn into a by-
path, lest the parties of walkers should see me blubbering for
imaginary beings, the creations of a ballad-maker who has
been dead two thousand seven hundred years. What is the
power and glory of Cæsar and Alexander to that? Think
what it would be to be assured that the inhabitants of Mono-
motapa would weep over one's writings Anno Domini 4551!"

Macaulay was so devoid of egotism, and exacted so little
deference and attention from those with whom he lived, that
the young people around him were under an illusion which to
this day it is pleasant to recall. It was long, very long, before
we guessed that the world thought much of one who appeared to think so little of himself. I remember telling my
school-fellows that I had an uncle who was about to publish a
"History of England" in two volumes, each containing six
hundred and fifty pages; but it never crossed my mind that
the work in question would have any thing to distinguish it
except its length. As years went on, it seemed strange and
unnatural to hear him more and more frequently talked of as
a great man; and we slowly, and almost reluctantly, awoke to
the conviction that "Uncle Tom" was cleverer, as well as
more good-natured, than his neighbors.

Among other tastes which he had in common with children
was an avidity for sight-seeing. "What say you," he asks
Mr. Ellis, "to a visit to the Chinese Museum? It is the most
interesting and curious sight that I know. If you like the
plan, I will call on you at four. Or will you call on me?
For I am half-way between the Temple and the wonders of
the Celestial empire." And again: "We treated the Clifton
Zoö much too contemptuously. I lounged thither, and found
more than sixpennyworth of amusement." "After breakfast
I went to the Tower," he writes in his journal of 1839: "I
found great changes. The wild beasts were all gone. The
Zoological Gardens have driven paved courts and dark narrow
cages quite out of fashion. I was glad for the sake of the
tigers and leopards."

He was never so happy as when he could spend an afternoon in taking his nieces and nephews a round of London
sights, until, to use his favorite expression, they "could not
drag one leg after the other." If he had been able to have
his own way, the treat would have recurred at least twice a
week. On these occasions we drove into London in time for
a sumptuous midday meal, at which every thing that we liked
best was accompanied by oysters, caviare, and olives, some of
which delicacies he invariably provided with the sole object
of seeing us reject them with contemptuous disgust. Then off
we set under his escort, in summer to the bears and lions;
in winter to the Panorama of Waterloo, to the Colosseum in
Regent's Park, or to the enjoyment of the delicious terror inspired by Madame Tussaud's Chamber of Horrors. When
the more attractive exhibitions had been exhausted by too
frequent visits, he would enliven with his irrepressible fun the
dreary propriety of the Polytechnic, or would lead us through
the lofty corridors of the British Museum, making the statues
live and the busts speak by the spirit and color of his innumerable anecdotes, paraphrased off-hand from the pages of
Plutarch and Suetonius. One of these expeditions is described
in a letter to my mother in January, 1845: "Fanny brought
George and Margaret, with Charley Cropper, to the Albany
at one yesterday. I gave them some dinner: fowl, ham, mar-
row-bones, tart, ice, olives, and Champagne. I found it difficult to think of any sight for the children: however, I took
them to the National Gallery, and was excessively amused
with the airs of connoisseurship which Charley and Margaret
gave themselves, and with Georgy's honestly avowed weariness: 'Let us go. There is nothing here that I care for at
all.' When I put him into the carriage, he said, half sulkily:
'I do not call this seeing sights. I have seen no sight to-day.'
Many a man who has laid out thirty thousand pounds on
paintings would, if he spoke the truth, own that he cared as
little for the art as poor Georgy."

Regularly every Easter, when the closing of the public offices drove my father from the Treasury for a brief holiday,
Macaulay took our family on a tour among cathedral-towns,

varied by an occasional visit to the universities. We started
on the Thursday; spent Good-Friday in one city and Easter
Sunday in another, and went back to town on the Monday.
This year it was Worcester and Gloucester; the next, York
and Lincoln; then Lichfield and Chester, Norwich and Peter-
borough, Ely and Cambridge, Salisbury and Winchester. Now
and then the routine was interrupted by a trip to Paris, or to
the great churches on the Loire; but in the course of twenty
years we had inspected at least once all the cathedrals of England, or indeed of England and Wales, for we carried our researches after ecclesiastical architecture as far down in the list
as Bangor. " Our party just filled a railway carriage," says
Lady Trevelyan, " and the journey found his flow of spirits
unfailing. It was a return to old times; a running fire of
jokes, rhymes, puns, never ceasing. It was a peculiarity of his
that he never got tired on a journey. As the day wore on he
did not feel the desire to lie back and be quiet, and he liked
to find his companions ready to be entertained to the last."

Any one who reads the account of Norwich and Bristol in
the third chapter, or the account of Magdalen College in the
eighth chapter, of the " History," may form an idea of Macaulay's merits as a cicerone in an old English provincial capital.
To walk with him round the walls of York, or through the
Rows of Chester; to look up at the towers of Lichfield from
the spot where Lord Brooke received his death-wound, or down
upon Durham from the brow of the hill behind Neville's
Cross; to hear him discourse on Monmouth and Bishop Ken
beneath the roof of Longleat Hall, or give the rein to all the
fancies and reminiscences, political, personal, and historical,
which were conjured up by a drive past Old Sarum to Stone-
henge, were privileges which a child could appreciate, but
which the most learned of scholars might have envied.

When we returned to our inn in the evening, it was only
an exchange of pleasures. Sometimes he would translate to us
choice morsels from Greek, Latin, Italian, or Spanish writers,
with a vigor of language and vivacity of manner which communicated to his impromptu version not a little of the air and
the charm of the original. Sometimes he would read from

the works of Sterne, or Smollett, or Fielding those scenes to
which ladies might listen, but which they could not well venture to pick out for themselves. And when we had heard
enough of the siege of Carthagena in "Roderick Random,"
or of Lieutenant Le Fevre's death in "Tristram Shandy," we
would fall to capping verses, or stringing rhymes, or amusing
ourselves with some game devised for the occasion which oft-
en made a considerable demand upon the memory or invention of the players. Of these games only a single trace remains. One of his nieces, unable to forecast the future of her
sex, had expressed a regret that she could never hope to go
in for a college examination. Macaulay thereupon produced
what he was pleased to call a paper of questions in divinity,
the contents of which afford a curious proof how constantly
the lighter aspects of English sectarianism were present to his
thoughts. The first three questions ran as follows :

> 1. "And this is law, I will maintain
> Until my dying day, sir,
> That whatsoever king shall reign,
> I'll be the Vicar of Bray, sir."

> "Then read Paul's epistles,
> You rotten Arminian !
> You won't find a passage
> To support your opinion."

> "When the lads of the village so merrily, ah !
> Sound their tabors, I'll hand thee along.
> And verily, verily, verily, ah !
> Thou and I will be first in the throng."

To what sects did the three persons belong who express their sentiments
in the three passages cited above? Is there any thing in the third passage at variance with the usages of the sect to which it relates? Which
of those three sects do you prefer? Which of the three bears the closest
resemblance to Popery? Where is Bray? Through what reigns did the
political life of the Vicar of Bray extend?

2. Define "Jumper," "Shaker," "Ranter," "Dunker."

3. Translate the following passage into the Quakeric dialect: "You and
Sir Edward Ryan breakfasted with me on Friday, the 11th of December."

Like all other men who play with a will, and who work to

a purpose, Macaulay was very well aware of the distinction between work and play. He did not carry on the business of his life by desultory efforts, or in the happy moments of an elegant inspiration. Men have disputed, and will long continue to dispute, whether or not his fame was deserved; but no one who himself has written books will doubt that, at any rate, it was hardly earned. "Take at hazard," says Thackeray, "any three pages of the 'Essays' or 'History;' and, glimmering below the stream of the narrative, you, an average reader, see one, two, three, a half-score of allusions to other historic facts, characters, literature, poetry, with which you are acquainted. Your neighbor, who has *his* reading and *his* little stock of literature stowed away in his mind, shall detect more points, allusions, happy touches, indicating not only the prodigious memory and vast learning of this master, but the wonderful industry, the honest, humble previous toil of this great scholar. He reads twenty books to write a sentence; he travels a hundred miles to make a line of description."

That this praise, though high, was not excessive, is amply proved by that portion of Macaulay's papers which extends over the period when his "History" was in course of preparation. Justice demands that, even at the risk of being tedious, a specimen should be given of the scrupulous care and the unflagging energy with which he conducted his investigations.

July 17th, 1848.

Dear Ellis,—Many thanks for your kindness. Pray let Dr. Hook know, whenever you have an opportunity, how much I am obliged to him.* The information which he has procured for me, I am sorry to say, is not such as I can use. But you need not tell him so. I feel convinced that he has made some mistake: for he sends me only a part of the Leeds burials in 1685; and yet the number is double that of the Manchester burials in the same year. If the ordinary rules of calculation are applied to these data, it will be found that Leeds must in 1685 have contained 16,000 souls or thereabouts.

---

* Mr. Ellis was Recorder of Leeds, and Dr. Hook its vicar.

Now, at the beginning of the American war Leeds contained only 16,000 souls, as appears from Dr. Hook's own letter. Nobody can suppose that there had been no increase between 1685 and 1775. Besides, neither York nor Exeter contained 16,000 inhabitants in 1685, and nobody who knows the state of things at that time can believe that Leeds was then a greater town than York or Exeter. Either some error has been committed, or else there was an extraordinary mortality at Leeds in 1685. In either case the numbers are useless for my purpose. Ever yours,   T. B. M.

July 27th, 1848.

Dear Ellis,—Many thanks. Wardell* is the man. He gives a much better thing than a list of burials; a list of the houses returned by the hearth-money collectors. It appears that Leeds contained, in 1663, just 1400 houses. And observe; all the townships are included. The average number of people to a house in a country town was, according to the best statistical writers of the seventeenth century, 4·3. If that estimate be just, Leeds must, in 1663, have contained about 6000 souls. As it increased in trade and wealth during the reign of Charles II., we may well suppose that in 1685 the population was near 8000; that is to say, about as much as the population of Manchester. I had expected this result from observing that by the writers of that time Manchester and Leeds are always mentioned as of about the same size. But this evidence proves to demonstration either that there was some mistake about the number of burials, or that the year 1685 was a singularly unhealthy year, from which no inference can be drawn. One person must have died in every third house within twelve months; a rate of mortality quite frightful. Ever yours,   T. B. Macaulay.

It must be remembered that these letters represent only a part of the trouble which Macaulay underwent in order to insure the correctness of five and a half lines of print. He had a right to the feeling of self-satisfaction which, a month later

---

* The author of the " Municipal History of the Borough of Leeds."

on, allowed him to say: "I am working intensely, and, I hope, not unsuccessfully. My third chapter, which is the most difficult part of my task, is done, and, I think, not ill done." Any one who will turn to the description of the town of Leeds, and will read the six paragraphs that precede it and the three that follow it, may form a conception of the pains which those clear and flowing periods must have cost an author who expended on the pointing of a phrase as much conscientious research as would have provided some writers who speak of Macaulay as showy and shallow with at least half a dozen pages of ostentatious statistics.

On the 8th of February, 1849, after the publication of his first two volumes, he writes in his journal: "I have now made up my mind to change my plan about my 'History.' I will first set myself to know the whole subject; to get, by reading and traveling, a full acquaintance with William's reign. I reckon that it will take me eighteen months to do this. I must visit Holland, Belgium, Scotland, Ireland, France. The Dutch archives and French archives must be ransacked. I will see whether any thing is to be got from other diplomatic collections. I must see Londonderry, the Boyne, Aghrim, Limerick, Kinsale, Namur again, Landen, Steinkirk. I must turn over hundreds, thousands, of pamphlets. Lambeth, the Bodleian, and the other Oxford libraries,* the Devonshire

---

* "*October 2d*, 1854.—I called on the warden of All Souls', who was the only soul in residence. He was most kind; got me the manuscript of Narcissus Luttrell's Diary—seven thick volumes in cramped writing—put me into a comfortable room; and then left me to myself. I worked till past five; then walked for an hour or so, and dined at my inn, reading Cooper's 'Pathfinder.'

"*October 3d*.—I went to All Souls' at ten, and worked till five. Narcissus is dreadfully illegible in 1696; but that matters the less, as by that time the newspapers had come in. I found some curious things. The Jacobites had a way of drinking treasonable healths by limping about the rooms with glasses at their lips.

To limp meant L. Lewis XIV.
　　　　　　　　　　I. James.
　　　　　　　　　　M. Mary of Modena.
　　　　　　　　　　P. Prince of Wales.

Papers, the British Museum, must be explored, and notes made: and then I shall go to work. When the materials are ready, and the History mapped out in my mind, I ought easily to write, on an average, two of my pages daily. In two years from the time I begin writing I shall have more than finished my second part. Then I reckon a year for polishing, retouching, and printing. This brings me to the autumn of 1853. I like this scheme much. I began to-day with Avaux's dispatches from Ireland, abstracted almost a whole thick volume, and compared his narrative with James's. There is much to be said as to these events."

This programme was faithfully carried out. He saw Glencoe in rain and in sunshine: "Yet even with sunshine what a place it is! The very valley of the shadow of death." He paid a second visit to Killiecrankie for the special purpose of walking up the old road which skirts the Garry, in order to verify the received accounts of the time spent by the English army in mounting the pass which they were to descend at a quicker rate. The notes made during his fortnight's tour through the scenes of the Irish war are equal in bulk to a first-class article in the *Edinburgh* or *Quarterly Reviews*. He gives four closely written folio pages to the Boyne, and six to Londonderry. It is interesting to compare the shape which each idea took as it arose in his mind, with the shape in which he eventually gave it to the world. As he drove up the river from Drogheda he notices that "the country looked like a flourishing part of England. Corn-fields, gardens, woods, succeeded each other just as in Kent and Warwickshire." And again: "Handsome seats, fields of wheat and clover, noble trees: it would be called a fine country even in Somerset-

---

"*October 4th.*—I have done with All Souls'. At ten I went to the Bodleian. I got out the Tanner MSS., and worked on them two or three hours. Then the Wharton MSS. Then the far more remarkable Nairne MSS. At three they rang me out. I do think that from ten to three is a very short time to keep so noble a library open.

"*October 5th.*—Pamphlets in abundance; but pamphlets I can get elsewhere; so I fell on the Nairne MSS. again. I could amuse myself here ten years without a moment of ennui."

shire." In the sixteenth chapter of the "History" these hasty jottings have been transmuted into the sentences: "Beneath lay a valley now so rich and so cheerful that an Englishman who gazes on it may imagine himself to be in one of the most highly favored parts of his own highly favored country. Fields of wheat, woodlands, meadows bright with daisies and clover, slope gently down to the edge of the Boyne."

Macaulay passed two days in Londonderry, and made the most of each minute of daylight. He penetrated into every corner where there still lurked a vestige of the past, and called upon every inhabitant who was acquainted with any tradition worth the hearing. He drove through the suburbs; he sketched a ground-plan of the streets; alone or in company, he walked four times round the walls of the city for which he was to do what Thucydides had done for Platæa. A few extracts from the voluminous records of those two days will give some notion of what Macaulay meant by saying that he had seen a town.

"*August* 31*st*, 1849.—I left a card for Captain Leach, of the Ordnance Survey, and then wandered round the walls, and saw the cathedral. It has been spoiled by architects, who tried to imitate the Gothic style without knowing what they were about.* The choir, however, is neat and interesting. Leach came, a sensible, amiable young officer, as far as I could judge. I went again round the walls with him. The circuit is a short one. It may be performed, I should say, in twenty minutes. Then we got into a car, crossed the wooden bridge, and took a view of the city from the opposite bank of the river. Walker's pillar† is well placed, and is not con-

---

* "On the highest ground stood the cathedral, a church which, though erected when the secret of Gothic architecture was lost, and though ill qualified to sustain a comparison with the awful temples of the Middle Ages, is not without grace and dignity."—*Macaulay's History of England*, ch. xii.

† "A lofty pillar, rising from a bastion which bore during many weeks the heaviest fire of the enemy, is seen far up and far down the Foyle. On the summit is the statue of Walker, such as when, in the last and most terrible emergency, his eloquence roused the fainting courage of his brethren. In one hand he grasps a Bible. The other, pointing down the river, seems to direct the eyes of his famished audience to the English topmasts in the distant bay."

temptible. The honest divine, in his canonicals, haranguing with vehemence, is at the top, and makes a tolerable figure at some distance. Then we crossed again, and drove to Boom Hall, so called from the memorable boom. The mistress of the house, a very civil lady, came out and acted as cicerone. We walked down to the very spot where the boom was fastened. It was secured by a chain which passed through the earth of the bank, and was attached to a huge stone. Our hospitable guide would insist that an iron ring fixed in one of the rocks close by had been part of the apparatus to secure the boom. I felt very skeptical, and my doubts were soon changed into certainties; for I lifted up my eyes, and, about fifty yards off, I saw just such another ring fastened to another rock. I did not tell the good lady what I thought, but, as soon as we had taken our leave, I told Leach that these rings were evidently put there for the same purpose, that of securing shipping. He quite agreed with me, and seemed to admire my sagacious incredulity a great deal more than it at all deserved."

" *Saturday, September 1st.*—As soon as I had breakfasted, Sir R. Ferguson came and walked round the walls with me. Then he took me to the reading-room, where I met Captain Leach, and a Mr. Gilmour, a great man here. They walked with me round the walls, which I have thus gone over four times. The bastions are planted as gardens. The old pieces of ordnance lie among the flowers and shrubs—strange, antique guns of the time of Elizabeth and Charles the First: Roaring Meg, a present of the fishmongers, with the date 1642; another piece of the same date, given by the vintners; and another by the merchant tailors. The citizens are to the last degree jealous of the integrity of these walls.*   No improvement which would deface them would be proposed without raising a storm: and I do not blame them. Every stone has some fact, or at least some legend, connected with it. I found no difficulty, sometimes, in separating the facts from the legends. The picture of the whole is in my mind, and I do not know that there would be any advantage in putting the plan on paper."

---

* "The wall is carefully preserved; nor would any plea of health or convenience be held by the inhabitants sufficient to justify the demolition of that sacred inclosure, which, in the evil time, gave shelter to their race and their religion........ It is impossible not to respect the sentiment which indicates itself by these tokens. It is a sentiment which belongs to the higher and purer part of human nature, and which adds not a little to the strength of States. A people which takes no pride in the noble achievements of remote ancestors will never achieve any thing to be remembered with pride by remote descendants. Yet it is impossible for the moralist or the statesman to look with unmixed complacency on the solemnities with which Londonderry commemorates her deliverance, and on the honors which she pays to those who saved her."

Put it on paper, however, he did; and indeed, when employed upon his "History," he habitually preserved in writing such materials as were gathered elsewhere than from the shelves of his own library, instead of continuing the facile, though hazardous, course which he had pursued as a reviewer, and trusting to his memory alone. The fruits of many a long hour passed among the Pepysian book-cases, the manuscripts at Althorp, or the archives of the French War Office, were garnered into a multitude of pocket-books of every possible shape and color. Of these a dozen still remain, ready to the hands of any among Macaulay's remote heirs, who may be tempted to commit the posthumous treachery of publishing the commonplace-book of a great writer.

His industry has had its reward. The extent and exactness of his knowledge have won him the commendation of learned and candid writers who have traveled over ground which he has trod before. Each, in his own particular field, recognizes the high quality of Macaulay's work; and there is no testimonial so valuable as the praise of an enlightened specialist. Such praise has been freely given by Mr. Bagehot, the editor of the *Economist*, in that delightful treatise which goes by the name of "Lombard Street." He commences one important section of the book with the sentence in which, except for its modesty, I am unwilling to find a fault: "The origin of the Bank of England has been told by Macaulay, and it is never wise for an ordinary writer to tell again what he has told so much better." And Mr. Buckle, who was as well acquainted with the social manners of our ancestors as is Mr. Bagehot with their finance, appends the following note to what is perhaps the most interesting chapter in his "History of Civilization:" "Every thing Mr. Macaulay has said on the contempt into which the clergy fell in the reign of Charles the Second is perfectly accurate;[*] and, from evidence which I have collected, I know that this very able writer, of whose immense

---

[*] "I shall soon have done this ecclesiastical part of my narrative. Some people may imagine that I infer too much from slight indications; but no one who has not soaked his mind with the transitory literature of the day is really entitled to judge."—*Macaulay's Journal.*

research few people are competent judges, has rather under-stated the case than overstated it. On several subjects I should venture to differ from Mr. Macaulay; but I can not re-frain from expressing my admiration of his unwearied dili-gence, of the consummate skill with which he has arranged his materials, and of the noble love of liberty which animates his entire work. These are qualities which will long survive the aspersions of his puny detractors—men who, in point of knowledge and ability, are unworthy to loosen the shoe-latchet of him they foolishly attack."

The main secret of Macaulay's success lay in this, that to extraordinary fluency and facility he united patient, minute, and persistent diligence. He well knew, as Chaucer knew before him, that

> There is na workeman
> That can bothe worken wel and hastilie.
> This must be done at leisure parfaitlie.

If his method of composition ever comes into fashion, books probably will be better, and undoubtedly will be shorter. As soon as he had got into his head all the information relating to any particular episode in his "History" (such, for instance, as Argyll's expedition to Scotland, or the attainder of Sir John Fenwick, or the calling in of the clipped coinage), he would sit down and write off the whole story at a headlong pace; sketching in the outlines under the genial and audacious im-pulse of a first conception; and securing in black and white each idea, and epithet, and turn of phrase, as it flowed straight from his busy brain to his rapid fingers. His manuscript, at this stage, to the eyes of any one but himself, appeared to con-sist of column after column of dashes and flourishes, in which a straight line, with a half-formed letter at each end and another in the middle, did duty for a word. It was from amidst a chaos of such hieroglyphics that Lady Trevelyan, after her brother's death, deciphered that account of the last days of William which fitly closes the "History."*

---

* Lord Carlisle relates how Mr. Prescott, as a brother historian, was much interested by the sight of these manuscript sheets, "in which words are as much abbreviated as 'cle' for 'castle.'"

As soon as Macaulay had finished his rough draft, he began to fill it in at the rate of six sides of foolscap every morning; written in so large a hand, and with such a multitude of erasures,* that the whole six pages were, on an average, compressed into two pages of print. This portion he called his "task," and he was never quite easy unless he completed it daily. More he seldom sought to accomplish; for he had learned by long experience that this was as much as he could do at his best; and, except when at his best, he never would work at all. "I had no heart to write," he says in his journal of March 6th, 1851. "I am too self-indulgent in this matter, it may be: and yet I attribute much of the success which I have had to my habit of writing only when I am in the humor, and of stopping as soon as the thoughts and words cease to flow fast. There are, therefore, few lees in my wine. It is all the cream of the bottle."†

---

* Mr. Woodrow, in the preface to his collection of the Indian Education minutes, says: "Scarcely five consecutive lines in any of Macaulay's minutes will be found unmarked by blots or corrections. He himself, in a minute dated November 3d, 1835, says, 'After blotting a great deal of paper, I can recommend nothing but a reference to the governor-general in Council.' My copyist was always able instantly to single out his writing by the multiplicity of corrections and blots which mark the page. These corrections are now exceedingly valuable. When the first master of the English language corrects his own composition, which appeared faultless before, the correction must be based on the highest rules of criticism."

† In small things as well as in great, Macaulay held that what was worth doing at all was worth doing well. He had promised to compose an epitaph for his uncle, Mr. Babington. In June, 1851, he writes: "My delay has not arisen from any want of respect or tenderness for my uncle's memory. I loved and honored him most sincerely. But the truth is, that I have not been able to satisfy myself. People who are not accustomed to this sort of literary exercise often imagine that a man can do it as he can work a sum in rule of three, or answer an invitation to dinner. But these short compositions, in which every word ought to tell strongly, and in which there ought to be at once some point and much feeling, are not to be produced by mere labor. There must be a concurrence of luck with industry. It is natural that those who have not considered the matter should think that a man, who has sometimes written ten or twelve effective pages in a day, must certainly be able to write five lines in less than a

Macaulay never allowed a sentence to pass muster until it was as good as he could make it. He thought little of recasting a chapter in order to obtain a more lucid arrangement, and nothing whatever of reconstructing a paragraph for the sake of one happy stroke or apt illustration. Whatever the worth of his labor, at any rate it was a labor of love.

> Antonio Stradivari has an eye
> That winces at false work, and loves the true.

Leonardo da Vinci would walk the whole length of Milan that he might alter a single tint in his picture of the Last Supper. Napoleon kept the returns of his army under his pillow at night, to refer to in case he was sleepless; and would set himself problems at the Opera while the overture was playing: "I have ten thousand men at Strasbourg; fifteen thousand at Magdeburg; twenty thousand at Wurtzburg. By what stages must they march so as to arrive at Ratisbon on three successive days?" What his violins were to Stradivarius, and his fresco to Leonardo, and his campaigns to Napoleon, that was his "History" to Macaulay. How fully it occupied his thoughts did not appear in his conversation; for he steadily and successfully resisted any inclination to that most subtle form of selfishness which often renders the period of literary creation one long penance to all the members of an author's family. But none the less his book was always in his mind; and seldom, indeed, did he pass a day, or turn over a volume, without lighting upon a suggestion which could be turned to useful purpose. In May, 1851, he writes: "I went to the Exhibition, and lounged there during some hours. I never knew a sight which extorted from all ages, classes, and nations such unanimous and genuine admiration. I felt a glow of eloquence, or something like it, come on me from the mere effect of the place, and I thought of some touches which will

---

year. But it is not so; and if you think over the really good epitaphs which you have read, and consider how small a proportion they bear to the thousands that have been written by clever men, you will own that I am right."

greatly improve my Steinkirk." It is curious to trace whence was derived the fire which sparkles through every line of that terse and animated narrative, which has preserved from unmerited oblivion the story of a defeat more glorious to the British arms than not a few of our victories.

Macaulay deserved the compliment which Cecil paid to Sir Walter Raleigh as the supreme of commendations: "I know that he can labor terribly." One example will serve for many, in order to attest the pains which were ungrudgingly bestowed upon every section of the "History:"

"*March 21st.*—To-morrow I must begin upon a difficult and painful subject, Glencoe."

"*March 23d.*—I looked at some books about Glencoe. Then to the Athenæum, and examined the Scotch Acts of Parliament on the same subject. Walked a good way, meditating. I see my line. Home, and wrote a little, but thought and prepared more."

"*March 25th.*—Wrote a little. Mr. Lovell Reeve, editor of the *Literary Gazette,* called, and offered to defend me about Penn. I gave him some memoranda. Then to Glencoe again, and worked all day with energy, pleasure, and, I think, success."

"*March 26th.*—Wrote much. I have seldom worked to better purpose than on these three days."

"*March 27th.*—After breakfast I wrote a little, and then walked through April weather to Westbourne Terrace, and saw my dear little nieces.* Home, and wrote more. I am getting on fast with this most horrible story. It is even worse than I thought. The Master of Stair is a perfect Iago."

"*March 28th.*—I went to the Museum, and made some extracts about Glencoe."

On the 29th, 30th, and 31st of March, and the 1st and 2d of April, there is nothing relating to the "History" except the daily entry, "Wrote."

"*April 3d.*—Wrote. This Glencoe business is infernal."

"*April 4th.*—Wrote; walked round by London Bridge, and wrote again. To-day I finished the massacre. This episode will, I hope, be interesting."

"*April 6th.*—Wrote to good purpose."

"*April 7th.*—Wrote and corrected. The account of the massacre is now, I think, finished."

---

* In the summer of 1849 my father changed house from Clapham Common to No. 20 Westbourne Terrace.

"*April 8th.*—I went to the Museum, and turned over the *Gazette de Paris,* and the Dutch dispatches of 1692. I learned much from the errors of the French Gazette, and from the profound silence of the Dutch ministers on the subject of Glencoe. Home, and wrote."

"*April 9th.*—A rainy and disagreeable day. I read a 'Life of Romney,' which I picked up uncut in Chancery Lane yesterday: a quarto. That there should be two showy quarto lives of a man who did not deserve a duodecimo! Wrote hard, rewriting Glencoe."

"*April 10th.*—Finished 'Don Carlos.' I have been long about it; but twenty pages a day in bed while I am waiting for the newspaper will serve to keep up my German. A fine play, with all its faults. Schiller's good and evil genius struggled in it; as Shakspeare's good and evil genius, to compare greater things with smaller, struggled in 'Romeo and Juliet.' 'Carlos' is half by the author of 'The Robbers' and half by the author of 'Wallenstein;' as 'Romeo and Juliet' is half by the author of 'Love's Labor Lost' and half by the author of 'Othello.' After 'Romeo and Juliet' Shakspeare never went back, nor Schiller after 'Carlos.' Wrote all the morning, and then to Westbourne Terrace. I chatted, played chess, and dined there."

"*April 11th.*—Wrote all the morning. Ellis came to dinner. I read him Glencoe. He did not seem to like it much, which vexed me, though I am not partial to it. It is a good thing to find sincerity."

That author must have had a strong head, and no very exaggerated self-esteem, who, while fresh from a literary success which had probably never been equaled, and certainly never surpassed—at a time when the book-sellers were waiting with almost feverish eagerness for any thing that he chose to give them—spent nineteen working days over thirty octavo pages, and ended by humbly acknowledging that the result was not to his mind.

When at length, after repeated revisions, Macaulay had satisfied himself that his writing was as good as he could make it, he would submit it to the severest of all tests, that of being read aloud to others. Though he never ventured on this experiment in the presence of any except his own family and his friend Mr. Ellis, it may well be believed that, even within that restricted circle, he had no difficulty in finding hearers. "I read," he says in December, 1849, "a portion of my 'History' to Hannah and Trevelyan with great effect. Hannah cried, and Trevelyan kept awake. I think what I have done as good as any part of the former volumes: and so thinks Ellis."

Whenever one of his books was passing through the press, Macaulay extended his indefatigable industry and his scrupulous precision to the minutest mechanical drudgery of the literary calling. There was no end to the trouble that he devoted to matters which most authors are only too glad to leave to the care and experience of their publisher. He could not rest until the lines were level to a hair's breadth, and the punctuation correct to a comma; until every paragraph concluded with a telling sentence, and every sentence flowed like running water.* I remember the pleasure with which he showed us a communication from one of the readers in Mr. Spottiswoode's office, who respectfully informed him that there was one expression, and one only, throughout the two volumes of which he did not catch the meaning at a glance. And it must be remembered that Macaulay's punctilious attention to details was prompted by an honest wish to increase the enjoyment, and smooth the difficulties, of those who did him the honor to buy his books. His was not the accuracy of those who judge it necessary to keep up a distinction in small mat-

---

* Macaulay writes to Mr. Longman about the edition of 1858: "I have no more corrections to make at present. I am inclined to hope that the book will be as nearly faultless, as to typographical execution, as any work of equal extent that is to be found in the world."

On another occasion he says: "I am very unwilling to seem captious about such a work as an Index. By all means let Mr. —— go on. But offer him, with all delicacy and courtesy, from me this suggestion: I would advise him to have very few heads except proper names. A few there must be, such as Convocation, Non-jurors, Bank of England, National Debt. These are heads to which readers who wish for information on those subjects will naturally turn. But I think that Mr. —— will, on consideration, perceive that such heads as Priestcraft, Priesthood, Party Spirit, Insurrection, War, Bible, Crown, Controversies, Dissent, are quite useless. Nobody will ever look at them; and if every passage in which party spirit, dissent, the art of war, and the power of the crown are mentioned is to be noticed in the Index, the size of the volumes will be doubled. The best rule is to keep close to proper names, and never to deviate from the rule without some special occasion."

ters between the learned and the unlearned. As little of a
purist as it is possible for a scholar to be, his distaste for Mr.
Grote's exalted standard of orthography interfered sadly with
his admiration for the judgment, the power, and the knowledge of that truly great historian. He never could reconcile
himself to seeing the friends of his boyhood figure as Kleon,
and Alkibiadês, and Poseidôn, and Odysseus; and I tremble
to think of the outburst of indignation with which, if he had
lived to open some of the more recent editions of the Latin
poets, he would have lighted upon the " Dialogue with Lydia,"
or the "Ode to Lyce," printed with a small letter at the head
of each familiar line.

Macaulay's correspondence in the summer and autumn of
1848 is full of allusions to his great work, the first volumes
of which were then in the hands of the publisher. On the
22d of June he writes to Mr. Longman: "If you wish to say,
'History of England from the Accession of James II.,' I have
no objection; but I can not consent to put in any thing about
an Introductory Essay. There is no Introductory Essay, unless you call the first Book of Davila, and the first three chapters of Gibbon, Introductory Essays." In a letter to his sister Selina he says: " Longman seems content with his bargain.
Jeffrey, Ellis, and Hannah all agree in predicting that the
book will succeed. I ought to add Marian Ellis's judgment;
for her father tells me that he can not get the proof-sheets
out of her hand. These things keep up my spirits: yet I see
every day more and more clearly how far my performance is
below excellence." On the 24th of October, 1848, he writes
to my mother: "I do not know whether you have heard how
pleasant a day Margaret passed with me. We had a long
walk, a great deal of chat, a very nice dinner, and a quiet,
happy evening. That was my only holiday last week. I
work with scarcely any intermission from seven in the morning to seven in the afternoon, and shall probably continue to
do so during the next ten days. Then my labors will become lighter, and, in about three weeks, will completely cease.
There will still be a fortnight before publication. I have
armed myself with all my philosophy for the event of a failure.

Jeffrey, Ellis, Longman, and Mrs. Longman seem to think that there is no chance of such a catastrophe. I might add Macleod, who has read the third chapter, and professes to be, on the whole, better pleased than with any other history that he has read. The state of my own mind is this: when I compare my book with what I imagine history ought to be, I feel dejected and ashamed; but when I compare it with some histories which have a high repute, I feel re-assured."

He might have spared his fears. Within three days after its first appearance the fortune of the book was already secure. It was greeted by an ebullition of national pride and satisfaction which delighted Macaulay's friends, and reconciled to him most who remained of his old political adversaries. Other hands than his have copied and preserved the letters of congratulation and approval which for months together flowed in upon him from every quarter of the compass; but prudence forbids me to admit into these pages more than a very few samples of a species of correspondence which forms the most uninviting portion of only too many literary biographies. It is, however, worth while to reproduce the phrases in which Lord Halifax expressed the general feeling that the "History" was singularly well-timed. "I have finished," he writes, "your second volume, and I can not tell you how grateful all lovers of truth, all lovers of liberty, all lovers of order and of civilized freedom, ought to be to you for having so set before them the History of our Revolution of 1688. It has come at a moment when the lessons it inculcates ought to produce great practical effects on the conduct of the educated leaders of what is now going on abroad; but I fear that the long education in the working of a constitution such as ours is not to be supplied by any reading or meditation. Jameses we may find; but Europe shows no likeness of William."

"My dear Macaulay," says Lord Jeffrey, "the mother that bore you, had she been yet alive, could scarcely have felt prouder or happier than I do at this outburst of your graver fame. I have long had a sort of parental interest in your glory; and it is now mingled with a feeling of deference to your intellectual superiority which can only consort, I take it, with the character of a female parent."

A still older friend even than Lord Jeffrey — Lord Auckland, the Bishop of Sodor and Man—wrote of him in more racy, but not less affectionate, language. "Tom Macaulay should be embalmed and kept. I delight in his book, though luckily I am not half through it, for I have just had an ordination, and my house is pervaded by Butler's 'Analogy' and young priests. Do you think that Tom is not a little hard on old Cranmer? He certainly brings him down a peg or two in my estimation. I had also hated Cromwell more than I now do; for I always agree with Tom; and it saves trouble to agree with him at once, because he is sure to make you do so at last. Since I have had this book I have hated the best insular friend we have for coming in and breaking up the evening. At any other crisis we should have embraced him on both sides of his face."

Among all the incidents connected with the publication of his "History," nothing pleased Macaulay so much as the gratification that he contrived to give to Maria Edgeworth, as a small return for the enjoyment which, during more than forty years, he had derived from her charming writings.* That lady, who was then in her eighty-third winter, and within a few months of her death, says, in the course of a letter addressed to Dr. Holland: "And now, my good friend, I require you to believe that all the admiration I have expressed of Macaulay's work is quite uninfluenced by the self-satisfaction, vanity, pride, surprise, I had in finding my own name in a note!!!!! I had formed my opinion, and expressed it to my friends who were reading the book to me, before I came to that note.† Moreover, there was a mixture of shame, and

---

* Macaulay on one occasion pronounces that the scene in the "Absentee," where Lord Colambre discovers himself to his tenantry and to their oppressor, is the best thing of the sort since the opening of the Twenty-second book of the "Odyssey."

† This note is in the sixth chapter, at the bottom of a page describing the habits of the old native Irish proprietors in the seventeenth century: "Miss Edgeworth's King Corny belongs to a later and much more civ-

a twinge of pain, with the pleasure and the pride I felt in
having a line in this immortal 'History' given to *me*, when
there is no mention of Sir Walter Scott throughout the work,
even in places where it seems impossible that the historian
could resist paying the becoming tribute which genius owes,
and loves to pay, to genius.   Perhaps he reserves himself for
the '45 ; and I hope in heaven it is so.   Meanwhile be so good
as to make my grateful and deeply felt thanks to the great
author for the honor which he has done me."

Macaulay's journal will relate the phases and gradations
which marked the growing popularity of his book, in so far
as that popularity could be measured by the figures in a publisher's ledger.   But, over and above Mr. Longman's triumphant bulletins, every day brought to his ears a fresh indication
of the hold which the work had taken on the public mind.
Some of the instances which he has recorded are quaint
enough.   An officer of good family had been committed for
a fortnight to the House of Correction for knocking down a
policeman.   The authorities intercepted the prisoner's French
novels, but allowed him to have the Bible, and Macaulay's
" History."*   At Dukinfield, near Manchester, a gentleman
who thought that there would be a certain selfishness in keeping so great a pleasure to himself, invited his poorer neighbors to attend every evening after their work was finished,
and read the " History " aloud to them from beginning to
end.   At the close of the last meeting, one of the audience
rose, and moved, in North-country fashion, a vote of thanks to

---

ilized generation; but whoever has studied that admirable portrait can
form some notion of what King Corny's great-grandfather must have
been."

* London gossip went on to say that the gallant captain preferred picking oakum to reading about the Revolution of 1688 ; gossip which avenged
Guicciardini for the anecdote told by Macaulay in the second paragraph of
his "Essay on Burleigh."

"There was, it is said, a criminal in Italy, who was suffered to make his
choice between Guicciardini and the galleys.   He chose the history.   But
the war of Pisa was too much for him.   He changed his mind, and went
to the oar."

Mr. Macaulay, "for having written a history which working-men can understand."*

The people of the United States were even more eager than the people of the United Kingdom to read about their common ancestors; with the advantage that, from the absence of an international copyright, they were able to read about them for next to nothing. On the 4th of April, 1849, Messrs. Harper, of New York, wrote to Macaulay: "We beg you to accept herewith a copy of our cheap edition of your work. There have been three other editions published by different houses, and another is now in preparation; so there will be six different editions in the market. We have already sold forty thousand copies, and we presume that over sixty thousand copies have been disposed of. Probably, within three months of this time, the sale will amount to two hundred thousand copies. No work, of any kind, has ever so completely taken our whole country by storm." An indirect compliment to the celebrity of the book was afforded by a desperate, and almost internecine, controversy which raged throughout the American newspapers as to whether the Messrs. Harper were justified in having altered Macaulay's spelling to suit the orthographical canons laid down in Noah Webster's dictionary.

Nor were the enterprising publishers of Paris and Brussels behindhand in catering for readers whose appetite for cheap literature made them less particular than they should have been as to the means by which they gratified it. *Punch* devoted half of one of his columns to a serio-comic review of Galignani's edition of the "History:"

"This is an extraordinary work. A miracle of cheapness. A handsomely printed book, in royal octavo (if any thing be royal in republican France), and all at the low charge of some 7s. 6d. of English money. Many thousands of this impression of Mr. Macaulay's works—it must delight his *amour propre* as an author to know it—have been circulated in England. 'Sir,' said a Boulogne book-seller, his voice slightly trembling

---

* Macaulay says in his journal, "I really prize this vote."

with emotion, 'Sir, it is impossible to supply travelers; but we expect a few thousand kilogrammes more of the work by to-morrow's train, and then, for a week, we may rub on.' It is cheering to find that French, Belgian, and American book-sellers are doing their best to scatter abroad, and at home too, the seeds of English literature. 'Sir,' said the French book-seller, holding up the tome, 'you will smuggle it thus: divide the book in two; spread it over your breast; button your waist-coat close; and, when you land, look the picture of innocence in the face of the searchers.'"

It is a characteristic trait in Macaulay that, as soon as his last proof-sheet had been dispatched to the printers, he at once fell to reading a course of historians, from Herodotus down-ward. The sense of his own inferiority to Thucydides did more to put him out of conceit with himself than all the un-favorable comments which were bestowed upon him (sparing-ly enough, it must be allowed) by the newspapers and reviews of the day. He was even less thin-skinned as a writer than as a politician. When he felt conscious that he had done his very best—when all that lay within his own power had been faithfully and diligently performed—it was not his way to chafe under hostile criticism, or to waste time and temper by engaging in controversies on the subject of his own works. Like Dr. Johnson, "he had learned, both from his own obser-vation and from literary history, in which he was deeply read, that the place of books in the public estimation is fixed, not by what is written about them, but by what is written in them; and that an author whose works are likely to live is very unwise if he stoops to wrangle with detractors whose works are certain to die." "I have never been able," Mac-aulay says, in a letter dated December, 1849, "to discover that a man is at all the worse for being attacked. One foolish line of his own does him more harm than the ablest pamphlets written against him by other people."

It must be owned that, as far as his "History" was con-cerned, Macaulay had not occasion to draw largely upon his stock of philosophy. Some few notes of disapprobation and detraction might here and there be heard; but they were for the most part too faint to mar the effect produced by so full a chorus of eulogy; and the only loud one among them was harsh and discordant to that degree that all the by-standers were fain to stop their ears. It was generally believed that Mr. Croker had long been praying that he might be spared to settle accounts with his old antagonist. His opportunity had now arrived; and people gave themselves up with a safer conscience to the fascination of the historian's narrative, because the *Quarterly Review* would be certain to inform them of all that could be said either against the book or against the author. But Macaulay's good fortune attended him even here. He could not have fared better had he been privileged to choose his own adversary, and to select the very weapons with which the assault was to be conducted. After spending four most unprofitable months in preparing his thunder, Mr. Croker discharged it in an article so bitter, so foolish, and, above all, so tedious, that scarcely any body could get through it, and nobody was convinced by it. Many readers, who looked to professional critics for an authoritative opinion on the learning and accuracy of a contemporary writer, came to the not unreasonable conclusion that the case against Macaulay had irretrievably broken down, when they saw how little had been made of it by so acrimonious and so long-winded an advocate. Nothing would have opened the pages of the *Quarterly Review* to that farrago of angry trash except the deference with which its proprietor thought himself bound to treat one who, forty years before, had assisted Canning to found the periodical. The sole effect which the article produced upon the public was to set it reading Macaulay's review of Croker's "Boswell," in order to learn what the injury might be which, after the lapse of eighteen years, had sting enough left to provoke a veteran writer, politician, and man of the world into such utter oblivion of common sense, common fairness, and common courtesy.

The Whig press, headed by the *Times* and the *Scotsman*, hastened to defend the historian; and the Tory press was at least equally forward to disown the critic. A subsequent page in this volume will show that Croker's arrow did not go

very far home. Indeed, in the whole of Macaulay's journal
for the year 1849 there can be detected but one single indication of his having possessed even the germ of an author's sensibility: "*February 17th.*—I went to the Athenæum, and saw
in a weekly literary journal a silly, spiteful attack on what
I have said about Procopius in the first pages of my first
chapter. I was vexed for a moment, but only for a moment.
Both Austin and Mahon had looked into Procopius, and were
satisfied that I was right; as I am. I shall take no notice."
A year later he wrote to Mr. Longman: "I have looked
through the tenth volume of Lingard's 'History' in the new
edition. I am not aware that a single error has been pointed
out by Lingard in my narrative. His estimate of men and of
institutions naturally differs from mine. There is no direct
reference to me, but much pilfering from me, and a little carping at me. I shall take no notice either of the pilfering or
the carping." After once his judgment had become mature,
Macaulay, at all times and under all temptations, acted in
strict accordance with Bentley's famous maxim (which, in
print and talk alike, he dearly loved to quote), that no man
was ever written down, except by himself.[*]

"Lord Macaulay," said an acute observer, who knew him
well, "is an almost unique instance of a man of transcendent

---

[*] Bentley's career was one long exemplification of his famous saying.
In the year 1856, Macaulay writes, after what was perhaps his tenth repe-
rusal of Bishop Monk's life of the great critic: "Bentley seems to me an
eminent instance of the extent to which intellectual powers of a most rare
and admirable kind may be impaired by moral defects. It was not on account of any obscuration of his memory, or of any decay in his inventive
faculties, that he fell from the very first place among critics to the third
or fourth rank. It was his insolence, his arrogance, his boundless confidence in himself and disdain of every body else, that lowered him. Instead of taking subjects which he thoroughly understood, and which he
would have treated better than all the other scholars in Europe together,
he would take subjects which he had but superficially studied. He ceased
to give his whole mind to what he wrote. He scribbled a dozen sheets of
Latin at a sitting, sent them to the press without reading them over, and
then, as was natural, had to bear the baiting of word-catching pedants
who were on the watch for all his blunders."

force of character, mighty will, mighty energy, giving all that
to literature instead of to practical work;" and it can not be
denied that, in his vocation of historian, he gave proof of qualities which would have commanded success in almost any field.
To sacrifice the accessory to the principal; to plan an extensive and arduous task, and to pursue it without remission and
without misgiving; to withstand resolutely all counter-attrac-
tions, whether they come in the shape of distracting pleasures
or of competing duties—such are the indispensable conditions
for attaining to that high and sustained excellence of artistic
performance which, in the beautiful words of George Eliot,
"must be wooed with industrious thought and patient renun-
ciation of small desires." At a period when the mere rumor
of his presence would have made the fortune of an evening in
any drawing-room in London, Macaulay consented to see less
and less, and at length almost nothing, of general society, in
order that he might devote all his energies to the work which
he had in hand. He relinquished that House of Commons
which the first sentence of his speeches hushed into silence,
and the first five minutes filled to overflowing. He watched,
without a shade of regret or a twinge of envy, men, who would
never have ventured to set their claims against his, rise one
after another to the summit of the State. "I am sincerely
glad," said Sir James Graham, "that Macaulay has so greatly
succeeded. The sacrifices which he has made to literature deserve no ordinary triumph; and, when the statesmen of this
present day are forgotten, the historian of the Revolution will
be remembered." Among men of letters there were some
who maintained that the fame of Macaulay's volumes exceeded their deserts; but his former rivals and colleagues in Parliament, one and all, rejoiced in the prosperous issue of an undertaking for the sake of which he had surrendered more than
others could ever hope to win.

CHAPTER XII.

1848–1852.

Extracts from Macaulay's Diary.—Herodotus.—Mr. Roebuck.—Anticipations of Failure and Success.—Appearance of the "History."—Progress
of the Sale.—Duke of Wellington.—Lord Palmerston.—Letters to Mr.
Ellis.—Lord Brougham on Euripides.—Macaulay is elected Lord Rector
of Glasgow University.—His Inaugural Address.—Good Resolutions.—
Croker.—Dr. Parr.—The Historical Professorship at Cambridge.—By-
ron.—Tour in Ireland.—Althorp.—Lord Sidmouth.—Lord Thurlow.—
Death of Jeffrey.—Mr. Richmond's Portrait of Macaulay.—Dinner at the
Palace.—Robert Montgomery.—Death of Sir Robert Peel.—The Prelude.
—Ventnor.—Letters to Mr. Ellis.—Plautus.—Fra Paolo.—Gibbon.—The
Papal Bull.—Death of Henry Hallam.—Porson's Letters to Archdeacon
Travis.— Charles Mathews. — Windsor Castle. — Macaulay sets up his
Carriage.—Opening of the Great Exhibition of 1851.—Cobbett.—Mal-
vern.—Letters to Mr. Ellis.—Wilhelm Meister.—The Battle of Worces-
ter.—Palmerston leaves the Foreign Office.—Macaulay refuses an Offer
of the Cabinet.—Windsor Castle.—King John.—Scene of the Assassination Plot.—Royal Academy Dinner.

"NOVEMBER 18th, 1848: *Albany.*—After the lapse of more than nine years
I begin my journal again.* What a change! I have been, since the last

---

* It must be remembered that whatever was in Macaulay's mind may be
found in his diary. That diary was written, throughout, with the unconscious candor of a man who freely and frankly notes down remarks which
he expects to be read by himself alone; and with the copiousness natural
to one who, except where it was demanded for the purpose of literary effect, did not willingly compress any thing which he had to say. It may,
therefore, be hoped that the extracts presented in these volumes possess
those qualities in which, as he has himself pronounced, the special merit of
a private journal lies. In a letter dated August 4th, 1853, he says: "The
article on the 'Life of Moore' is spiteful. Moore, however, afforded but
too good an opportunity to a malevolent assailant. His diary, it is evident
to me, was written to be published, and this destroys the charm proper to
diaries."

lines were written, a member of two Parliaments and of two Cabinets. I have published several volumes with success. I have escaped from Parliament, and am living in the way best suited to my temper. I lead a college life in London, with the comforts of domestic life near me; for Hannah and her children are very dear to me. I have an easy fortune. I have finished the first two volumes of my 'History.' Yesterday the last sheets went to America, and within a fortnight, I hope, the publication will take place in London. I am pretty well satisfied. As compared with excellence, the work is a failure; but, as compared with other similar books, I can not think so. We shall soon know what the world says. To-day I enjoyed my new liberty, after having been most severely worked during three months in finishing my 'History' and correcting proofs. I rose at half after nine, read at breakfast Fearon's 'Sketches of America,' and then finished Lucian's critique on the bad historians of his time, and felt my own withers unwrung. Ellis came to dinner at seven. I gave him a lobster curry, woodcock, and macaroni. I think that I will note dinners, as honest Pepys did."

"*Monday, November 20th.*—Read Pepys at breakfast, and then sat down to Herodotus, and finished 'Melpomene' at a sitting. I went out, looked into the Athenæum, and walked about the streets for some time; came home, and read 'Terpsichore,' and began 'Erato.' I never went through Herodotus at such a pace before. He is an admirable artist in many respects; but undoubtedly his arrangement is faulty."

"*November 23d.*—I received to-day a translation of Kant from Ellis's friend at Liverpool. I tried to read it, but found it utterly unintelligible, just as if it had been written in Sanskrit. Not one word of it gave me any thing like an idea except a Latin quotation from 'Persius.' It seems to me that it ought to be possible to explain a true theory of metaphysics in words which I can understand. I can understand Locke, and Berkeley, and Hume, and Reid, and Stewart. I can understand Cicero's Academics, and most of Plato: and it seems odd that in a book on the elements of metaphysics, by a Liverpool merchant, I should not be able to comprehend a word. I wrote my acknowledgments, with a little touch of the Socratic irony.

"Roebuck called, and talked to me about the West Riding. He asked me to stand. I told him that it was quite out of the question; that I had made up my mind never again to make the smallest concession to fanatical clamor on the subject of Papal endowment. I would not certainly advise the Government to propose such endowment, but I would say nothing tending to flatter the absurd prejudices which exist on that subject. I thanked him for his good-will, and asked him to breakfast on Monday. I find that Macculloch and Hastie have a wager on the sale of my 'History.' Macculloch has betted that it will sell better than Lord Campbell's book. Hastie bets on Lord Campbell. Green, of Longman's house, is to be arbiter."

"*November 25th.*—Read my book while dressing, and thought it better than Campbell's, with all deference to Mr. Hastie. But these things are a strange lottery. After breakfast I went to the British Museum. I was in the chair. It is a stupid, useless way of doing business. An hour was lost in reading trashy minutes. All boards are bad, and this is the worst of boards. If I live, I will see whether I can not work a reform here. Home, and read Thucydides. I admire him more than ever. He is the great historian. The others one may hope to match: him, never."

"*November 29th,* 1848, *Wednesday.*—I was shocked to learn the death of poor Charles Buller. It took me quite by surprise. I could almost cry for him.* I found copies of my 'History' on my table. The suspense must now soon be over. I read my book, and Thucydides's, which, I am sorry to say, I found much better than mine."

"*November 30th.*—Tufnell† sent for me, and proposed Liskeard to me. I hesitated; and went home, leaving the matter doubtful. Roebuck called at near seven to ask about my intentions, as he had also been thought of. This at once decided me; and I said that I would not stand, and wrote to Tufnell telling him so. Roebuck has on more than one occasion behaved to me with great kindness and generosity, and I did not choose to stand in his way."

"*December 4th,* 1848.—Staid at home all the day, making corrections for the second edition. Shaw, the printer, came to tell me that they are wanted with speed, and that the first edition of three thousand is nearly out. Then I read the eighth book of Thucydides. On the whole, he is the first of historians. What is good in him is better than any thing that can be found elsewhere. But his dry parts are dreadfully dry, and his arrangement is bad. Mere chronological order is not the order for a complicated narrative.

"I have felt to-day somewhat anxious about the fate of my book. The sale has surpassed expectation: but that proves only that people have formed a high idea of what they are to have. The disappointment, if there is disappointment, will be great. All that I hear is laudatory. But who can trust to praise which is poured into his own ear? At all events, I have aimed high; I have tried to do something that may be remembered;

---

* "In Parliament I shall look in vain for virtues which I loved, and for abilities which I admired. Often in debate, and never more than when we discuss those questions of colonial policy which are every day acquiring a new importance, I shall remember with regret how much eloquence and wit, how much acuteness and knowledge, how many engaging qualities, how many fair hopes, are buried in the grave of poor Charles Buller."— *Macaulay's Speech at Edinburgh in* 1852.

† Mr. Tufnell was then patronage secretary, or, in more familiar parlance, treasury whip.

I have had the year 2000, and even the year 3000, often in my mind; I have sacrificed nothing to temporary fashions of thought and style; and if I fail, my failure will be more honorable than nine-tenths of the successes that I have witnessed."

"*December 12th*, 1848.—Longman called. A new edition of three thousand copies is preparing as fast as they can work. I have reason to be pleased. Of the 'Lay of the Last Minstrel' two thousand two hundred and fifty copies were sold in the first year; of 'Marmion' two thousand copies in the first month; of my book three thousand copies in ten days. Black says that there has been no such sale since the days of 'Waverley.' The success is in every way complete beyond all hope, and is the more agreeable to me because expectation had been wound up so high that disappointment was almost inevitable. I think, though with some misgivings, that the book will live. I put two volumes of Foote into my pockets, and walked to Clapham. They were reading my book again. How happy their praise made me, and how little by comparison I care for any other praise! A quiet, happy, affectionate evening. Mr. Conybeare makes a criticism, in which Hannah seems to agree, that I sometimes repeat myself. I suspect there is truth in this. Yet it is very hard to know what to do. If an important principle is laid down only once, it is unnoticed or forgotten by dull readers, who are the majority. If it is inculcated in several places, quick-witted persons think that the writer harps too much on one string. Probably I have erred on the side of repetition. This is really the only important criticism that I have yet heard.

"I looked at the 'Life of Campbell,' by a foolish Dr. Beattie: a glorious specimen of the book-making of this age. Campbell may have written in all his life three hundred good lines, rather less than more. His letters, his conversation, were mere trash.* A life such as Johnson has written

---

* This was rather ungrateful to Campbell, who had provided Macaulay with an anecdote, which he told well and often, to illustrate the sentiment with which the authors of old days regarded their publishers. At a literary dinner Campbell asked leave to propose a toast, and gave the health of Napoleon Bonaparte. The war was at its height, and the very mention of Napoleon's name, except in conjunction with some uncomplimentary epithet, was in most circles regarded as an outrage. A storm of groans broke out, and Campbell with difficulty could get a few sentences heard. "Gentlemen," he said, "you must not mistake me. I admit that the French emperor is a tyrant. I admit that he is a monster. I admit that he is the sworn foe of our own nation, and, if you will, of the whole human race. But, gentlemen, we must be just to our great enemy. We must not forget that he once shot a book-seller." The guests, of whom two out of every three lived by their pens, burst into a roar of laughter, and Campbell sat down in triumph.

of Shenstone, or Akenside, would have been quite long enough for the subject; but here are three mortal volumes. I suppose that, if I die to-morrow, I shall have three volumes. Really, I begin to understand why Coleridge says that life in death is more horrible than death.

"I dined with Miss Berry. She and her guests made an idol of me: but I know the value of London idolatry, and how soon these fashions pass away."*

"*January 11th*, 1849.—I am glad to find how well my book continues to sell. The second edition of three thousand was out of print almost as soon as it appeared, and one thousand two hundred and fifty of the third edition are already bespoken. I hope all this will not make me a coxcomb. I feel no intoxicating effect; but a man may be drunk without knowing it. If my abilities do not fail me, I shall be a rich man; as rich, that is to say, as I wish to be. But that I am already, if it were not for my dear ones. I am content, and should have been so with less. On the whole, I remember no success so complete; and I remember all Byron's poems and all Scott's novels."

"*Saturday, January 27th*.—Longman has written to say that only sixteen hundred copies are left of the third edition of five thousand, and that two thousand more copies must be immediately printed, still to be called the third edition. I went into the City to discuss the matter, and found William Longman and Green. They convinced me that the proposed course was right; but I am half afraid of this strange prosperity. Thirteen thousand copies, they seem quite confident, will have been taken off in less than six months.† Of such a run I had never dreamed. But I had thought that the book would have a permanent place in our literature; and I see no reason to alter that opinion. Yet I feel extremely anxious about the second part. Can it possibly come up to the first? Does the subject admit of such vivid description and such exciting narrative? Will not the judgment of the public be unduly severe? All this disturbs me. Yet the risk must be run; and whatever art and labor can do shall be done."

"*February 2d*.—Mahon sent me a letter from Arbuthnot, saying that the Duke of Wellington was enthusiastic in admiration of my book. Though

---

* "There is nothing," Macaulay says elsewhere, "more pitiable than an ex-lion or ex-lioness. London, I have often thought, is like the sorceress in the 'Arabian Nights,' who, by some mysterious law, can love the same object only forty days. During forty days she is all fondness. As soon as they are over, she not only discards the poor favorite, but turns him into some wretched shape—a mangy dog or spavined horse. How many hundreds of victims have undergone this fate since I was born! The strongest instances, I think, have been Betty, who was called the young Roscius; Edward Irving; and Mrs. Beecher Stowe."

† As a matter of fact, they were taken off in less than four months.

I am almost callous to praise now, this praise made me happy for two minutes. A fine old fellow! The Quakers have fixed Monday at eleven for my opportunity.* Many a man, says Sancho, comes for wool, and goes home shorn. To dinner at Lansdowne House. All were kind and cordial. I thought myself agreeable, but perhaps I was mistaken. Lord Lansdowne almost made up his mind to come to the interview with the Quakers; but a sense of decorum withheld him. Lord Shelburne begged so hard to be admitted that I could not refuse him, though I must provide myself with a different kind of second in such a combat. Milman will come if he can."

"*Saturday, February 3d.*—Longman came. He brought two reviews of my book, *North British* and *British Quarterly*. When he was gone I read both. They are more than sufficiently eulogistic. In both there are squeezes of acid. Part of the censure I admit to be just, but not all. Much of the praise I know to be undeserved. I began my second part, and wrote two foolscap sheets. I am glad to see how well things are going in Parliament. Stanley is surely very foolish and inconsiderate. What would he have done if he had succeeded? He is a great debater; but as to every thing else he is still what he was thirty years ago, a clever boy. All right in the Commons. Excellent speech of Palmerston. What a knack he has for falling on his feet! I never will believe, after this, that there is any scrape out of which his cleverness and his good fortune will not extricate him. And I rejoice in his luck most sincerely; for, though he now and then trips, he is an excellent minister, and I can not bear the thought of his being a sacrifice to the spite of foreign powers."

Of all English statesmen, Macaulay liked Lord Palmerston the best; and never was that liking stronger than during the crisis through which the nations of the Continent were passing in 1848 and 1849. His heart was entirely with the minister who, whenever and wherever the interests of liberty and humanity were at stake, was eager to prove that those to whom the power of England was committed did not wield the pen, and on occasion did not bear the sword, in vain. But Palmerston's foreign policy was little to the taste of some among his political opponents. They had not been able to digest his civility to republican governments; nor could they forgive him for having approved the conduct of the admiral who anchored British men-of-war between the broadsides of

---

* A deputation from the Society of Friends proposed to wait upon Macaulay to remonstrate with him about his treatment of William Penn in the fifth and eighth chapters of the "History."

the King of Naples's ships and the defenseless streets of Palermo. An amendment on the Address was moved in both Houses, humbly representing to her majesty that her affairs were not in such a state as to justify Parliament in addressing her in the language of congratulation. The Peers, dazzled by Lord Stanley's reckless eloquence, ran the ministry within two votes of a defeat which, in the then existing condition of affairs abroad, would have been nothing short of a European calamity. In the Commons, Lord Palmerston opposed the amendment in a speech of extraordinary spirit,* which at once

---

* "If you say that you can not congratulate us, I say 'Wait till you are asked.' It would be highly improper to ask the House to express on the present occasion any opinion on the foreign relations of the country....... The real fault found with her majesty's Government is that we are not at war with some of our allies. Our great offense is that we have remained on amicable terms with the republican government of France. There are those who think that the government of a republic is not sufficiently good company for the government of a monarchy. Now, I hold that the relations between governments are, in fact, the relations between those nations to which the governments belong. What business is it of ours to ask whether the French nation thinks proper to be governed by a king, an emperor, a president, or a consul? Our object, and our duty, is to cement the closest ties of friendship between ourselves and our nearest neighbor —that neighbor who in war would be our most formidable enemy, and in peace our most useful ally....... This, then, is the state of the matter. We stand here charged with the grave offense of having preserved a good understanding with the republic of France, and of having thereby essentially contributed to the maintenance of peace in Europe. We are charged with having put an end to hostilities in Schleswig-Holstein which might have led to a European war. We are accused of having persuaded Austria and Sardinia to lay down their arms, when their differences might have involved the other powers of Europe in contention. We are reproached with having prevented great calamities in Sicily, and with laboring to restore friendly relations between the King of Naples and his subjects. These are the charges which the House is called upon to determine for, or against, us. We stand here as men who have labored assiduously to prevent war, and, where it had broken out, to put an end to it as soon as was practicable. We stand here as the promoters of peace under charges brought against us by the advocates of war. I leave it to the House to decide between us and our accusers, and I look forward with confidence to the verdict which the House will give."

decided the fortune of the debate; a motion for adjournment was thrown out by 221 votes to 80; and Mr. Disraeli, rightly interpreting the general feeling of the House, took the judicious course of withdrawing the hostile amendment.

"*Sunday, February 4th.*—I walked out to Clapham yesterday afternoon; had a quiet, happy evening; and went to church this morning. I love the church for the sake of old times. I love even that absurd painted window with the dove, the lamb, the urn, the two cornucopias, and the profusion of sunflowers, passion-flowers, and peonies. Heard a Puseyite sermon, very different from the oratory which I formerly used to hear from the same pulpit."

"*February 5th,* 1849.—Lord Shelburne, Charles Austin, and Milman to breakfast. A pleasant meal. Then the Quakers, five in number. Never was there such a rout. They had absolutely nothing to say. Every charge against Penn came out as clear as any case at the Old Bailey. They had nothing to urge but what was true enough: that he looked worse in my 'History' than he would have looked on a general survey of his whole life. But that is not my fault. I wrote the history of four years during which he was exposed to great temptations; during which he was the favorite of a bad king, and an active solicitor in a most corrupt court. His character was injured by his associations. Ten years before, or ten years later, he would have made a much better figure.* But was I to begin my book ten years earlier or ten years later for William Penn's sake? The Quakers were extremely civil. So was I. They complimented me on my courtesy and candor."

This will, perhaps, be the most convenient place to insert some extracts from Macaulay's letters to Mr. Ellis.

"Albany, January 10th, 1849.

"I have had a pastoral epistle in three sheets from St. Henry, of Exon, and have sent him three sheets in answer. We are the most courteous and affectionate of adversaries. You can not think how different an opinion I entertain of him since he has taken to subscribing himself, 'with very high esteem, my admiring reader.' How is it possible to hold out against a man whose censure is conveyed in the following sort of phrase?

---

* If Macaulay's "History" was not a Life of William Penn, this book is still less so. Those who are honorably jealous for Penn's reputation will forgive me if I do not express an opinion of my own with regard to the controversy; an opinion which, after all, would be valueless. In my uncle's papers there can be found no trace of his ever having changed his mind on the merits of the question.

'Pardon me if I say that a different course would have been more generous, more candid, more philosophical, all which I may sum up in the words, more like yourself.' This is the extreme point of his severity. And to think how long I have denied to this man all share of Christian charity!"*

"March 6th, 1849.

"Pray tell Adolphus how much obliged I am to him for his criticisms. I see that I now and then fell into error. I got into a passion with the Stuarts, and consequently did less damage than I should have done if I had kept my temper.

"I hear that Croker has written a furious article against me, and that Lockhart wishes to suppress it, declaring that the current of public opinion runs strongly on my side, and that a violent attack by a personal enemy will do no harm to me and much harm to the *Quarterly Review.* How they settle the matter I care not, as the duke says, one two-penny damn."†

"March 8th, 1849.

"At last I have attained true glory. As I walked through Fleet Street the day before yesterday, I saw a copy of Hume at a book-seller's window with the following label: 'Only £2 2s. Hume's "History of England," in eight volumes, highly valuable as an introduction to Macaulay.' I laughed so convulsively that the other people who were staring at the books took me for a poor demented gentleman. Alas for poor David! As for me, only one height of renown yet remains to be attained. I am not yet in Madame Tussaud's wax-work. I live, however, in hope of seeing one day an advertisement of a new group of figures—Mr. Macaulay, in one of

---

* Unfortunately, these were only the preliminaries of the combat. When the bishop passed from compliments to arguments, he soon showed that he had not forgotten his swashing blow. Macaulay writes with the air of a man whose sole object is to be out of a controversy on the shortest and the most civil terms. "Before another edition of my book appears, I shall have time to weigh your observations carefully, and to examine the works to which you have called my attention. You have convinced me of the propriety of making some alterations. But I hope that you will not accuse me of pertinacity if I add that, as far as I can at present judge, the alterations will be slight, and that on the great point at issue my opinion is unchanged." To this the bishop rejoins: "Do not think me very angry, when I say that a person *willing* to come to such a conclusion would make an invaluable foreman of a jury to convict another Algernon Sidney. Sincerely, I never met so monstrous an attempt to support a foregone conclusion."

† It was the Duke of Wellington who invented this oath, so disproportioned to the greatness of its author.

his own coats, conversing with Mr. Silk Buckingham in Oriental costume, and Mr. Robert Montgomery in full canonicals."

"March 9th, 1850.

"I hope that Roebuck will do well. If he fails, it will not be from the strength of his competitors. What a nerveless, milk-and-water set the young fellows of the present day are! —— —— declares that there is not in the whole House of Commons any stuff, under five-and-thirty, of which a junior lord of the treasury can be made. It is the same in literature, and, I imagine, at the bar. It is odd that the last twenty-five years, which have witnessed the greatest progress ever made in physical science —the greatest victories ever achieved by man over matter—should have produced hardly a volume that will be remembered in 1900, and should have seen the breed of great advocates and Parliamentary orators become extinct among us.

"One good composition of its kind was produced yesterday;* the judgment in Gorham's case. I hope you like it. I think it excellent, worthy of D'Aguesseau or Mansfield. I meant to have heard it delivered; but, when I came to Whitehall, I found the stairs, the passages, and the very street so full of parsons, Puseyite and Simeonite, that there was no access even for privy councilors; and, not caring to elbow so many successors of the apostles, I walked away.

"I have seen the hippopotamus, both asleep and awake; and I can assure you that, awake or asleep, he is the ugliest of the works of God. But you must hear of my triumphs. Thackeray swears that he was eye-witness and ear-witness of the proudest event of my life. Two damsels were just about to pass that door-way which we, on Monday, in vain attempted to enter, when I was pointed out to them. 'Mr. Macaulay!' cried the lovely pair. 'Is that Mr. Macaulay? Never mind the hippopotamus.' And, having paid a shilling to see Behemoth, they left him in the very moment at which he was about to display himself to them, in order to see—but spare my modesty. I can wish for nothing more on earth, now that Madame Tussaud, in whose Pantheon I once hoped for a place, is dead."

"*February 12th.*—I bought a superb sheet of paper for a guinea, and wrote on it a Valentine for Alice. I dined at Lady Charlotte Lindsay's with Hallam and Kinglake. I am afraid that I talked too much about my book. Yet really the fault was not mine. People would introduce the subject. I will be more guarded; yet how difficult it is to hit the right point! To turn the conversation might look ungracious and affected."

"*February 13th*, 1849.—I sent off Alice's Valentine to Fanny to be forwarded.† The sale keeps up—eighty or more a day. It is strange. Peo-

---

* On March 8th, 1850, Lord Langdale delivered the judgment of the Judicial Committee of the Privy Council.

† The Miss Macaulays resided at Brighton. The many weeks which

ple tell me that Miss Aikin abuses my book like a fury, and can not forgive my treatment of her 'Life of Addison.' Poor creature! If she knew how little I deserve her ill-will, and how little I care for it, she would be quieter. If she would have let me save her from exposing herself, I would have done so;* and, when she rudely rejected my help, and I could not escape from the necessity of censuring her, I censured her more leniently, I will venture to say, than so bad a book was ever censured by any critic of the smallest discernment. From the first word to the last, I never forgot my respect for her petticoats. Even now, I do not reprint one of my best reviews for fear of giving her pain. But there is no great magnanimity in all this."

"*February* 14*th*.—At three came Fanny and the children. Alice was in perfect raptures over her Valentine. She begged quite pathetically to be told the truth about it. When we were alone together she said, 'I am going to be very serious.' Down she fell before me on her knees, and lifted up her hands: 'Dear uncle, do tell the truth to your little girl. Did you send the Valentine?' I did not choose to tell a real lie to a child even about such a trifle, and so I owned it."

"*February* 15*th*.—To dinner with Baron Parke. Brougham was noisily friendly. I know how mortally he hates and how bitterly he reviles me. But it matters little. He has long outlived his power to injure. He has not, however, outlived his power to amuse. He was very pleasant, but, as usual, excessively absurd, and exposed himself quite ludicrously on one subject. He maintained that it was doubtful whether the tragic poet was Euripĭdes or Euripīdes. It was Euripīdes in his Ainsworth. There was, he said, no authority either way. I answered by quoting a couple of lines from Aristophanes. I could have overwhelmed him with quotations. 'Oh!' said this great scholar, 'those are iambics. Iambics are very capricious and irregular; not like hexameters.' I kept my countenance, and so did Parke. Nobody else who heard the discussion understood the subject."

In November, 1848, Macaulay had been elected Lord Rector of the University of Glasgow. The time was now approaching for the ceremony of his installation—one of those occasions which are the special terror of an orator, when much is

their brother spent there in their company added much to his health and comfort. For the most part he lived at the Norfolk Hotel, but he sometimes took a lodging in the neighborhood of their house. His article on Bunyan in the "Encyclopædia Britannica" was written in one of the houses in Regency Square.

* See pages 115 and 116.

expected, and every thing has been well said many times before. His year of office fortunately chanced to be the fourth centenary of the body over which he had been chosen to preside; and he contrived to give point and novelty to his inaugural address by framing it into a retrospect of the history and condition of the University at the commencement of each successive century of its existence.

"*March* 12*th*.—I called on the lord advocate, settled the date of my journey to Glasgow, and consulted him about the plan of my speech. He thought the notion very good; grand, indeed, he said; and I think that it is striking and original, without being at all affected or eccentric. I was vexed to hear that there is some thought of giving me the freedom of Glasgow in a gold box. This may make it necessary for me to make a speech, on which I had not reckoned. It is strange, even to myself, to find how the horror of public exhibitions grows on me. Having made my way in the world by haranguing, I am now as unwilling to make a speech as any timid stammerer in Great Britain."

The event proved that his apprehensions were superfluous. "I took the oath of office," he writes in his journal of March 21st, 1849; "signed my name, and delivered my address. It was very successful; for, though of little intrinsic value, it was not unskillfully framed for its purpose, and for the place and time. The acclamations were prodigious."

"*March* 22*d*.—Another eventful and exciting day. I was much annoyed and anxious, in consequence of hearing that there were great expectations of a fine oration from me at the town-hall. I had broken rest, partly from the effect of the bustle which was over, and partly from the apprehension of the bustle which was to come. I turned over a few sentences in my head, but was very ill satisfied with them. Well or ill satisfied, however, I was forced to be ready when the lord provost called for me. I felt like a man going to be hanged; and, as such a man generally does, plucked up courage to behave with decency. We went to the city hall, which is a fine room, and was crowded as full as it could hold. Nothing but huzzaing and clapping of hands. The provost presented me with a handsome box, silver-gilt, containing the freedom of the city, and made a very fair speech on the occasion. I returned thanks with sincere emotion, and, I hope, with propriety. What I said was very well received, and I was vehemently applauded at the close. At half-past two I took flight for Edinburgh, and, on arriving, drove straight from the station to Craig

Crook. I had a pleasant, painful half-hour with Jeffrey—perhaps the last. He was in almost hysterical excitement. His kindness and praise were quite overwhelming. The tears were in the eyes of both of us."

"*March 26th.*—Longman has written to say that the third edition is all sold off to the last copy. I wrote up my journal for the past week: an hour for fourteen pages, at about four minutes a page. Then came a long call from Macleod, with whom I had much good talk, which occupied most of the morning. I must not go on in this dawdling way. Soon the correspondence to which my book has given occasion will be over; the correcting of proof-sheets for fresh editions will also be over; the mornings will be mild; the sun will be up early; and I will try to be up early too. I should like to get again into the habit of working three hours before breakfast. Once I had it, and I may easily recover it. A man feels his conscience so light during the day when he has done a good piece of work with a clear head before leaving his bedroom. I think I will fix Easter Tuesday for the beginning of this new system. It is hardly worth while to make the change before we return from our tour."*

"*April 13th.*—To the British Museum. I looked over the 'Travels of the Duke of Tuscany,' and found the passage the existence of which Croker denies. His blunders are really incredible. The article has been received with general contempt. Really, Croker has done me a great service. I apprehended a strong reaction, the natural effect of such a success; and, if hatred had left him free to use his very slender faculties to the best advantage, he might have injured me much. He should have been large in acknowledgment; should have taken a mild and expostulatory tone; and should have looked out for real blemishes, which, as I too well know, he might easily have found. Instead of that, he has written with such rancor as to make every body sick. I could almost pity him. But he is a bad, a very bad, man: a scandal to politics and to letters.

"I corrected my article on Addison for insertion in the collected Essays. I shall leave out all the animadversions on Miss Aikin's blunders. She has used me ill, and this is the honorable and gentleman-like revenge."

"*Friday, May 5th*, 1849.—A lucky day on which to begin a new volume of my journal. Glorious weather. A letter from Lord John to say that he has given my brother John the living of Aldingham, worth eleven hundred pounds a year, in a fine country, and amidst a fine population. Was there ever such prosperity? I wrote a few lines of warm thanks to Lord John. To Longman's. A thousand of the fifth edition bespoken. Longman has sent me Southey's 'Commonplace Book'—trash, if ever there was trash in a book-seller's shop.

"I read some of Dr. Parr's correspondence while I dressed. I have been dawdling, at odd moments, over his writings, and over the memoirs of him,

---

* At Easter, 1849, we went to Chester, Bangor, and Lichfield.

during the last week. He certainly was very far from being all humbug. Yet the proportion of humbug was so great that one is tempted to deny him the merit which he really possessed. The preface to the Warburtonian Tracts is, I think, the best piece."

"*June* 28*th.*—After breakfast to the Museum, and sat till three, reading and making extracts. I turned over three volumes of newspapers and tracts—*Flying Posts, Postboys,* and *Postmen.* I found some curious things which will be of direct service; but the chief advantage of these researches is that the mind is transported back a century and a half, and gets familiar with the ways of thinking, and with the habits, of a past generation. I feel that I am fast becoming master of my subject; at least, more master of it than any writer who has yet handled it."

"*June* 29*th.*—To the British Museum, and read and extracted there till near five. I find a growing pleasure in this employment. The reign of William the Third, so mysterious to me a few weeks ago, is beginning to take a clear form. I begin to see the men, and to understand all their difficulties and jealousies."

"*June* 30*th.*—To-day my yearly account with Longman is wound up. I may now say that my book has run the gauntlet of criticism pretty thoroughly. I have every reason to be content. The most savage and dishonest assailant has not been able to deny me merit as a writer. All critics who have the least pretense to impartiality have given me praise which I may be glad to think that I at all deserve. My present enterprise is a more arduous one, and will probably be rewarded with less applause. Yet I feel strong in hope.

"I received a note from Prince Albert. He wants to see me at Buckingham Palace at three to-morrow. I answered like a courtier; yet what am I to say to him? For, of course, he wants to consult me about the Cambridge professorship.* How can I be just at once to Stephen and to Kemble?"

"*Saturday, July* 1*st.*—To the Palace. The prince, to my extreme astonishment, offered me the professorship; and very earnestly, and with many flattering expressions, pressed me to accept it. I was resolute, and gratefully and respectfully declined. I should have declined, indeed, if only in order to give no ground to any body to accuse me of foul play; for I have had difficulty enough in steering my course so as to deal properly both by Stephen and by Kemble; and if I had marched off with the prize, I could not have been astonished if both had entertained a very unjust suspicion of me. But, in truth, my temper is that of the wolf in the fable. I can not bear the collar, and I have got rid of much finer and richer collars than this. It would be strange if, having sacrificed for liberty a seat in the

---

* The Professorship of Modern History. The chair was eventually filled by Sir James Stephen.

Cabinet and twenty-five hundred pounds a year, I should now sacrifice liberty for a chair at Cambridge and four hundred pounds a year. Besides, I never could do two things at once. If I lectured well, my 'History' must be given up; and to give up my 'History' would be to give up much more than the emoluments of the professorship—if emolument were my chief object, which it is not now, nor ever was. The prince, when he found me determined, asked me about the other candidates."

"*July 21st.*—I went to a shop near Westminster Bridge, where I yesterday remarked some volumes of the *Morning Chronicle,* and bought some of them to continue my set. I read the *Morning Chronicle* of 1811. How scandalously the Whig press treated the Duke of Wellington, till his merit became too great to be disputed! How extravagantly unjust party spirit makes men!

"Some scribbler in the *Morning Post* has just now a spite to Trevelyan, and writes several absurd papers against him every week. He will never hear of them, probably, and will certainly not care for them. They can do him no harm; and yet I, who am never moved by such attacks on myself, and who would not walk across the room to change all the abuse that the *Morning Post* has ever put forth against me into panegyric, can not help being irritated by this low, dirty wickedness. To the Museum, and passed two or three hours usefully and agreeably over maps and tracts relating to Londonderry. I can make something of that matter, unless I have lost my cunning."

"*August 3d.*—I am now near the end of Tom Moore's 'Life of Byron.' It is a sad book. Poor fellow! Yet he was a bad fellow, and horribly affected. But then what, that could spoil a character, was wanting? Had I at twenty-four had a peerage, and been the most popular poet and the most successful Lovelace of the day, I should have been as great a coxcomb, and possibly as bad a man. I passed some hours over 'Don Juan,' and saw no reason to change the opinion which I formed twenty-five years ago. The first two cantos are Byron's masterpieces. The next two may pass as not below his average. Then begins the descent, and at last he sinks to the level of his own imitators in the magazines."

Macaulay spent the last half of August in Ireland,* and, as his custom was, employed himself during the days that preceded his tour in studying the literature of the country. He turned over Swift's "Correspondence," and at least a shelf-full of Irish novels; and read more carefully Moore's "Life of Sheridan," and the "Life of Flood," which did not at all meet his fancy. "A stupid, ill-spelled, ill-written book it is. He

---

* See pages 194–196.

was a remarkable man; but one not much to be esteemed or loved. I looked through the 'Memoirs of Wolfe Tone.' In spite of the fellow's savage, unreasonable hatred of England, there is something about him which I can not help liking. Why is it that an Irishman's, or Frenchman's, hatred of England does not excite in me an answering hatred? I imagine that my national pride prevents it. England is so great that an Englishman cares little what others think of her, or how they talk of her."

"*August* 16*th*, 1849.—The express train reached Holyhead about seven in the evening. I read, between London and Bangor, the 'Lives of the Emperors,' from Maximin to Carinus inclusive, in the Augustan History, and was greatly amused and interested. It is a pity that Philip and Decius are wanting to the series. Philip's strange leaning toward Christianity, and the vigor and ability of Decius, and his inveterate hostility to the new religion, would be interesting even in the worst history; and certainly worse historians than Trebellius Capitolinus and Vopiscus are not easily to be found. Yet I like their silliest garrulity. It sometimes has a Pepyslike effect.

"We sailed as soon as we got on board. The breeze was fresh and adverse, and the sea rough. The sun set in glory, and then the starlight was like the starlight of the Trades. I put on my great-coat, and sat on deck during the whole voyage. As I could not read, I used an excellent substitute for reading. I went through 'Paradise Lost' in my head. I could still repeat half of it, and that the best half. I really never enjoyed it so much. In the dialogue at the end of the fourth book, Satan and Gabriel became to me quite like two of Shakspeare's men. Old Sharp once told me that Henderson, the actor, used to say to him that there was no better acting scene in the English drama than this. I now felt the truth of the criticism. How admirable is that hit in the manner of Euripides:

> But wherefore thou alone? Wherefore with thee
> Came not all hell broke loose?

I will try my hand on the passage in Greek iambics; or set Ellis to do it, who will do it better.

"I had got to the end of the conversation between Raphael and Adam, admiring more than ever the sublime courtesy of the Archangel, when I saw the lights of Dublin Bay. I love entering a port at night. The contrast between the wild, lonely sea, and the life and tumult of a harbor when a ship is coming in, have always impressed me much."

"*August* 17*th*.—Off to Dublin by railway. The public buildings, at this first glance, struck me as very fine, and would be considered fine even at Paris. Yet the old Parliament House, from which I had expected most, fell below my expectations. It is handsome, undoubtedly; indeed, more than handsome; but it is too low. If it were twice as high as it is, it would be one of the noblest edifices in Europe. It is remarkable that architecture is the only art in which mere bulk is an element of sublimity. There is more grandeur in a Greek gem of a quarter of an inch diameter, than in the statue of Peter the Great at Petersburg. There is more grandeur in Raphael's 'Vision of Ezekiel' than in all West's and Barry's acres of spoiled canvas. But no building of very small dimensions can be grand, and no building as lofty as the Pyramids or the Colosseum can be mean. The Pyramids are a proof; for what on earth could be viler than a pyramid thirty feet high?

"The rain was so heavy that I was forced to come back in a covered car. While in this detestable vehicle, I looked rapidly through the correspondence between Pliny and Trajan, and thought that Trajan made a most creditable figure. I saw the outside of Christ Church Cathedral, and felt very little inclination to see the inside. Not so with St. Patrick's. Ruinous, and ruinous in the worst way—undergoing repairs which there are not funds to make—it is still a striking church; but the interest which belongs to it is chiefly historical. In the choir I saw Schomberg's grave, and Swift's furious libel* written above. Opposite hang the spurs of St. Ruth, and the chain-ball which killed him; not a very Christian-like ornament for the neighborhood of an altar. In the nave Swift and Stella are buried. Swift's bust is much the best likeness of him that I ever saw; striking and full of character. Going away through Kevin Street I saw the Deanery; not Swift's house, though on the same site. Some of the hovels opposite must have been standing in his time; and the inmates were probably among the people who borrowed small sums of him, or took off their hats to him in the street."

"*August* 24th, *Killarney*.—A busy day. I found that I must either forego the finest part of the sight, or mount a pony. Ponies are not much in my way. However, I was ashamed to flinch, and rode twelve miles, with a guide, to the head of the Upper Lake, where we met the boat which had been sent forward with four rowers. One of the boatmen gloried in having rowed Sir Walter Scott and Miss Edgeworth, twenty-four years ago. It was, he said, a compensation to him for having missed a hanging which took place that very day. Nothing can exceed the beauty of the Upper

---

* The inscription on Schomberg's tablet relates, in most outspoken phrases, how the Dean and Chapter of St. Patrick's in vain importuned the duke's heirs to erect him a monument, and how at length they were induced to erect one themselves. The last line runs thus: "Plus potuit fama virtutis apud alienos, quam sanguinis proximitas apud suos."

Lake.* I got home after a seven hours' ramble, during which I went twelve miles on horseback, and about twenty by boat. I had not crossed a horse since in June, 1834, I rode with Captain Smith through the Mango Garden, near Arcot. I was pleased to find that I had a good seat; and my guide, whom I had apprised of my unskillfulness, professed himself quite an admirer of the way in which I trotted and cantered. His flattery pleased me more than many fine compliments which have been paid to my 'History.'†

After his fortnight in Ireland, Macaulay took another fortnight in France, and then applied himself, sedulously and continuously, to the completion of his twelfth chapter. For weeks together the account of each day ends or begins with the words: "My task;" "Did my task;" "My task, and something over."

---

* " Killarney is worth some trouble," Macaulay writes to Mr. Ellis. " I never in my life saw any thing more beautiful; I might say, so beautiful. Imagine a fairer Windermere in that part of Devonshire where the myrtle grows wild. The ash-berries are redder, the heath richer, the very fern more delicately articulated than elsewhere. The wood is everywhere. The grass is greener than any thing that I ever saw. There is a positive sensual pleasure in looking at it. No sheep is suffered to remain more than a few months on any of the islands of the lakes. I asked why not. I was told that they would die of fat; and, indeed, those that I saw looked like aldermen who had passed the chair."

† In a letter written from Dublin on his way home, Macaulay says: " I was agreeably disappointed with what I saw of the condition of the people in Meath and Louth, when I went to the Boyne, and not much shocked by any thing that I fell in with in going by railway from Dublin to Limerick. But from Limerick to Killarney, and from Killarney to Cork, I hardly knew whether to laugh or cry. Hundreds of dwellings in ruins, abandoned by the late inmates, who have fled to America; the laboring people dressed literally, not rhetorically, worse than the scarecrows of England; the children of whole villages turning out to beg of every coach and car that goes by. But I will have done. I can not mend this state of things, and there is no use in breaking my heart about it. I am comforted by thinking that between the poorest English peasant and the Irish peasant there is ample room for ten or twelve well-marked degrees of poverty. As to political agitation, it is dead and buried. Never did I see a society apparently so well satisfied with its rulers. The queen made a conquest of all hearts."

"*September 22d.*—Wrote my regular quantity—six foolscap pages of my scrawl, which will be about two pages in print. I hope to hold on at this pace through the greater part of the year. If I do this, I shall, by next September, have rough-hewn my third volume. Of course, the polishing and retouching will be an immense labor."

"*October 2d.*—Wrote fast and long. I do not know that I ever composed with more ease and pleasure than of late. I have got far beyond my task. I will only mention days when I fall short of it; and I hope that it will be long before I have occasion to make such an entry."

"*October 9th.*—Sat down again to write, but not in the vein. I hope that I shall not break my wholesome practice to-day, for the first time since I came back from France. A Frenchman called on me, a sort of man of letters, who has translated some bits of my 'History.' When he went, I sat down doggedly, as Johnson used to say, and did my task, but somewhat against my will."

"*October 25th*, 1849.—My birthday. Forty-nine years old. I have no cause of complaint. Tolerable health; competence; liberty; leisure; very dear relations and friends; a great, I may say a very great, literary reputation.

Nil amplius oro,

Maiâ nate, nisi ut propria hæc mihi munera faxis.*

But how will that be? My fortune is tolerably secure against any thing but a great public calamity. My liberty depends on myself, and I shall not easily part with it. As to fame, it may fade and die; but I hope that mine has deeper roots. This I can not but perceive, that even the hasty and imperfect articles which I wrote for the *Edinburgh Review* are valued by a generation which has sprung up since they were first published. While two editions of Jeffrey's papers, and four of Sydney's, have sold, mine are reprinting for the seventh time. Then, as to my 'History,' there is no change yet in the public feeling of England. I find that the United States, France, and Germany confirm the judgment of my own country. I have seen not less than six German reviews, all in the highest degree laudatory. This is a sufficient answer to those detractors who attribute the success of my book here to the skill with which I have addressed myself to mere local and temporary feelings. I am conscious that I did not mean to address myself to such feelings, and that I wrote with a remote past, and a remote future, constantly in my mind. The applause of people at Charleston, people at Heidelberg, and people at Paris has reached me this very week; and this consent of men so differently situated leads me to hope that I have really achieved the high adventure which I undertook, and produced something which will live. What a long rigma-

---

* " My only prayer is, O son of Maia, that thou wilt make these blessings my own."

role! But on a birthday a man may be excused for looking backward and forward.

"Not quite my whole task; but I have a grand purple patch to sew on,* and I must take time. I have been delighted to hear of Milman's appointment to St. Paul's—honestly delighted, as much as if a good legacy had been left me."

"*December 5th.*—In the afternoon to Westbourne Terrace. I read my Irish narrative to Hannah. Trevelyan came in the middle. After dinner I read again. They seemed much, very much, interested. Hannah cried. I could not at all command my voice. I think that if I ever wrote well, I have done so here. But this is but a small part of my task. However, I was pleased at the effect which I produced; and the more so as I am sensible that I do not read my own compositions well."

"*December 7th.*—I bought Thiers's new volume, and read it in the street. He is fair enough about Vimiera and Corunna, and just to the English officers, but hardly so to the private soldiers. After dinner I read Thiers again, and finished him. I am afraid of saying to other people how much I miss in historians who pass for good. The truth is that I admire no historians much except Herodotus, Thucydides, and Tacitus. Perhaps, in his way, a very peculiar way, I might add Fra Paolo. The modern writers who have most of the great qualities of the ancient masters of history are some memoir writers; St. Simon, for example. There is merit, no doubt, in Hume, Robertson, Voltaire, and Gibbon. Yet it is not the thing. I have a conception of history more just, I am confident, than theirs. The execution is another matter. But I hope to improve."

In a letter of December 19th, 1849, Macaulay writes: "Lord Spencer has invited me to rummage his family papers; a great proof of liberality, when it is considered that he is the lineal descendant of Sunderland and Marlborough. In general, it is ludicrous to notice how sore people are at the truth being told about their ancestors. I am curious to see that noble library; the finest private library, I believe, in England."

"*December 20th: Althorp.*—This is a very early house. We had breakfast at nine, preceded by prayers in the chapel. I was just in time for them. After breakfast I went to the library. The first glance showed what a vast collection it was. Mr. Appleyard was cicerone. Though not much given to admire the merely curious parts of libraries, I was greatly pleased with the old block-printing; the very early specimens of the art at Mentz; the Caxtons; the Florence Homer; the Alduses; the famous

---

* The Relief of Londonderry.

Boccaccio. I looked with particular interest into the two editions of Chaucer by Caxton, and at the preface of the latter. Lord Spencer expressed his regret that his sea education had kept him ignorant of much that was known to scholars, and said that his chief pleasure in his library was derived from the pleasure of his friends. This he said so frankly and kindly that it was impossible not to be humbled by his superiority in a thing more important even than learning. He reminded me of his brother, my old friend and leader."

"*December 21st.*—After breakfast to-day I sat down to work. Appleyard showed me the pamphlet corner, and I fell to vigorously. There is here a large collection of pamphlets, formerly the property of General Conway. The volumes relating to William's reign can not have been fewer than fourteen or fifteen; the pamphlets, I should think, at least a dozen to a volume. Many I have, and many are, to my knowledge, at the British Museum. But there were many which I had never seen; and I found abundant, and useful, and pleasing occupation for five or six hours. I filled several sheets of paper with notes. Though I do not love country-house society, I got pleasantly through the evening. In truth, when people are so kind and so honest, it would be brutal not to be pleased. To-day I sent ten pounds to poor ——'s family. I do not complain of such calls; but I must save in other things in order to meet them."

"*December 26th.*—I bought Thackeray's 'Rebecca and Rowena'—a very pretty, clever piece of fooling; but I doubt whether every body will taste the humor as I do. I wish him success heartily. I finished the 'Life of Lord Sidmouth.' Addington seems to me to have had more pluck than I had given him credit for. As to the rest, he was narrow-minded and imbecile, beyond any person who has filled such posts since the Revolution. Lord Sidmouth might have made a highly creditable figure if he had continued to be speaker, as he well might have done, twenty years longer. He would then have left as considerable a name as Onslow's. He was well qualified for that sort of work. But his sudden elevation to the highest place in the State not only exposed his incapacity, but turned his head. He began to think highly of himself exactly at the moment when every body else began to think meanly of him. There is a punctiliousness, a sense of personal dignity, an expectation of being consulted, a disposition to resent slights, to the end of his life. These were the effects, I apprehend, of his having been put above his station. He had a dream like Abou Hassan's, and was the worse for it all his days. I do not wonder at the contempt which Pitt felt for him; but it was below Pitt to be angry."

"*December 27th.*—Disagreeable weather, and disagreeable news. —— is in difficulty again. I sent fifty pounds, and I shall send the same to ——, who does not ask it. But I can not help being vexed. All the fruits of my book have for this year been swallowed up. It will be all that I can

do to make both ends meet without breaking in upon capital. In the
mean time, people who know my incomings, and do not know the drains,
have no scruple about boring me for subscriptions and assistance.

"I read 'Romilly's Memoirs.' A fine fellow; but too stoical for my
taste. I love a little of the Epicurean element in virtue."

"*January 12th*, 1850.—To the Board at the Museum, and shook hands
with Peel. We did business—board-fashion. Would it were otherwise!
I went home, worked some hours, and got on tolerably. No doubt what I
am writing will require much correction; but in the main, I think, it will
do. How little the all-important art of making meaning pellucid is studied now! Hardly any popular writer, except myself, thinks of it. Many
seem to aim at being obscure. Indeed, they may be right enough in one
sense; for many readers give credit for profundity to whatever is obscure,
and call all that is perspicuous, shallow. But, coraggio! and think of A.D.
2850. Where will your Emersons be then? But Herodotus will still be
read with delight. We must do our best to be read too.

"A letter from Campbell with news that I am a bencher of Lincoln's
Inn. I am pleased and amused.* I read some of Campbell's 'Lives.' To
Thurlow's abilities he is surely unjust. It is idle to question powers of
mind which a generation of able men admitted. Thurlow was in the
House of Commons when Fox and Burke were against him, and made a
great figure there. He dominated over the Lords, in spite of Camden,
Mansfield, and Loughborough. His talents were acknowledged by the
writers of the 'Rolliad,' and even by Peter Pindar. It is too late to dispute them now."

"*January 28th.*—Jeffrey is gone. Dear fellow! I loved him as much
as it is easy to love a man who belongs to an older generation. And how
good, and kind, and generous he was to me! His goodness, too, was the
more precious because his perspicacity was so great. He saw through and
through you. He marked every fault of taste, every weakness, every ridi-
cule; and yet he loved you as if he had been the dullest fellow in England.
He had a much better heart than Sydney Smith. I do not mean that
Sydney was in that respect below par. In ability I should say that Jeffrey
was higher, but Sydney rarer. I would rather have been Jeffrey; but
there will be several Jeffreys, before there is a Sydney. After all, dear
Jeffrey's death is hardly matter for mourning. God grant that I may die
so! Full of years; full of honors; faculties bright, and affections warm,

---

* A benchership of Lincoln's Inn has rarely fallen to a stuff gown; and
to a stuff gown whose wearer had, in the course of his life, earned but one
solitary guinea. The notion of conferring this high honor upon Macaulay
was mooted by Lord Justice Knight Bruce, who had been one of his most
determined adversaries in the House of Commons during the heat of the
great controversies of 1832.

to the last; lamented by the public, and by many valuable private friends. This is the euthanasia.

"I dined at home, and read in the evening Rousseau's 'Letter to the Archbishop of Paris,' and 'Letter to D'Alembert.' In spite of my hatred of the fellow, I can not deny that he had great eloquence and vigor of mind. At the same time, he does not amuse me, and to me a book which is not amusing wants the highest of all recommendations."

"*February* 19*th.*—Went with Hannah to Richmond's studio, to see my picture. He seemed anxious and excited; but at last, when he produced his work, she pronounced it excellent. I am no judge of the likeness, but the face is characteristic. It is the face of a man of considerable mental powers, great boldness and frankness, and a quick relish for pleasure. It is not unlike Mr. Fox's face in general expression. I am quite content to have such a physiognomy. Home, and counted my books. Those which are in front are, in round numbers, six thousand one hundred. There are several hundreds behind, chiefly novels. I may call the whole collection at least seven thousand. It will probably amount to ten thousand by the time that my lease of these chambers expires; unless, indeed, I expire first, which I think very probable. It is odd how indifferent I have become to the fear of death; and yet I enjoy life greatly. I looked at some Spanish ballads, and was struck by the superiority of Lockhart's versions to the originals.

"To dinner at the Club, and very pleasant it was."*

"*March* 2*d.*—I was pained by hearing at Westbourne Terrace that —— is deeply hurt by the failure of his portrait of me.† I am very sorry for it. He seemed a good fellow, and a pleasing painter; and I have a great tenderness for the sensibility of artists whose bread depends on their success. I have had as few checks to my vanity in my own line as most men; but I have felt enough to teach me sympathy. I have been reading a book called 'Les Gentilshommes Chasseurs.' The old régime would have been a fine thing if the world had been made only for gentlemen, and if gentlemen had been made only for hunting."

"*March* 9*th,* 1850.—To dinner at the Palace. The queen was most gracious to me. She talked much about my book, and owned that she had

---

* Lord Carlisle says, in his diary of February 19th, 1850: "Dined at the Club. Hallam in the chair. It was remarkably pleasant, except once, when we got on Scotch entails. I saw Pemberton Leigh look amused when Macaulay turned on him: Don't you remember—as he always begins —then something in 'Don Gusman d'Alfarache.' He said Dryden had three great dialogues in his plays: Sebastian and Dorax; Antony and Ventidius (I forget the third); but he considers all immeasurably below the Brutus and Cassius."

† This does not refer to Mr. Richmond's picture.

nothing to say for her poor ancestor, James the Second. 'Not your majesty's ancestor,' said I; 'your majesty's predecessor.' I hope this was not an uncourtly correction. I meant it as a compliment, and she seemed to take it so."

In the year 1839 Macaulay dined at the Palace for the first time, and described his entertainment in a letter to one of his sisters. "We all spoke in whispers; and, when dinner was over, almost every body went to cards or chess. I was presented; knelt down; kissed her majesty's hand; had the honor of a conversation with her of about two minutes, and assured her that India was hot, and that I kept my health there." It may well be believed that Macaulay did not relish a society where he fancied himself bound to condense his remarks into the space of two minutes, and to speak in the nearest approach to a whisper which he had at his command. But, in truth, the restraint under which he found himself was mainly due to his own inexperience of court life; and, as time went on, he began to perceive that he could not make himself more acceptable than by talking as he talked elsewhere. Before long, a lady who met him frequently at the Palace, whether in the character of a cabinet minister or of a private guest, writes: "Mr. Macaulay was very interesting to listen to; quite immeasurably abundant in anecdote and knowledge."

"*March* 11*th.*—I wrote the arrival of the news of the Boyne at Whitehall. I go on slowly, but, I think, pretty well. There are not many weeks in which I do not write enough to fill seven or eight printed pages. The rule of never going on when the vein does not flow readily would not do for all men, or for all kinds of work. But I, who am not tied to time, who do not write for money, and who aim at interesting and pleasing readers whom ordinary histories repel, can hardly do better. How can a man expect that others will be amused by reading what he finds it dull to compose?

"Still north-east wind. Alas for the days when N.E. and S.W. were all one to me! Yet I have compensations, and ought to be contented; and so I am, though now and then I wince for a moment."

"*March* 21*st.*—I have been plagued to know what to do about a letter from that poor creature, Robert Montgomery. He has written to me begging, in fact, that I will let him out of the pillory. I wrote, and re-wrote my answer. It was very difficult to hit the exact point—to refuse all concession without offering any new offense, and, without any fresh asperity, to defend the asperity of my article."

"*April* 15*th.*—After breakfast I fell to work on the conspiracy of the Jacobites in 1690. This is a tough chapter. To make the narrative flow along as it ought, every part naturally springing from that which precedes —to carry the reader backward and forward across St. George's Channel without distracting his attention—is not easy. Yet it may be done. I believe that this art of transition is as important, or nearly so, to history, as the art of narration. I read the last volume of 'Clarissa,' which I have not opened since my voyage from India in the *Lord Hungerford*. I nearly cried my eyes out."

"*April* 27*th.*—To Westbourne Terrace, and passed an hour in playing with Alice. A very intelligent and engaging playfellow I found her. I was Dando at a pastry-cook's, and then at an oyster-shop.* Afterward I was a dog-stealer, who had carried away her little spaniel, Diamond, while she was playing in Kensington Gardens, and who came to get the reward advertised in the *Times*. Dear little creature! How such things twine themselves about our hearts!

"To dinner with Inglis. Hardinge told some good campaigning stories; and, among others, the cold language which the duke used about a brave officer on the staff, who was killed by exposing himself injudiciously. 'What business had he larking there? I shall not mention his name. I shall teach officers that, dead or alive, they shall not be praised if they throw their lives away.' William the Third all over.†

"Longman gives a capital account of the sale of my works. The sixth edition of the 'History' is gone. That makes 22,000 copies."

"*May* 9*th.*—To the British Museum. We put Peel into the chair. Very handy he is, to use the vulgar phrase. A capital man of business. We got on fast."

"*May* 14*th.*—To the Museum. Peel brought his project of a report. I admire the neatness and readiness with which he does such things. It is

---

* A generation has arisen of whom not one in fifty knows Dando, the "bouncing, seedy swell," hero of a hundred ballads, who was at least twice in every month brought before the magistrates for having refused to settle his bill after overeating himself in an oyster-shop.

† "Walker was treated less respectfully. William thought him a busy-body who had been properly punished for running into danger without any call of duty, and expressed that feeling with characteristic bluntness, on the field of battle. 'Sir,' said an attendant, 'the Bishop of Derry has been killed by a shot at the ford.' 'What took him there?' growled the king." See likewise, in the twenty-first chapter of the "History," the whole paragraph containing the account of the death of Mr. Godfrey at the siege of Namur.

of a piece with his Parliamentary performances. He and I get on wonderfully well together."

"*June 1st.*—Dined with Peel. How odd!"*

Three weeks afterward, Macaulay started for his tour to Glencoe and Killiecrankie.

"*July 3d.*—As we drove into Glasgow, I saw 'Death of Sir Robert Peel' placarded at a newsman's. I was extremely shocked. Thank God, I had shaken hands cordially with the poor fellow, after all our blows given and received."†

"*July 4th.*—Poor Peel's death in the *Times*. I have been more affected by it than I could have believed. It was in the dining-room that he died. I dined with him there for the first, and the last, time about a month ago. If he is buried publicly, I will certainly follow his coffin. Once I little thought that I should have cried for his death."

"*July 28th.*—My account of the Highlands is getting into tolerable shape. To-morrow I shall begin to transcribe again, and to polish. What trouble these few pages will have cost me! The great object is that, after all this trouble, they may read as if they had been spoken off, and may seem to flow as easily as table-talk. We shall see.

"I brought home, and read, the 'Prelude.' It is a poorer 'Excursion;' the same sort of faults and beauties; but the faults greater and the beauties fainter, both in themselves and because faults are always made more offensive, and beauties less pleasing, by repetition. The story is the old story. There are the old raptures about mountains and cataracts; the old

---

* The strangeness consisted in Macaulay's dining under Sir Robert Peel's roof. He had, at least once before this, met his old antagonist at the house of a common friend. "*April 2d* (1839).—I dined at Inglis's, and met Peel. He was pleasant enough; not a brilliant talker, but conversible and easy, with a little turn in private, as in public, to egotism. We got on very well. I recollect only his account of Sir William Scott's excessive timidity about speaking in Parliament. 'My dear young friend, how does the House seem? Is Brougham there? Does he look very savage?'"

† "I shall hardly know the House of Commons without Sir Robert Peel....... His figure is now before me: all the tones of his voice are in my ears; and the pain with which I think that I shall never hear them again would be imbittered by the recollection of some sharp encounters which took place between us, were it not that at last there was an entire and cordial reconciliation, and that, only a very few days before his death, I had the pleasure of receiving from him marks of kindness and esteem, of which I shall always cherish the recollection."—*Macaulay's Speech at Edinburgh in* 1852.

flimsy philosophy about the effect of scenery on the mind; the old crazy,
mystical metaphysics; the endless wildernesses of dull, flat, prosaic twaddle; and here and there fine descriptions and energetic declamations interspersed.   The story of the French Revolution, and of its influence on
the character of a young enthusiast, is told again at greater length, and
with less force and pathos, than in the 'Excursion.'   The poem is to the
last degree Jacobinical, indeed Socialist.   I understand perfectly why
Wordsworth did not choose to publish it in his life-time.

"I looked over 'Coleridge's Remains.'   What stuff some of his criticisms
on style are!   Think of his saying that scarcely any English writer before
the Revolution used the Saxon genitive, except with a name indicating a
living being, or where a personification was intended!   About twenty lines
of Shakspeare occurred to me in five minutes.   In 'King John,'

In dreadful trial of our kingdom's king:

"Again,

Nor let my kingdom's rivers take their course.

"In 'Hamlet:'

The law's delay.

"In 'Romeo and Juliet,'

My bosom's lord sits lightly on his throne.

"In 'Richard the Third,' strongest of all,

Why, then, All-souls-day is my body's doomsday."

Macaulay spent the September of 1850 in a pleasant villa
on the south coast of the Isle of Wight.   The letters in which
he urges Mr. Ellis to share his retreat may lack the poetical
beauty of Horace's invitation to Mæcenas and Tennyson's invitation to Mr. Maurice; but it is probable that the entertainment, both material and intellectual, which awaited a guest at
Madeira Hall, did not yield in quality to that provided either at
Tibur or at Freshwater.

Madeira Hall, Ventnor, September 3d, 1850.

DEAR ELLIS,—Here I am, lodged most delightfully.   I look
out on one side to the crags and myrtles of the Undercliff,
against which my house is built.   On the other side I have a
view of the sea, which is at this moment as blue as the sky
and as calm as the Serpentine.   My little garden is charming.
I wish that I may not, like Will Honeycomb, forget the sin
and sea-coal of London for innocence and hay-cocks.   To be
sure, innocence and hay-cocks do not always go together.

When will you come? Take your own time: but I am rather anxious that you should not lose this delicious weather, and defer your trip till the equinoctial storms are setting in. I can promise you plenty of water and of towels; good wine; good tea; good cheese from town; good eggs, butter, and milk from the farm at my door; a beautiful prospect from your bedroom window; and (if the weather keeps us within doors), Plautus's "Comedies," Plutarch's "Lives," twenty or thirty comedies of Calderon, Fra Paolo's "History," and a little library of novels—to say nothing of my own compositions, which, like Ligurinus, I will read to you *stanti, sedenti*, etc., etc.

I am just returned from a walk of near seven hours, and of full fifteen miles; part of it as steep as the Monument. Indeed, I was so knocked up with climbing Black Gang Chine that I lay on the turf at the top for a quarter of an hour.

Ever yours,   T. B. MACAULAY.

Ventnor, September 8th, 1850.

DEAR ELLIS,—I shall be at Ryde to meet you next Saturday. I only hope that the weather may continue to be just what it is. The evenings are a little chilly out-of-doors; but the days are glorious. I rise before seven; breakfast at nine; write a page; ramble five or six hours over rocks and through copse-wood, with Plutarch in my hand; come home; write another page; take Fra Paolo, and sit in the garden reading till the sun sinks behind the Undercliff. Then it begins to be cold; so I carry my Fra Paolo into the house and read on till dinner. While I am at dinner the *Times* comes in, and is a good accompaniment to a delicious dessert of peaches, which are abundant here. I have also a novel of Theodore Hook by my side, to relish my wine. I then take a short stroll by starlight, and go to bed at ten. I am perfectly solitary; almost as much so as Robinson Crusoe before he caught Friday. I have not opened my lips, that I remember, these six weeks, except to say "Bread, if you please," or, "Bring a bottle of soda-water;" yet I have not had a moment of ennui. Nevertheless I am heartily glad that you can give me nine days. I wish it were eighteen. Ever yours,   T. B. MACAULAY.

"*September 9th.*—Up soon after six, and read Cobbett with admiration, pleasure, and abhorrence.* After breakfast I gave orders about culinary preparations for Ellis, who is more of an Apicius than I am. Then, after writing a little, I put a volume of Plautus in my pocket, and wandered through the thickets under Bonchurch. I sat down here and there, and read the 'Pœnulus.' It is amusing; but there is a heavy, lumbering way about honest Plautus which makes him as bad a substitute for the Attic masters of the later comedy as the ass was for the spaniel in the fable. You see every now and then that what he does coarsely and blunderingly was done in the original with exquisite delicacy. The name of Hanno in the play reminded me of Hanno in my lay of Virginia,† and I went through it all during the rest of my ramble, and was pretty well pleased with it. Those poems have now been eight years published. They still sell, and seem still to give pleasure. I do not rate them high; but I do not remember that any better poetry has been published since.

"On my return home I took Fra Paolo into the garden. Admirable writer! How I enjoy my solitude—the sunshine, the fresh air, the scenery, and quiet study! I do not know why I have suffered myself to get into the habit of thinking that I could not live out of London. After dinner I walked again, looking at the stars, and thinking how I used to watch them on board the *Asia*. Those were unhappy times compared with these. I find no disposition in myself to regret the past by comparison with the present."

"*September 16th.*—I walked again in the beautiful thicket under Bonchurch, and turned the dialogue in the Rudens between Gripus and Dæmones, 'O Gripe, Gripe,' back again into Greek—nineteen lines, which I should not be ashamed to send in for a university scholarship, or a medal. They were made under every disadvantage, for there is no Greek book

---

* "I read Cobbett," Macaulay writes. "Interesting; but the impression of a prolonged perusal of such venomous invective and gross sophistry becomes painful. After he came into Parliament, he was nothing. He spoke freely there when I heard him, which was often. He made, I believe, one successful speech—mere banter on Plunkett—when I was absent. He proved that he was quite incapable of doing any thing great in debate; and his Parliamentary attendance prevented him from doing any thing great with his pen. His *Register* became as stupid as the *Morning Herald*. In truth, his faculties were impaired by age; and the late hours of the House probably assisted to enfeeble his body, and consequently his mind. His egotism and his suspicion that every body was in a plot against him increased, and at last attained such a height that he was really as mad as Rousseau. I could write a very curious article on him, if I chose."

† The money-changer Crispus, with his long silver hairs,
　　And Hanno from the stately booth glittering with Punic wares.

within my reach except a Plutarch and a New Testament, neither of which is of much use here."*

Macaulay was of opinion that men, the business of whose lives lies elsewhere than among the classics, may easily amuse themselves to more purpose than by turning good English poetry into Greek and Latin verses which may have merit, but can not possibly have any value. It has been well said that "Greek iambics, of which Euripides wrote ten at a sitting—Latin hexameters, of which Virgil wrote five in a day—are not things to be thrown off by dozens" in the course of an afternoon's walk by an English lawyer or statesman who is out for a holiday. Indeed, Macaulay went farther still, and held that the incongruities between modern and ancient modes of feeling and expression are such as to defy the skill of the most practiced and industrious translator — working, as he must work, in a language which is not his own. It was in accordance with this notion that the only experiment in Greek composition, which he made since the day that he left college, took the shape of an attempt to reproduce a lost antique original.

"*September 28th.*—I read part of the 'Life of Fra Paolo' prefixed to his history. A wonderful man; but the biographer would have done better to have softened down the almost incredible things which he relates. According to him Fra Paolo was Galileo's predecessor in mathematics, Locke's in metaphysics—this last, I think, is true—and the real discoverer of the circulation of the blood. This is a little too much. To have written the 'History of the Council of Trent,' and the tracts on the Venetian dispute with Rome, is enough for one man's fame. As to the attempt to make out that he was a real Roman Catholic, even according to the lowest Gallican notions, the thing is impossible. Bossuet, whom the ultramontane divines regard as little better than a heretic, was himself a bigoted ultramontane when compared with Fra Paolo."†

---

* These lines may be found at the end of the 'Miscellaneous Writings.' A Greek drama, which is no longer extant, by the poet Diphilus, is supposed to have been the original of the Rudens.

† Macaulay says, in a letter dated September, 1850: "Fra Paolo is my favorite modern historian. His subject did not admit of vivid painting; but what he did, he did better than any body. I wish that he had not kept his friar's gown; for he was undoubtedly at heart as much a Protestant as Latimer."

" *October 9th.*—I picked up Whitaker's criticism on Gibbon. Pointless spite, with here and there a just remark. It would be strange if in so large a work as Gibbon's there were nothing open to just remark. How utterly all the attacks on his 'History' are forgotten!* this of Whitaker; Randolph's; Chelsum's; Davies's; that stupid beast, Joseph Milner's;† even Watson's. And still the book, with all its great faults of substance and style, retains, and will retain, its place in our literature; and this though it is offensive to the religious feeling of the country, and really most unfair where religion is concerned. But Whitaker was as dirty a cur as I remember."

" *October 14th.*—In the morning ——— called. He seems to be getting on well. He is almost the only person to whom I ever gave liberal assistance without having reason to regret it. Of course I do not speak of my own family; but I am confident that, within the last ten years, I have laid out several hundreds of pounds in trying to benefit people whose own vices and follies have frustrated every attempt to serve them. I have had a letter from a Miss ———, asking me to lend, that is, to give her, a hundred

---

* "A victory," says Gibbon, "over such antagonists was a sufficient humiliation. They were, however, rewarded in this world. Poor Chelsum is indeed neglected; and I dare not boast the making Dr. Watson a bishop. He is a prelate of a large mind and liberal spirit. But I enjoyed the pleasure of giving a royal pension to Dr. Davies, and of collating Dr. Apthorpe to an archiepiscopal living."

† Macaulay's view of Milner is pretty strongly expressed on the margin of his copy of the "History of the Church." "My quarrel with you," he says in one place, "is that you are ridiculously credulous; that you wrest every thing to your own purpose in defiance of all the rules of sound construction; that you are profoundly ignorant of your subject; that your information is second-hand, and that your style is nauseous." On the margin of the passage where Basil says of Gregory Thaumaturgus (in whose miraculous powers Milner devoutly believed), "He never allowed himself to call his brother fool," Macaulay writes: "He never knew such a fool as Milner, then."

Dean Milman, writing for the public eye, indicates the same opinion in terms more befitting the pen of a clergyman: "Milner's 'History of the Church' enjoys an extensive popularity with a considerable class of readers, who are content to accept fervent piety and an accordance with their own religious views, instead of the profound original research, the various erudition, and dispassionate judgment which more rational Christians consider indispensable to an historian. In his answer to Gibbon, Milner unfortunately betrays the incapacity of his mind for historical criticism. When he enters into detail, it is in general on indefensible points, long abandoned by sound scholars."

pounds. I never saw her; I know nothing of her; her only claim on me is that I once gave her money. She will, of course, hate me and abuse me for not complying with this modest request. Except in the single case of ——, I never, as far as I know, reaped any thing in return for charities, which have often been large for my means, except positive ill-will. My facility has tempted those whom I have relieved to make one unreasonable request after another. At last I have been forced to stop, and then they thought themselves wronged.

"I picked up a tract on the Blockade of Norway, by Sir Philip Francis: Junius all over, but Junius grown old. Among other things I read Newman's 'Lectures,' which have just been published. They are ingenious enough, and, I dare say, cogent to those people who call themselves Anglo-Catholics; but to me they are futile as any Rabbinical tradition. One lecture is evidently directed against me, though not by name: and I am quite willing that the public should judge between us.

"I walked to Westbourne Terrace, and talked with Hannah about setting up a brougham. I really shall do it. The cost will be small, and the comfort great. It is but fair, too, that I should have some of the advantage of my own labor."

"*October 25th,* 1850.—My birthday. I am fifty. Well, I have had a happy life. I do not know that any body, whom I have seen close, has had a happier. Some things I regret; but, on the whole, who is better off? I have not children of my own, it is true; but I have children whom I love as if they were my own, and who, I believe, love me. I wish that the next ten years may be as happy as the last ten. But I rather wish it than hope it."

"*November 1st.*—I was shocked to find a letter from Dr. Holland, to the effect that poor Harry Hallam is dying at Sienna. What a trial for my dear old friend! I feel for the lad himself, too. Much distressed. I dined, however. We dine, unless the blow comes very, very near the heart indeed.

"Holland is angry and alarmed about the Papal Bull and the Archbishop of Westminster. I am not; but I am not sorry that other people take fright, for such fright is an additional security to us against that execrable superstition. I begin to feel the same disgust at the Anglo-Catholic and Roman Catholic cant which people after the Restoration felt for the Puritan cant. Their saints' days affect me as the Puritan Sabbath affected drunken Barnaby. Their dates of letters—the Eve of St. Bridget—the Octave of St. Swithin—provoke me as I used to be provoked by the First Month and First Day of the Quakers. I shall not at all wonder if this feeling should become general, and these follies should sink amidst a storm of laughter. Oh for a Butler!"*

---

* It is, perhaps, needless to say that this prayer refers to the author of "Hudibras," and not to the author of the "Analogy."

"*November 2d.*—At breakfast I was comforted by a line from Holland saying that young Hallam is better, and likely to do well. God send it! To Brooks's, and talked on the Wiseman question. I made my hearers very merry."

"*November 4th.*—I am deeply concerned to hear that poor Harry Hallam is gone. Alas! alas! He died on my birthday. There must have been near a quarter of a century between us. I could find it in my heart to cry. Poor Hallam! what will he do? He is more stoical than I am, to be sure. I walked, reading Epictetus in the streets. Anointing for broken bones! Let him try how Hallam will be consoled by being told that the lives of children are οὐκ ἐφ' ἡμῖν."*

"*November 5th.*—I went to poor Hallam's. The servants had heard from him to-day. He was at Florence, hastening home, perhaps with the body. He brought home his son Arthur.† Alas! Looked at the 'Life of Hugh Blair'—a stupid book, by a stupid man, about a stupid man. Surely it is strange that so poor a creature as Blair should ever have had any literary reputation at all. The 'Life' is in that very vile fashion which Dugald Stewart set—not a life, but a series of disquisitions on all sorts of subjects."

"*December 2d.*—To poor Hallam's. He was much as before. At first he wept, and was a good deal affected. Then he brightened up, and we talked, as in old times, for the best part of an hour."

"*December 10th.*—I wrote, or rather transcribed and corrected, much. The declamatory disquisition which I have substituted for the orations of the ancient historians seems to me likely to answer.‡ It is a sort of composition which suits my style, and will probably take with the public. I met Sir Bulwer Lytton, or Lytton Bulwer. He is anxious about some scheme for some association of literary men. I detest all such associations. I hate the notion of gregarious authors. The less we have to do with each other, the better."

"*December 25th.*—In bed, and at breakfast, I read Porson's 'Letters to Archdeacon Travis,' and compared the collected letters with the *Gentleman's Magazine*, in which they originally appeared. The book has a little

---

* "Matters beyond our control."

> "Fair ship, that from the Italian shore
>   Sailest the placid ocean's plains
>   With my lost Arthur's loved remains,
> Spread thy full wings, and waft him o'er."—*In Memoriam.*

‡ Macaulay was then employed upon the controversy about the lawfulness of swearing allegiance to William and Mary, which split the Highchurch divines of 1689 into two parties. See Chapter XIV. of the "History."

suffered from the awkwardness of turning what were letters to Sylvanus Urban* into letters to Archdeacon Travis; but it is a masterly work. A comparison between it and the 'Phalaris' would be a comparison between Porson's mind and Bentley's mind. Porson's more sure-footed, more exact, more neat; Bentley's far more comprehensive and inventive. While walking, I read Bishop Burgess's trash in answer to Porson. Home, and read Turton's defense of Porson against Burgess; an impenetrable dunce, to reason with whom is like kicking a wool-pack. Was there ever such an instance of the blinding power of bigotry as the fact that some men, who were not absolute fools, continued, after reading Porson and Turton, to believe in the authenticity of the text of the 'Three Witnesses?'"

"*January 10th*, 1851.—Rain. Rain. Wrote a little, but am out of heart. The events take new shapes. I find that what I have done must be done over again. Yet so much the better. This is the old story. How many times it was so with the first two volumes, and how well it ended at last! I took heart again, and worked.

"I finished the 'Life of Mathews.' It is a strange book; too much of it, but highly interesting. A singular man; certainly the greatest actor that I ever saw; far greater than Munden, Dowton, Liston, or Fawcett; far greater than Kean, though there it is not so easy to make a comparison. I can hardly believe Garrick to have had more of the genuine mimetic genius than Mathews. I often regret that I did not see him more frequently. Why did I not? I can not tell; for I admired him, and laughed my sides sore whenever I saw him."

"*January 13th*.—At breakfast came a summons to Windsor Castle for to-morrow. I feel a twinge at the name. Was ever man so persecuted for such a trifle as I was about that business? And, if the truth were known, without the shadow of a reason. Yet my life must be allowed to have been a very happy one, seeing that such a persecution was among my greatest misfortunes."

"*January 14th*.—To Windsor, and walked up to the Castle. I found my room very comfortable, and read a volume of Jacobite pamphlets by a blazing fire. At eight I went into the Corridor, and was struck by its immense length, and the number and beauty of the objects which it contains. It is near twelve years since I was here. How changed is every thing, and myself among other things! I had a few words with the prince about the Regius professorship of medicine at Cambridge, now vacant by Haviland's death. I remarked that it was impossible to make either Oxford or Cambridge a great medical school. He said, truly enough, that Oxford and Cambridge are larger towns than Heidelberg, and yet that

---

* Sylvanus Urban was the *nom de plume* adopted by the editor of the *Gentleman's Magazine*. In another part of his diary Macaulay says: "Read Porson's 'Letters to Francis.' I am never weary of them."

Heidelberg is eminent as a place of medical education. He added, however, something which explained why this was. There was hardly, he said, a physician in Germany, even at Berlin, even at Vienna, who made one thousand pounds a year by his profession. In that case, a professorship at Heidelberg may well be worth as much as the best practice in the great cities. Here, where Brodie and Bright make more than ten thousand pounds a year, and where, if settled at Cambridge or Oxford, they probably could not make fifteen hundred pounds, there is no chance that the academic chairs will be filled by the heads of the profession.

"At table I was between the Duchess of Norfolk and a foreign woman who could hardly speak English intelligibly. I got on as well as I could. The band covered the talk with a succession of sonorous tunes. 'The Campbells are Coming' was one.* When we went into the drawing-room, the queen came to me with great animation, and insisted on my telling her some of my stories, which she had heard at second-hand from George Grey. I certainly made her laugh heartily. She talked on for some time, most courteously and pleasantly. Nothing could be more sensible than her remarks on German affairs. She asked me about Merle d'Aubigné's book; and I answered that it was not to be implicitly trusted; that the writer was a strong partisan, and too much of a colorist; but that his work well deserved a perusal, and would greatly interest and amuse her. Then came cards, during which I sat and chatted with two maids of honor. The dinner was late, and, consequently, the evening short. At eleven precisely the queen withdrew."

"*January 16th.*—To the station. Lord Aberdeen and George Grey went with me. Throughout this visit we have been inseparable, and have agreed perfectly. We talked much together till another party got into the carriage—a canting fellow, and a canting woman. Their cant was not religious, but philanthropical and phrenological. I never heard such stuff. It was all that we could do to avoid laughing out loud. The lady pronounced that the Exhibition of 1851 would enlarge her ideality, and exercise her locality. Lord Aberdeen had a little before told us some droll stories of the old Scotch judges. Lord Braxfield, at whist, exclaimed to a lady with whom he was playing, 'What are ye doing, ye d—d auld —— ?' and then, recollecting himself, 'Your pardon's begged, madam. I took ye for my ain wife.'

"At half-past seven the brougham came, and I went to dine at Lord John Russell's, pleased and proud, and thinking how unjustly poor Pepys was abused for noting in his diary the satisfaction it gave him to ride in his own coach. This is the first time I ever had a carriage of my own, except when in office."

---

* This is the only authentic instance on record of Macaulay's having known one tune from another.

"*February 5th.*—At breakfast I read the correspondence between Voltaire and Frederic; a precious pair! I looked over my paper on Frederic. It contains much that is just, and much that is lively and spirited; but, on the whole, I think I judged rightly in not reprinting it.* I bought a superb valentine in the Colonnade, and wrote my lines to Miss Stanhope. Pretty lines they are. Then to Westbourne Terrace, and picked up by the way a well-remembered volume, which I had not seen for many years; a translation of some Spanish comedies, one of the few bright specks in our very sullen library at Clapham. Hannah was in delight at seeing it again.

"I read a good deal of what I have written, and was not ill-pleased, especially with the account of the Treason Trials Bill in the eighteenth chapter. These abstracts of Parliamentary debates will be a new, and, I hope, a striking feature in the book."

"*Thursday, May 1st,* 1851.—A fine day for the opening of the Exhibition. A little cloudy in the morning, but generally sunny and pleasant. I was struck by the number of foreigners in the streets. All, however, were respectable and decent people. I saw none of the men of action with whom the Socialists were threatening us. I went to the Park, and along the Serpentine. There were immense crowds on both sides of the water. I should think that there must have been near three hundred thousand people in Hyde Park at once. The sight among the green boughs was delightful. The boats and little frigates darting across the lake; the flags; the music; the guns; every thing was exhilarating, and the temper of the multitude the best possible. I fell in with Punch Greville, and walked with him for an hour. He, like me, thought the outside spectacle better worth seeing than the pageant under cover. He showed me a letter from Madame de Lieven, foolish, with an affectation of cleverness and profundity, just like herself. She calls this Exhibition a bold, a rash experiment. She apprehends a horrible explosion : 'You may get through it safe; and, if you do, you will give yourselves more airs than ever.' And this woman is thought a political oracle in some circles! There is just as much chance of a revolution in England as of the falling of the moon.

"I made my way into the building : a most gorgeous sight; vast; graceful; beyond the dreams of the Arabian romances.† I can not think that the Cæsars ever exhibited a more splendid spectacle. I was quite dazzled,

---

* Macaulay changed his mind before long, and the essay on Frederic took its place in the collected edition.

† In October Macaulay writes : "As the Exhibition is drawing toward its close the crowd becomes greater and greater. Yesterday I let my servants go for the last time. I shall go no more. Alas! alas! It was a glorious sight; and it is associated in my mind with all whom I love most. I am glad that the building is to be removed. I have no wish to see the corpse when the life has departed."

and I felt as I did on entering St. Peter's. I wandered about, and elbowed my way through the crowd which filled the nave, admiring the general effect, but not attending much to details.

"Home, and finished 'Persuasion.' I have now read over again all Miss Austin's novels. Charming they are; but I found a little more to criticise than formerly. Yet there are in the world no compositions which approach nearer to perfection."

"*May* 26*th*.—To-day the Exhibition opens at a shilling. It seems to be the fate of this extraordinary show to confound all predictions, favorable and unfavorable. Fewer people went on the shilling day than on the five-shilling day. I got a letter from ——, who is in great distress about his son's debts. I am vexed and sorry; but I wrote, insisting on being allowed to settle the matter; and I was pleased that (though there have been, and will be, other calls on me) I made this offer from the heart and with the wish to have it accepted.

"I finished 'Joan of Arc.' The last act is absurd beyond description. The monstrous violation of history which every body knows is not to be defended. Schiller might just as well have made Wallenstein dethrone the emperor, and reign himself over Germany—or Mary become Queen of England, and cut off Elizabeth's head—as make Joan fall in the moment of victory."

"*June* 12*th*.—After breakfast —— called. I must make one more effort to save him, and it shall be the last.* Margaret came, to take me to Thackeray's lecture. He is full of humor and imagination, and I only wish that these lectures may answer both in the way of fame and money. He told me, as I was going out, that the scheme had done wonders for him; and I told him, and from my heart, that I wished he had made ten times as much. Dear Lord Lansdowne was there, looking much better; much. I dined at Baron Parke's. It was pleasant, and I thought that I pleased; but perhaps was mistaken. Then to Lady Granville's rout, where I found many friends, and all kind. I seldom appear, and therefore am the better received. This racketing does not suit me; but civility requires me to go once for ten times that I am asked to parties."

"*June* 9*th*.—I picked up the volumes of 1832 and 1833 of Cobbett's *Register*. His style had then gone off, and the circumstance that he was in Parliament was against him. His mind was drawn away from that which he did well to that which he did very poorly. My own name often appears in these volumes. Many people thought that he had a peculiar animosity to me; but I doubt it. He abuses me; but less than he abused almost every other public man whom he mentioned.

---

* It was not the last, by a good many. The person of whom Macaulay writes thus had no claim whatever upon him except their common humanity.

"An American has written to me from Arkansas, and sent me a copy of Bancroft's 'History.' Very civil and kind; but by some odd mistake he directs to me at Abbotsford. Does he think that all Britishers who write books live there together?"

Macaulay spent August and September at Malvern, in a pleasant villa, embowered in "a wood full of blackbirds." Mr. Ellis gave him ten days of his company, timing his visit so as to attend the Musical Festival at Worcester.

Malvern, August 21st, 1851.

DEAR ELLIS,—I shall expect you on Wednesday next. I have got the tickets for the "Messiah." There may be some difficulty about conveyances during the festival. But the supply here is immense. On every road round Malvern coaches and flies pass you every ten minutes, to say nothing of irregular vehicles. For example, the other day I was overtaken by a hearse as I was strolling along, and reading the night expedition of Diomede and Ulysses. "Would you like a ride, sir?" said the driver. "Plenty of room." I could not help laughing. "I dare say I shall want such a carriage some day or other. But I am not ready yet." The fellow, with the most consummate professional gravity, answered, "I meant, sir, that there was plenty of room on the box."

I do not think that I ever, at Cambridge or in India, did a better day's work in Greek than to-day. I have read at one stretch fourteen books of the "Odyssey," from the Sixth to the Nineteenth inclusive.* I did it while walking to Worcester and back. I have a great deal to say about the old fellow. I admire him more than ever; but I am now quite sure that the "Iliad" is a piece of mosaic, made very skillfully long

---

* In his journal of August 19th Macaulay writes: "I walked far into Herefordshire, and read, while walking, the last five books of the 'Iliad,' with deep interest and many tears. I was afraid to be seen crying by the parties of walkers that met me as I came back; crying for Achilles cutting off his hair; crying for Priam rolling on the ground in the court-yard of his house: mere imaginary beings, creatures of an old ballad-maker who died near three thousand years ago."

after his time out of several of his lays, with bits here and there of the compositions of inferior minstrels.

I am planning various excursions. We can easily see Hereford between breakfast and dinner one day, and Gloucester on another. Cheltenham, and Tewkesbury, with its fine church, are still more accessible. The rain is over; the afternoon has been brilliant, and I hope that we have another glorious month before us. You shall have water in plenty. I have a well-polished ἀσάμινθος* for you, into which going you may wash, and out of which you may come, looking like a god.

Ever yours,   T. B. MACAULAY.

                                          Malvern, September 12th, 1851.

DEAR ELLIS,—I have sent William to look after your business. In the mean time, I must own that your ill-luck rather titillates the malicious parts of my nature. The taking of a place by a railway train, which the vulgar, myself included, perform in thirty seconds, is with you an operation requiring as much thought and time as the purchase of an estate. On two successive days did I kick my heels in the street, first before the railway office, and then before the Bellevue Hotel, while you were examining and cross-examining the book-keepers, and arranging and rearranging your plans. I must say that your letter is well calculated to make me uneasy as to my own return to London. For if all your forethought and anxiety, your acute inquiries and ingenious combinations, have ended thus, how can such a careless fellow as I am hope to reach town without immeasurable disappointment and losses?

Here is William at last with a letter from the coach-office, but no money. As to the three shillings, οὔποτε ἥξουσι πρὸς σε· οὔποτε ἥξουσιν.† I send the book-keeper's explanation. You took your place in one coach: you rode to Worcester in another: you have paid the full fare to both: and you will not recover a half-penny from either. Your case, if that is

---

* The Homeric word for a bath. The sentence is, of course, a ludicrously literal translation from the Greek.

† "You will never get them back: never."

any comfort, is not a rare one. Indeed, it seems to be the
common practice at Malvern to travel in this way. And here
we have an explanation of the extraordinary number of
coaches at this place. There is room for a great many rival
establishments, when passengers pay both for the conveyance
by which they go and for that by which they do not go.

Good-bye. I miss you much, and console myself as well as
I can with Demosthenes, Goethe, Lord Campbell, and Miss
Ferrier. Ever yours,   T. B. MACAULAY.

"*September* 19*th.*—I put 'Wilhelm Meister' into my pocket; walked to
the Cleaveland Ferry; crossed the Severn, and rambled along the eastern
bank to Upton. The confessions of the pious Stiftsdame interested me, as
they have always done, more than I can well explain. I felt this when I
read them first on the Indian Ocean, and I felt it again when I read them
at the inn at Hereford in 1844. I think that the cause of the interest
which I feel in them is that Goethe was here exerting himself to do, as an
artist, what, as far as I know, no other mere artist has ever tried to do.
From Augustin downward, people strongly under religious impressions
have written their confessions, or, in the cant phrase, their experience;
and very curious many of their narratives are. John Newton's, Bunyan's,
Will Huntington's, Cowper's, Wesley's, Whitefield's, Scott's—there is no
end of them. When worldly men have imitated these narratives, it has
almost always been in a satirical and hostile spirit. Goethe is the single
instance of an unbeliever who has attempted to put himself into the person of one of these pious autobiographers. He has tried to imitate them,
just as he tried to imitate the Greek dramatists in his 'Iphigenia,' and the
Roman poets in his elegies. A vulgar artist would have multiplied texts
and savory phrases. He has done nothing of the kind; but has tried to
exhibit the spirit of piety in the highest exaltation; and a very singular
performance he has produced.*

"What odd things happen! Two gentlemen, or at least two men in
good coats and hats, overtook me as I was strolling through one of the
meadows close to the river. One of them stared at me, touched his hat,
and said, 'Mr. Macaulay, I believe.' I admitted the truth of the imputa-
tion. So the fellow went on: 'I suppose, sir, you are come here to study

---

* When Macaulay was at Frankfort he went to Goethe's house, and
"found it with some difficulty. I was greatly interested; not that he is
one of my first favorites; but the earlier books of his life of himself have
a great charm for me; and the old house plays a great part in the narrative. The house of Wilhelm Meister's father, too, is evidently this house
at Frankfort."

the localities of the battle of Worcester. We shall expect a very fine account of the battle of Worcester.' I hinted with all delicacy that I had no more to do with the battle of Worcester than with the battle of Marathon. 'Of course not, sir, of course not. The battle of Worcester certainly does not enter into your plan.' So we bowed and parted. I thought of the proverb,* and I thought, too, that on this occasion the name of Tom Fool might be properly applied to more than one of the parties concerned."

"*September* 21*st*.—I saw in the hedge the largest snake that I remember to have seen in wild natural liberty. I remembered the agonies of terror into which the sight of a snake, creeping among the shrubs at Barley Wood, threw me when I was a boy of six. It was a deep, and really terrible, impression. My mother feared that it would make me ill. It was to no purpose that they told me, and that I told myself, that there was no danger. A serpent was to me like a giant or a ghost—a horrible thing which was mentioned in story-books, but which had no existence in England; and the actual sight affected me as if a hobgoblin had really appeared. I followed the snake of to-day for some distance. He seemed as much afraid of me as I was of his kinsman forty-four years ago. During this long walk I read 'Wilhelm Meister' occasionally. I never liked it so little. Even the account of Aurelia's and Marianne's deaths, which used to break my heart, moved me as little as it moved those brutes Lothario and Wilhelm."

At the close of 1851 Palmerston was ejected from the Foreign Office. The Government needed no small accession of prestige in order to balance so heavy a loss, and overtures were made, without much hope of success, to induce Macaulay to accept a seat in the Cabinet.

"*December* 24*th*.—Palmerston is out. It was high time; but I can not help being sorry. A daring, indefatigable, high-spirited man; but too fond of conflict, and too ready to sacrifice every thing to victory when once he was in the ring. Lord Granville, I suppose, will succeed. I wish him well. 1851 has done a great deal for him."

"*December* 25*th*.—I met Lord Granville at Brooks's. I congratulated him, and gave him good wishes warmly and sincerely; but I spoke kindly, and with regret, as I felt, about Palmerston. From Granville's answer, guarded as it very properly was, I judge that we have not yet seen the true explanation. He told me that anxiety had kept him awake two nights."

"*December* 31*st*.—I met Peacock; a clever fellow, and a good scholar.†

---

* "More people know Tom Fool than Tom Fool knows."

† This passage refers to the author of "Headlong Hall," and not to the Dean of Ely, as some readers might possibly suppose.

I am glad to have an opportunity of being better acquainted with him. We had out Aristophanes, Æschylus, Sophocles, and several other old fellows, and tried each other's quality pretty well. We are both strong enough in these matters for gentlemen. But he is editing the 'Supplices.' Æschylus is not to be edited by a man whose Greek is only a secondary pursuit."

"*January* 18*th*, 1852.—At dinner I received a note from Lord John asking to see me to-morrow at eleven."

"*January* 19*th.* — I was anxious; but determined, if I found myself hard pressed, to beg a day for consideration, and then to send a refusal in writing. I find it difficult to refuse people face to face. I went to Chesham Place. He at once asked me to join the Cabinet. I refused, and gave about a quarter of my reasons, though half a quarter would have been sufficient. I told him that I should be of no use; that I was not a debater; that it was too late for me to become one; that I might once have turned out effective in that way, but that now my literary habits, and my literary reputation, had made it impossible. I pleaded health, temper, and tastes. He did not urge me much, and I think has been rather induced by others, than by his own judgment, to make the proposition. I added that I would not sit for any nomination borough, and that my turn of mind disqualified me for canvassing great constituent bodies. I might have added that I did not wish to be forced to take part against Palmerston in a personal dispute; that I much doubt whether I should like the new Reform Bill; and that I had no reason to believe that all that I think right will be done as respects national defense. I did speak very strongly on this point, as I feel."

"*January* 31*st.*—I see that Lord Broughton retires, and that Maule goes to the India Board. I might have had that place, I believe; the pleasantest in the Government, and the best suited to me; but I judged far better for my reputation and peace of mind."

In February, Macaulay paid another visit to Windsor Castle.

"*February* 6*th.*—We breakfasted at nine. I strolled up and down the fine gallery for an hour; then with Mahon to the Library; and then to the top of the Round Tower, and enjoyed a noble view. In the Library, taking up by the merest chance a finely bound book, it proved to be Ticknor's—a presentation copy, with a letter from the author to the queen saying that he had sent his volumes because he had been told by the American minister that an eminent literary man had recommended them to her majesty. I was the eminent literary man; and I dare say that I could find the day in my journal. It is an odd coincidence that I should light on his letter. Dinner was at a quarter to seven, on account of the play which was to follow. The theatre was handsome, the scenery good, and the play 'King John.' There were faults in the acting, as there are great faults in the play, considered as an acting play; but there was great effect likewise. Constance made me cry. The scene between King John and Hubert, and that between Hubert and Arthur, were very telling. Faulconbridge swaggered well. The allusions to a French invasion and to the Popish encroachments would have been furiously applauded at Drury Lane or Covent Garden. Here we applauded with some reserve. The little girl who acted Arthur did wonders.*   Lord Salisbury seemed not to like the part which his namesake performed in the play."†

"*February 16th.*—I finished 'St. Simon's Memoirs,' and am more struck with the goodness of the good parts than ever. To be sure, the road from fountain to fountain lies through a very dry desert."

"*May 1st.*—A cold 1st of May. After breakfast I went to Turnham Green, to look at the place. I found it after some search; the very spot beyond all doubt, and admirably suited for an assassination.‡

"On my return I looked into Shakspeare, and could not get away from him. I passed the whole day, till it was time to dress, in turning him over. Then to dine with the Royal Academy.§   A great number of my friends, and immense smiling and shaking of hands. I got a seat in a pleasant situation near Thesiger, Hallam, and Inglis. The scene was lively, and many of the pictures good. I was charmed by Stanfield's Rochelle, and Roberts's three paintings. It is the old duke's birthday: he is eighty-three to-day. I never see him now without a painful interest. I look at him every time with the thought that this may be the last. We drank

---

* It is almost worth while to be past middle life in order to have seen Miss Kate Terry in Arthur.

†   "*Sal.* Stand by, or I shall gall you, Faulconbridge.
         Bast. Thou wert better gall the devil, Salisbury.
   If thou but frown on me, or stir thy foot,
   Or teach thy hasty spleen to do me shame,
   I'll strike thee dead.   Put up thy sword betime;
   Or I'll so maul you and your toasting-iron
   That you shall think the devil is come from hell."

‡ See the account of the assassination plot in chapter xxi. of the "History." "The place and time were fixed. The place was to be a narrow and winding lane leading from the landing-place on the north of the river to Turnham Green. The spot may still easily be found. The ground has since been drained by trenches. But in the seventeenth century it was a quagmire, through which the royal coach was with difficulty tugged at a foot's pace. The time was to be the afternoon of Saturday, the 15th of February."

§ Macaulay attended the dinner in his character of Professor of Ancient Literature to the Royal Academy.

his health with immense shouting and table - banging. He returned thanks, and spoke of the loss of the *Birkenhead*. I remarked (and Lawrence, the American minister, said that he had remarked the same thing) that, in his eulogy of the poor fellows who were lost, the duke never spoke of their courage, but always of their discipline and subordination. He repeated it several times over. The courage, I suppose, he treated as a thing of course. Lord Derby spoke with spirit, but with more hesitation than on any occasion on which I have heard him. Disraeli's speech was clever. In defiance of all rule, he gave Lord John Russell's health. Lord John answered good-humoredly and well. I was glad of it. Although a speech at the Royal Academy is not much, it is important that, whatever he does now, should be well done."

CHAPTER XIII.

1852-1856.

The Magnetoscope, and Table-turning.—Macaulay's Re-election for Edinburgh, and the General Satisfaction which it occasioned.—He has a Serious Attack of Illness.—Clifton.—Extracts from Macaulay's Journal.—His Strong Feelings for Old Associations.—Barley Wood.—Letters to Mr. Ellis.—Great Change in Macaulay's Health and Habits.—His Speech at Edinburgh.—The House of Commons.—Mr. Disraeli's Budget.—Formation of Lord Aberdeen's Ministry.—The Judges' Exclusion Bill.—The India Bill.—The Annuity Tax.—Macaulay ceases to take an Active Part in Politics.—Letters to Mr. Ellis.—Mrs. Beecher Stowe.—Tunbridge Wells.—Plato.—Mr. Vizetelly.—Macaulay's Patriotism.—The Crimean War.—Open Competition.—The "History."—Thames Ditton.—Publication of Macaulay's Third and Fourth Volumes.—Statistics of the Sale of the "History."—Honors conferred on Macaulay.—The British Museum.

THE year 1852 opened very pleasantly for Macaulay. From January to July his diary presents a record of hopeful and uninterrupted literary labor, and of cheerful dinners and breakfasts at the houses which he cared to frequent. About this period the friends among whom he lived were much given to inquiries into fields of speculation that may not unfairly be classed under the head of the occult sciences; allusions to which more than once occur both in Lord Carlisle's and in Macaulay's journals. Lord Carlisle writes:

"*May* 19*th*, 1852.—Breakfasted with the Mahons. We talked a good deal of the magnetoscope, which has received a staggerer from Dufferin, who went rather disguised a second time, and got quite a different character. The man told Macaulay that he was an historical painter, which the Bishop of Oxford thinks a very just character. Macaulay, I hear, denounces the wretched quack without measure. At twelve there was a large assemblage at the bishop's to see a clairvoyant, brought by Sir David Brewster very much for the purpose of encountering Whewell, who is an arch-skeptic. About twelve of us in turns put our hands upon her eyes, and in every instance she read without mistake one, two, or three lines from books taken at random. We believed, except Whewell; who has very resilient eyes himself, which he thinks can see through every thing."

Macaulay held the same opinion about his own eyes, at any rate so far as concerned the magnetoscope, as the following extract from his diary will show:

"*May* 18*th*, 1852.—Mahon came, and we went to a house in —— Street, where a Dr. —— performs his feats of phrenology and mesmerism. I was half ashamed of going, but Mahon made a point of it. The Bishop of Oxford, and his brother Robert, came soon after us. Never was there such paltry quackery. The fraud was absolutely transparent. I can not conceive how it should impose upon a child. The man knew nothing about me, and therefore his trickery completely failed him. He made me out to be a painter—a landscape painter or a historical painter. He had made out Hallam to be a musician. I could hardly restrain myself from expressing my contempt and disgust while he was pawing my head, and poring over the rotations and oscillations of his pendulum, and the deviations to different points of the compass. Dined at the club. We have taught Lord Aberdeen to talk. He is really quite gay."

"*May* 19*th*.—To dine with the Bishop of London. The party should have been pleasant: the Bishop of Oxford, Milman, Hallam, and Rajah Brooke. But unluckily we got into a somewhat keen argument about clairvoyance. The two bishops lost their temper. Indeed, we were all too disputatious, though I hope I was not offensively so. The ladies, who wanted to be off to the queen's ball, wished us, I dare say, at Jericho."

Macaulay writes on a subsequent occasion: "A breakfast-party at my chambers. There was talk about electricity, and the rotatory motion of tables under electrical influence. I was very incredulous. We tried the experiment on my table; and there certainly was a rotatory motion, but probably impressed by the Bishop of Oxford, though he declared that he was not quite certain whether he had pushed or not. We tried again; and then, after we had given it up, he certainly pushed, and caused a rotatory motion exactly similar to what we had seen before. The experiment therefore failed. At the same time, I would not confidently say in this case, as I say in cases of clairvoyance, that there must be deception. I know too little of electricity to judge."*

Equable and tranquil as was the course of Macaulay's life during the earlier months of 1852, that year had still both good and evil in store for him. The Parliamentary session had been fruitful in events. "I met Greville in the street," Macaulay writes. "He is going to Broadlands, and seems persuaded that Palmerston has nothing but revenge on Lord John in his head and heart, and that he will soon be leader of the House of Commons under Lord Derby. I doubt." He might well doubt. The late Foreign Secretary was not the man to sit down under a grievance; but he knew how to pay off old scores in accordance with the rules of political decency. By his powerful aid, the Conservatives succeeded in defeating the ministry on a detail of the Militia Bill; and Lord Derby came in with a minority, and scrambled through the session as best he might. While the summer was yet young, Parliament was dissolved, and the general election took place in July, with no very great issue definitely at stake. The ministerial programme was not of a nature to arouse enthusiasm. Lord Derby confined himself to vague hints, which might be construed to mean either that protection was capable of being

---

* Macaulay did not love charlatans; and he included in that category some who pretty confidently arrogated to themselves the title of philosophers. "There came," he once writes to Lady Trevelyan, "a knock at my door, and in walked that miserable old impostor ——, who, I hoped, had been hanged or guillotined years ago. You must have heard of him. He is a votary of Spurzheim; a compound of all the quackeries, physiological and theological, of half a century. I always detested the fellow; but I could not turn him out of the room; for he came up with, 'Do you not remember? You are so like the dear man, Zachary. It was just so that he used to look on me.' (I looked, by-the-bye, as sulky as a bear.) 'I felt your dear skull when you was a child, and I prophesied that you should be a minister of state. Paff! That is a demonstration. I keep my eye on you ever since. Paff! It come true!' So I desired the man to sit down, and was as civil as I could be to one whom I know to be a mere Dousterswivel." Macaulay, very characteristically, ended his letter by regretting that his visitor did not ask for pecuniary assistance, in order that he might have given him a ten-pound note.

revived, or that he personally had not ceased to be a mourner for its death; but he made up for his reticence on the question of the day by entreating the country to believe that his government had every intention of upholding the Established Church. The country, which was very well aware that the Church could keep on its feet without the assistance of a Tory administration, but which was sincerely anxious to be re-assured that the Cabinet had no wish to tamper with free trade, did not respond to the appeal, and the electioneerers of the Carlton failed to make any marked impression upon the borough constituencies.

Edinburgh was one of the places where the Conservatives resolved to try an almost desperate chance. The Liberals of that city were at odds among themselves; and the occurrences of 1847 had not been such as to attract any candidate who enjoyed the position and reputation which would have enabled him to unite a divided party. Honorably ambitious to obtain a worthy representative for the capital of Scotland, and sincerely desirous to make amends for their harsh usage of a great man who had done his best to serve them, the electors turned their eyes toward Macaulay. A resolution in favor of taking the necessary measures for furthering his return was carried in a crowded public meeting by unanimous acclamation. The speeches in support of that resolution did honor to those who made them. " No man," said Mr. Adam Black, " has given stronger pledges than Mr. Macaulay that he will defend the rights of the people against the encroachments of despotism and the licentiousness of democracy. His pledges have not been given upon the hustings during the excitement of an election; but they have been published to the world in the calm deliberation of the closet; and he stands and falls by them. If Mr. Macaulay has a fault, it is that he is too straightforward, too open; that he uses no ambiguities to disarm opposition. By many his early, his eloquent, his constant, his consistent advocacy of civil liberty is forgotten, while a few unconsidered words are harped upon. Will you lose the most powerful defender for a piece of etiquette? Will you rob the British Senate of one of its brightest ornaments ? Will you deprive Edinburgh of the honor of association with one of the most illustrious men of the day ? Will you silence that voice whose tones would sustain the sinking spirits of the friends of constitutional liberty in Europe ? No. I know the inhabitants of Edinburgh are not so unwise. It is in their power to secure the most able advocate of their own cause, and of the cause of truth and liberty in the world; and they will secure him." The resolution, proposed in these words by the chief of the Edinburgh Whigs, was seconded by a Radical; a fine fellow, whose remarks were very brief, as is almost universally the case in Scotland and in the North of England with local leaders who have any real influence over the political conduct of their fellow-citizens. " The vexatious question," he said, " being long ago settled upon which alone I, along with several hundred other electors, felt reluctantly constrained to withhold our support from Mr. Macaulay at the last election, I have great pleasure in having this opportunity afforded me of returning to my first love by seconding the nomination of that illustrious historian and statesman."

To Miss Macaulay.

Albany, June 19th, 1852.

DEAR FANNY,—I have not made, and do not mean to make, the smallest move toward the people of Edinburgh. But they, to my great surprise, have found out that they treated me ill five years ago, and that they are now paying the penalty. They can get nobody to stand who is likely to do them credit; and it seemed as if they were in danger of having members who would have made them regret not only me, but Cowan. Then, without any communication with me, it was suggested by some of the most respectable citizens that the town might solve its difficulties by electing me without asking me to go down, or to give any pledges, or even any opinion, on political matters. The hint was eagerly taken up; and I am assured that the feeling in my favor is strong, and that I shall probably be at the head of the poll. All that I have been asked to do is to say that, if I am chosen on those terms, I will sit. On full consideration, I did not think that I could, consistently with my duty, decline the invitation.

To me, personally, the sacrifice is great. Though I shall not make a drudge of myself, and though I certainly shall never, in any event, accept office, the appearance of my next volumes may be postponed a year, or even two. But it seems to me to be of the highest importance that great constituent bodies should learn to respect the conscience and the honor of their representatives; should not expect slavish obedience from men of spirit and ability; and should, instead of catechising such men, and caviling at them, repose in them a large confidence. The way in which such bodies have of late behaved has driven many excellent persons from public life, and will, unless a remedy is found, drive away many more. The conduct of Edinburgh toward me was not worse than that of several other places to their members; but it attracted more notice, and has been often mentioned, in Parliament and out of Parliament, as a flagrant instance of the caprice and perverseness of even the most intelligent bodies of electors. It is, therefore, not an unimportant nor an undesirable thing that Edinburgh should, quite spontaneously, make a very signal, I may say, an unprecedented, reparation.

Do not talk about this more than you find absolutely necessary; but treat it lightly, as I do in all companies where I hear it mentioned. Ever yours,   T. B. MACAULAY.

Macaulay's diary amply proves that in this letter to his sister he had written about the Edinburgh election exactly as he had felt; if, indeed, he had been capable of writing otherwise to any person, or on any subject.

"*May* 15*th*.—I met Dundas in Bond Street, and went with him to Brooks's. Craig showed me a letter from Adam Black, by which it appears that some of the people at Edinburgh think of putting me up without applying to me. I said a little to discourage the notion, but thought it best not to appear to treat it seriously. I dined with Lord Broughton. Lord John and I sat together, and got on very well. I can not help loving him; and I regret the diminution of his weight and popularity both for his own sake and for that of the country."

"*May 27th.*—Breakfast with Mahon. Very pleasant it was. I had a letter from Hannah, inclosing one from Craig about Edinburgh. She has acquitted herself with true feminine skill and tact. I feel quite indifferent about the matter. I should like the *amende.* I should dislike the trouble. The two feelings balance each other; so I have only to follow a perfectly straightforward course, which indeed is always best."

"*June 9th.*—I received a letter from James Simpson about the election, and answered him as I resolved. I am fully determined that no trace of vacillation or inconsistency shall be discerned in what I write and say. I shall stick to one plain story."

Little as he wished it, Macaulay soon had to tell that story to the public at large. The Committee of the Scottish Reformation Society, insisting on their privilege as electors, wrote to him in respectful terms to inquire whether, in the event of his being returned to Parliament, he was prepared to vote against the grant to Maynooth. He replied as follows:

To the Secretary of the Scottish Reformation Society.

June 23d, 1852.

Sir,—I must beg to be excused from answering the questions which you put to me. I have great respect for the gentlemen in whose name you write, but I have nothing to ask of them. I am not a candidate for their suffrages; I have no desire to sit again in Parliament, and I certainly shall never again sit there, except in an event which I did not till very lately contemplate as possible, and which even now seems to me highly improbable. If, indeed, the electors of such a city as Edinburgh should, without requiring from me any explanation or any guarantee, think fit to confide their interests to my care, I should not feel myself justified in refusing to accept a public trust offered me in a manner so honorable and so peculiar. I have not, I am sensible, the smallest right to expect that I shall on such terms be chosen to represent a great constituent body; but I have a right to say that on no other terms can I be induced to leave that quiet and happy retirement in which I have passed the last four years.

I have the honor to be yours, etc.,

T. B. MACAULAY.

The dignified minuteness with which Macaulay defined his position did not altogether meet the views of his supporters; and yet it is not easy to see how, under circumstances of such extreme delicacy, the letter could have been better written.

"*June 30th.*—I heard from Adam Black, who is alarmed about the effect which my answer to the Reformation Society may have upon the election. It is very odd that, careless as I am about the result of the whole business, a certain disagreeable physical excitement was produced by Black's letter. All day I have felt unstrung; a weight at my heart, and an indescribable sense of anxiety. These are the penalties of advancing life. My reason is as clear as ever, and tells me that I have not the slightest cause for uneasiness. I answered Adam, using language much gentler than I should have used except out of consideration for him."

"*July 5th.*—I see in *The Scotsman* my answer to Adam, or most of it. I hardly like this; but no doubt it was done for the best. I can not bear any thing that looks like stooping."

It is difficult to imagine how even Macaulay could discern any trace of obsequiousness in the language of his letter to Mr. Black. "I despair," he writes, "of being able to use words which will not be distorted. How stands the case? I say that such a distinction is so rare that I lately thought it unattainable, and that even now I hardly venture to expect that I shall attain it; and I am told that I hold it cheap. I say that to be elected member for Edinburgh, without appearing as a candidate, would be a high and peculiar honor—an honor which would induce me to make a sacrifice such as I would in no other case—and I am told that this is to treat the electors contemptuously. My language, naturally construed, was respectful—nay, humble. If any person finds an insult in it, the reason must be that he is determined to find an insult in every thing I write."

"*July 7th.*—Broken sleep at night, and then an eventful day. The *Times* is full of election oratory. All is right, on the whole. The City is well; the Tower Hamlets well; at Greenwich a check, but very slight; gains at Reading, Aylesbury, Horsham, and Hertford; but for the gain at Hertford I am sorry, from personal regard for Mahon. I am glad that Strutt heads the poll at Nottingham."

"*July 8th.*—Another day of excitement, following another bad night.

Immediately after breakfast I went to Golden Square, and polled for Shelley and Evans. All the day was taken up with questioning, and answering questions; waiting for news, and devouring it. Brooks's was quite like a bee-hive. We were anxious to the last about Westminster. I have had news from Black and Craig—welcome, and unwelcome. My success, if it is to be so called, seems certain. I shall not go down to the declaration of the poll. I can not travel all night in my present state of health; and, as to starting on Tuesday morning, and going as far as Berwick with the chance of having to turn back in case of a reverse, the thing is not to be thought of. I have held my head pretty high; and this would be a humiliation aggravated tenfold by the reserve, approaching to haughtiness, which I have hitherto maintained."

In spite of Mr. Black's friendly apprehensions, Macaulay's high and rigid bearing had not been distasteful to the Edinburgh electors. They justly considered that the self-respect of a member of Parliament reflects itself upon his constituents; and they were rather proud, than not, of voting for a candidate who was probably the worst electioneerer since Coriolanus. The enthusiasm in his favor was not confined to his own party. Professor Wilson, the most distinguished survivor from the old school of Scotch Toryism, as Toryism was understood by Lord Melville and Sir Walter Scott, performed the last public act of his bustling and jovial existence by going to the poll for Macaulay. At the close of the day the numbers stood:

Macaulay	1846
Cowan	1753
M'Laren	1561
Bruce	1068
Campbell	625

It is no exaggeration to say that from one end of the island to the other the tidings were received with keen and all but universal satisfaction.* Amidst the passions and ambitions and

---

* "All over the country the news of his election was received with a burst of joy. Men congratulated each other as if some dear friend or relation of their own had received so signal an honor. People who had never seen his face shook hands with one another in an unreasoning way on the receipt of such glorious news."—*The Public Life of Lord Macaulay.* By the Rev. Frederick Arnold, B.A.

jealousies of a general election that was to decide the fate of
a ministry, the combatants on both sides found time to rejoice
over an event which was regarded, not as a party victory, but
as the triumph of intellectual eminence and political integrity.
I well remember blushing and trembling with a boy's delight
when Albert Smith, in two or three dashing couplets inserted
off-hand into the best of his admirable songs, announced that
Edinburgh had at last put itself right with Mr. Macaulay;
and I still seem to hear the prolonged and repeated cheering
that broke forth from every corner of an audience which, unless it differed from every other London audience of its class,
must have been at least three-fourths Tory.

But the very same week which honored Macaulay with so
marked a proof of the esteem and admiration of his countrymen brought with it likewise sad and sure indications that
the great labors to which his fame was due had not been undertaken with impunity. "In the midst of my triumphs,"
he writes, "I am but poorly;" and he was one who never complained lightly. For some months past such ominous passages
as these had been frequent in his journal: "I turned over the
new volumes of Thiers's book — the Austrian campaign of
1809. It is heavy. I hope that my volumes will be more attractive reading. I am out of sorts, however, at present, and
can not write. Why? I can not tell. I will wait a day or
two, and then try anew." And again: "I wrote some of my
'History;' not amiss; but I am not in the stream yet. I feel
quite oppressed by the weight of the task. How odd a thing
the human mind is! Mine, at least. I could write a queer
Montaignish essay on my morbidities. I sometimes lose
months, I do not know how; accusing myself daily, and yet
really incapable of vigorous exertion. I seem under a spell of
laziness. Then I warm, and can go on working twelve hours
at a stretch. How I worked a year ago! And why can not
I work so now?"

He was soon to know. On the 15th of July, two days after the election was decided, he describes himself as extremely
languid and oppressed; hardly able to walk or breathe. A
week later he says: "I was not well to-day; something the

matter with the heart. I felt a load on my breast. I was much unstrung, and could hardly help shedding tears of mere weakness: but I did help it. I shrink from the journey to Edinburgh, and the public appearance. I am sure that, in the state in which I am, I shall be forced to sit down in five minutes; if, indeed, I do not faint, which I have repeatedly expected to do of late."

The day on which he was to address his constituents was close at hand, and there was no time to be lost. "I sent for Bright. He came with a stethoscope; pronounced that the action of the heart was much deranged, and positively forbade me to think of going to Edinburgh. I went out, but could hardly get along with the help of my stick; so I took a cab to Westbourne Terrace, and returned in the same way. Their society and kindness keep up my spirits, which are but low. I am vexed with myself for having suffered myself to be enticed back to public life. My book seems to me certain to be a failure. Yet, when I look up any part, and read it, I can not but see that it is better than the other works on the same subject. That, to be sure, is not saying much; for Ralph, Smollett, Kennett, Somerville, Belsham, Lord Dungannon, are all of them wretched writers of history; and Burnet, who down to the Revolution is most valuable and amusing, becomes dull as soon as he reaches the reign of William. I should be sorry to leave that reign unfinished."

For some weeks to come Macaulay was very ill indeed; and he never recovered the secure and superabundant health which he had hitherto enjoyed. It is needless to say that the affection which he had passed his life in deserving did not fail him now. Lady Trevelyan saw Dr. Bright, and learned that the case was more serious than she believed her brother himself to be aware of; a belief which was quite erroneous, as his journal proves, but under which he very willingly allowed her to lie. She took upon herself the arrangements necessary for the postponement of the Edinburgh meeting, and then accompanied Macaulay down to Clifton; where she saw him comfortably settled, and staid with him until he began to mend.

" *Clifton, August 8th,* 1852.—I went out, reading ' Julius Cæsar ' in Suetonius, and was overtaken by heavy rain and thunder. I could not get under a tree for fear of lightning, and could not run home for fear of bringing on the palpitation; so I walked through the rain as slowly and gravely as if I had been a mourner in a funeral. The slightest excitement or
anxiety affects the play of my heart. In spite of myself my spirits are
low; but my reason tells me that hardly any man living has so much to
be thankful for. And I will be thankful, and firm, as far as I am master
of myself. Hannah and I did not venture out after dinner, but chatted
over old times, affectionately, and very pleasantly."

" *Sunday, August 15th.*—To Christ Church. I got a place among the free
seats, and heard not a bad sermon on the word ' Therefore.' The preacher
disclaimed all intention of startling us by oddity, after the fashion of the
seventeenth century; but I doubt whether he did not find in St. Paul's
' therefore ' much more than St. Paul thought of. There was a collection
for church-building, and I slipped my sovereign into the plate the more
willingly because the preacher asked for our money on sensible grounds,
and in a manly manner."

"*August 16th.*—The *Times* brought the news of Sir James Parker's death.
He died of heart-complaint. Poor fellow! I feel for him. The attack
came on just as he was made vice-chancellor. Mine came on just as I
was elected for Edinburgh. Mine may, very likely, end as his has ended;
and it may be for the best that it should do so. My eyes fill with tears
when I think of those whom I must leave; but there is no mixture of
pusillanimity in my tenderness. I long to see Hannah and Margaret. I
wish that they were back again from the Continent; but I do not think
that the end is so near. To-day I wrote a pretty fair quantity of ' History.' I should be glad to finish William before I go. But this is like the
old excuses that were made to Charon."

Some fastidious critics think it proper to deny Macaulay the
title of a poet; and it was a title which he did not claim. No
one was more ready than himself to allow that the bay-tree
does not grow kindly in the regions among which his lot had
been cast. He had lived in the world, and had held his own
there; and a man who would hold his own in the world must
learn betimes to think, as well as write, in prose. Downing
Street and Calcutta, the *Edinburgh Review* and the House of
Commons, had exercised his judgment and curbed his fancy;
but those who knew his inner mind never doubted that, however much it had been overlaid by the habits and the acquirements of an active and varied career, the poetic nature was

there. If any one will read the story of the copying-clerk who found himself unexpectedly transformed into a poet, as told in Hans Andersen's exquisite little fairy tale, he will get an exact picture of the manner in which Macaulay's memory and imagination worked during the greater part of his idle hours. He positively lived upon the associations of his own past. A sixpenny print which had hung in a Clapham nursery or school-room gave him more real delight than any masterpiece of Reynolds. The day on which he detected, in the darkest recesses of a Holborn book-stall, some trumpery romance that had been in the Cambridge circulating libraries of the year 1820, was a date marked with a white stone in his calendar. He exults in his diary over the discovery of a wretched novel called "Conscience," which he himself confesses to be "execrable trash," as triumphantly as if it had been a first folio edition of Shakspeare, with an inch and a half of margin. But nothing caused him so much pleasure (a pleasure which frequent repetition did not perceptibly diminish) as a visit to any scene that he had known in earlier years. It mattered not with what period of his existence that scene was connected, or whether the reminiscences which it conjured up were gay or gloomy, utterly trivial or profoundly interesting. The inn at Durham, where he had dined badly when on circuit; the court-house at Lancaster, where as a briefless barrister he had listened to Brougham exchanging retorts with Pollock; the dining-room in Great George Street, in a corner of which he had written his articles on Lord Holland and Warren Hastings; the church at Cheddar, where as a child he had sat of a Sunday afternoon, longing to get at the great blackletter volume of the "Book of Martyrs" which was chained to the neighboring reading-desk, while the vicar, whom Mrs. Hannah More had pronounced to be a poor "preacher and not at all a Gospel minister," was droning unheeded overhead—these, and others such as these, were localities possessing in his eyes a charm far surpassing that which the most stately and famous cities derive from historic tradition or architectural splendor. Never had he a better opportunity of indulging himself in his favorite amusement of hunting up old recollec-

tions than when he was living at Clifton, within a short drive
of the cottage which had once been Mrs. Hannah More's, and
under the strictest orders from his physicians to do nothing
but amuse himself.

"*August 21st.*—A fine day. At eleven, the Harfords of Blaise Castle
called in their barouche to take Margaret and me to Barley Wood. The
Valley of Wrington was as rich and lovely as ever. The Mendip ridge,
the church tower, the islands in the distance, were what they were forty
years ago, and more. But Barley Wood itself is greatly changed. There
has been no want of care, or taste, or respect for old recollections; but the
trees would grow, and the summer-houses would decay. The cottage itself, once visible from a considerable distance, is now so completely surrounded with wood that you do not see it until you actually drive up to
the door. The shrubs, which were not as high as I was at eleven years
old, have become great masses of verdure; and at many points from which
there once was an extensive prospect nothing can now be seen. The
house, and the esplanade of turf just before it, are the least changed. The
dining-room and drawing-room are what they were, the old engravings excepted, the place of almost every one of which I well remembered. The
old roses run up the old trellis-work, or up trellis-work very like the old.
But the Temple of the Winds is in ruins; and the root house, which was
called the 'Tecta pauperis Evandri,' has quite disappeared. That was my
favorite haunt. The urn of Locke has been moved. The urn of Porteus
stands where it did. The place is improved; but it is not the place where
I passed so many happy days in my childhood."

"*September 14th.*—A beautiful day. After breakfast Ellis and I drove to
Wrington in an open carriage and pair. We first paid a visit to the church.
I recognized the old pew, and one of the epitaphs; but I missed the pulpit-
cloth of scarlet velvet, with an inscription in remarkably long gold letters.
The sexton recollected it. There were the books chained to the desks;
and, to my surprise, the 'Book of Martyrs' was among them. I did not
remember that there was one here, though I perfectly remember that at
Cheddar. I saw my dear old friend's grave, with a foolish, canting inscription. We then walked to Barley Wood. They very kindly asked me to
go upstairs. We saw Mrs. Hannah More's room. The bed is where her
sofa and desk used to stand. The old book-cases, some of them at least,
remain. I could point out the very place where the 'Don Quixote,' in four
volumes, stood, and the very place from which I took down, at ten years
old, the 'Lyrical Ballads.' With what delight and horror I read the 'Ancient Mariner!' Home, much pleased with this second visit."

"*September 16th.*—A knock, and a carriage. Who should it be but my
old Trinity tutor, Monk, the bishop of the diocese! I was really glad to

see him and to shake hands with him; for he was kind to me when I was young, and I was ungrateful and impertinent to him."

"*October 4th.*—I finished 'Uncle Tom's Cabin,' a powerful and disagreeable book; too dark and Spagnoletto-like for my taste, when considered as a work of art. But, on the whole, it is the most valuable addition that America has made to English literature."

While in the West of England, Macaulay read as much as ever, but he wrote little except his weekly letter to Mr. Ellis.

　　　　　　　　　　　　　　　16 Caledonia Place, Clifton.

Here I am; not the worse, on the whole, for the journey. I already feel the influence of this balmy air. Remember that you are booked for the 10th of September. You will find a good bedroom, a great tub, a tolerably furnished book-case, lovely walks, fine churches, a dozen of special sherry, half a dozen of special hock, and a tureen of turtle soup. I read this last paragraph to Hannah, who is writing at the table beside me. She exclaimed against the turtle: "Such gluttons men are!" "For shame!" I said; "when a friend comes to us, we ought to kill the fatted calf." "Yes," says she; "but from the fatted calf you will get only mock turtle."

Rely on it that I shall never be in office again. Every motive is against it; avarice and ambition, as well as the love of ease and the love of liberty. I have been twice a Cabinet minister, and never made a farthing by being so. I have now been four years out of office, and I have added ten thousand pounds to my capital. So much for avarice. Then, as for ambition, I should be a far greater man as M.P. for Edinburgh, supporting a Liberal government cordially, but not servilely, than as chancellor of the duchy or pay-master of the forces. I receive congratulations from all quarters. The most fervent, perhaps, are from Graham. My own feelings are mixed. If I analyze them strictly, I find that I am glad and sorry; glad to have been elected, sorry to have to sit. The election was a great honor. The sitting will be a great bore.

　　　　　　　　　　　　　　　　　　August 12th, 1852.

I am better than when I left town, but still far from well. The weather has been against me as yet. During the last forty-eight hours I have been close prisoner to the house. The Deluge, which Lord Maidstone told us was to come after Lord Derby, has come already; so that we are cursed with Derby and the Deluge too. I have very little to complain of. I suffer no pain. My mind is unclouded. My temper is not soured. I sleep sound. I eat and drink heartily. Nothing that care or tenderness can do for me is wanting. Indeed, it would be unjust and selfish in me to accept all the sacrifices which those whom I love are eager to make.

　　　　　　　　　　　　　　　　　　September 25th, 1852.

On Thursday I walked to Leigh Court, on the other side of the ferry, to see the famous collection of pictures, and found that report had not done them justice. Nothing struck me so much as Rubens's "Woman taken in Adultery." The figures have a look of life which I do not know that I ever saw elsewhere on canvas. On the road between Leigh Court and the ferry, however, I saw a more delightful picture than any in the collection. In a deep shady lane was a donkey-cart driven by a lad; and in it were four very pretty girls from eleven to six, evidently sisters. They were quite mad with spirits at having so rare a treat as a ride; and they were laughing and singing in a way that almost made me cry with mere sense of the beautiful. They saw that I was pleased, and answered me very prettily when I made some inquiry about my route. I begged them to go on singing; and they all four began caroling, in perfect concert, and in tones as joyous as a lark's. I gave them the silver that I had about me to buy dolls. I should like to have a picture of the cart and the cargo. Gainsborough would have been the man. But I should not like to have an execrably bad poem on the subject, such as Wordsworth would have written. I am really quite well; though my Clifton doctor adjures me not to take liberties, and Bright writes, advising me to ask for the Chiltern Hundreds.

Dr. Bright had good reason for the advice which he gave. So far from being quite well, it may be said that Macaulay never was well again. "Last July was a crisis in my life," he writes in March, 1853. "I became twenty years older in a week. A mile is more to me now than ten miles a year ago." In the winter that followed his re-election at Edinburgh he had a severe attack of bronchitis; and during all his remaining years he suffered from confirmed asthma, and was tormented by frequent and distressing fits of violent coughing. One after another, in quick succession, his favorite habits were abandoned, without any prospect of being resumed. His day-long rambles, in company with Homer or Goethe, along river banks, and over ridge and common; his afternoons spent in leisurely explorations of all the book-stalls and print-shops between Charing Cross and Bethnal Green; his Sunday walks from the Albany to Clapham, and from Clapham to Richmond or Blackwall, were now, during long periods together, exchanged for a crawl along the sunny side of the street in the middle hours of any day which happened to be fine. Instead of writing, as on a pinch he loved to write, straight on from his late and somewhat lazy breakfast until the moment of dinner found him hungry and complacent, with a heavy task successfully performed, he was condemned, for the first time in his life, to the detested necessity of breaking the labors of the day by luncheon. He was forced, sorely against his will, to give up reading aloud, which, ever since he was four years old, he had enjoyed even more than reading to himself. He was almost totally debarred from general society; for his doctor rarely permitted him to go out of an evening, and often forbade him to go out at all. In February, 1855, he writes to Mr. Ellis: "I am still a prisoner; I have now had nearly three months of it, with rather less range than Sir Francis Burdett had in the Tower, or Leigh Hunt at Newgate." In May, 1854, Lord Carlisle writes: "I met Macaulay at a few breakfasts, and was sorry to think his health less good." And again: "It was tolerably pleasant — always so when Macaulay talked. The 'flashes of silence' come much more frequently now."*

The change for the worse in Macaulay's health was apparent even to those who watched him less closely and less anxiously than did Lord Carlisle; but, though that change might be read on his countenance, it was seldom, indeed, that any allusion to it passed his lips. Sufficient for himself, he made no demands upon the compassion of others. His equanimity had never been found wanting amidst the difficulties and reverses of a not uncheckered public career; and it now stood the severer test of a life which, for long periods together, was the life of an invalid who had to depend largely upon his own fortitude for support, and upon his own mental resources for occupation and amusement. It might have been expected that he would have made his private journal the safety-valve for that querulousness which an egotist vents upon his relatives, and a self-conscious author upon his readers. But as each birthday and each New-year's recurs, instead of peevishly

---

* "Yes," said Sydney Smith, "he is certainly more agreeable since his return from India. His enemies might perhaps have said before (though I never did so) that he talked rather too much; but now he has occasional flashes of silence, that make his conversation perfectly delightful."

mourning over the blessings which had departed from him, he
records in manly terms his gratitude for those that had been
left to him.

"*December 31st*, 1853.—Another day of work and solitude. I enjoy this
invalid life extremely. In spite of my gradually sinking health, this has
been a happy year. My strength is failing. My life will not, I think, be
long. But I have clear faculties, warm affections, abundant sources of
pleasure."

At very distant intervals, he gives expression, in two or
three pathetic sentences, to the dejection which is the inevitable attendant upon the most depressing of all ailments: "I
am not what I was, and every month my heart tells it me more
and more clearly. I am a little low; not from apprehension,
for I look forward to the inevitable close with perfect seren-
ity; but from regret for what I love. I sometimes hardly
command my tears when I think how soon I may leave them.
I feel that the fund of life is nearly spent." But, throughout
the volumes of his journals, Macaulay never for a single instant assumes the air of an unfortunate or an ill-used man.
One or two of his contemporaries, who grudged him his prosperity, have said that discontent was a sin to which he had
small temptation. At any rate, it was a sin of which he never
was guilty. Instead of murmuring and repining, we find him
exhorting himself to work while it was day, and to increase his
exertions as the sand sunk ever lower in the glass; rescuing
some from the poverty from which he long ago had set himself free, and consoling others for the pangs of disappointed
ambition from which he had never suffered; providing the
young people around him only too lavishly with the pleasures
that he could no longer enjoy, and striving by every possible
method to make their lives all the brighter, as the shadows
deepened down upon his own. To admit the world unreserv-
edly behind the scenes of Macaulay's life would be an act
which the world itself would blame; but those who have special reason to cherish his memory may be allowed to say, that,
proud as they are of his brilliant and elaborate compositions,
which in half a score of languages have been the delight of a
million readers, they set a still higher value upon the careless

pages of that diary which testifies how, through seven years of trying and constant illness, he maintained his industry, his courage, his patience, and his benevolence unimpaired and unbroken to the last.

By the end of October, 1852, Macaulay had recovered his health sufficiently to fulfill his engagements with the people of Edinburgh. After spending some days there in the society of his friends, both old and new, he delivered an address in the Music Hall on the 2d of November. He began, as became an historian, by reviewing the events of the past five years, both foreign and domestic, in a strain of lofty impartiality, to which his audience listened with respectful and not dissatisfied attention; and then, of a sudden, he changed his tone, and did his best to satisfy the expectations of his constituents by giving them forty minutes of as rattling a party speech as ever was delivered from the Westminster hustings, or the platform of the Free-trade Hall at Manchester. And yet, party speech as it was, it occasioned very little offense in any quarter; for its easy flow of raillery was marked by an absence of asperity which betokened to experienced eyes that Macaulay, as far as modern politics were concerned, had ceased to be at heart a party man. As an author, he had met with so much indulgence from his Conservative fellow-countrymen that he was thenceforward most unwilling, as a statesman, to say any thing which could hurt their feelings or shock their sincere convictions. The most determined Tory found little to quarrel with in the spirit of the speech, and thought himself justified in laughing, as heartily as if he had been a Whig, over the jokes about Lord Maidstone's hexameters, and the enfranchising clause which Lord Derby's Cabinet had proposed to tack on to the Militia Bill.*

---

* This clause gave a vote to every man who had served for two years in the militia. "And what," said Macaulay, " is the qualification? Why, the first qualification is youth. These electors are not to be above a certain age; but the nearer you can get them to eighteen, the better. The second qualification is poverty. The elector is to be a person to whom a shilling a day is an object. The third qualification is ignorance; for I venture to say that, if you take the trouble to observe the appearance of

"*Sunday, October 31st, Edinburgh.*—This is a Sunday—a Presbyterian Sunday—a Presbyterian Sacrament Sunday. The town is as still as if it were midnight. Whoever opposes himself to the prevailing humor would run a great risk of being affronted. There was one person, whom Christians generally mention with respect, who, I am sure, could not have walked Prince's Street in safety, and who would have addressed some very cutting rebukes to my grave constituents.*

"I have just been to Guthrie's church. I had once before seen the Presbyterian administration of the Eucharist, in July, 1817. There was much appearance of devotion, and even of religious excitement, among the communicants; and the rite was decently performed; but, though Guthrie is a man of considerable powers, his prayers were at a prodigious distance from those of our liturgy. There was nothing which, even for a moment, rose to the level of 'Therefore with angels and archangels.' There were some fine passages, in the midst of much that was bad, in his sermon. The man is a noble, honest, courageous specimen of humanity.† I staid at home all

---

those young fellows who follow the recruiting-sergeant in the streets, you will at once say that, among your laboring classes, they are not the most educated, they are not the most intelligent. And, then, a young man who goes from the plow-tail into the army is generally rather thoughtless, and disposed to idleness. Oh! but there is another qualification which I had forgotten: the voter must be five feet two. There is a qualification for you! Only think of measuring a man for the franchise! And this is the work of a Conservative government—this plan which would swamp all the counties in England with electors who possess the qualifications of youth, poverty, ignorance, a roving disposition, and five feet two. Why, what right have people who have proposed such a change as this to talk about—I do not say Lord John Russell's imprudence—but the imprudence of Ernest Jones, or of any other Chartist? The Chartists, to do them justice, would give the franchise to wealth as well as to poverty, to knowledge as well as to ignorance, to mature age as well as to youth. But to make a qualification compounded of disqualifications is a feat of which the whole glory belongs to our Conservative rulers."

* "Your old parson is a dunce," Macaulay writes to one of his sisters. "There is nothing in Homer, or in Hesiod either, about the observation of every seventh day. Hesiod, to be sure, says that the seventh day of every month (a very different thing) is a holiday; and the reason which he gives is that, on the seventh day of the month, Latona brought Apollo into the world. A pretty reason for Christians!"

† Some years before this, Macaulay had found himself in Scotland on a fast-day, without the luck of being in the same town with Guthrie. "A kirk-fast. The place had all the aspect of a Puritan Sunday. Every shop was shut, and every church open. I heard the worst and longest sermon

the afternoon, dined alone, and stole out in the dark for a walk. The view of the Old Town at night from my windows is the finest thing in the world. They have taken to lighting their houses with gas, and the effect is wonderful."

"*Tuesday, November 2d.*—A great day. Very fine; a splendid specimen of St. Martin's little summer. I was pretty well prepared for the exhibition, and doubted only about my bodily strength. People were too considerate to call this morning. At half-past twelve came my escort, and brought me to the Hall, which was as full as it could hold. Multitudes had gone away, unable to find room. At one we went in. A vast gathering. They received me with a prodigious uproar of kindness. Black took the chair, on Craig's motion, and said a very few words. Then I rose, and spoke more than an hour, always with the sympathy and applause of the whole audience. I found that I could not go on longer; so I contrived to leave off at a good moment, and to escape from some dangerous topics. Nothing could be more successful. There was immense acclamation, in the midst of which I retired, exhausted, but relieved from a weight which has been pressing on my heart during four months. I dined at Moncrieff's with a large party. Lord Ivory talked loud, with Cowan at his elbow, about the disgrace of 1847, and the recovered character of the city. I felt for Cowan, who has been very civil to me, and to whom I have not, and never have had, any unkind feelings. As I was undressing, came the proofs of *The Scotsman's* report of my speech. I was too much exhausted to correct them, and sent them back with a civil line to the editor, who is both a good and a clever fellow."

The new Parliament assembled early in November, and on the 3d of December Mr. Disraeli opened his budget. "It was well done," writes Macaulay, "both as to manner and language. The statement was lucid, though much too long. I could have said the whole as clearly, or more clearly, in two hours; and Disraeli was up five. The plan was nothing but taking money out of the pockets of people in towns, and putting it into the pockets of growers of malt. I greatly doubt

---

that I ever remember. Every sentence was repeated three or four times over, and nothing in any sentence deserved to be said once. I withdrew my attention, and read the Epistle to the Romans. I was much struck by the eloquence and force of some passages, and made out the connection and argument of some others which had formerly seemed to me unmeaning; but there were others, again, which I was still quite unable to comprehend. I know few things finer than the end of the first chapter, and the 'Who shall separate us from the love of Christ?'"

whether he will be able to carry it; but he has raised his reputation for practical ability."

During the first six weeks of his renewed experience of the
House of Commons, Macaulay, as befitted a re-enlisted veteran, thought that the standard of speaking was lower than of
old. But he soon had reason to change his mind: 1832 itself could boast few more animated and exciting scenes than
that which was enacted during the first three hours in the
morning of the 17th of December, 1852; when the Tory
leader, more formidable than ever in the audacity of despair,
turned to bay in defense of his doomed budget; and when,
at the moment that friends and foes alike thought that the
last word had been spoken on either side, Mr. Gladstone
bounded on to the floor amidst a storm of cheering and coun-
ter-cheering such as the walls of Parliament have never re-
echoed since, and plunged straight into the heart of an oration which, in a single day, doubled his influence in Parliament and his popularity in the country. "At half-past ten,"
says Macaulay, "I went to the House, and staid till near four;
generally in the library, or the division lobby, reading. I
heard a little of Disraeli, who was clever, but inconclusive;
and most unhandsome. A little of Gladstone, gravely and
severely bitter. At last came the division. There was an
immense crowd; a deafening cheer, when Hayter took the
right hand of the row of tellers; and a still louder cheer
when the numbers were read—305 to 286. In the midst of
the shouting I stole away, got to my carriage, and reached
home just at four, much exhausted."

Then came the change of government, with all that accom-
panies the process of forming a cabinet. The stir; the gossip; the political clubs, swarming with groups of talkers, who
exchange morsels of news and of criticism in eager whispers;
the hansom cabs dashing about Belgravia and Mayfair, or
waiting for hours together at the door of the incoming Pre-
mier; the ever-increasing discomfort of eminent statesmen
who sit in their studies, waiting for the possible arrival of a
Treasury messenger; the cozy dinners at the houses of the
new ministers, growing larger and merrier daily, as another,

and yet another, right honorable gentleman is added to the number of the elect. "I doubt," says Macaulay, "whether so many members of the two Houses have been in town on Christmas-day since 1783, sixty-nine years ago. Then, as now, there was a change of ministry in Christmas week. Indeed, there was a great debate in a full House of Commons on the 22d of December, and Lord North made, on that occasion, a very celebrated speech."

"*December 20th.*—An eventful day. After breakfast, at the Athenæum, I met Senior, who told me that he had been at my chambers to beg me to go to Lansdowne House; that Lord Lansdowne wished to see me before half-past twelve. I went. I found him and Lord John closeted together. Lord John read us a letter which he had received from the queen; very good, like all her letters that I have seen. She told him that she saw hope of making a strong and durable government, at once conservative and reforming; that she had asked Lord Aberdeen to form such a government; that great exertions and sacrifices would be necessary, and that she relied on the patriotism of Lord John not to refuse his valuable aid. They asked me what I thought. I said that I could improve the queen's letter neither in substance nor in language, and that she had expressed my sentiments to a tittle. Then Lord John said that of course he should try to help Lord Aberdeen—but how? There were two ways. He might take the lead of the Commons with the Foreign Office, or he might refuse office, and give his support from the back benches. I adjured him not to think of this last course, and I argued it with him during a quarter of an hour with, I thought, a great flow of thoughts and words. I was encouraged by Lord Lansdowne, who nodded, smiled, and rubbed his hands at every thing that I said. I reminded him that the Duke of Wellington had taken the Foreign Office, after having been at the Treasury, and I quoted his own pretty speech on the duke. 'You said, Lord John, that we could not all win battles of Waterloo; but that we might all imitate the old man's patriotism, sense of duty, and indifference to selfish interests and vanities when the public welfare was concerned; and now is the time for you to make a sacrifice. Your past services and your name give us a right to expect it.' He went away evidently much impressed by what had been said, and promising to consult others. When he was gone, Lord Lansdowne told me that I had come just as opportunely as Blücher did at Waterloo. He told me also, what affected me and struck me exceedingly, that, in the last resort, he would himself, in spite of the danger to his health and the destruction of his comfort, take the Treasury, if in no other way Lord John could be induced to lead the Commons. But this he keeps wisely secret for the present."

When the question of the leadership in the Commons had once been settled, Macaulay's interest in the personal arrangements of Lord Aberdeen's ministry did not go further than the sympathy, not unmixed with amusement, with which he listened to the confidences of his old Whig colleagues. " I went to Brooks's," he says, "and heard not a little grumbling about the large share of the spoil which had been allotted to the Peelites. I myself think that we ought to have had either the Lord-lieutenant, or the Secretary for Ireland. How glad I am that I so positively announced at Edinburgh my resolution never again to hold office! Otherwise people might fancy that I was disappointed. I went home, but wrote nothing. I never can work in these times of crisis."

Macaulay did well to stand aside from official life. He never opened his lips in Parliament without receiving a fresh proof that his authority there could gain nothing even from a seat in the Cabinet. Lord Hotham, a much-respected member of the Conservative party, had introduced a measure whose chief object was to exclude the Master of the Rolls from the House of Commons. He had brought it unopposed through all its stages but the last; and when, on the 1st of June, 1853, he rose to move the third reading, he was fully justified in regarding his success as a foregone conclusion. But the ultimate fate of the bill was curiously at variance with the anticipations which were entertained by its promoter, and, indeed, by all other members of Parliament who knew that such a bill was in existence. The story was told at the time in the *Leader* newspaper, with a minuteness of circumstance which calls for some degree of abridgment:

"It was pleasanter talking on Wednesday, when the position of Mr. Macaulay in Great Britain was measured in a great way. On a Wednesday the House, and the committees, are sitting at once. The talk was not interesting—on a Wednesday it seldom is—and you were loitering along the committee lobby upstairs, wondering which of the rooms you should take next, when, as you paused uncertain, you were bumped against by somebody. He begged your pardon, and rushed on; a member; a stout member; a man you couldn't conceive in a run, and yet he's running like mad. You are still staring at him, when two more men trot past you, one

on each side, and they are members too. The door close to you, marked
'Members' Entrance,' is flung open, and five members dash from it, and
plunge furiously down the lobby. More doors open; more members rush
out; members are tearing past you, from all points, but in one direction.
Then wigs and gowns appear. Their owners tell you, with happy faces,
that their committees have adjourned; and then come a third class, the
gentlemen of the Press, hilarious. Why, what's the matter? Matter?
Macaulay is up! It was an announcement that one had not heard for
years, and the passing of the word had emptied the committee-rooms as,
of old, it emptied clubs.

"You join the runners in a moment, and are in the gallery in time to
see the senators, who had start of you, perspiring into their places. It
was true. He was up, and in for a long speech. He was in a new place;
standing in the second row above the Treasury Bench; and looking and
sounding all the better for the elevation, and the clearer atmosphere for
an orator. The old voice, the old manner, and the old style—glorious
speaking! Well prepared, carefully elaborated, confessedly essayish; but
spoken with perfect art and consummate management; the grand conversation of a man of the world, confiding his learning, his recollections,
and his logic to a party of gentlemen, and just raising his voice enough to
be heard through the room. Such it was while he was only opening his
subject, and waiting for his audience; but as the House filled, which it did
with marvelous celerity, he got prouder and more oratorical; and then he
poured out his speech, with rapidity increasing after every sentence, till it
became a torrent of the richest words, carrying his hearers with him into
enthusiasm, and yet not leaving them time to cheer. A torrent of words
—that is the only description of Macaulay's style, when he has warmed
into speed. And such words! Why, it wasn't four in the afternoon;
lunch hardly digested; and the quiet, reserved English gentlemen were as
wild with delight as an opera-house, after Grisi, at ten. You doubt it?
See the division; and yet, before Mr. Macaulay had spoken, you might
have safely bet fifty to one that Lord Hotham would have carried his bill.
After that speech the bill was not thrown out, but pitched out. One began to have a higher opinion of the House of Commons, seeing, as one did,
that, if the Macaulay class of minds would bid for leadership, they would
get it. But it was not all congratulation. Mr. Macaulay had rushed
through his oration of forty minutes with masterly vigor; but the doubts
about his health, which arise when you meet him in the street—when you
take advantage of his sphinx-like reverie,

Staring right on with calm, eternal eyes,

to study the sickly face—would be confirmed by a close inspection on
Wednesday. The great orator was trembling when he sat down; the excitement of a triumph overcame him; and he had scarcely the self-posses-

sion to acknowledge the eager praises which were offered by the ministers and others in the neighborhood."

Lord Hotham, with the courage of a man who had been wounded at Salamanca, did his best, in his reply, to stem the cataract of arguments and illustrations with which his unfortunate measure had been overwhelmed. But all was in vain. There were at least two hundred men in the House who had been brought there to hear Macaulay, and who knew nothing about the question except what he had thought fit to tell them. The bill was thrown out by 224 votes to 123. After the lapse of twenty years, the act which created the Supreme Court of Judicature at length gave effect to Lord Hotham's policy. That portion of the act which provided for the exclusion of, the Master of the Rolls from the House of Commons was carried through the Parliament of 1873 without opposition, and without discussion. "Clauses 9 to 11, inclusive, agreed to," is the sole notice which Hansard takes of the proceedings which reversed the decision of 1853. The enthusiastic adhesion to Macaulay's views of a House of Commons which had heard those views stated by himself, as compared with the silent unanimity, in the opposite direction, of a House of Commons which he was not there to persuade, together constitute as high, and at the same time as unintentional, a compliment as ever was paid to the character and the genius of an orator.

Macaulay's own account of the affair proves how short a time he gave to the preparation of a speech, conspicuous, even among his speeches, for wealth of material and perfection of finish. He spent exactly two mornings' work over the arrangement of what he intended to say on an occasion which he regarded as critical, for personal as well as for public reasons. On the evening preceding the debate, he writes: "I thought of Lord Hotham's bill. Craig called, and sat for two hours. His account of the state of things at Edinburgh is as good as possible. In the evening I again thought of the bill. I was anxious, and apprehensive of complete failure; and yet I must stand the hazard."

"*Wednesday, June 1st.*—A day of painful anxiety and great success. I thought that I should fail, and, though no failure can now destroy my reputation, which rests on other than Parliamentary successes, it would have mortified me deeply. I was vexed to find how much expectation had been excited. I was sure that I should not speak well enough to satisfy that expectation. However, down I went. First we were three hours on an Irish criminal law bill, and then the Judges Exclusion Bill came on. Drummond moved to put off the third reading for six months, and spoke tersely and keenly, but did not anticipate any thing at all important that had occurred to me. When he sat down, nobody rose. There was a cry of 'Divide!' Then I stood up. The House filled, and was as still as death —a severe trial to the nerves of a man returning, after an absence of six years, to an arena where he had once made a great figure. I should have been more discomposed if I had known that my dear Hannah and Margaret were in the gallery. They had got tickets, but kept their intention strictly secret from me, meaning, if I failed, not to let me know that they had witnessed my failure. I spoke with great ease to myself, great applause, and, better than applause, complete success. We beat Lord Hotham by more than a hundred votes, and every body ascribes the victory to me. I was warmly congratulated by all my friends and acquaintances. In the midst of the first tumult of applause, a note was handed to me from Margaret, to say that she and her mamma were above. I went up to them, and they were very kind and very happy. To have given them pleasure is to me the best part of this triumph. To be sure, I am glad to have stopped a most mischievous course of legislation, and to find that, even for public conflict, my faculties are in full vigor and alertness. Craig, I hear, was in the gallery; and his kind heart will be pleased with my success. But I was knocked up."

Just twenty years had passed since Macaulay won his spurs as a minister by the workman-like style in which he conducted through Parliament the India Bill of 1833. In 1853 the time had again come round for the periodical revision of our relations with our Eastern dependency; and Sir Charles Wood, as President of the Board of Control, introduced a bill which met with Macaulay's warmest approbation. He recognized the courage and public spirit which prompted the minister to call upon Parliament to enact that a nomination for the Civil Service of India should thenceforward become the reward of industry and ability, instead of being the price of political support, or the appanage of private interest and family connection. He had himself imported into the act of 1833 clauses

which re-arranged the system of appointment to the Civil
Service on a basis of competition.* But the Directors of the
East India Company had then been too strong for him. They
were not going to resign without a struggle the most valuable
patronage which had existed in the world since the days when
the Roman senate sent proconsuls and proprætors to Syria,
Sicily, and Egypt. Back-stairs influence in Leadenhall Street

---

* The passage in which Macaulay explained and defended these clauses
is still worth reading : "It is said, I know, that examinations in Latin, in
Greek, and in mathematics are no tests of what men will prove to be in
life. I am perfectly aware that they are not infallible tests ; but that they
are tests I confidently maintain. Look at every walk of life, at this House,
at the other House, at the Bar, at the Bench, at the Church, and see whether it be not true that those who attain high distinction in the world were
generally men who were distinguished in their academic career. Indeed,
sir, this objection would prove far too much even for those who use it. It
would prove that there is no use at all in education. Education would be
a mere useless torture, if, at two or three and twenty, a man who had neglected his studies were exactly on a par with a man who had applied himself to them—exactly as likely to perform all the offices of public life with
credit to himself and with advantage to society. Whether the English
system of education be good or bad is not now the question. Perhaps I
may think that too much time is given to the ancient languages and to
the abstract sciences. But what then ? Whatever be the languages, whatever be the sciences, which it is, in any age or country, the fashion to teach,
the persons who become the greatest proficients in those languages and
those sciences will generally be the flower of the youth ; the most acute,
the most industrious, the most ambitious of honorable distinctions. If the
Ptolemaic system were taught at Cambridge instead of the Newtonian, the
senior wrangler would, nevertheless, be in general a superior man to the
wooden spoon. If, instead of learning Greek, we learned the Cherokee,
the man who understood the Cherokee best, who made the most correct
and melodious Cherokee verses, who comprehended most accurately the
effect of the Cherokee particles, would generally be a superior man to him
who was destitute of those accomplishments. If astrology were taught at
our universities, the young man who cast nativities best would generally
turn out a superior man. If alchemy were taught, the young man who
showed most activity in the pursuit of the philosopher's stone would generally turn out a superior man."

When Macaulay was correcting this speech for the press in 1853, he says
with pardonable complacency, " Every subject has a striking and interesting side to it, if people could find it out."

contrived that the clauses embodying Macaulay's plan lay dormant in a pigeon-hole at the Board of Control, until backstairs influence in Parliament at length found an opportunity to procure their repeal.

Unfortunately, the India Bill of 1853 fell short of Mr. Bright's expectations. That statesman, in his generous enthusiasm for the welfare of the Indian people, pronounced that the ministerial scheme did little or nothing to promote those salutary reforms which, in his opinion, our duty as a nation imperatively demanded of us to effect without delay. The discussion in the House of Commons on the first reading damaged the prospects of Sir Charles Wood's measure. The effect of cold water, when thrown by Mr. Bright, is never very bracing; and Macaulay was seriously alarmed for the future of a bill, the positive advantages of which, in his opinion, outweighed all defects and shortcomings whatsoever. "I read Wood's speech," he writes on the 6th of June; "and thought the plan a great improvement on the present system. Some of Bright's objections are groundless, and others exaggerated; but the vigor of his speech will do harm. On the second reading I will try whether I can not deal with the Manchester champion."

The second reading of the India Bill was moved on the 23d of June. Sir Charles Wood urged Macaulay to speak as early in the debate as possible; but his health was already in a state which required that special arrangements should be made in order to enable him to speak at all. The oppression on his chest would not allow him to exert his voice for some hours after eating; and, on the other hand, with his tendency to faintness, he could not go far into the evening without the support of food. There was a general wish that he should take the first place on the afternoon of the 24th; but the ministers were not sufficiently on the alert; and, late at night on the 23d, Mr. Joseph Hume moved the adjournment, and secured the precedence for himself.

When the morrow came, the House was crammed. Every one who could venture to remonstrate with the member for Montrose on so delicate a subject entreated him not to stand between Macaulay and his audience; but Mr. Hume replied that his own chest was weak; that his health was as important as that of any other person; that he knew just as much about India as Mr. Macaulay; and, in short, that speak he would. In spite of his assurances that he would detain honorable gentlemen for no "great length of time," the House, which had very little compassion for an invalid who had been on his legs six times within the last ten days, received him with signs of impatience so marked that Hansard has thought it incumbent upon him to record them with greater minuteness than he has bestowed upon the speech itself. Hume and his hearers had different notions as to length of time; and the clock was well on toward eight before Macaulay rose. "It was the deadest time of the evening," he writes; "but the House was very well filled. I spoke for an hour and a half, pretty well—others say very well. I did not satisfy myself; but, on the whole, I succeeded better than I expected. I was much exhausted, though I had by no means exhausted my subject."

As a consequence of his having been forced to bring his speech to an abrupt and premature conclusion, Macaulay did not judge it worthy of a place in the collected edition. He was too much an artist to consent to rest his reputation upon unfinished work, and too much a man of the world to print what he had never spoken. But it would have been well if he had done some violence to his literary taste by publishing, as a fragment, the most masterly vindication of the principle of appointment by competition that ever was left unanswered. He began by a few remarks about the relations between the Board of Control and the Court of Directors, and then glided off, by a happy transition, from that portion of the bill which related to the men who were to rule India from home to that portion which related to the men who were to rule it on the spot. "The test," he said, "by which I am inclined to judge of the present bill is the probable effect it will have upon the Civil Service in India. Is it likely to raise, or is it likely to lower, the character and spirit of that distinguished body which furnishes India with its judges and collectors?" The question for the House was to consider the process by

which these functionaries were henceforward to be selected.
There had been talk of giving the governor-general an unlim-
ited power of appointing whom he chose.

"There is something plausible in the proposition that you
should allow him to take able men wherever he finds them.
But my firm opinion is, that the day on which the Civil Service of India ceases to be a close service will be the beginning
of an age of jobbing—the most monstrous, the most extensive,
and the most perilous system of abuse in the distribution of
patronage that we have ever witnessed. Every governor-general would take out with him, or would soon be followed by,
a crowd of nephews, first and second cousins, friends, sons of
friends, and political hangers-on; while every steamer arriving from the Red Sea would carry to India some adventurer
bearing with him testimonials from people of influence in England. The governor-general would have it in his power to
distribute residencies, seats at the council board, seats at the
revenue board, places of from four thousand to six thousand
pounds a year, upon men without the least acquaintance
with the character or habits of the natives, and with only
such knowledge of the language as would enable them to call
for another bottle of pale ale, or desire their attendant to pull
the punka faster. In what way could you put a check on
such proceedings? Would you, the House of Commons, control them? Have you been so successful in extirpating nepotism at your own door, and in excluding all abuses from
Whitehall and Somerset House, that you should fancy that
you could establish purity in countries the situation of which
you do not know, and the names of which you can not pronounce? I believe most fully that, instead of purity resulting
from that arrangement to India, England itself would soon be
tainted; and that before long, when a son or brother of some
active member of this House went out to Calcutta, carrying
with him a letter of recommendation from the prime minister
to the governor-general, that letter would be really a bill of
exchange drawn on the revenues of India for value received
in Parliamentary support in this House.

"We are not without experience on this point. We have only to look back to those shameful and lamentable years which followed the first establishment of our power in Bengal. If you turn to any poet, satirist, or essayist of those times, you may see in what manner that system of appointment operated. There was a tradition in Calcutta that, during Lord Clive's second administration, a man came out with a strong letter of recommendation from one of the ministers. Lord Clive said in his peculiar way, 'Well, chap, how much do you want?' Not being accustomed to be spoken to so plainly, the man replied that he only hoped for some situation in which his services might be useful. 'That is no answer, chap,' said Lord Clive. 'How much do you want? will a hundred thousand pounds do?'* The person replied that he should be delighted if, by laborious service, he could obtain that competence. Lord Clive at once wrote out an order for the sum, and told the applicant to leave India by the ship he came in, and, once back in England, to remain there. I think that the story is very probable, and I also think that India ought to be grateful for the course which Lord Clive pursued; for, though he pillaged the people of Bengal to enrich this lucky adventurer, yet, if the man had received an appointment, they would have been pillaged, and misgoverned as well. Against evils like these there is one security, and, I believe, but one; and that is, that the Civil Service should be kept close."

Macaulay then referred to Sir Charles Wood's proposal, that admissions to the Civil Service of India should be distributed according to the result of an open competitive examination. He expressed his satisfaction at the support which that proposal had received from the present Earl of Derby,

---

* I have kept the amount of money as it stands in Hansard; but it is more than probable that Macaulay said "a hundred thousand rupees," in accordance with the version which in his day was current at Calcutta. A hundred thousand rupees was a favorite sum with Lord Clive. When he was called upon for a sentiment after dinner, he used to give "Alas and a-lackaday!" (a lass, and a lac a day).

and the surprise and disappointment which had been aroused in his mind by the nature of Lord Ellenborough's opposition to it.

"If I understand the opinions imputed to that noble lord, he thinks that the proficiency of a young man in those pursuits which constitute a liberal education is not only no indication that he is likely to make a figure in after-life, but that it positively raises a presumption that he will be passed by those whom he overcame in these early contests. I understand that the noble lord holds that young men who gain distinction in such pursuits are likely to turn out dullards, utterly unfit for an active career; and I am not sure that the noble lord did not say that it would be wiser to make boxing or cricket a test of fitness than a liberal education. It seems to me that there never was a fact proved by a larger mass of evidence, or a more unvaried experience than this: that men who distinguish themselves in their youth above their contemporaries almost always keep, to the end of their lives, the start which they have gained. This experience is so vast that I should as soon expect to hear any one question it as to hear it denied that arsenic is poison, or that brandy is intoxicating. Take down, in any library, the Cambridge calendar. There you have the list of honors for a hundred years. Look at the list of wranglers and of junior optimes; and I will venture to say that, for one man who has in after-life distinguished himself among the junior optimes, you will find twenty among the wranglers. Take the Oxford calendar, and compare the list of first-class men with an equal number of men in the third class. Is not our history full of instances which prove this fact? Look at the Church or the Bar. Look at Parliament, from the time that Parliamentary government began in this country; from the days of Montague and St. John to those of Canning and Peel. Look to India. The ablest man who ever governed India was Warren Hastings, and was he not in the first rank at Westminster? The ablest civil servant I ever knew in India was Sir Charles Metcalfe, and was he not of the first standing at Eton? The most eminent member of the aristocracy who ever governed India was Lord Wellesley.

What was his Eton reputation? What was his Oxford reputation? I must also mention—I can not refrain from mentioning—another noble and distinguished governor-general.
A few days ago, while the memory of the speech to which I
have alluded was still fresh in my mind, I read in the 'Musæ
Cantabrigienses' a very eloquent and classical ode by a young
poet of seventeen, which the University of Cambridge rewarded with a gold medal; and with pleasure, not altogether unmingled with pain, I read at the bottom of that composition
the name of the Honorable Edward Law, of St. John's College.
I saw with pleasure that the name of Lord Ellenborough may
be added to the long list of men who, in early youth, have by
success in academical studies given the augury of the part
which they were afterward to play in public life; and, at the
same time, I could not but feel some concern and surprise that
a nobleman so honorably distinguished in his youth by attention to those studies should, in his maturer years, have descended to use language respecting them which would have better
become the lips of Ensign Northerton,* or the captain in
Swift's poem, who says:

> A scholard when first from his college broke loose
> Can hardly tell how to cry *boh!* to a goose.
> Your Noveds, and Bluturchs, and Omurs, and stuff,
> By George, they don't signify this pinch of snuff.
> To give a young gentleman right education
> The army's the only good school in the nation.
> My school-master called me a dunce and a fool;
> But at cuffs I was always the cock of the school.

If a recollection of his own early triumphs did not restrain
the noble earl from using this language, I should have thought
that his filial piety would have had that effect. I should have

---

* It was Ensign Northerton who, on a certain famous occasion, comment-
ed over the mess-table upon Homer and Corderius in language far too
strong for quotation, and with an audacious misapplication of epithets as
ludicrous as any thing in Fielding. It can not be said that the young officer's impertinence was unprovoked. Tom Jones's observations about the
Greeks and Trojans would have been voted a gratuitous piece of pedantry
even in a college common-room.

thought that he would have remembered how splendid was the academical career of that great and strong-minded magistrate, the late Lord Ellenborough. . . . . It is no answer to say that you can point—as it is desirable that you should be able to point—to two or three men of great powers who, having idled when they were young, stung with remorse and generous shame, have afterward exerted themselves to retrieve lost time. Such exceptions should be noted; for they seem intended to encourage those who, after having thrown away their youth from levity or love of pleasure, may be inclined to throw their manhood after it from despair; but the general rule is, beyond all doubt, that the men who were first in the competition of the schools have been first in the competition of the world."

Macaulay clearly explained to the House how a system of competitive examination, by an infallible and self-acting process, maintains, and even raises, the standard of excellence, and how a system of pass examination tends surely and constantly to lower it. He supported his view by a chain of reasoning which has often been employed since, but to which no advocate of the old mode of appointment by private interest has even so much as attempted to reply.* He said something

---

* His argument ran thus: Under a system of competition every man struggles to do his best; and the consequence is that, without any effort on the part of the examiner, the standard keeps itself up. But the moment that you say to the examiner, not, "Shall A or B go to India?" but "Here is A. Is he fit to go to India?" the question becomes altogether a different one. The examiner's compassion, his good nature, his unwillingness to blast the prospects of a young man, lead him to strain a point in order to let the candidate in if he possibly can. That would be the case even if we suppose the dispensers of patronage left merely to the operation of their own minds; but you would have them subjected to solicitations of a sort which it would be impossible to resist. The father comes with tears in his eyes; the mother writes the most pathetic and heart-breaking letters. Very firm minds have often been shaken by appeals of that sort. But the system of competition allows nothing of the kind. The parent can not come to the examiner and say, "I know very well that the other boy beat my son; but please be good enough to say that my son beat the other boy!"

against the superstition that proficiency in learning implies a
want of energy and force of character; which, like all other
superstitions, is cherished only by those who are unwilling to
observe facts, or unable to draw deductions. A man who has
forced his way to the front of English politics has afforded at
least a strong presumption that he can hold his own in practical affairs; and there has been a Cabinet in which six out of
the seven ministers in the House of Commons, who had been
educated at the English universities, were either first-class or
double-first-class men.

Macaulay did not vouchsafe more than a passing allusion to
the theory that success in study is generally attended by physical weakness and dearth of courage and animal spirits. As
if a good place in an examination-list were any worse test of
a sound constitution than the possession of family or political
interest! As if a young fellow who can get the heart out of
a book, and concentrate his faculties over a paper of questions,
must needs be less able to sit a horse or handle a bat, and, if
need be, to lead a forlorn-hope or take charge of a famine-
stricken district, than the son of a person of fashion who has
the ear of a minister, or the nephew of an influential constituent who owns twenty public-houses in a Parliamentary borough! The Royal Engineers, the select of the select—every
one of whom, before he obtains his commission, has run the
gantlet of an almost endless series of intellectual contests—
for years together could turn out the best foot-ball eleven in
the kingdom, and within the last twelvemonth gained a success at cricket absolutely unprecedented in the annals of the
game.* But special examples are not needed in order to con-
fute the proposition that vigor of mind necessarily, or even
frequently, goes with feebleness of body. It is not in deference to such sophistry as this that the fathers of Great Britain
will ever surrender what is now the acknowledged birthright

---

* The match in question was played on the 20th and 21st of August,
1875, against an eleven of I Zingari. Eight wickets of the Royal Engineers fell for an average of more than ninety runs a wicket; and this stu-
pendous score was made against good bowling and excellent fielding.

of their sons—the privilege of doing their country's work, and
eating their country's bread, if only, in a fair and open trial,
they can win for themselves the right to be placed on the roll
of their country's servants.

Before he sat down, Macaulay had shown how little faith
his opponents themselves had in their own arguments. "The
noble lord," he said, "is of opinion that by encouraging natives to study the arts and learning of Europe we are preparing the way for the destruction of our power in India. I am
utterly at a loss to understand how, while contemning education when it is given to Europeans, he should regard it with
dread when it is given to natives. This training, we are told,
makes a European into a book-worm, a twaddler, a man unfit
for the active duties of life; but give the same education to
the Hindoo, and it arms him with such an accession of intellectual strength, that an established government, with an
army of two hundred and fifty thousand men, backed by the
whole military and naval force of England, are to go down inevitably before its irresistible power."

Macaulay had done his duty by India; and it now remained for him to show his gratitude to his constituents. The Established Church in Edinburgh was mainly supported by the
proceeds of a local impost which went by the name of the annuity tax. This tax was paid as reluctantly as church-rates
were paid in England during the ten years that preceded their
abolition; and, indeed, even more reluctantly; for it was lev-
ied on an inequitable and oppressive system. In the session
of 1853 a bill was before Parliament which embodied a scheme
for providing the stipends of the Edinburgh clergy by a less
unjust, or, at any rate, a less invidious, method. The bill was
supported on grounds of expediency by the lord provost and
the majority of the town council; but it was vigorously opposed by that party which objected on principle to making
grants of public money for religious purposes of any amount,
and under any disguise, whatsoever. Macaulay, who, as might
be expected, took the Whig view of the matter, was very glad
to have an opportunity of obliging his supporters, and not
sorry to say his say on the general question of Church and

State. On the 18th of July (during which month he was rusticating at Tunbridge Wells), he records his intention of trying " to make a Lysias-like speech on it." It is not easy for a Scotch member, who knows by experience what an annuity-tax debate is, to picture for himself the figure which an old Greek orator would make in so grim an argument. There is, indeed, very little in common between the controversies which engage the British Parliament on a Wednesday afternoon, and the glowing topics of war and diplomacy and high imperial state-craft that were discussed on a spring or autumn morning beneath the shadow of the Parthenon, and in full view of Pentelicus and Hymettus.*

"*July 19th.*—I was early at the railway station. On reaching town, I drove instantly to the House of Commons, and found the lord provost, Baillie Morrison, and Maitland, in the lobby, and had a short talk with them. There is a ridiculous mistake in the votes. Some fool has given an absurd notice about yachting, and my name has been put to it. At twelve business began. The lord advocate opened the matter; and then Smith, the member for Stockport, made a strong speech against the Edinburgh clergy, and proposed to read the bill again on that day three months. Hadfield seconded him; and I followed Hadfield, speaking without any preparation as to language, but with perfect fluency, and with considerable effect. I was heartily glad to have got it over. I have now done the handsome thing by my constituents. The bitterness of the voluntaries surprised me. I have no particular love for establishments or for priests; but I was irritated, and even disgusted, by the violence with which the bill was assailed."

It was the old Maynooth difficulty under a new aspect. " There is a rumor," said Mr. Hadfield, " that the right honorable and eloquent gentleman, the member for Edinburgh, intends to give his support to the bill; and curious shall I be to

---

* It is probable that by the epithet "Lysias-like," Macaulay meant nothing more than a short, unpretentious speech, on which he should bestow less pains than usual. He only began to think the subject over on the day preceding the debate; and on that day he likewise wrote out a good part of his speech of the 28th of February, 1832, on the representation of the Tower Hamlets; finished the "Nigrinus" of Lucian; and began to read Plato's "Gorgias," which he pronounced to be "my favorite dialogue, or nearly so, since my college days."

hear a defense of it from such eloquent lips. No man has more to lose in character, either in this House or the country, than the right honorable gentleman." "The honorable member for Sheffield," replied Macaulay, "must expect to hear nothing that deserves the name of eloquence from me." In truth, his speech was framed with the view of convincing, rather than of dazzling, his audience; and the peroration (if so it might be called) contained nothing which could arouse the disapprobation of even the most resolute voluntary. "The unpopularity of an Established Church is a very different thing from the unpopularity of the preventive service, of the army, of the police. The police, the army, and the coast-guard may be unpopular from the nature of the work which they have to do; but of the Church it may be said that it is worse than useless if it is unpopular; for it exists only to inspire affection and respect; and, if it inspires feelings of a character opposite to respect and affection, it had better not exist at all. Most earnestly, therefore, I implore the House not to support an institution which is useless unless it is beloved by means which can only cause it to be hated."

These were the last words which Macaulay spoke in the House of Commons. It would have been well for his comfort if, to use a favorite quotation of his own, he had never again quit for politics "la maison d'Aristippe, le jardin d'Épicure." The first two debates in which he took part after his return to Parliament proved to him by infallible indications that he must renounce the career of an orator, unless he was prepared to incur a risk which no man has a right to run. The biographer of another famous student* has told us that "when the brain is preoccupied, and the energy is drawn off into books, calls for efforts of external attention alarm and distress;" and to distress of that nature the state of his heart rendered Macaulay peculiarly susceptible. He had at every period of his career his full share in those tremors of anticipation from which no good speaker is free—the nature of which it is hard to analyze, and harder still to reconcile with reason

---

* Isaac Casaubon.

and experience; and during his later years his strength was quite unequal to the exertion and excitement of the speech itself.* When he re-entered the House of Commons in 1852 he had no intention of again aspiring to be a leader; and he very soon was taught that he must not even hope to count as an effective among the rank and file of politicians. He was slow to learn so painful a lesson. As regarded his attendance at Westminster, the indulgence of his constituents knew no bounds; but he himself had very little inclination to presume upon that indulgence. In the matter of party divisions, Macaulay's conscience was still that of a Whig who had served through the Committee of the great Reform Bill, and who had sat in the Parliament of Lord Melbourne, when a vote was a vote, and the fate of the ministry trembled daily in the balance. But the very first late night in the winter session of 1852 showed him that he was no longer the man of 1832 and 1841. On the 26th of November he writes: "We divided twice, and a very wearisome business it was. I walked slowly home at two in the morning, and got to bed much exhausted. A few such nights will make it necessary for me to go to Clifton again." After the defeat of Mr. Disraeli's budget he says: "I did not seem to be much the worse for yesterday's exertion until I went out; and then I found myself very weak, and felt as I used to do at Clifton." On an evening in January, he writes: "I was in pain and very poorly. I went down to the House, and paired. On my return, just as I was getting into bed, I received a note from Hayter to say that he had paired me. I was very unwilling to go out at that hour, and afraid of the night air; but I have a horror of the least suspicion of foul play; so I dressed, and went again to the House; settled the matter about the pairs; and came back at near twelve o'clock."†

---

* "This speech," he writes when the Indian debate of June, 1853, was in prospect, "which I must make, and which for many reasons can not be good, troubles me." And again: "I thought all day over my speech. I was painfully anxious; although, as usual, I recovered courage as the time drew near."

† It would, of course, be highly irregular for one member to be paired against two of his opponents.

If it had been a question of duty, Macaulay would have cared little whether or not his constitution could stand the strain of the House of Commons. He was no niggard of health and ease. To lavish on his work all that he had to give—to toil on, against the advice of physicians, and the still surer and more urgent warning of his own bodily sensations —to shorten, if need be, his life by a year, in order that his "History" might be longer by a volume — were sacrifices which he was ready to make, like all men who value their time on earth for the sake of what they accomplish, and not of what they enjoy. But he could not conceal from himself, and his friends would not suffer him to do so, that it was grievous waste, while the reign of Anne still remained un-written, for him to consume his scanty stock of vigor in the tedious but exhausting routine of a political existence; wait-ing whole evenings for the vote, and then walking half a mile at a foot's pace round and round the crowded lobbies; dining amidst clamor and confusion, with a division of twen-ty minutes long between two of the mouthfuls; trudging home at three in the morning through the slush of a Feb-ruary thaw; and sitting behind ministers in the centre of a closely packed bench during the hottest weeks of a London summer.

It was, therefore, with good reason that Macaulay spared himself as a member of Parliament. He did not economize his energies in order to squander them in any other quarter. The altered character of his private correspondence hencefor-ward indicates how carefully he husbanded his powers, with the view of employing them exclusively upon his books. When writing to publishers or editors, he never again allowed his pen to revel in that picturesque amplitude of literary de-tail which rendered many of his business letters to Mr. Napier as readable as so many passages from Sainte-Beuve. When writing to his relations, he never again treated them to those spirited imitations of Richardson, in which he described to his delighted sisters the routs, the dinner parties, and the debates of the London season of 1831. With Mr. Ellis he continued to correspond as frequently as ever. His letters sometimes consisted in little more than an invitation to dinner, imbedded in a couple of racy sentences; but for the most part they were not deficient in length. Flowing, or rather meandering on, in the easy and almost desultory style of an unrestrained familiarity—like the talk of a bachelor, in dressing-gown and slippers, over his morning coffee—they contain occasional passages which may be read with pleasure by those who care to know Macaulay as he showed himself to his chosen friend.

"Albany, December 8th, 1852.

"DEAR EMPSON,—I meant dear Ellis; but my mind is full of poor Empson. He is dying. I expect every hour to hear that all is over. Poor fellow! He was a most kind, generous friend to me, and as unselfish and unenvious as yourself. Longman has just been here; sorry for Empson, and anxious about the *Review*.* I recommended Cornewall Lewis; and I have little doubt that the offer will be made to him."

"December 13th, 1852.

"Poor Empson died with admirable fortitude and cheerfulness. I find that his wife was lately brought to bed. He spoke to her, to his friends, and to his other children with kindness, but with perfect firmness; but when the baby was put on his bed he burst into tears. Poor fellow! For my part, I feel that I should die best in the situation of Charles the First, or Lewis the Sixteenth, or Montrose—I mean, quite alone, surrounded by enemies, and nobody that I cared for near me. The parting is the dreadful thing. I do not wonder at Russell's saying, 'The bitterness of death is past.'"†

"December 30th, 1852.

"I am glad that you like Beaumarchais. The result was that the Goëzmans were utterly ruined; the husband forced to quit his office; the wife driven to a convent. Beaumarchais was blâmé by the Court. The effect of that blâme was very serious. It made a man legally infamous, I believe, and deprived him of many civil rights. But the public feeling was so strongly with Beaumarchais that he paraded his stigma as if it had been a mark of honor. He gave himself such airs that somebody said to him, 'Monsieur, ce n'est pas assez que d'être blâmé: il faut être modeste.' Do you see the whole finesse of this untranslatable *mot?* What a quanti-

---

* Mr. Empson had succeeded Mr. Napier as editor of the *Edinburgh Review*.

† The famous scene between Lord Russell and his wife is described, briefly enough, by Hume: "With a tender and decent composure they took leave of each other on the day of his execution. 'The bitterness of death is now past,' said he, when he turned from her."

ty of French words I have used! I suppose that the subject Frenchifies my style.*

"I am disengaged all next week. Fix some day for dining with me in honor of 1853. I hope that it will be as happy a year as, in spite of some bodily suffering, 1852 has been to me. It is odd that, though time is stealing from me perceptibly my vigor and my pleasures, I am growing happier and happier. As Milnes says, it is shocking, it is scandalous, to enjoy life as I do."

"Albany, July 11th, 1853.

"Read Haydon's memoirs. Haydon was exactly the vulgar idea of a man of genius. He had all the morbid peculiarities which are supposed by fools to belong to intellectual superiority—eccentricity, jealousy, caprice, infinite disdain for other men; and yet he was as poor, commonplace a creature as any in the world. He painted signs, and gave himself more airs than if he had painted the Cartoons....... Whether you struck him or stroked him, starved him or fed him, he snapped at your hand in just the same way. He would beg you in piteous accents to buy an acre and a half of canvas that he had spoiled. Some good-natured lord asks the price. Haydon demands a hundred guineas. His lordship gives the money out of mere charity, and is rewarded by some such entry as this in Haydon's journal: 'A hundred guineas, and for such a work! I expected that, for very shame, he would have made it a thousand. But he is a mean, sordid wretch.' In the mean time the purchaser is looking out for the most retired spot in his house to hide the huge daub which he has bought, for ten times its value, out of mere compassion."

"Tunbridge Wells, July 28th, 1853.

"I hope that you are looking forward to our tour. On Tuesday, the 23d, I shall be at the Albany, and shall proceed to hire a courier, and to get passports. My present notions of a route is Dover; Ostend; Cologne; the Rhine to Strasburg; the railway to Basle; voiture or diligence to Berne, and from Berne to Lausanne; steamboat on the Lake of Geneva; post to

---

* Mr. Goëzman was the judge who threw Beaumarchais over, after Madame Goëzman had accepted a present from him. The unsuccessful suitor got his present back, "and those who had disappointed him probably thought that he would not, for the mere gratification of his malevolence, make public a transaction which was discreditable to himself as well as to them. They knew little of him. He soon taught them to curse the day in which they had dared to trifle with a man of so revengeful and turbulent a spirit, of such dauntless effrontery, and of such eminent talents for controversy and satire." Macaulay's account of the Goëzman scandal, in his essay on Bacon, makes it evident that to write about Beaumarchais did not necessarily Frenchify his style.

Lyons; up the Saône by steam to Chalons; railway to Paris; three or four days at Paris; and back to London in one day. But I shall readily agree to any modification which you may propose. We could easily, I think, do all this, and be in town on the 18th of September with a great stock of pleasant recollections, and images of fine objects, natural and artificial. I dare say you will despise me for saying that, on the whole, I expect more pleasure from the cathedrals of Cologne and Strasburg than from the Bernese Alps or the Lake of Geneva."*

"Tunbridge Wells, August 16th, 1853.

"I am glad to find that we shall have a clear three weeks for our expedition. I hope to secure Wolmar. At all events, I shall have a good courier. I can afford to indulge myself; for Longman informs me that he shall have more than thirteen hundred pounds to pay me on the 1st of December, besides five hundred pounds in the first week of January; so that my whole income this year will be about three thousand six hundred pounds, clear of property tax. Like Dogberry, I shall have two gowns, and every thing handsome about me. But, alas! like Dogberry, I have had losses. The East India Company is going to pay me off some thousands; and I must take four per cent. instead of five, and be thankful even to get four. How justly has an ancient poet observed that

Crescentem sequitur cura pecuniam!

However, as my Lord Smart says, 'Hang saving! We'll have a penn'orth of cheese.'† I say, 'Hang saving! We'll have a jolly three weeks on the Continent.'

"I send you a treasure. I do believe that it is the autograph of the great Robert Montgomery. Pray let me have it again. I would not lose

---

* Like many other people, Macaulay was disappointed with the cathedral of Cologne. "My expectations," he says in his journal, "had been raised too high, and perhaps nothing could quite have satisfied me. It will never be equal to St. Ouen, and, I think, hardly to York Minster." Of the tower at Strasburg he writes: "I thought it the most exquisite morsel of Gothic architecture that I ever saw. The interior is grand, but has faults. The side aisles are too broad for their height. Even the central aisle would be better if it were narrower. The end of the vista is wretched. Nevertheless, it is a church of the first rank." He thoroughly enjoyed his tour. "So ends this journal of my travels. Very pleasant travels they were. I had good health, generally good weather, a good friend, and a good servant."

† Lord Smart is one of the characters in Swift's "Polite Conversations;" a book strangely neglected by a generation which ransacks the world from California to Calcutta for something to laugh at.

such a jewel on any account. I have read it, as Mr. Montgomery desires, in the presence of God; and in the presence of God I pronounce it to be incomparable.*

"Glorious news! Robert Montgomery writes to Longman that there is a point at which human patience must give way. Since the resignation and Christian fortitude of a quarter of a century have made no impression on the hard heart and darkened conscience of Mr. Macaulay, an injured poet must appeal to the laws of his country, which will doubtless give him a redress the more signal because he has been so slow to ask for it. I retain you. Consider yourself as feed. You shall choose your own junior. I shall put nobody over your head in this cause. Will he apply for a criminal information? Imagine Jack!† 'I have *thee graitest* respect for the very eminent poet who makes this application, and for the very eminent critic against whom it is made. It must be very satisfactory to Mr. Montgomery to have had an opportunity of denying on oath the charge that he writes nonsense. But it is not the practice of this court to grant criminal informations against libels which have been a quarter of a century before the world.' I send you some exquisite lines which I saw placarded on a wall the other day. The versification and diction seem to me perfect. Byrom's 'My time, oh ye Muses,' is not so complete in its kind."‡

> Although it is wrong, I must frankly confess,
> To judge of the merits of folks by their dress,
> I can not but think that an ill-looking hat
> Is a very bad sign of a man, for all that;
> Especially now, when James Johnson is willing
> To touch up our old ones in style for a shilling,
> And gives them a gloss of so silky a hue
> As makes them look newer than when they were new.

---

* "Robert Montgomery," Macaulay says in his journal, "has written to ask that he may be taken out of the pillory. Never, with my consent. He is the silliest scribbler of my time; and that his book sells among a certain class is a reason for keeping my protest on record. Besides, he has calumniated me in print, and I will not seem to be bullied into a concession."

† It is to be feared that this unceremonious reference is to no less a personage than Lord Campbell.

‡ Byrom's lines,

> My time, oh ye Muses, was happily spent
> When Phœbe went with me wherever I went,

were addressed to Joanna Bentley, the daughter of the great critic, and constitute the 603d paper of the *Spectator*. The effect which this little poem produces upon the reader may best be described by one of its prettiest couplets; for it resembles

> The fountain that wont to run sweetly along,
> And dance to soft murmurs the pebbles among.

In the spring of 1853 the expectation of Mrs. Beecher
Stowe's visit to England created some apprehension in the
minds of those eminent men who were pretty sure to come
within the circuit of her observation, and quite sure to find
themselves in her book of travels.

"*March* 16*th*, 1853.—To dinner, after a long interval, at Westbourne Terrace.   Gladstone, Lord Glenelg, and Goulburn.   There was much laughing about Mrs. Beecher Stowe, and what we were to give her.   I referred
the ladies to Goldsmith's poems for what I should give.   Nobody but Hannah understood me; but some of them have since been thumbing Goldsmith to make out the riddle."*

A year later, Macaulay writes: "A mighty foolish, impertinent book this of Mrs. Stowe.   She puts into my mouth a
great deal of stuff that I never uttered, particularly about
cathedrals.   What blunders she makes!   Robert Walpole for
Horace Walpole.   Shaftesbury, the author of the Habeas-
corpus Act, she confounds with Shaftesbury, the author of
the 'Characteristics.'   She can not even see.   Palmerston,
whose eyes are sky-blue, she calls dark-eyed.   I am glad that
I met her so seldom, and sorry that I met her at all."   The
passage in Mrs. Stowe's book to which Macaulay took exception, runs as follows:

"Macaulay made some suggestive remarks on cathedrals
generally.   I said that I thought that we so seldom know
who were the architects that designed these great buildings,
that they appeared to me the most sublime efforts of human
genius.

"He said that all the cathedrals of Europe were undoubtedly the result of one or two minds; that they rose into existence very nearly contemporaneously, and were built by traveling companies of masons, under the direction of some sys-
tematic organization.   Perhaps you knew all this before, but
I did not; and so it struck me as a glorious idea.   And, if it
is not the true account of the origin of cathedrals, it certainly

* The riddle is not difficult; and its solution is well worth the pleasing
trouble of turning over the few dozen pages of Goldsmith's poems.

ought to be; and, as our old grandmother used to say, 'I'm going to believe it!'"*

Macaulay spent part of the summer of 1853 at Tunbridge Wells. On the 11th of July he writes to Mr. Ellis that he has taken a house "in a delightful situation. The drawing-room is excellent; the dining-room so much overshadowed by trees and a veranda that it is dark even in the brightest noon. The country looks lovely. The heath is close to the door. I have a very pleasant room for you; a large tub; half a dozen of the best sherry, and a dozen of good Champagne; and Plato and Lucian." Macaulay had known Tunbridge Wells in his boyhood; and he now found a plentiful source of enjoyment in reviving his recollections of the past. He was pleased at feeling once more beneath his feet the red-brick pavement of the Pantiles, an ancient centre of social resort which, with a strange disregard for literary and historical associations where-of any town might well be proud, the inhabitants have lately rechristened by the title of "The Parade." As if a name that satisfied Johnson and Garrick, Richardson and Cibber, the Earl of Chatham and Mr. Speaker Onslow, were not good enough to serve for us! On Sundays, Macaulay went to church "in the well-remembered old building; the same that was erected in Charles the Second's days, and which the Tan-tivies wished to dedicate to St. Charles the Martyr."† And on more than one week-day he sat "in Nash's reading-room, in the old corner looking out upon the heath," and was

---

* "Sunny Memories in Foreign Lands," Letter xix. It certainly would be difficult even to manufacture a less adequate representation than this of Macaulay's talk, either as regarded manner or matter. But Mrs. Beecher Stowe has unfortunately shown herself only too ready to rush into print when she has lighted upon what she conceives to be curious information about the private life of a great English author.

† "In 1665 a subscription had just been raised among those who fre-quented the Wells for building a church, which the Tories, who then domi-neered everywhere, insisted on dedicating to St. Charles the Martyr." The third chapter of the "History" contains, within the compass of a page, a pleasant little picture of the Tunbridge Wells of the Restoration, as bright-ly colored as one of Turner's vignettes.

"amused by finding among the books the 'Self-tormentor,' published in 1789, and Sally More's novel, unseen since 1816."

But during his stay at Tunbridge Wells he was better engaged than in renewing his acquaintance with the dog-eared romances of a former day which still lingered on the back shelves of the circulating library. "I have determined," he writes to Mr. Ellis, "to read through Plato again. I began with the 'Phædrus' yesterday; one of the most eloquent, ingenious, fantastic, and delicately ironical of the dialogues. I doubt whether there be any of Plato's works which has left so many traces in the literature and philosophy of Europe. And this is the more remarkable, because no ancient work is so thoroughly tainted with what in modern times is regarded as the most odious of all kinds of immorality."* Some days later he says: "I have read a good deal of Plato; and the more I read, the more I admire his style, and the less I admire his reasonings."

Macaulay's diary for the month of July, 1853, is full of Plato. "I read the 'Protagoras' at dinner. The childish quibbling of Socrates provokes me. It is odd that such trumpery fallacies should have imposed on such powerful minds. Surely Protagoras reasoned in a better and more manly strain. I am more and more convinced that the merit of Plato lies in his talent for narrative and description, in his rhetoric, in his humor, and in his exquisite Greek. The introductions to the

---

* "I read Plato's 'Phædrus,'" he says in his journal. "Wonderful irony, eloquence, ingenuity, fancy. But what a state of morals! What a distortion of the imagination!" Macaulay felt a hearty detestation for the perverted sentiment (to use the mildest phrase) which disfigures some of the most beautiful works of antiquity. Below the twelfth Idyl of Theocritus he writes, "A fine poem on an odious subject;" and at the end of the third Idyl, "A pretty little poem; but it is inferior to Virgil's second Eclogue, in spite of the great inferiority of Virgil's subject." When Demosthenes rebuked his brother embassadors by the words "οὐκ εἶπον ὡς καλὸς εἶ · γυνὴ γὰρ τῶν ὄντων ἐστι κάλλιστον," Macaulay expresses in the margin his delight at meeting with a Greek who had the feelings of a man, and who was not ashamed to avow them. "I am glad," he writes, "that Demosthenes had so good a taste."

'Phædrus,' the 'Lysis,' and the 'Protagoras' are all three first-rate; the 'Protagoras' best."* And again: "I came home, and

---

* For the sake of readers who do not know Greek, I venture to give a very inadequate translation, or rather paraphrase, of some portion of what Macaulay calls the "introduction" to the "Protagoras." Socrates and his friend Hippocrates had gone to call at the house of Callias, an Athenian person of quality, much given to letters. The purpose of their visit was to have a look at three famous sophists from foreign parts—Protagoras of Abdera, Hippias of Elis, and Prodicus of Ceos. "When we had arrived within the porch," says Socrates, "we stopped there to finish a discussion which had been started in the course of our walk. And I suppose that the porter heard us talking away outside the threshold; which was unfortunate; as he was already in a bad temper on account of the number of sophists who were about the premises. So when we knocked, he opened the door, and directly he saw us he cried, 'More sophists! eh! Master's not at home,' and slammed the door to. We, however, persevered, and beat the panels vigorously with both hands: upon which he bawled through the key-hole, 'I tell you, master's not at home.' 'But, my good fellow,' said I, 'we don't want your master, and we do not happen to be sophists. We have come to see Protagoras; so just send in our names.' And then he grumbled a good deal, and let us in.

"And when we were inside we found Callias and his friends walking about in the corridor, seven abreast, with Protagoras in the middle. And behind them came a crowd of his disciples, chiefly foreigners, whom the great man drags about in his train from city to city, listening with all their ears to whatever was said. And what amused me most was to observe how carefully these people avoided getting in the way of their master, for, whenever he and the rest of the vanguard came to the end and turned round, his followers parted to right and left, let him pass through, and then wheeled about, and fell into the rear with admirable regularity and discretion.

"'And after him I was aware,' as Homer says, of Hippias sitting on a chair in the opposite corridor; and around him were seated on footstools Eryximachus and Phædrus, and a group of citizens and strangers. And they appeared to be putting questions to Hippias concerning natural science, and the celestial bodies; and he, sitting on his chair, answered them in turn, and cleared up their several difficulties. And Prodicus was occupying a closet, which Callias ordinarily uses as a still-room; but on this occasion, what with his sophists and their disciples, he was so hard put to it for space, that he had turned out all his stores, and made it into a bedchamber. So Prodicus was lying there, rolled up in an immense number of blankets and counterpanes, while his hearers had planted themselves on

finished the 'Apology,' and looked through the 'Crito.' Fine
they are ; but the stories of the oracle, the divine monitor, and
the dream are absurd.   I imagine that, with all his skill in
logomachy, Socrates was a strange, fanciful, superstitious old
fellow.   Extreme credulity has often gone with extreme logical subtlety.   Witness some of the school-men.   Witness John
Wesley.   I do not much wonder at the violence of the hatred
which Socrates had provoked.   He had, evidently, a thorough
love for making men look small.   There was a meek mali-
ciousness about him which gave wounds such as must have
smarted long, and his command of temper was more provoking than noisy triumph and insolence would have been."
Macaulay, who loved Plato for the sake of what he called
the " setting " of his dialogues, ranked them according to their
literary beauty rather than their philosophical excellence.   By
the time that he had got through the 'Hippias Major' and
the best part of the 'Republic,' and had nothing before him
more entertaining than the 'Laws,' the 'Ephebus,' and the
'Sophistes,' he allowed his attention once more to be diverted by modern books.   "I walked on the heath," he says, "in
glorious weather, and read the 'Mystères de Paris.'   Sue has
quite put poor Plato's nose out of joint."

The month that Macaulay passed at Tunbridge Wells was
not all play-time.   An event had occurred which gave him
great and just annoyance, and imposed upon him a considerable amount of unexpected though well-invested labor.   "I
have," he writes, " some work to do at Tunbridge Wells which
I had not reckoned upon.   A book-seller, named Vizetelly, a
sort of Curll,* has advertised an edition of my speeches *by*

---

the neighboring beds.   But without going in I could not catch the subject of their conversation, though I was anxious to hear what was said
(for I consider Prodicus a wonderfully wise personage), because his voice
was so deep that the closet seemed full of a sort of humming noise which
rendered his words indistinguishable."

* Macaulay, who took a warm interest in the great historical scandals
and mysteries of literature, had at his fingers' ends all that was known in
his own day concerning the relations between Pope and the notorious publisher whom he accused of having printed his correspondence—relations

special license, and had the brazen impudence to write to
Lord Lansdowne, and to ask his lordship to accept the dedica-
tion." In order to checkmate this proceeding, Mr. Longman
advised Macaulay to prepare forthwith for publication a selection of his best speeches; and, under the stress of circumstances, he had no choice but to give an instant, though reluctant, assent. "I found," he says, "that people really wished
to have the speeches. I therefore, much against my will, determined to give a revised and corrected edition. The preparing of this edition will occupy me two or three hours a
day during my holiday. Many of the speeches must be re-
written from memory, and from the hints given by the reports. I think of adding two or three state papers—my minute on the education of the natives of India, and my minute
on the Black Act."* "It will take some time," he writes in
his diary; "but I do not know that I should have given that
time to my 'History.' I can retouch a speech as well in the
country as in town. The 'History' is quite a different matter." The day after his arrival at Tunbridge Wells he fell
to work, transcribing every speech from beginning to end, at
the rate of from nine to fifteen printed pages a day. On
July the 14th, he says: "Heaps of letters. I sent eight or
nine answers, and then employed myself upon the Reform
speech of July the 5th, 1831. I wrote vigorously during several hours. I could not go out; for the rain was falling by
pailfuls, and the wind blowing a hurricane. I wrote with
spirit, as it seemed to me, and made a speech very like the
real one in language, and in substance exactly the real one. I
had half performed my task at five." And again, on the 4th
of August, "I went on with the Somnauth speech, which is
among my very best. I can not help expecting that the vol-

---

which were of a far more dubious character than his own with Mr. Vizetelly. He had a strong relish for Pope's celebrated pasquinade; which, in its
own rather questionable class, he held to be inferior only to Voltaire's Dia-
tribe of Doctor Akakia.

* In January, 1853, he notes in his journal: "I got from Westbourne
Terrace a copy of my Education minute of 1835, and was pleased to see it
again after eighteen years. It made a great revolution."

ume will have some success. At all events, it will, I really
think, deserve success."

It was not until Mr. Vizetelly's publication appeared that
his victim knew the full extent of the injury which had so
gratuitously been inflicted upon him. How serious that injury
was, and how peculiarly it was adapted to mortify and provoke
Macaulay, may be seen in the preface to Mr. Longman's edition of the " Speeches." Readers, who have a taste for strong
food, will find that the time which they may spend over that
preface will not be thrown away. " The substance of what I
said," writes Macaulay, " is perpetually misrepresented. The
connection of the arguments is altogether lost. Extravagant
blunders are put into my mouth in almost every page. An
editor who was not grossly ignorant would have perceived
that no person to whom the House of Commons would listen
could possibly have been guilty of such blunders. An editor
who had the smallest regard for truth, or for the fame of the
person whose speeches he had undertaken to publish, would
have had recourse to the various sources of information which
were readily accessible, and, by collating them, would have
produced a book which would at least have contained no absolute nonsense. But I have unfortunately had an editor whose
only object was to make a few pounds, and who was willing
to sacrifice to that object my reputation and his own."

*   *   *   *   *   *   *

" I could fill a volume with instances of the injustice with
which I have been treated. But I will confine myself to a
single speech, the speech on the Dissenters' Chapels Bill. I
have selected that speech, not because Mr. Vizetelly's version
of that speech is worse than his version of thirty or forty other speeches, but because I have before me a report of that
speech which an honest and diligent editor would have
thought it his first duty to consult. The report of which I
speak was published by the Unitarian Dissenters, who were
naturally desirous that there should be an accurate record of
what had passed in a debate deeply interesting to them."
Macaulay, infusing into his style a certain grim humor which
was not usual with him, then proceeds to give a detailed list

of absurdities which had been deliberately presented to the world as having been spoken by himself. "These samples," he goes on to say, "will probably be found sufficient. They all lie within the compass of seven or eight pages. It will be observed that all the faults which I have pointed out are grave faults of substance. Slighter faults of substance are numerous. As to faults of syntax and of style, hardly one sentence in a hundred is free from them.

"I can not permit myself to be exhibited in this ridiculous and degrading manner for the profit of an unprincipled man. I therefore unwillingly, and in mere self-defense, give this volume to the public..... I have only, in conclusion, to beg that the readers of this preface will pardon an egotism which a great wrong has made necessary, and which is quite as disagreeable to myself as it can be to them."

By the time that Macaulay's speeches were in print he had already ceased to be a politician. Absorbed in his "History," he paid little attention to what was passing at Westminster. Mr. Gladstone's plan for the consolidation of the national debt was far less to him than Montague's scheme for restoring the standard of the coinage by calling in the clipped silver; and the abortive Triennial Bill of 1692 was far more to him than the abortive Reform Bill of 1854. "To-day," he writes on the 13th of February, "Lord John is to bring in his new Reform Bill. I had meant to go down, but did not venture. This east wind keeps me a prisoner. How different a world from that which was convulsed by the first Reform Bill! How different a day this from the 1st of March, 1831, an epoch in my life as well as in that of the nation!" He now was so seldom at the House of Commons that his presence there was something of an event. Old members recollect how, if ever he was seen standing behind the Speaker's chair, some friend or acquaintance would undertake the easy task of drawing him into conversation; and very soon the space around him was as crowded as during the five minutes which precede a stand-and-fall division. He was very unwilling to continue to call himself a member of Parliament. "The feeling that I ought not to be in the House of Commons" (so he wrote to Mr. Black) "preys upon my mind. I think that I am acting ungenerously and ungratefully to a constituent body which has been most indulgent to me." But the people of Edinburgh thought otherwise; and the earnest and repeated solicitations of his leading supporters prevailed upon him to retain for a while the title of representative of their city.

Although, as a statesman, his day was past and gone, Macaulay watched with profound emotion the course of his country's fortunes during the momentous years 1854 and 1855. He was a patriot, if ever there was one.* It would be difficult to find any body, whether great or small, who more heartily and more permanently enjoyed the consciousness of being an Englishman. "When I am traveling on the Continent," he used to say, "I like to think that I am a citizen of no mean city." He hailed every sign which told that the fighting strength of the nation was undecayed, and its spirit as high as ever. Long before affairs in the east of Europe had assumed a threatening aspect, he had been unfeignedly anxious about the condition of our armaments. In November, 1852, he writes: "Joe Hume talked to me very earnestly about the necessity of a union of Liberals. He said much about ballot and the franchise. I told him that I could easily come to some compromise with him and his friends on these matters, but that there were other questions about which I feared that there was an irreconcilable difference, particularly the vital question of national defense. He seemed quite confounded, and had absolutely nothing to say. I am fully determined to make them eat their words on that point, or to have no political connection with them."

---

* *"August* 28*th*, 1859.—Monsieur de Circourt has thrown some scurrilous reflections on the national character of the English into one of his pamphlets. He ought not to have sent such a work to me. I was a good deal perplexed, being unwilling to act uncourteously toward a person who to me personally has shown the most marked civility; and being, on the other hand, unwilling to put up with affronts to my country in consideration of compliments to myself. I wrote him a letter which, I am sure, ought not to offend him, but which, I really think, must make him a little ashamed of himself."

Macaulay followed the progress of the Russian war through all its stages with intense but discriminating interest. He freely expressed his disdain of the gossip which accused Prince Albert of having played an underhand part in the negotiations that preceded the outbreak of hostilities. In a letter dated the 17th January, 1854, he says: " The yelping against Prince Albert is a mere way of filling up the time till Parliament meets. If he has the sense and fortitude to despise it, the whole will blow over and be forgotten. I do not believe that he has done any thing unconstitutional; and I am sure that those who are loudest in bawling know neither what he has done nor what is unconstitutional." And on the day that the queen opened Parliament he writes in his diary: " I was pleased to find that the prince was not ill received. The late attacks on him have been infamous and absurd to the last degree. Nothing so shameful since the Warming-pan story. I am ashamed for my country. However, the reaction has begun."

The Baltic fleet sailed early in March, under the command of Sir Charles Napier, who, a few days before his departure, had been entertained at a public banquet, which was attended by some leading members of the Government. The speeches which were made upon this occasion can not even now be read without a sensation of shame. Their tone and substance are best described by the epithet un-English. It has never been the habit of British statesmen to declaim boastfully and passionately against a foreign power with whom war has not been declared, and still less has it been the way with British sailors to exult beforehand over a victory which is yet to be won. Mr. Bright referred in the House of Commons to the fact that cabinet ministers had been present at this unlucky festival. " I have read," he said, " the proceedings of that banquet with pain and humiliation. The reckless levity displayed is, in my own opinion, discreditable to the grave and responsible statesmen of a civilized and Christian nation." There was very little trace either of statesmanship or Christianity in Lord Palmerston's reply. He began by alluding to Mr. Bright as " the honorable and reverend gentleman." He was called to order for this gross violation of the ordinary courtesies of debate; but, instead of taking advantage of the interruption to recover his temper and self-respect, he continued his remarks in a strain which, though it did not justify the interference of the Speaker, was most repugnant to the taste and feeling of his brother members. For the first and last time in his life Macaulay had nothing to say in defense of his hero. "I went to the House on Monday," he writes; "but for any pleasure I got, I might as well have staid away. I heard Bright say every thing that I thought; and I heard Palmerston and Graham expose themselves lamentably. Palmerston's want of temper, judgment, and good-breeding was almost incredible. He did himself more harm in three minutes than all his enemies and detractors throughout the world have been able to do him in twenty years. I came home quite dispirited."

Though Macaulay was not inclined by premature jubilation to discount triumphs which were still in the future, no one was more ready to feel an Englishman's pride as soon as our army should give him something to be proud of. He had not long to wait. "Glorious news!" he says, on the 4th of October, 1854. "Too glorious, I am afraid, to be all true. However, there is room for a large abatement. One effect, and a most important one, of these successes is that the war, which has not yet been national in France, will become so; and that, consequently, neither the death of the emperor nor any revolution which may follow will easily dissolve the present alliance." Throughout the winter months his journal shows how constantly the dangers and sufferings of our soldiers were present to his mind, and with what heart-felt admiration he regarded each successive proof of the discipline, the endurance, and the intrepidity which those dangers and sufferings so cruelly but so effectually tested. "I am anxious," he writes, on the 13th of November, "about our brave fellows in the Crimea, but proud for the country, and glad to think that the national spirit is so high and unconquerable. Invasion is a bugbear indeed while we retain our pluck." Macaulay viewed with great and increasing satisfaction the eagerness of his fellow-countrymen to make all the sacrifices which the war demanded. He was fond of reminding himself and others that the prosperity and the independence of England had not been bought for nothing, and could be retained only so long as we were willing to pay the price. A full and clear expression of this sentiment was evoked from him by the tidings of the great battle that tried, more severely than it had been tried since Albuera, that British courage which, to use his own words, "is never so sedate and stubborn as toward the close of a doubtful and murderous day." These were the terms in which he wrote, with the gazette containing the account of Inkermann on the table before him : "The interest excited by the war is as great as that which in my boyish days used to be excited by the Duke of Wellington's operations. I am well pleased, on the whole. It is impossible not to regret so many brave men, and to feel for the distress of so many families. But it is a great thing that, after the longest peace ever known, our army should be in a higher state of efficiency than at the end of the last war. The spirit of the soldiers, and of the whole country, is a complete guarantee against those dangers with which we were threatened two or three years ago. Nobody will be in a hurry to invade England for a long time to come."*

---

* Macaulay says, in a letter dated August, 1857 : "Lord Panmure has asked me to write an inscription for a column which is building at Scutari, in honor of our soldiers and sailors who died in the East during the last war. It is no easy task, as you may guess. Give me your opinion of what I have written. It is, as you will see, concise and austerely simple. There is not a single adjective. So far I believe that I am right. But whether the execution be in other respects good is a matter about which I feel great misgivings.

TO THE MEMORY
OF THE BRITISH SOLDIERS AND SAILORS
WHO,
DURING THE YEARS 1854 AND 1855,
DIED FAR FROM THEIR COUNTRY
IN DEFENSE OF THE LIBERTIES OF EUROPE,
THIS MONUMENT IS ERECTED
BY THE GRATITUDE
OF QUEEN VICTORIA AND HER PEOPLE
1857."

The occasion had now arrived for carrying into effect that part of the India Act of 1853 which related to the appointment of civil servants by open competition. Sir Charles Wood intrusted the duty of making the necessary arrangements to a committee of distinguished men, with Macaulay as chairman.* "I am to draw the report," he writes on the 1st of July, 1854. "I must and will finish it in a week." He completed his rough draft on the 7th of July, wrote it out fair on Saturday, the 8th, and read it to his brother-in-law on the Sunday. "Trevelyan," he says, "was much pleased;" and no wonder; for Macaulay had so framed his plan as to bring out all the strong points of the competitive system, and avoid its perils. He provided a simple but effective machinery for admitting into the service men of energy and ability, whose faculties were keen and whose acquirements were solid, and for excluding those who rested their hopes of success upon masses of half-digested, heterogeneous learning.

"Nothing," he wrote, "can be further from our wish than to hold out premiums for knowledge of wide surface and of small depth. We are of opinion that a candidate ought to be allowed no credit at all for taking up a subject in which he is a mere smatterer. Profound and accurate acquaintance with a single language ought to tell more than bad translations and themes in six languages. A single paper which shows that the writer thoroughly understands the principles of the differential calculus ought to tell more than twenty superficial and incorrect answers to questions about chemistry, botany, mineralogy, metaphysics, logic, and English history.....

"The marks ought, we conceive, to be distributed among the subjects of examination in such a manner that no part of the kingdom, and no class of schools, shall exclusively furnish servants to the East India Company. It would be grossly unjust, for example, to the great academical institutions of England, not to allow skill in Greek and Latin versification to have a considerable share in determining the issue of the com-

---

* Macaulay's colleagues were Lord Ashburton; Dr. Melvill, the Principal of Haileybury College; Dr. Jowett; and Sir John Shaw Lefevre.

petition. Skill in Greek and Latin versification has, indeed, no direct tendency to form a judge, a financier, or a diplomatist. But the youth who does best what all the ablest and most ambitious youths about him are trying to do well, will generally prove a superior man; nor can we doubt that an accomplishment by which Fox and Canning, Grenville and Wellesley, Mansfield and Tenterden, first distinguished themselves above their fellows, indicates powers of mind which, properly trained and directed, may do great service to the State. On the other hand, we must remember that in the north of this island the art of metrical composition in the ancient languages is very little cultivated, and that men so eminent as Dugald Stewart, Horner, Jeffrey, and Mackintosh would probably have been quite unable to write a good copy of Latin alcaics, or to translate ten lines of Shakspeare into Greek iambics. We wish to see such a system of examination established as shall not exclude from the service of the East India Company either a Mackintosh or a Tenterden, either a Canning or a Horner. We have, with an anxious desire to deal fairly by all parts of the United Kingdom, and by all places of liberal education, framed the following scale, which we venture to submit to your consideration."

There follows hereupon a complete list of subjects of examination, with the proportion of marks that was to be allotted to each. The Indian Government adopted this list in its integrity; and the same very practical compliment was paid to all the recommendations of the committee, whether they related to the age of the candidates, the abolition of the Company's college at Haileybury, or to the training of the probationers during the two years which were to intervene between their first selection and their final departure for India. One other passage in the report deserves quotation, as testifying to the confidence with which Macaulay anticipated that in nicety of honor and uprightness of character the young civilians of the future would be inferior to no class of public servants in the world.

"We hope and believe, also, that it will very rarely be necessary to expel any probationer from the service on account of grossly profligate habits, or of any action unbecoming a man of honor. The probationers will be young men superior to their fellows in science and literature; and it is not among young men superior to their fellows in science and literature that scandalous immorality is generally found to prevail. It is notoriously not once in twenty years that a student who has attained high academical distinction is expelled from Oxford or Cambridge. Indeed, early superiority in science and literature generally indicates the existence of some qualities which are securities against vice — industry, self-denial, a taste for pleasures not sensual, a laudable desire of honorable distinction, a still more laudable desire to obtain the approbation of friends and relations. We therefore believe that the intellectual test which is about to be established will be found in practice to be also the best moral test that can be desired."

Macaulay had hopes, but not very strong hopes, that the example of the Indian Government would be followed in the offices at Whitehall. "There is good public news," he writes in January, 1854. "The plan for appointing public servants by competition is to be adopted on a large scale, and mentioned in the queen's speech." "I had a long talk," he says again, "about the projected examination with Trevelyan. I am afraid that he will pay the examiners too high, and turn the whole thing into a job.* I am anxious on this head. If the thing succeeds, it will be of immense benefit to the country." Civil Service reform had Mr. Gladstone for a champion in the Cabinet; and the introduction of open competition had been earnestly recommended in a report drawn up by Sir Charles Trevelyan and Sir Stafford Northcote, who had been associated together in a comprehensive and searching revision of our public departments. But it soon became evident that very few of our leading politicians had their hearts in the

---

* Any such danger was eventually obviated by the appointment of Sir Edward Ryan to the post of Chief Civil Service Commissioner. That truly eminent man, who to the authority and experience of age united the vigor and enthusiasm which too seldom survive the prime of life, nursed the infant system through its troubled childhood, until from a project and an experiment it had grown into an institution.

matter. It was one thing for them to deprive the East India Directors of their patronage, and quite another to surrender their own. The outcry of the dispensers and expectants of public employment was loud and fierce, and the advocates of the new system were forced to admit that its hour had not come. "I went to Brooks's," says Macaulay on the 4th of March, "and found every body open-mouthed, I am sorry to say, against Trevelyan's plans about the Civil Service. He has been too sanguine. The pear is not ripe. I always thought so. The time will come, but it is not come yet. I am afraid that he will be much mortified."

He was mortified, and had good cause to be alarmed, for his career was seriously threatened by the hostility of some of the most powerful men of the day. But he did not lose his courage or composure. Accustomed, according to the frequent fate of permanent officials, to be pushed to the front in the moment of jeopardy, and thrust into the rear in the moment of triumph, he had weathered more formidable storms than that which was now growling and blustering through all the clubs and board-rooms between Piccadilly and Parliament Street. Macaulay, who lived sufficiently behind the scenes to discern the full gravity of the situation, was extremely uneasy on his brother-in-law's account. "The news is worse," he writes, "about Trevelyan. There is a set made at him by men who will not scruple to do their utmost. But he will get through his difficulties, which he feels less than I should in his place; less, indeed, than I feel them for him. I was nervous about him, and out of spirits the whole evening." During the next few weeks Macaulay was never so depressed as when he had been spending part of his afternoon at Brooks's. Such were the views which then prevailed at the head-quarters of the great party that has long ere this identified itself with the maintenance of a system to which, more than to any other cause, we owe it that our political morality grows purer as our political institutions become more popular —a system which the most far-seeing of American statesmen already regard with a generous envy, knowing, as they have only too good reason to know, that it is the one and only specific against the jobbery and corruption which are fast undermining the efficiency of their administration, and debasing their standard of national virtue.*

When Macaulay had finished the business of preparing his speeches for the press, he returned to his "History," and continued to work upon it almost without intermission for two years, from November, 1853, onward. His labors, during this period of his life, were always too severe for his strength, and sometimes even for his happiness. He felt the strain most painfully during the early months of 1854.

"*Sunday, January 1st,* 1854.—This will, I hope, be a year of industry. I began pretty well. Chapter XIV. will require a good deal of work. I toiled on it some hours, and now and then felt dispirited. But we must be resolute, and work doggedly, as Johnson said. I read some of his Life with great delight, and then meditated a new arrangement of my 'History.' Arrangement and transition are arts which I value much, but which I do not flatter myself that I have attained. I amused myself with making out a Laponian New Testament by the help of a Norwegian dictionary. With time I could learn a good deal of the two languages in this way."

"*February 6th.*—I worked hard at altering the arrangement of the first three chapters of the third volume. What labor it is to make a tolerable book, and how little readers know how much trouble the ordering of the parts has cost the writer! I have now finished reading again most of Burke's works. Admirable! The greatest man since Milton."

"*Thursday, February 16th.*—I staid at home and did nothing. An unprofitable day. I tried to write, but had a feeling of impotence and despondency to which I am subject, but which I have not had now for some time. I sent twenty pounds to —— and ——. I thought that these high prices might pinch them. Then I sat down doggedly to work, and got on very tolerably—the state of England at the time of William's re-

---

* The whole question of patronage as bearing upon the official system of the United States is most ably and frankly discussed in the *North American Review* of January, 1871. The author of the article, speaking of the proposal to introduce competition into his own country, says distinctly: "There should be no attempt to disguise the fact that it is the purpose of this theory of administration to prevent the public service from being used in any manner or to any extent as a means of party success." It is to be hoped that this is a case in which, instead of Americanizing our own institutions, we shall induce our transatlantic cousins to Anglicize theirs.

turn from the Continent in 1692. I read Monk Lewis's Life. A very odd fellow! One of the best of men, if he had not had a trick of writing profane and indecent books. Excellent son, excellent master; and in the most trying circumstances; for he was the son of a vile brace of parents, and the master of a stupid, ungrateful gang of negroes."

"*March* 3d.—I staid at home all day. In the morning there was a fog which affected my breath, and made me cough much. I was sad and desponding all day. I thought that my book would be a failure; that I had written myself out; that my reputation would go down in my life-time; and that I should be left, like Hayley and other such men, among people who would wonder why I had ever been thought much of. These clouds will pass away, no doubt."

They passed away when the warm weather came, and did not return with the returning winter. Macaulay's health was confirmed by a fine summer, spent under circumstances which exactly suited his notions of enjoyment; and, for a good while to come, he was a stronger man than he had been since his first great illness. His brother-in-law had taken a house in the village of Esher; and Macaulay accordingly settled himself, with infinite content, exactly in the middle of the only ugly square mile of country which can be found in that delightful neighborhood. "I am pretty well pleased," he says, "with my house. The cabin, for a cabin it is, is convenient." "Here I am," he writes to Mr. Ellis, "in a pleasant, small dwelling, surrounded by geraniums and roses; the house so clean that you might eat off the floor. The only complaint I have to make is that the view from my front windows is blocked by a railway embankment. The Trevelyans have a very pleasant place only a mile and a half off." Macaulay's cottage, which stood in Ditton Marsh, by the side of the high-road from Kingston to Esher, was called Greenwood Lodge. An occasional extract from his journal will show how smoothly ran the current of his days.

"*July* 23d, 1854.—Tremendous heat. I put the first volume of Wilberforce's Life into my pocket, went by ferry across the Thames to Hampton Court, and lounged under the shade of the palace gardens and of Bushey Park during some hours. A hot walk back. I don't know that I ever felt it hotter."

"*August* 12th.—I wrote to Longman. I think that I must take till Oc-

tober next.* By that time the book may be not what I wish, but as good
as I can hope to make it. I read Dickens's 'Hard Times.' One excessively touching, heart-breaking passage, and the rest sullen socialism. The
evils which he attacks he caricatures grossly, and with little humor. Another book of Pliny's letters. Read 'Northanger Abbey;' worth all Dickens and Pliny together. Yet it was the work of a girl. She was certainly
not more than twenty-six. Wonderful creature! Finished Pliny. Capital fellow, Trajan, and deserving of a better Panegyric."

"*September 22d.*—I am glad that our troops have landed in the Cherso-
nese. As I walked back from Esher a shower came on. Afraid for my
chest, which at best is in no very good state, I turned into a small ale-
house, and called for a glass of ginger-beer. I found there a party of hop-
pickers, come back from the neighborhood of Farnham. They had had
but a bad season, and were returning, nearly walked off their legs. I liked
their looks, and thought their English remarkably good for their rank of
life. It was in truth the Surrey English, the English of the suburbs of
London, which is to the Somersetshire and Yorkshire what Castilian is to
Andalusian, or Tuscan to Neapolitan. The poor people had a foaming pot
before them; but as soon as they heard the price, they rose, and were going
to leave it untasted. They could not, they said, afford so much. It was
but fourpence-half-penny. I laid the money down; and their delight and
gratitude quite affected me. Two more of the party soon arrived. I ordered another pot, and when the rain was over left them, followed by more
blessings than, I believe, were ever purchased for ninepence. To be sure,
the boon, though very small, was seasonable; and I did my best to play
the courteous host."

During his residence in Surrey, Macaulay kept Mr. Ellis
regularly informed of all that a friend would wish to know;
but his letters contain little of general interest. On the 11th
of July he writes: "I have been working four or five days at
my report on the Indian Civil Service, and have at last finished it. It is much longer than I anticipated that it would be,
and has given me great trouble. To-morrow I go vigorously
to work on my 'History.' I have been so busy here with my
report that I have read nothing but comedies of Goldoni and
novels of Eugene Sue.

"I walked yesterday to Hampton Court along the Middlesex bank of the Thames, and lounged among the avenues and

---

* He underrated by fully three-quarters of a year the duration of the
work which was still before him..

flower-beds about an hour. I wonder that no poet has thought of writing a descriptive poem on the Thames. Particular spots have been celebrated; but surely there is no finer subject of the sort than the whole course of the river from Oxford downward — the noble University; Clifden; Windsor; Chertsey, the retreat of Cowley; St. Anne's Hill, the retreat of Fox; Hampton Court, with all the recollections of Wolsey, Cromwell, William and Mary, Belinda's hair, the Cartoons, the Beauties; then Strawberry Hill; then Twickenham and Pope's grotto; then Richmond; and so on to the great City, the forest of masts, the Tower, Greenwich Hospital, Tilbury Fort, and the Armada. Is there any river in the world which, in so short a space, affords such subjects for poetry? Not the Tiber, I am sure, nor the Seine."

From the summer of 1854, until his third and fourth volumes were published, the composition of his "History" was to Macaulay a source of almost unmingled interest and delight; "a work which never presses, and never ceases," as he called it in a letter to his sister; "a work which is the business and the pleasure of my life," as he described it in the preface to his speeches. By September, 1854, he was so far forward that he thought himself justified in saying, after a visit to the Windsor collection: "I was told that there was scarcely any thing of earlier date than George 1. A good hearing. I have now got to a point at which there is no more gratifying discovery than that nothing is to be discovered." As the months went on he worked harder, and ever harder. His labor, though a labor of love, was immense. He almost gave up letter-writing; he quite gave up society; and at last he had not leisure even for his diary.

"*January 1st*, 1855.—A new year. May it be as happy as the last! To me it will probably be more eventful, as it will see, if I live and am well, the publication of the second part of my 'History.'"

"*January 10th*.—I find that I am getting out of the habit of keeping my journal. I have, indeed, so much to do with my 'History' that I have little inclination for any other writing. My life, too, is very uneventful. I am a prisoner to my room, or nearly so. I do nothing but write or read. I will, however, minute down interesting things from time to time. Some day the taste for journalizing may return."

"*January* 29*th*, 1855.—I open this book again after an interval of near three weeks; three weeks passed by the fireside. Once I dined out; on Tuesday, the 16th, at Westbourne Terrace, to meet Gladstone. Nothing could be more lamentable than his account of affairs in the Crimea.

"To-night there will, I suppose, be a vote against the Government, and to-morrow a change of Administration.* I am content that it should be so, and well pleased that my illness dispenses me from voting. I have made great progress with my book of late, and see no reason to doubt that I shall go to press in the summer. I am now deep in Chapter XIX. Odd that here, within a few yards of all the bustle of politics, I should be as quiet as a hermit; as quiet as Cowper was at Olney; much more quiet, thank God, than my old friend Hannah More at Barley Wood; buried in old pamphlets and broadsides; turning away from the miseries of Balaklava to the battle of Steinkirk, on which I was busied to-day. The fates have spun me not the coarsest thread, as old Ben says. Hannah, Margaret, Alice, Trevelyan, and George are as kind as possible. I want no more; but I have other very kind visitors. I can not think that this can go on long. But I hope that I shall bring out my two volumes. I am conscious of no intellectual decay. My memory I often try, and find it as good as ever; and memory is the faculty which it is most easy to bring to decisive tests, and also the faculty which gives way first."

"*November* 6*th*, 1855.—After an interval of eight months I begin my journal again. My book is almost printed. It will appear before the middle of December, I hope. It will certainly make me rich, as I account riches. As to success I am less certain; but I have a good hope. I mean to keep my journal as regularly as I did seven years ago when the first part came out. To-day I went to call on poor Hallam. How much changed! In the evening a proof of Chapter XX. came from Spottiswoode's."

During the ensuing fortnight the entries in Macaulay's diary relate almost exclusively to the proof-sheets, which generally occupied him both morning and afternoon, and to the books which he turned over for his amusement after the appearance of the lamp had given him the signal to leave his desk, and draw his easy-chair to the hearth-rug. On the 13th of November, to take an instance, he read " 'Welsted's Life and Remains;' mostly trash. At dinner the 'Love Match.'

---

* On the 29th of January Mr. Roebuck carried his motion for a Committee of Inquiry into the condition of our army before Sebastopol, by 305 votes to 148. Lord Aberdeen at once resigned.

In the evening Jesse's 'Selwyn Correspondence,' Skelton's 'Deism Revealed,' and a great deal of Bolingbroke's stupid infidelity."

At length, on the 21st of November, he writes: "I looked over and sent off the last twenty pages. My work is done, thank God! and now for the result. On the whole, I think that it can not be very unfavorable. At dinner I finished 'Melpomene.'" The first effect upon Macaulay of having completed an installment of his own "History" was now, as in 1848, to set him reading Herodotus.

"*November 23d.*—Longman came. All the twenty-five thousand copies are ordered. Monday, the 27th of December, is to be the day; but on the evening of the preceding Saturday those book-sellers who take more than a thousand are to have their books. The stock lying at the book-binders' is insured for ten thousand pounds. The whole weight is fifty-six tons. It seems that no such edition was ever published of any work of the same bulk. I earnestly hope that neither age nor riches will narrow my heart."

"*November 27th.*—I finished Prescott's 'Philip the Second.' What strikes me most about him is, that, though he has had new materials, and tells his story well, he does not put any thing in a light very different from that in which I had before seen it; and I have never studied that part of history deeply. To-day I received from Longman the first copy of my book in the brown livery. I sent him yesterday the list of presentation copies."

"*November 28th.*—I dawdled over my book most of the day, sometimes in good, sometimes in bad spirits about it. On the whole, I think that it must do. The only competition which, as far as I perceive, it has to dread, is that of the two former volumes. Certainly no other history of William's reign is either so trustworthy or so readable."

"*November 29th.*—I was again confined to my room all day, and again dawdled over my book. I wish that the next month were over. I am more anxious than I was about the first part, for then I had no highly raised expectations to satisfy, and now people expect so much that the Seventh Book of Thucydides would hardly content them. On the other hand, the general sterility, the miserably enervated state of literature, is all in my favor. We shall see. It is odd that I should care so very little about the money, though it is full as much as I made by banishing myself for four and a half of the best years of my life to India."

"*December 4th.*—Another bleak day passed in my chambers. I am never tired of reading. Read some of Swift's 'Polite Conversations,' and Arbuthnot's 'John Bull.' One never wearies of these excellent pieces."*

---

* In Chapter XXIV. of his "History," Macaulay calls the "History of

"*December 6th.*—Fine, but cold. I staid at home all day, read ten cantos of the 'Morgante Maggiore,' and was languidly amused. A Yankee publisher sends me very coolly an enormous folio in two closely printed columns, a 'Dictionary of Authors,' and asks me to give my opinion of it—that opinion, of course, to be printed as a puff. He has already used the opinions of Everett, Washington Irving, and others in that way. I sent it back with a note saying that I could not form an opinion of such a work at a glance, and that I had not time for a full examination. I hate such tricks. *A propos* of puffing, I see that Robert Montgomery is gathered to Bavius and Blackmore. How he pestered me with his alternate cries for mercy and threats of vengeance!"

"*December 9th.*—Colder and more gloomy than ever. I staid at home, and enjoyed my liberty, though a prisoner to my room. I feel much easier about my book; very much. I read a great deal of Photius with much zest.* His account of Isocrates induces me to take down Isocrates again. I have not read him since I was in India. I looked at several speeches. He was never a favorite of mine, and I see no reason to change my opinion. I have found one serious mistake in my 'History.' I wonder whether any body else will find it out."

The presentation copies were delivered on the 15th of December. On Sunday, the 16th, which Macaulay, as usual, spent within-doors, " Sir Henry Holland called; very kind. He had read the first chapter, and came to pay compliments, which were the more welcome because my chief misgivings are about that chapter."

"*Monday, December* 17th.—An article on my book in the *Times;* in tone

---

John Bull" " the most ingenious and humorous political satire in our language." His own imitation of it well deserves a reading. It appeared first in *Knight's Quarterly Magazine,* in April, 1824, under the title, " Some Account of the Great Lawsuit between the Parishes of St. Dennis and St. George in the Water," and may now be found in his " Miscellaneous Writings."

* Macaulay first attacked Photius during his country rambles round Thames Ditton, without the aid of notes or of a Latin version. " I do not get on with Photius," he says. " I read chiefly while walking, and my copy is not one which I can conveniently carry in my hand." The rumor that he read Photius for pleasure was current in the Athenæum Club, and was never mentioned without awe. The very name of the patriarch's great work, the " Myriobiblon," or " Bibliotheca," is enough for most scholars of our degenerate day.

what I wished, that is to say, laudatory without any appearance of puffing. I had letters from Stephen and Adolphus—kind; but neither of them can as yet have read enough to judge. Longman called to-day and told me that they must print more copies. He was for five thousand. I insisted that there should be only two thousand."

"*December 18th.*—There came one of Longman's clerks, with news that the first two volumes of the 'History' must be reprinted at once, as the sale of them has during the last few days been very great.* I wrote to —— and —— about money matters. I am glad that I am now able to make them quite comfortable."

"*Sunday, December 23d.*—More of Photius. He sent me to 'Lysias;' and I read with the greatest delight some of those incomparable speeches; incomparable, I mean, in their kind, which is not the highest kind. They are wonderful—Scarlett speaking in the style of Addison."

"*Wednesday, December 26th.*—Read 'Cicero De Divinatione.' The second book is excellent. What a man he was! To think that the 'Divinatione,' the 'De Fato,' and the 'De Officiis' should all have been the fruits of his leisure during the few months that he outlived the death of Cæsar. During those months Cicero was leader of the Senate, and as busy a man as any in the republic. The finest of his senatorial speeches, spoken or not, belongs to that time. He seems to have been at the head of the minds of the second order."†

"*Tuesday, January 1st,* 1856.—A new year. I am happy in fame, fortune, family affection—most eminently so. Under these heads I have nothing to ask more; but my health is very indifferent. Yet I have no pain. My faculties are unimpaired. My spirits are very seldom depressed; and I am not without hopes of being set up again. I read miscellaneous trifles from the back rows of my books; Nathan's 'Reminiscences of Byron;' Colman's 'Broad Grins;' Strange's 'Letter to Lord Bute;' Gibbon's 'Vindication,' and his answer to Warburton about the Sixth Æneid. Letters and criticisms still pour in. Praise greatly preponderates, but there is a strong admixture of censure. I can, however, see no sign that these volumes excite less interest than their predecessors. Fanny tells me that a sermon was preached at Brighton to my praise and glory last Sunday, and the Londonderry people seem in great glee."

"*Friday, January 4th.*—To-day I gave a breakfast to Jowett, Ellis, Hannah, Margaret, and Montagu Butler and Vaughan Hawkins, young Fel-

---

* The sale of the first two volumes rose, from eleven hundred and seventy-two copies in 1854–'55, to four thousand nine hundred and one copies in 1855–'56; and this, be it observed, in the large library edition.

† Macaulay had of late been reading "Cicero De Finibus." "I always liked it," he says, "the best of his philosophical works; and I am still of the same mind."

lows of Trinity. A pleasant party; at least I thought so. After long silence and solitude, I poured myself out very freely and generally. They
staid till past one; a pretty good proof that they were entertained. I
have a letter from Guizot, full of kind compliments. He asks a question
about the place where the Lords received Charles the Second on May 29th,
1660. It is odd that a foreigner should trouble himself about so minute a
matter. I went to the Royal Institution, got down the Journals, and soon
found that the Lords were in the drawing-room at Whitehall. The Commons were in the Banqueting House."

"*Monday, January 7th.*—Yesterday and to-day I have been reading over
my old journals of 1852 and 1853. What a strange interest they have!
No kind of reading is so delightful, so fascinating, as this minute history
of a man's self. I received another heap of criticisms—praise and blame.
But it matters little. The victory is won. The book has not disappointed the very highly raised expectations of the public. The first fortnight
was the time of peril. Now all is safe."

The event more than justified Macaulay's confidence. The
ground which his book then gained has never been lost since.
"I shall not be satisfied," he wrote in 1841, "unless I produce something which shall for a few days supersede the last
fashionable novel on the tables of young ladies." It may be
said, for the credit of his countrymen no less than for his own,
that the annual sale of his "History" has frequently since
1857 surpassed the sale of the fashionable novel of the current
year. How firm a hold that "History" has obtained on the
estimation of the reading world is well known to all whose
business makes them acquainted with the intellectual side of
common English life; but the figures which testify to Macaulay's stable and increasing popularity may well surprise even
the guardian of a free library or the secretary of a mechan-
ics' institute. Those figures shall be given in the simplest
and the most precise shape. "Round numbers are always
false," said Dr. Johnson; and a man need not be as conversant as Dr. Johnson with the trade secrets of literature in order to be aware that what are called "new editions" are sometimes even more misleading than round numbers. Messrs.
Longman's books show that, in an ordinary year, when nothing is done to stimulate the public appetite by novelty of form
or reduction of price, their stock of the "History" goes out

of their hands at the rate of seventy complete copies a week. But a computation founded on this basis would give a very inadequate notion of the extent to which Macaulay's most important work is bought and read; for no account would have been taken of the years in which large masses of new and cheap editions were sold off in the course of a few months: 12,024 copies of a single volume of the "History" were put into circulation in 1858, and 22,925 copies of a single volume in 1864. During the nine years ending with the 25th of June, 1857, Messrs. Longman disposed of 30,478 copies of the first volume of the "History;" 50,783 copies during the nine years ending with June, 1866; and 52,392 copies during the nine years ending with June, 1875. Within a generation of its first appearance, upward of a hundred and forty thousand copies of the "History" will have been printed and sold in the United Kingdom alone.

But the influence of the work and the fame of its author were not confined to the United Kingdom. "I have," writes Macaulay, "a most intoxicating letter from Everett. He says that no book has ever had such a sale in the United States, except (note the exception) the Bible and one or two school-books of universal use. This, he says, he has been assured by book-sellers of the best authority."* On the continent of Eu-

---

* With reference to the first two volumes of the "History," Macaulay wrote to Mr. Everett: "It would be mere affectation in me not to own that I am greatly pleased by the success of my 'History' in America. But I am almost as much puzzled as pleased; for the book is quite insular in spirit. There is nothing cosmopolitan about it. I can well understand that it might have an interest for a few highly educated men in your country; but I do not at all understand how it should be acceptable to the body of a people who have no king, no lords, no Established Church, no Tories, nay (I might say), no Whigs in the English sense of the word. The dispensing power, the ecclesiastical supremacy, the doctrines of Divine right and passive obedience, must all, I should have thought, seemed strange, unmeaning things to the vast majority of the inhabitants of Boston and Philadelphia. Indeed, so very English is my book, that some Scotch critics, who have praised me far beyond my deserts, have yet complained that I have said so much of the crotchets of the Anglican High-churchmen—crotchets which scarcely any Scotchman seems able to comprehend."

rope, within six months after the third and fourth volumes
appeared, Baron Tauchnitz had sold near ten thousand copies;
"which proves," writes Macaulay, "that the number of persons who read English in France and Germany is very great."
"The incomparable man" (says of him Professor Von Ranke),
"whose works have a European, or rather a world-wide, circulation, to a degree unequaled by any of his contemporaries."
Six rival translators were engaged at one and the same time
on the work of turning the "History" into German. It has
been published in the Polish, the Danish, the Swedish, the
Italian, the French, the Dutch, the Spanish, the Hungarian,
the Russian, the Bohemian languages, and is at this moment
in course of translation into Persian.

Macaulay received frequent and flattering marks of the
respect and admiration with which he was regarded by the
foreigner. He was made a member of the Academies of
Utrecht, Munich, and Turin. The King of Prussia named
him a Knight of the Order of Merit, on the presentation of
the Royal Academy of Sciences at Berlin; and his nomination was communicated to him in a letter from the Baron
Von Humboldt, the chancellor of the order.* Guizot wrote
to inform him that he had himself proposed him for the Institute of France. On one and the same day of February,
1853, the official announcement of his election came from
Paris, and his badge of the Order of Merit from Berlin.

---

* The Prussian Order of Merit is, to other honors, what its founder Frederic the Great was to other kings. The following paragraph appeared
lately in *The Academy*:

"It has excited some surprise that Mr. Carlyle should have declined the
Grand Cross of the Bath, after having accepted the *Ordre pour le Mérite*.
There is, however, a great difference between the two. The *Ordre pour le Mérite* is not given by the sovereign or the minister, but by the knights themselves. The king only confirms their choice. The number of the knights
of the *Ordre pour le Mérite* is strictly limited (there are no more than thirty German and thirty foreign knights), so that every knight knows who
will be his peers. In Germany, not even Bismarck is a knight of the *Ordre
pour le Mérite*. Moltke was elected simply as the best representative of
military science; nor does he rank higher as a knight of that order than
Bunsen, the representative of physical science, or Ranke, the historian."

In the following June, Macaulay was presented to the degree of Doctor of Civil Law at Oxford, where he was welcomed enthusiastically by the crowd in the body of the theatre, and not unkindly even by the under-graduates, who almost forgot to enter a protest against the compliment that their university had thought fit to bestow on the great Whig writer.* In 1854 he was chosen president of the Philosophical Institution of Edinburgh, to the duties of which post he could give little of his time, though the Institution owes to his judgment and liberality some important additions to its stock of curious and valuable books. He showed himself, however, most assiduous in his attendance at the British Museum, both as a trustee and as a student. His habit was to work in the King's Library; partly for quiet, and partly in order to have George the Third's wonderful collection of pamphlets within an easy walk of his chair. He did his writing at one of the oak tables which stand in the centre of the room, sitting away from the outer wall, for the sake of the light. He availed himself of his official authority to search the shelves at pleasure without the intervention of a librarian; and (says the attendant) "when he had taken down a volume, he generally looked as if he had found something in it." A manuscript page of his "History," thickly scored with dashes and erasures — it is the passage in the twenty-fifth chapter where Sir Hans Sloane is mentioned as "the founder of the magnificent museum which is one of the glories of our country"—is preserved at that museum in a cabinet, which may truly be called the place of honor; within whose narrow limits are gathered together a rare collection of objects such as Englishmen of all classes and parties regard with a common reverence and pride. There may be seen Nelson's hasty

---

* The batch of new doctors included Mr. Grote, Mr. Disraeli, Sir Edward Bulwer Lytton, and the present Lord Derby. "I congratulated Grote with special warmth," says Macaulay, "for, with all his faults of style, he has really done wonders....... I was pleased with Lord Derby's reception of his son. 'Fili mi dilectissime,' he called him. When I entered somebody called out 'History of England!' Then came a great tumult of applause and hissing; but the applause greatly predominated."

sketch of the line of battle at the Nile; and the sheet of paper on which Wellington computed the strength of the cavalry regiments that were to fight at Waterloo; and the notebook of Locke; and the autographs of Samuel Johnson's "Irene," and Ben Jonson's "Masque of Queens;" and the rough copy of the translation of the "Iliad," written, as Pope loved to write, on the margin of frayed letters and the backs of tattered envelopes. It is pleasant to think what Macaulay's feelings would have been if, when he was rhyming and castle-building among the summer-houses at Barley Wood, or the laurel-walks at Aspenden, or under the limes and horse-chestnuts in the Cambridge Gardens, he could have been assured that the day would come when he should be invited to take his place in such a noble company.

CHAPTER XIV.

1856–1858.

MACAULAY's first care in the year 1856 was to make his arrangements for retiring from Parliament. He bid farewell to the electors of Edinburgh in a letter which, as we are told by his successor in the representation of the city, was received by them with "unfeigned sorrow." "The experience," he writes, "of the last two years has convinced me that I can not reasonably expect to be ever again capable of performing, even in an imperfect manner, those duties which the public has a right to expect from every member of the House of Commons. You meanwhile have borne with me in a manner which entitles you to my warmest gratitude. Had even a small number of my constituents hinted to me a wish that I would vacate my seat, I should have thought it my duty to comply with that wish. But from not one single elector have

I ever received a line of reproach or complaint." This letter
was dispatched on the 19th of January; on the 21st he applied for the Chiltern Hundreds; and on the 2d of February
he notes in his journal: "I received a letter from the Lord
Provost of Edinburgh, inclosing an address from the electors
unanimously voted in a great meeting. I was really touched."

And now Macaulay, yielding a tardy obedience to the advice of every one who had an interest in his welfare, began to
enjoy the ease which he had so laboriously earned. He had
more than once talked of shifting his quarters to some residence less unsuited to his state of health than a set of chambers on a second floor between Vigo Street and Piccadilly.
At one time he amused himself with the idea of renting one
of the new villas on Weybridge Common; and at another he
was sorely tempted to become the purchaser of a large man-
sion and grounds at "dear old Clapham." But in January,
1856, Dean Milman wrote to inform him that the lease of a
very agreeable house and garden at Kensington was in the
market. The immediate effect of this letter was to suggest to
Macaulay the propriety of giving his old friend's book another reading. "I began," he says, "Milman's 'Latin Christianity,' and was more impressed than ever by the contrast between the substance and the style. The substance is excellent. The style very much otherwise."* On the morrow he
heard from the Duchess of Argyll, who, knowing the place in
question as only a next-door neighbor could, urged him not
to miss what was indeed an excellent opportunity. Accordingly, on the 23d of January, he says: "I went with Hannah
and Margaret to see the house about which the duchess and
the dean had written to me. It is in many respects the very
thing; but I must know more, and think more, before I decide." He soon made up his mind that he had lighted on the
home which he wanted. Without more ado he bought the
lease, and with great deliberation, and after many a pleasant

---

* A few months after this Macaulay writes: "I was glad to hear that a
new edition of Milman's History is called for. It is creditable to the age.
I began to read it again."

family discussion, he refurnished his new abode in conformity with his sister's taste and his own notions of comfort.

"*May 1st*, 1856.—The change draws very near. After fifteen happy years passed in the Albany, I am going to leave it, thrice as rich a man as when I entered it, and far more famous; with health impaired, but with affections as warm and faculties as vigorous as ever. I have lost nothing that was very near my heart while I was here. Kind friends have died, but they were not part of my daily circle. I do not at all expect to live fifteen years more. If I do, I can not hope that they will be so happy as the last fifteen. The removal makes me sad, and would make me sadder but for the extreme discomfort in which I have been living during the last week. The books are gone, and the shelves look like a skeleton. To-morrow I take final leave of this room where I have spent most of the waking hours of so many years. Already its aspect is changed. It is the corpse of what it was on Sunday. I hate partings. To-day, even while I climbed the endless steps, panting and weary, I thought that it was for the last time, and the tears would come into my eyes. I have been happy at the top of this toilsome stair. Ellis came to dinner—the last of probably four hundred dinners, or more, that we have had in these chambers. Then to bed. Every thing that I do is colored by the thought that it is for the last time. One day there will come a last in good earnest."

I well remember that, about this period, my uncle used to speak of the affinity which existed between our feeling for houses and our feeling for people. "Nothing," he said, "would at one time have reconciled me to the thought of leaving the Albany; but, when I go home, and see the rooms dismantled, and the book-cases empty, and the whole place the ghost of its former self, I acknowledge that the end can not come too soon." And then he spoke of those sad changes, the work of age and illness, which prepare us gradually, and even mercifully, for the loss of those from whom it once seemed as if we could never have borne to part. He was thinking of a very dear friend who was just then passing quietly, and very slowly, through the antechamber of death. On the 13th of February in this year he says: "I went to call on poor Hallam. I found him quite prisoner to his sofa, unable to walk. To write legibly he has long been unable. But in the conversation between us—not, to be sure, a trying conversation—he showed no defect of memory or apprehen-

sion. Poor dear fellow! I put a cheerful face on the matter; but I was sad at heart.

> Let me not live
> After my flame lacks oil, to be the scoff
> Of meaner spirits.

Mean they must be indeed who scoff in such a case."*

Macaulay was now lodged as his friends wished to see him.
He could not well have bettered his choice. Holly Lodge,
now called Airlie Lodge, occupies the most secluded corner of
the little labyrinth of by-roads, which, bounded to the east by
Palace Gardens and to the west by Holland House, constitutes
the district known by the name of Campden Hill. The villa,
for a villa it is, stands in a long and winding lane, which, with
its high black paling concealing from the passer-by every thing
except a mass of dense and varied foliage, presents an appearance as rural as Roehampton and East Sheen presents still,
and as Wandsworth and Streatham presented twenty years
ago. The only entrance for carriages was at the end of the
lane farthest from Holly Lodge; and Macaulay had no one
living beyond him except the Duke of Argyll, who loved quiet
as much as himself, and for the same reasons.

The rooms in Holly Lodge were for the most part small.
The dining-room was that of a bachelor who was likewise
something of an invalid; and the drawing-room, which, from
old habit, my uncle could seldom bring himself to use, was
little more than a vestibule to the dining-room. But the
house afforded in perfection the two requisites for an author's
ideal of happiness, a library and a garden. The library was a
spacious and commodiously shaped room, enlarged, after the
old fashion, by a pillared recess. It was a warm and airy retreat in winter; and in summer it afforded a student only too

---

* Mr. Hallam lived into 1859. In the January of that year Macaulay
wrote: "Poor Hallam! To be sure, to me he died some years ago. I then
missed him much and often. Now the loss is hardly felt. I am inclined
to think that there is scarcely any separation, even of those separations
which break hearts and cause suicides, which might not be made endurable
by gradual weaning. In the course of that weaning there will be much
suffering, but it will at no moment be very acute."

irresistible an inducement to step from among his book-shelves on to a lawn whose unbroken slope of verdure was worthy of the country-house of a lord-lieutenant. Nothing in the garden exceeded thirty feet in height; but there was in abundance all that hollies, and laurels, and hawthorns, and groves of standard roses, and bowers of lilacs and laburnums could give of shade and scent and color. The charms of the spot were not thrown away upon its owner. "How I love," he says, "my little paradise of shrubs and turf!" "I remember no such May," he writes in 1857. "It is delicious. The lilacs are now completely out; the laburnums almost completely. The brilliant red flowers of my favorite thorn-tree began to show themselves yesterday. To-day they are beautiful. To morrow, I dare say, the whole tree will be in a blaze." And again, a few days later: "The rhododendrons are coming out; the mulberry-tree, which, though small, is a principal object in the view of the garden from my library window, is staring into leaf." In the following September, when fresh from a tour down the Moselle and up the Rhine, through the glen of Vaucluse and across the pastures of the Italian Alps, he writes in high content, after his return to Holly Lodge: "My garden is really charming. The flowers are less brilliant than when I went away, but the turf is perfect emerald. All the countries through which I have been traveling could not show such a carpet of soft, rich green herbage as mine."

The beauty of the objects around him, combined with the novel sense of possession, inspired Macaulay with an interest in small every-day matters to which he had hitherto been a stranger. He began to feel the proprietor's passion for seeing things in order within doors and without. He says in one place: "To-day I cleared my tables of a vast accumulation of books and pamphlets. This process I must carry a good deal further. The time so spent is not time lost. It is, as Bacon would say, *luciferum*, if not directly *fructiferum*." One of the most fortunate consequences arising from his change of residence was that, if it were for only ten minutes in the day, he accustomed himself to do something besides write and talk and read. It must be admitted that his efforts at gardening were sufficiently humble. Far beneath any thing which is re-corded of such scientific horticulturists as Pope and Shenstone, his first attempts might have aroused the mild scorn even of Wordsworth and of Cowper. "I have ordered," he says, "the dead sprigs to be cleared from the lilacs, and the grass to be weeded of dandelions;" and, shortly after, "I had an hour's walk, and exterminated all the dandelions which had sprouted up since yesterday."* But he soon became more ambitious. "I chose places for rhododendron-beds, and directed the work-men to set creepers in my xystus.† On Christmas-day, 1856, he writes to his sister Fanny: "The holiday interrupts my gardening. I have turned gardener; not indeed working-gar-dener, but master-gardener. I have just been putting creep-ers round my windows, and forming beds of rhododendrons round my fountain. In three or four summers, if I live so long, I may expect to see the results of my care."

The hospitality at Holly Lodge had about it a flavor of pleasant peculiarity. Macaulay was no epicure on his own

---

* These unlucky weeds play a leading part in Macaulay's correspondence with his youngest niece. "My dear little Alice," he writes, "I quite for-got my promised letter, but I assure you that you were never out of my mind for three waking hours together. I have, indeed, had little to put you and yours out of my thoughts; for I have been living, these last ten days, like Robinson Crusoe in his desert island. I have had no friends near me but my books and my flowers, and no enemies but those execrable dan-delions. I thought that I was rid of the villains; but the day before yes-terday, when I got up and looked out of my window, I could see five or six of their great, impudent, flaring, yellow faces turned up at me. ' Only you wait till I come down,' I said. How I grubbed them up! How I enjoyed their destruction! Is it Christian-like to hate a dandelion so savagely? That is a curious question of casuistry."

† The word "xystus" was a reminiscence from the letters of Cicero and Pliny. According to Dr. William Smith it signifies an "open colonnade or portico, for recreation, conversation, and philosophical discussion." The easier life which Macaulay henceforward led gave him a fresh lease of health, or, at any rate, of comfort. "I am wonderfully well," he writes; "my sleep is deeper and sweeter than it has been for years." And again: "I had an excellent night. What a blessing to regain, so late, the refresh-ing sleep of early years! I am altogether better than I have been since 1852."

account. In his Reform Bill days, as many passages in his
letters show, he enjoyed a banquet at the house of a Cabinet
minister or a City magnate with all the zest of a hungry un-
der-graduate; but there never was a time when his daily wants
would not have been amply satisfied by a couple of eggs with
his coffee in the morning, and a dinner such as is served at a
decent sea-side lodging-house. He could not, however, endure
to see guests, even of the most tender age, seated round his
board, unless there was upon it something very like a feast.
He generally selected, by a half-conscious preference, dishes of
an established, and, if so it may be called, an historical reputation. He was fond of testifying to his friendliness for
Dissenters by treating his friends to a fillet of veal, which he
maintained to be the recognized Sunday dinner in good old
Non - conformist families. He liked still better to prove his
loyalty to the Church by keeping her feasts, and keeping
them in good company; and by observing her fasts, so far,
that is to say, as they could be observed by making additions
to the ordinary bill of fare. A Michaelmas-day on which he
did not eat goose, or ate it in solitude, was no Michaelmas
to him; and regularly on Christmas - eve there came to our
house a cod-fish, a barrel of oysters, and a chine, accompanied
by the heaviest turkey which diligence could discover and
money could purchase. If he were entertaining a couple of
school-boys who could construe their fourth satire of Juvenal,
he would reward them for their proficiency with a dish of
mullet that might have passed muster on the table of an augur
or an emperor's freedman. If he succeeded in collecting a
party of his own Cambridge contemporaries, he took care that
they should have no cause to remember with regret the Trinity butteries.*   "I should be much obliged to you," so he

* Macaulay liked nothing better than a Trinity gathering. In February, 1852, he says: "To the Clarendon at seven, where I had ordered dinner for a party of ex-fellows of the dear old college. Malden came first;
then the Lord Chief Baron, Baron Parke, Waddington, Lefevre, and Ellis.
We had an excellent dinner. The Dean of Durham's favorite dish, filet
de bœuf sauté au vin de Madère aux truffes, was there. We all tried it,
applauded it, and drank his health in Champagne recommended by him."

writes to Mr. Ellis, "to lend me a bottle or two of that excellent audit ale which you produced the last time that I dined with you. You shall have in return two bottles which still require time to make them perfect. I ask this, because our party on Tuesday will consist exclusively of old fellows and scholars of Trinity; and I should like to give them some of our own nectar."* With regard to the contents of his cellar, Macaulay prided himself on being able to say with Mr. John Thorpe, "Mine is famous good stuff, to be sure;" and if my mother took him to task for his extravagance, he would reply, in the words used by another of their favorite characters in fiction, that there was "a great deal of good eating and drinking" in seven hundred a year, if people knew how to manage it.†

But he never was so amusing as when it pleased him to season a family repast by a series of quotations from the "Almanach des Gourmands"— that wonderful monument of the outrageous self-indulgence prevalent in French society during the epoch of luxury and debauchery which succeeded to the surly discomfort of the Revolution,‡ and ushered in the vulgar magnificence of the First Empire. He had by heart the choice morsels of humor and extravagance that are so freely scattered through the eight fat little volumes; and he was at all times ready to undertake the feat of detailing the ceremonies of a Parisian banquet, from those awkward complications of arrangement, "que les personnes bien avisées ont l'attention

---

* The party in question turned out a complete success. "*November 9th.* —Lord Mayor's Day ; and I had a dinner as well as the lord-mayor. I did my best as host. The dinner was well cooked ; the audit ale perfect. We had so much to say about auld lang-syne that great powers of conversation were not wanted. I have been at parties of men celebrated for wit and eloquence which were much less lively. Every body seemed to be pleased."

† See Miss Ferrier's "Marriage," chapter xx.

‡ "Les tables d'hôte," says the "Almanach," "ne se rouvrirent point alors. On continua d'aller manger isolément et tristement chez les restaurateurs, où chacun, assis à une petite table, et séparé des autres, consomme en silence sa portion, sans se mêler de ce que dit ou de ce que fait son voisin."

d'abréger en mettant d'avance le nom de chaque convive sur chaque couvert, dans l'ordre de leur appétit connu ou présumé," to the "visite de digestion" on the morrow, the length of which was supposed to be proportioned to the excellence of the entertainment. He could follow the repast through the whole series of delicacies, from the "potage brûlant, tel qu'il doit être," on to the "biscuit d'ivrogne;" taking care to impress upon the unwilling ears of his younger hearers that "tout bon mangeur a fini son dîner après le rôti." He would assure us on the same high authority that, after the sixth dozen, oysters ceased to whet the appetite; and he would repeat with infinite gusto the sentence that closes the description of a breakfast such as, during the last years of the century, a high official of the republic took pride in giving : "Ceux qui veulent faire grandement les choses, finissent par parfumer la bouche de leurs convives (ou plutôt de leurs amis, car c'est ainsi que s'appellent les convives d'un déjeûner), avec deux ou trois tasses de glaces; on se la rinse ensuite avec un grand verre de marasquin; et puis chacun se retire en hâte chez soi—pour aller manger la soupe."*

It must be owned that even a "grand déjeûner" at the hôtel of Cambaceres or Barras could hardly have lasted longer than a breakfast at Holly Lodge; but Macaulay's guests were detained at table by attractions less material than those which were provided by the Amphitryons of the Directory and the Consulate. Long after the cutlets and the potted char had been forgotten the circle would sit entranced, while their host disposed of topic after topic, and fetched from his shelves volume after volume, until the noon-day sun invited the party to spare yet another hour for a stroll round the garden, so gay in its winter dress that it seemed "very enjoyable" even to the

---

* Macaulay's favorite passage in the "Almanach des Gourmands" was that which prescribes the period (varying from a week to six months, according to the goodness of the dinner) during which the guests may not speak ill of their host; who has, moreover, the privilege of chaining their tongues afresh by sending out a new set of invitations before the full time has expired. "On conviendra que, de toutes les manières d'empêcher de mal parler de soi, celle-ci n'est pas la moins aimable."

master of Castle Howard.   Lord Carlisle says in his journal of
December 19th, 1856: "Walked to Campden Hill on a beautiful morning.   David Dundas had invited me to breakfast
there.   Was received with surprise, but with warm welcome,
by Macaulay.   I never knew his memory more brilliant or
surprising.   A casual mention of the lion on the Howard
shield brought down a volume of Skelton with his finger on
the passage.   Then there was a long charade on Polyphemus,
which he remembered from an *Age* newspaper in 1825.   He
seemed to me to have gained in health by his transfer to his
pleasant villa."

So pleasant was it, that its occupant did not care to seek for
pleasure elsewhere.   Months would pass away without Macaulay's having once made his appearance in London society;
and years, during which he refused all invitations to stay with
friends or acquaintances in the country.   One or two nights
spent at Windsor Castle, and one or two visits to Lord Stanhope's seat in Kent, formed almost the sole exceptions to a
rule which the condition of his health imperatively prescribed,
and against which his inclinations did not lead him to rebel.

" *Chevening, July* 16*th*, 1856.—After breakfast Lord Stanhope very kindly
and sensibly left me to rummage his library.   A fine old library it is, of, I
should guess, fifteen thousand volumes: much resembling a college library
both in appearance and in the character of the books.   I was very agreeably entertained till two in the afternoon.   Then we set off for Mountstuart
Elphinstone's, six miles off.   I saw him probably for the last time; still
himself, though very old and infirm.   A great and accomplished man as
any that I have known.   In the evening Darwin, a geologist and traveler,
came to dinner."

"*July* 17*th*.—The morning again in the library.   In the afternoon to a
pretty spot of common land which has fallen to Lord Stanhope under a
late inclosure act; fine wood and heath, and a fine prospect.   My Valentine* was with us, dancing about among the flowers; gathering fox-gloves
and whortleberries, and very gay and happy.   I love all little girls of that
age for the sake of my own nieces; and Lady Mary is a very amiable child.
In the evening Lord Stanhope produced a tragedy written by Pitt, and his
brother Lord Chatham, in 1772; detestable of course, but well enough for
a boy of thirteen.   Odd that there was no love at all in the plot: a dis-

---

* See page 185.

pute about a regency, during the absence of the king, and the minority
of his son Prince Florus.   There were several passages which reminded
me of 1789."

There is a characteristic notice in Macaulay's diary of a winter visit to Bowood.

"*January* 31*st*.—A fine frosty day.   Lord Lansdowne proposed a walk,
and we went up to the hill where the old moat and the yew-tree are.   The
way lay through a perfect Slough of Despond.   I, like Pliable, should have
turned back, but Lady Mahon's courage shamed me.   After lunch I went
to walk alone in the pleasure-ground, but was pestered by a most sociable
cur who would not be got rid of.   I went into a plantation, railed off with
gates at each end, and shut the brute out; but he perfectly understood
my tactics—curse his intelligence!—and waited for me at the other gate.
After vainly trying to escape him in this way, I shut him in, and staid outside myself.   When I walked away, he saw that he had been outgeneraled
by human reason, and set up the most ludicrous howl that I ever heard in
my life."

It is to be hoped, for Macaulay's sake, that the biographers
of great men who were partial to the company of animals over-
state their case when they assert that the love of dogs is the
surest test of a good heart.   In 1850, when staying with some
friends in the country, he writes: "After breakfast I walked
with the young ladies; nice, intelligent girls they are.   A
couple of ill-conditioned curs went with us, whom they were
foolish enough to make pets of; so that we were regaled by
a dog-fight, and were very near having on our hands two or
three other fights.   How odd that people of sense should find
any pleasure in being accompanied by a beast who is always
spoiling conversation!"*   It must be said that my uncle was

---

* In July, 1856, Macaulay writes: "I went to Oatlands and walked with
Margaret and Alice to a most singular monument of human folly.   The
Duchess of York had made a cemetery for her dogs.   There is a gate-way
like that under which coffins are laid in the church-yard of this part of the
country; there is a sort of chapel; and there are the grave-stones of sixty-
four of her royal highness's curs.   On some of these mausoleums were inscriptions in verse.   I was disgusted by this exceeding folly.   Humanity
to the inferior animals I feel and practice, I hope, as much as any man; but
seriously to make friends of dogs is not my taste.   I can understand, how-

very kind to the only dog which ever depended on him for kindness; a very pretty and very small Mexican spaniel, that belonged to one of his nieces. He treated the little animal exactly as he treated children, bringing it presents from the toy-shops, and making rhymes about it by the quarter of an hour together.

Little as Macaulay liked to spend his time under other people's roofs, he had no objection to hotels, and to foreign hotels least of all. Nothing short of a Continental war, or the impossibility of getting Mr. Ellis's company, would ever have prevented him from taking his autumn tour. In 1856 he once more crossed the Alps, and was at Milan by the end of August. "From the balcony we caught sight of the cathedral, which made us impatient to see the whole. We went. I never was more delighted and amazed by any building except St. Peter's. The great façade is undoubtedly a blunder: but a most splendid and imposing blunder. I wish to heaven that our Soanes, and Nashes, and Wilkinses had blundered in the same way." Venice, with which, ever since his boyhood, he had been as familiar as book and picture could make him, when seen at length in her own sad grandeur, seemed to him "strange beyond all words." He did not fail to admire "the succession of palaces, towering out of the green salt water; now passing into decay, yet retaining many traces of their

---

ever, that even a sensible man may have a fondness for a dog. But sixty-four dogs! Why, it is hardly conceivable that there should be warm affection in any heart for sixty-four human beings. I had formed a better opinion of the duchess." It is difficult to say whether his opinion of the duchess was raised or lowered by some information which reached him a few days later, when he was dining with Lord Lyveden, "very agreeably seated between two clever women, Lady Morley and Lady Dufferin." The latter told him that she and Mrs. Norton had been much at Oatlands when they were girls of twelve or thirteen; that the epitaphs were not, as Macaulay had supposed, the mature efforts of Monk Lewis's genius, but the childish productions of herself and her sister; and that the great multitude of the graves might be accounted for by the fact that the duchess was plagued to death with presents of dogs, which she did not like to refuse, and which would have turned her house into a kennel, if she had not given them a dose of opium, and sent them to the cemetery.

ancient magnificence—rich carvings, incrustations of rare marbles, faint remains of gilding and fresco-painting. Of these great mansions there is scarcely one so modern as the oldest house in St. James's Square. Many were built, and crowded with brilliant company, in the days of Henry the Eighth and Elizabeth; some as far back as the days of Richard the Second and Henry the Fourth. For Venice then was to London what London now is to Sydney or Toronto."

St. Mark's Church, without impairing his loyalty to the great Roman basilica, affected him in a manner which was beyond, or rather beside, his expectations. "I do not think it, nobody can think it, beautiful, and yet I never was more entertained by any building. I never saw a building except St. Peter's where I could be content to pass so many hours in looking about me. There is something attractive to me in the very badness of the rhyming monkish hexameters, and in the queer designs and false drawing of the pictures. Every thing carries back the mind to a remote age; to a time when Cicero and Virgil were hardly known in Italy; to a time compared with which the time of Politian and even the time of Petrarch is modern. I returned in the course of the day, and spent an hour in making out the histories of Moses and Joseph, and the mottoes. They amused me as the pictures in very old Bibles used to amuse me when I was a child."

After his first visit to the Academy, Macaulay makes some remarks which, with the fear of Mr. Ruskin before my eyes, I almost tremble to transcribe: "The glow, the blaze, of warm Venetian coloring produces a wonderful effect. But there are few pieces which, considered separately as works of art, give me much pleasure. There is an eternal repetition of the same subjects—nine Holy Families, for example, in one small room. Then the monstrous absurdity of bringing doges, archangels, cardinals, apostles, persons of the Trinity, and members of the Council of Ten into one composition shocks and disgusts me. A spectator who can forgive such faults for the sake of a dexterous disposition of red tints and green tints must have improved his eye, I think, at the expense of his understanding." Macaulay's last day at Venice was devoted to the Ducal Palace.

"I was more indignant," he writes, "than I chose to show when I found not only that Petrarch's legacy of books had been suffered to perish, but that the public library of Venice did not contain a copy of one of Aldus's great editions of the Greek classics. I am sorry to leave this fascinating city; forever, I suppose. I may now often use the word 'forever' when I leave things."

He had brought with him instructions from his nieces to report at length upon Juliet's tomb; and he accordingly writes to them from Verona to express his delight at finding himself in a city so rich in its matchless variety of beauties and associations. "You have an amphitheatre which very likely Pliny may have frequented; huge old palaces and towers, the work of princes who were contemporary with our Edward the First; and most charming and graceful architecture of the time of Michael Angelo and Raphael; and all this within a space not larger than Belgrave Square." At the same time he threatens them with a Popish aunt, who will be able to assist them in their Italian studies. "But perhaps the questions of religion and residence may be as hard to get over in the case of the Chevalier Macaulay as in the case of the Chevalier Grandison; and I may be forced to leave the too charming Giuseppa here with a blister on her head and a strait-waistcoat on her back."

During his journeys abroad Macaulay always made a point of reading the literature of the country. He began his Italian tour with Cicero's "Letters,"* and ended it with "I Promessi Sposi." "I finished Manzoni's novel, not without many tears. The scene between the archbishop and Don Abbondio is one of the noblest that I know. The parting scene between the lovers and Father Cristoforo is most touching. If the Church of Rome really were what Manzoni represents her to be, I should be tempted to follow Newman's example."

The next year, while traveling through France to the cities

---

* "I have been reading," he says, "those letters of Cicero which were written just after Cæsar had taken up arms. What materials for history! What a picture of a mind which well deserves to be studied! No novel ever interested me more. Often as I have read them, every sentence seems new."

of the Rhine and the Moselle, he bought on the way Chateaubriand's "Génie du Christianisme." "I was astonished," he
says, "at the utter worthlessness of the book, both in matter
and manner. The French may be beautiful, as far as mere
selection and arrangement of words go. But in the higher
graces of style—those graces which affect a foreigner as much
as a native—those graces which delight us in Plato, in Demosthenes, and in Pascal—there is a lamentable deficiency. As
to the substance, it is beneath criticism. Yet I have heard
men of ten times Chateaubriand's powers talk of him as the
first of French writers. He was simply a great humbug."

On the last day of February, 1856, Macaulay writes in his
journal: "Longman called. It is necessary to reprint. This
is wonderful. Twenty-six thousand five hundred copies sold
in ten weeks! I should not wonder if I made twenty thousand pounds clear this year by literature. Pretty well, considering that, twenty-two years ago, I had just nothing when
my debts were paid; and all that I have, with the exception
of a small part left me by my uncle the general, has been made
by myself, and made easily and honestly, by pursuits which
were a pleasure to me, and without one insinuation from any
slanderer that I was not even liberal in all my pecuniary dealings."

"*March 7th.*—Longman came, with a very pleasant announcement. He
and his partners find that they are overflowing with money, and think that
they can not invest it better than by advancing to me—on the usual terms
of course—part of what will be due to me in December. We agreed that
they shall pay twenty thousand pounds into Williams's bank next week.
What a sum to be gained by one edition of a book! I may say, gained in
one day. But that was harvest-day. The work had been near seven
years in hand. I went to Westbourne Terrace by a Paddington omnibus,
and passed an hour there, laughing and laughed at. They are all much
pleased. They have, indeed, as much reason to be pleased as I, who am
pleased on their account rather than on my own, though I am glad that
my last years will be comfortable. Comfortable, however, I could have
been on a sixth part of the income which I shall now have."

The check is still preserved as a curiosity among the archives of Messrs. Longman's firm. "The transaction," says

Macaulay, "is quite unparalleled in the history of the book-trade; and both the people at Smith, Payne, & Smith's who are to pay the money, and my friends who are to receive it, have been much amused. I went into the City to-day to give instructions, and was most warmly congratulated on being a great moneyed man. I said that I had some thoughts of going to the chancellor of the exchequer as a bidder for the next loan."

My uncle was a great favorite with his bankers. Mr. Henry Thornton, who was, and is, a partner in Messrs. Williams & Deacon's, carefully encouraged him in his fixed idea that business could only be done by word of mouth, and many a pleasant hour the two old college friends had together in the back parlor at Bircham Lane. On one occasion Mr. Thornton, by Macaulay's request, explained to him at some length the distinction between the different classes of Spanish stock—Active, Passive, and Deferred. "I think," said my uncle, "that I catch your meaning. Active Spanish bonds profess to pay interest now, and do not. Deferred Spanish bonds profess to pay interest at some future time, and will not. Passive Spanish bonds profess to pay interest neither now, nor at any future time. I think that you might buy a large amount of Passive Spanish bonds for a very small sum."

It mattered nothing to Macaulay personally whether or not Spain pretended to be solvent; for he never touched crazy securities. He was essentially an investor, and not a speculator. "He had as sound a judgment in City matters," said Mr. Thornton, "as I ever met with. You might safely have followed him blindfold." "I have," my uncle writes in his journal, "a great turn for finance, though few people would suspect it. I have a pleasure in carrying on long arithmetical operations in my head. I used to find amusement, when I was secretary at war, in the army estimates. I generally went through my pecuniary statements without book, except when it was necessary to come to pence and farthings."

Macaulay so arranged his affairs that their management was to him a pastime, instead of being a source of annoyance and anxiety. His economical maxims were of the simplest—to treat official and literary gains as capital,* and to pay all bills within the twenty - four hours. "I think," he says, "that prompt payment is a moral duty; knowing, as I do, how painful it is to have such things deferred." Like other men who have more money than time, his only account-book was that which his banker kept for him; and, to assist himself in making up his yearly balance-sheet, he embodied a list of his investments, and the main items of his expenditure, in a couple of irregular, but not inharmonious, stanzas.

> North-west; South-west; South-east; Two Irish Greats;
> 　　Denmark; Bengal; Commercial; London Dock;
> Insurance; Steamship; and United States;
> 　　Slave-state; and Free-state; and Old English Stock.

> Taxes; Rent; Sisters; Carriage; Wages; Clo'es;
> 　　Coals; Wine; Alms; Pocket-cash; Subscriptions; Treats;
> Bills, weekly these, and miscellaneous those.
> 　　Travel the list completes.

The wealth which Macaulay gathered prudently he spent royally; if to spend royally is to spend on others rather than yourself. From the time that he began to feel the money in his purse, almost every page in his diary contains evidence of his inexhaustible, and sometimes rather carelessly regulated, generosity.

"Mrs. X—— applied to me, as she said, and as I believe, without her husband's knowledge, for help in his profession. He is a clergyman; a good one, but too Puritanical for my

---

* Macaulay had good historical authority for this method of proceeding. We are told by an admirer of the Right Honorable George Grenville that it was the unvaried practice of that statesman, in all situations, to live upon his private fortune, and save the emoluments of whatever office he possessed. "He had early accustomed himself to a strict appropriation of his income, and an exact economy in its expenditure, as the only sure ground on which to build a reputation for public and private integrity, and to support a dignified independence." The moral results which were expected to flow from the observance of these excellent precepts were not very visible in the case of Grenville, who ratted more shamelessly than any public man even of his own century.

taste. I could not promise to ask any favors from the Government; but I sent him twenty-five pounds to assist him in supporting the orphan daughters of his brother. I mean to let him have the same sum annually." "I have been forced to refuse any further assistance to a Mrs. Y——, who has had thirty-five pounds from me in the course of a few months, and whose demands come thicker and thicker. I suppose that she will resent my refusal bitterly. That is all that I ever got by conferring benefits on any but my own nearest relations and friends." "H—— called. I gave him three guineas for his library subscription. I lay out very little money with so much satisfaction. For three guineas a year, I keep a very good, intelligent young fellow out of a great deal of harm, and do him a great deal of good." "I suppose," he writes to one of his sisters, "that you told Mrs. Z—— that I was not angry with her; for to-day I have a letter from her begging for money most vehemently, and saying that, if I am obdurate, her husband must go to prison. I have sent her twenty pounds; making up what she has had from me within a few months to a hundred and thirty pounds. But I have told her that her husband must take the consequences of his own acts, and that she must expect no further assistance from me. This importunity has provoked me not a little." In truth, the tone in which some of Macaulay's most regular pensioners were accustomed to address him contrasts almost absurdly with the respect paid toward him by the public at large. "That wretched K——," he writes, "has sent a scurrilous begging letter in his usual style. He hears that I have made thirty thousand pounds by my malignant abuse of good men. Will I not send some of it to him?"

To have written, or to pretend to have written, a book, whether good or bad, was the surest and shortest road to Macaulay's pocket. "I sent some money to Miss ——, a middling writer, whom I relieved some time ago. I have been giving too fast of late—forty pounds in four or five days. I must pull in a little." "Mrs. —— again, begging and praying. 'This the last time; an execution; etc., etc.' I will send her five pounds more. This will make fifty pounds in a few

months to a bad writer whom I never saw." "I have received," he writes to Mr. Longman, "a rather queer letter, pur-
porting to be from the wife of Mr. D——, the author of ——,
and dated from Greenwich. Now, I have once or twice received similar letters which have afterward turned out to be
forgeries. I sent ten pounds to a sham Mary Howitt, who
complained that an unforeseen misfortune had reduced her to
poverty; and I can hardly help suspecting that there may be
a sham Mrs. D——. If, however, the author of —— is really in distress, I would gladly assist him, though I am no admirer of his poetry. Could you learn from his publishers
whether he really lives at Greenwich? If he does, I will send
him a few pounds. If he does not, I will set the police to
work."

The Rev. Mr. Frederick Arnold tells the story of a German
gentleman, the husband of a lady honorably connected with
literature, who had fallen from affluence to unexpected poverty. He applied to Macaulay for assistance, and, instead of the
guinea for which he had ventured to hope, he was instantly
presented with thirty pounds. During the last year of my
uncle's life, I called at Holly Lodge to bid him good-bye before my return to the university. He told me that a person
had presented himself that very morning, under the name of
a Cambridge fellow of some mark, but no great mark, in the
learned world. This gentleman (for such he appeared to be)
stated himself to be in distress, and asked for pecuniary aid.
Macaulay, then and there, gave him a hundred pounds. The
visitor had no sooner left the room than my uncle began to
reflect that he had never set eyes on him before. He accordingly desired me, as soon as I got back to Cambridge, to
make, with all possible delicacy, such inquiries as might satisfy
him that, when wishing to relieve the necessities of a brother
scholar, he had not rewarded the audacity of a professional
impostor.*

---

* "*September 14th*, 1859.—A Dr. —— called, and introduced himself as a
needy man of letters. I was going to give him a sovereign, and send him
away, when I discovered that he was the philologist, whom I should never
have expected to see in such a plight. I felt for him, and gave him a hun-

If he was such with regard to people whose very faces were strange to him, it may well be believed that every valid claim upon his liberality was readily acknowledged. He was handsome in all his dealings, both great and small. Wherever he went (to use his own phrase), he took care to make his mother's son welcome. Within his own household he was positively worshiped, and with good reason; for Sir Walter Scott himself was not a kinder master. He cheerfully and habitually submitted to those petty sacrifices by means of which an unselfish man can do so much to secure the comfort and to earn the attachment of those who are around him; marching off in all weathers to his weekly dinner at the club, in order to give his servants their Sunday evening; going far out of his way to make such arrangements as would enable them to enjoy and to prolong their holidays; or permitting them, if so they preferred, to entertain their relations under his roof for a month together. "To-day," he says, "William and Elizabeth went off to fetch William's father. As I write, here come my travelers; the old man with a stick. Well? It is good to give pleasure and show sympathy. There is no vanity in saying that I am a good master."

It would be superfluous to dwell upon Macaulay's conduct toward those with whom he was connected by the ties of blood, and by the recollections of early days which had not been exempt from poverty and sorrow. Suffice it to say that he regarded himself as the head of his family; responsible (to speak plainly) for seeing that all his brothers and sisters were no worse off than if his father had died a prosperous man. It was only in this respect that he assumed the paternal relation. In his ordinary behavior there was nothing which betokened that he was the benefactor of all with whom he had to do. He never interfered; he never obtruded advice; he never demanded that his own tastes or views should be consulted, and he was studiously mindful of the feelings,

---

dred pounds. A hard pull on me, I must say. However, I have been prosperous beyond the common lot of men, and may well assist those who have been out of luck."

and even the fancies, of others. With the omission of only
two words, we may justly apply to him the eulogy pronounced upon another famous author by one who certainly
had the best of reasons for knowing that it was deserved: " It
is Southey's almost unexampled felicity to possess the best
gifts of talent and genius, free from all their characteristic
defects. As son, brother, husband, father, master, friend, he
moves with firm yet light steps, alike unostentatious, and alike
exemplary."*

It is pleasant to reflect that Macaulay's goodness was repaid,
as far as gratitude and affection could suffice to repay it. He
was contented with the share of domestic felicity which had
fallen to his lot. "To-morrow," he says in one place, "the
Trevelyans go to Weybridge. I feel these separations, though
they are for short times, and short distances; but a life is happy of which these are the misfortunes."† From graver calamities and longer partings he was mercifully spared; most
mercifully, because, as will soon be seen, he was quite unfitted
to bear them. Already he was painfully aware that the mal-
adies under which he suffered had relaxed the elasticity of his
spirits, had sapped his powers of mental endurance, and had
rendered his happiness more dependent than ever upon the
permanence of blessings which no human foresight could secure. The prayer that most often came to his lips was that
he might not survive those whom he loved. "God grant,"
he writes on the 1st of January, 1858, "that, if my dear little

---

* This passage is from a letter written by Coleridge, which forms part
of the extraordinarily interesting collection published by Mr. Cottle, the
Bristol book-seller. The correspondence presents a winning picture of
Southey's silent and unconscious heroism. "I feel," he once said (and his
life showed how truly he felt it), "that duty and happiness are inseparable." Neither he nor Macaulay laid claim to what are called the "privileges of genius." In a note on the margin of Nichols's "Literary Anecdotes" my uncle says: "Genius! What had Perceval Stockdale to do
with genius? But, as it is, the plea of genius is but a poor one for immorality, and nine-tenths of those who plead it are dunces."

† He consoled himself on this occasion by reading Crabbe "during some
hours, with pleasure ever fresh."

circle is to be diminished this year by any death, it may be by
mine! Not that I am weary of life. I am far from insensible to the pleasure of having fame, rank, and this opulence
which has come so late." His imagination was deeply impressed by an old Roman imprecation, which he had noticed
long ago in a Gallery of Inscriptions: "'Ultimus suorum
moriatur;' an awful curse!"

Once, and once only, during many years, he had any real
ground for alarm.

"*January 29th*, 1855.—The severest shock that I have had since January,
1835.* A note from Margaret to say that Hannah has scarlet fever. Margaret, too, is exposed. I was quite overset. They begged me not to go,
but I could not stay away. I saw them both, and was much relieved. It
seems that the crisis is over, and that the worst was past before the nature of the disease was known." A few days afterward he says: "I went
to Westbourne Terrace, and saw Margaret. I begin to be nervous about
her, now that her mother is safe. Alas that I should have staked so much
on what may be so easily lost! Yet I would not have it otherwise!"

He assuredly had no cause to wish it otherwise; for he enjoyed the satisfaction of feeling, not only that his affection
was appreciated and returned, but that those of whom he was
fondest never wearied of his company. Full and diversified
always, and often impassioned or profound, his conversation
was never beyond the compass of his audience; for his talk,
like his writing, was explanatory rather than allusive; and,
born orator that he was, he contrived without any apparent
effort that every sentence which he uttered should go home
to every person who heard it. He was admirable with young
people. Innumerable passages in his journals and correspondence prove how closely he watched them; how completely he
understood them; and how, awake or asleep, they were for-

---

* It was in January, 1835, that he heard of his youngest sister's death.
He writes, in April, 1856: "I passed the day in burning and arranging papers. Some things that met my eyes overcame me for a time. Margaret.
Alas! alas! And yet she might have changed to me. But no; that could
never have been. To think that she has been near twenty-two years dead;
and I am crying for her as if it were yesterday."

ever in his thoughts. On the fragment of a letter to Mr. Ellis there is mention of a dream he had about his younger niece, " so vivid that I must tell it. She came to me with a penitential face, and told me that she had a great sin to confess; that 'Pepys's Diary' was all a forgery, and that she had forged it. I was in the greatest dismay. 'What! I have been quoting in reviews, and in my " History," a forgery of yours as a book of the highest authority. How shall I ever hold my head up again?' I woke with the fright, poor Alice's supplicating voice still in my ears." He now and then speaks of his wish to have some serious talk with one or another of the lads in whom he was specially interested "in a quiet way," and " without the forms of a lecture." His lectures were, indeed, neither frequent nor formidable. I faintly remember his once attempting to shame me out of a fit of idleness by holding himself up as an awful example of the neglect of mathematics. It must not, however, be supposed that Macaulay spoiled the children of whom he was fondest. On the contrary, he had strict notions of what their behavior should be; and, in his own quiet way, he took no little pains to train their dispositions. He was visibly pained by any outbreak on their part of willfulness, or bad temper, or, above all, of selfishness. But he had very seldom occasion to give verbal expression to his disapprobation. His influence over us was so unbounded—there was something so impressive in the displeasure of one whose affection for us was so deep, and whose kindness was so unfailing—that no punishment could be devised one half as formidable as the knowledge that we had vexed our uncle. He was enabled to reserve his spoken reproofs for the less heinous sins of false rhymes, misquotations, and solecisms (or what he chose to consider as such), in grammar, orthography, and accentuation—for saying " The tea is being made," and not " The tea is a-making;" for writing " Bosphorus " instead of " Bosporus," and " Syren " instead of " Siren;" and, above all, for pronouncing the penultimate of " Metamorphosis " short. This was the more hard upon us because, in conforming to the fashion of the world, we were acting in accordance with the moral of the best among his

many stories about Dr. Parr. A gentleman who had been
taken to task for speaking of the ancient capital of Egypt as
" Alexandrīa " defended himself by the authority and example of Dr. Bentley. " Dr. Bentley and I," replied Dr. Parr,
" may call it Alexandrīa; but I think you had better call it
Alexandrĭa."

It was a grievous loss to Macaulay when we grew too old for
sight-seeing; or, at any rate, for seeing the same sight many
times over. As the best substitute for Madame Tussaud and
the Colosseum he used, in later years, to take his nieces the
round of the picture-galleries; and, though far from an unim-
peachable authority on matters of art, he was certainly a most
agreeable cicerone. In painting, as in most things, he had
his likes and dislikes, and had them strongly. In 1857 he
writes : " Preraphaelitism is spreading, I am glad to see—glad,
because it is by spreading that such affectations perish." He
saw at the Frankfort Museum " several chefs-d'œuvre, as they
are considered, of modern German art; all, to my thinking,
very poor. There is a 'Daniel in the Den of Lions,' which
it is a shame to exhibit. I did not even like the John Huss,
and still less Overbeck's trashy allegory. One of Stanfield's
landscapes or of Landseer's hunting pieces is worth all the
mystic daubs of all the Germans."

Macaulay looked at pictures as a man of letters, rather than
as a connoisseur; judging them less by their technical merits
than with reference to the painter's choice and treatment of
his subject. " There was a Salvator," he says in one place,
" which I was pleased to see, because the thought had occurred to me in Horatius—an oak struck by lightning, with the
augurs looking at it in dismay." In 1853 he writes: " The Exhibition was very good indeed; capital Landseers; one excellent Stanfield; a very good Roberts. Ward was good; but I
was struck by one obvious fault in his picture of Montrose's
execution—a fault, perhaps, inseparable from such subjects.
Montrose was a mean-looking man, and Ward thought it necessary to follow the likeness, and perhaps he was right. But
all the other figures are imaginary, and each is, in its own way,
striking. The consequence is that the central figure is not

only mean in itself, but is made meaner by contrast. In pictures where all the figures are imaginary this will not occur, nor in pictures where all the figures are real." Macaulay's sentence about Dr. Johnson's literary verdicts might perhaps be applied to his own criticisms on art: "At the very worst, they mean something; a praise to which much of what is called criticism in our time has no pretensions."*

Macaulay may not have been a reliable guide in the regions of high art, but there was one department of education in which, as an instructor, he might have challenged comparison with the best. A boy whose classical reading he watched, and in some degree directed, might, indeed, be lazy, but could not be indifferent to his work. The dullest of tyros would have been inspired by the ardor of one whose thoughts were often for weeks together more in Latium and Attica than in Middlesex; who knew the careers and the characters of the great men who paced the forum, and declaimed in the Temple of Concord, as intimately as those of his own rivals in Parliament and his own colleagues in the Cabinet; to whom Cicero was as real as Peel, and Curio as Stanley; who was as familiar with his Lucian and his Augustan histories as other men of letters are with their Voltaire and their Pepys; who cried over Homer with emotion, and over Aristophanes with laughter, and could not read the "De Coronâ" even for the twentieth time without striking his clenched fist at least once a minute on the arm of his easy-chair. As he himself says of

---

* Macaulay had a great admiration for that fine picture, the "Lady's Last Stake," which, strange to say, is not included in the ordinary editions of Hogarth. He suggested that an engraving of it should be prefixed as frontispiece to a collection of Mrs. Piozzi's papers which Mr. Longman talked of publishing. "There is a great deal," he writes, "about that picture in Mrs. Piozzi's life of herself. The lady who is reduced to the last stake was a portrait of her; and the likeness was discernible after the lapse of more than fifty years." The expression of puzzled amusement on the lady's face is as good as any thing in the breakfast scene of the "Marriage à la Mode;" and the effect of the background—a plain parlor, with the ordinary furniture of the day—is a remarkable instance of the amount of pleasure that may be afforded to the spectator by the merest accessories of a picture which is the careful work of a great artist.

Lord Somers, "he had studied ancient literature like a man;" and he loved it as only a poet could. No words can convey a notion of the glamour which Macaulay's robust and unaffected enthusiasm threw over the books or the events which had aroused and which fed it; or of the permanent impression which that enthusiasm left upon the minds of those who came within its influence. All the little interviews that took place between us as master and pupil, to which a multitude of notices in his diary refer, are as fresh in my memory as if they had occurred last summer, instead of twenty years ago. "Home, and took a cabful of books to Westbourne Terrace for George — Scapula, Ainsworth, Lucian, Quintus Curtius." And again: "George was at home, with a hurt which kept him from returning to school. I gave him a lecture on the tragic metres, which will be well worth a day's schooling to him if he profits by it." Macaulay's care of my classics ceased with the holidays, for he knew that at school I was in safe hands. He writes to his sister in December, 1856: "I am truly glad that Vaughan remains for the present at Harrow. After next October, the sooner he is made a bishop the better." This last opinion was shared by all who wished well to the Church of England, with the most unfortunate exception of Dr. Vaughan himself.

Macaulay wrote to me at Harrow pretty constantly, sealing his letters with an amorphous mass of red wax, which, in defiance of post-office regulations, not unfrequently concealed a piece of gold. "It is said" (so he once began), "that the best part of a lady's letter is the postscript. The best part of an uncle's is under the seal."

Tunbridge Wells, August 1st, 1853.

DEAR GEORGE,—I am glad that you are working hard. Did you ever read "Paradise Lost?" If not, I would advise you to read it now; for it is the best commentary that I know on the "Prometheus." There was a great resemblance between the genius of Æschylus and the genius of Milton; and this appears most strikingly in those two wonderful creations of the imagination, Prometheus and Satan. I do not believe that Milton borrowed Satan from the Greek drama. For, though he was an excellent scholar after the fashion of his time, Æschylus was, I suspect, a little beyond him. You can not conceive how much the facilities for reading the Greek writers have increased within the last two hundred years, how much better the text is now printed, and how much light the successive labors of learned men have thrown on obscure passages. I was greatly struck with this when, at Althorp, I looked through Lord Spencer's magnificent collection of Aldine editions. Numerous passages which are now perfectly simple were mere heaps of nonsense. And no writer suffered more than Æschylus.

Note particularly in the "Prometheus" the magnificent history of the origin of arts and sciences. That passage shows Æschylus to have been not only a poet of the first order, but a great thinker. It is the fashion to call Euripides a philosophical poet; but I remember nothing in Euripides so philosophical as that rapid enumeration of all the discoveries and inventions which make the difference between savage and civilized man. The latter part of the play is glorious.

I am very busy here getting some of my speeches ready for the press, and during the day I get no reading, except while I walk on the heath, and then I read Plato, one of the five first-rate Athenians. The other four are your friends Æschylus and Thucydides, Sophocles and Demosthenes. I know of no sixth Athenian who can be added to the list. Certainly not Euripides, nor Xenophon, nor Isocrates, nor Æschines. But I forgot Aristophanes. More shame for me. He makes six, and I can certainly add nobody else to the six. How I go on gossiping about these old fellows when I should be thinking of other things! Ever yours,

T. B. MACAULAY.

During my last year at school my uncle did me the honor of making me the vehicle for a compliment to Lord Palmerston. "George's Latin Poem," he writes to Mr. Ellis, in the spring of 1857, "is an account of a tour up the Rhine in imitation of the Fifth Satire of Horace's First Book. The close does not please Vaughan, and, indeed, is not good. I have suggested what I think a happier termination. The travelers get into a scrape at Heidelberg, and are taken up. How to extricate them is the question. I advise George to represent himself as saying that he is an Englishman, and that there is one who will look to it that an Englishman shall be as much respected as a Roman citizen. The name of Palmerston at once procures the prisoners their liberty. Palmerston, you remember, is a Harrow man. The following termination has occurred to me:

> Tantum valuit prænobile nomen,
> Quod noster collis, nostra hæc sibi vindicat aula;
> Quod Scytha, quod tortâ redimitus tempora mitrâ
> Persa timet, diroque gerens Ser bella veneno.

"Do not mention this. It might lead people to think that I have helped George, and there is not a line in any of his exercises that is not his own."

It may be imagined amidst what a storm of applause these spirited verses (redolent, perhaps, rather of Claudia than of Horace) were declaimed, on the Harrow speech-day, to an audience as proud of Palmerston as ever an Eton audience was of Canning.*

"*August 28th*, 1857.—A great day in my life. I staid at home, very sad about India.† Not that I have any doubt about the result; but the news is heart-breaking. I went, very low, to dinner, and had hardly begun to eat when a messenger came with a letter from Palmerston. An offer of a peerage; the queen's pleasure already taken. I was very much surprised. Perhaps no such offer was ever made without the slightest solicitation, direct or indirect, to a man of humble origin and moderate fortune, who had long quitted public life. I had no hesitation about accepting, with many respectful and grateful expressions; but God knows that the poor women at Delhi and Cawnpore are more in my thoughts than my coronet.

---

* It is necessary, in order to explain the allusions in Macaulay's lines, to remind the reader that in July, 1857, Palmerston's Russian laurels were still fresh; and that he had within the last few months brought the Persian difficulty to a successful issue, and commenced a war with China. Hostilities began with an attempt on the part of a Hong-Kong baker, of the suggestive name of A-lum, to poison Sir John Bowring.

† The Sepoy Mutiny was then at its very worst. Something like the truth of the Cawnpore story was beginning to be known in England.

It was necessary for me to choose a title off-hand. I determined to be Baron Macaulay of Rothley. I was born there; I have lived much there; I am named from the family which long had the manor; my uncle was rector there. Nobody can complain of my taking a designation from a village which is nobody's property now."

Macaulay went abroad on the 1st of September. After his return from the Continent he says: "On my way from the station to Holly Lodge yesterday, I called at the Royal Institution, and saw the papers of the last fortnight. There is a general cry of pleasure at my elevation. I am truly gratified by finding how well I stand with the public, and gratified by finding that Palmerston has made a hit for himself in bestowing this dignity on me." "I think" (so my mother writes) "that his being made a peer was one of the very few things that every body approved. I can not recall any opinion adverse to it. He enjoyed it himself, as he did every thing, simply and cordially. We were making a tour in the Tyrol that summer; and, on our return, we stopped at Paris, I and my children, to spend a few days at the Louvre Hotel with your uncle and Mr. Ellis. I often think of our arrival at eleven at night; the well-spread board awaiting us; his joyous welcome; and then his desiring us to guess what his news was, and my disappointing him by instantly guessing it. Then our merry time together; the last unbroken circle; for change began the following year, and change has since been the order of my life."

To the Rev. Dr. Whewell.

Holly Lodge, Kensington, October 9th, 1857.

My dear Master,—Thanks for your kindness, which is what it has always been. Unhappily I have so bad a cold, and Trevelyan has so much to do, that neither of us will be able to accompany our boy—for we are equally interested in him—to Cambridge next week. It is pleasant to me to think that I have now a new tie to Trinity. Ever yours,

MACAULAY.

My uncle had long been looking forward to the period of

my residence at the university as an opportunity for renewing those early recollections and associations which he studiously cultivated, and which, after the lapse of five-and-thirty
years, filled as large a space as ever in his thoughts. I have
at this moment before me his Cambridge Calendar for 1859.
The book is full of his handwriting. He has been at the
pains of supplementing the Tripos lists, between 1750 and
1835, with the names of all the distinguished men who took
their degrees in each successive year, but who, failing to go
out in honors, missed such immortality as the Cambridge
Calendar can give. He has made an elaborate computation,
which must have consumed a whole morning, in order to ascertain the collective annual value of the livings in the gift of
the several colleges; from the twenty-four thousand pounds
a year of St. John's and the eighteeen thousand of Trinity,
down to the hundreds a year of St. Catherine's and of Downing. Many and many an entry in his diary proves that he
never ceased to be proud of having won for himself a name
at Cambridge. On the 11th of June, 1857, he writes: "I
dined with Milnes, and sat between Thirlwall and Whewell—
three Trinity fellows together; and not bad specimens for a
college to have turned out within six years, though I say it."

If Macaulay's reverence for those personal anecdotes relating to the habits and doings of famous students, which have
come down to us from the Golden Age of classical criticism,
was any indication of his tastes, he would willingly have once
more been a member of his old college, leading the life of a
senior fellow, such as it was, or such as he imagined it to have
been, in the days of Porson, Scholefield, or Dobree. Gladly
(at least so he pretended to believe) would he have passed his
summers by the banks of the Cam editing the "Pharsalia;"
collating* the manuscripts of the "Hecuba" which are among
the treasures of the University Library; and "dawdling over
Tryphiodorus, Callimachus's Epigrams, and Tacitus's Histo-

---

* Macaulay had a sincere admiration for that old scholar, who, when
condoled with upon the misfortune of an illness which had injured his
sight, thanked God that he had kept his "collating eye."

ries." He was always ready for a conversation, and even for a
correspondence, on a nice point of scholarship; and I have seldom seen him more genuinely gratified than by the intelligence that an emendation which he had suggested upon an
obscure passage in Euripides was favorably regarded in the
Trinity combination room.*

During the May term of 1858 he paid me the first of those
visits which he had taught me to anticipate with delight ever
since I had been old enough to know what a college was. He
detained a large breakfast-party of under-graduates far into the
day, while he rolled out for their amusement and instruction
his stores of information on the history, customs, and traditions of the university; and I remember that after their departure he entertained himself with an excessively droll comparison of his own position with that of Major Pendennis
among the young heroes of St. Boniface. But, proud as I was
of him, I can recall few things more painful than the contrast between his strength of intellect and of memory, and his
extreme weakness of body. In July, 1858, Lord Carlisle expressed himself as distressed "to see and hear Macaulay much
broken by cough;" and in the previous May the symptoms
of failing health were not less clearly discernible. With a
mind still as fresh as when, in 1820, he wore the blue gown
of Trinity, and disputed with Charles Austin till four in the
morning over the comparative merits of the Inductive and the
à priori method in politics, it was already apparent that a
journey across Clare Bridge, and along the edge of the great
lawn at King's, performed at the rate of half a mile in the
hour, was an exertion too severe for his feeble frame.†

---

* τί δῆτ' ἔτι ζῶ; τιν' ὑπολείπομαι τύχην;
γάμους ἑλομένη τῶν κακῶν ὑπαλλαγὰς,
μετ' ἀνδρὸς οἰκεῖν βαρβάρου, πρὸς πλουσίαν
τράπεζαν ἴζουσ'; ἀλλ' ὅταν πόσις πικρὸς
ξυνῇ γυναικὶ, καὶ τὸ σῶμ' ἐστὶν πικρόν.

The difficulty of this passage lies in the concluding line. One editor reads
"τὸ σῶν ἐστίν," another "τὸ σώζεσθαι." Macaulay proposed to substitute
"βρῶμ'" for "σῶμ'."

† In November, 1857, Macaulay received invitations from Edinburgh and

In the autumn of 1857 the high-stewardship of the Borough of Cambridge became vacant by the death of Earl Fitzwilliam, and Macaulay was elected in his place by the unanimous vote of the Town Council. "I find," he says, "that the office has been held by a succession of men of the highest eminence in political and literary history—the Protector Somerset; Dudley Duke of Northumberland; Ellesmere; Bacon; Coventry; Finch; Oliver Cromwell; Clarendon; and Russell, the La Hogue man. Very few places have been so filled." The ceremony of Macaulay's inauguration as high-steward was deferred till the warm weather of 1858.

"*Tuesday, May 11th.*—I was at Cambridge by ten. The mayor was at the station to receive me; and most hospitable he was, and kind. I went with him to the Town-hall, was sworn in, and then was ushered into the great room, where a public breakfast was set out. I had not been in that room since 1820, when I heard Miss Stephens sing there, and bore part in a furious contest between 'God save the King' and 'God save the Queen.' I had been earlier in this room. I was there at two meetings of the Cambridge Bible Society; that of 1813, and that of 1815. On the later occasion I bought at Deighton's Scott's 'Waterloo,' just published, and read it on a frosty journey back to Aspenden Hall. But how I go on wandering! The room now looked smaller than in old times. About forty municipal functionaries, and as many guests, chiefly of the university, were present. The mayor gave my health in a very graceful manner. I replied concisely, excusing myself, with much truth, on the plea of health, from haranguing longer. I was well received; very well. Several speeches followed; the vice-chancellor saying very handsomely that I was a pledge of the continuance of the present harmony between town and gown."

Macaulay had good reason to shrink from the exertion of a long speech, as was only too evident to his audience in the Cambridge Assembly-room. There was a touch of sadness in the minds of all present as they listened to the brief but expressive phrases in which he reminded them that the time had

Glasgow to take part in the ceremonies of the Burns centenary. "I refused both invitations," he says, "for fifty reasons; one of which is that, if I went down in the depth of winter to harangue in Scotland, I should never come back alive."

been when he might have commanded a hearing "in larger and stormier assemblies," but that any service which he could henceforward do for his country must be done in the quiet of his own library. "It is now five years," he said, "since I raised my voice in public; and it is not likely—unless there be some special call of duty—that I shall ever raise it in public again."

That special call of duty never came. Macaulay's indifference to the vicissitudes of party politics had by this time grown into a confirmed habit of mind. His correspondence during the spring of 1857 contains but few and brief allusions even to catastrophes as striking as the ministerial defeat upon the China war, and the overwhelming reverse of fortune which ensued when the question was transferred to the polling booths. "Was there ever any thing," he writes, "since the fall of the rebel angels, like the smash of the Anti-Corn-law League? How art thou fallen from heaven, O Lucifer! I wish that Bright and Cobden had been returned." Macaulay's opinion in the matter, as far as he had an opinion, was in favor of the Government, and against the coalition. "I am glad," he wrote on the eve of the debate, "that I have done with politics. I should not have been able to avoid a pretty sharp encounter with Lord John." But his days for sharp encounters were over, and his feelings of partisanship were reserved for the controversies about standing armies and royal grants which convulsed the last two Parliaments of the seventeenth century. He was, to describe him in his own words, "a vehement ministerialist of 1698," who thought "more about Somers and Montague than about Campbell and Lord Palmerston."

A faint interest, rather personal than political, in the proceedings of the Upper House was awakened in his breast when, sitting for the first time on the red benches, he found himself in the presence of the most eminent among his ancient rivals, adversaries, and allies. "Lord Derby," he writes, "was all himself—clever, keen, neat, clear; never aiming high, but always hitting what he aims at." A quarter of a century had not changed Macaulay's estimate of Lord Brougham, nor softened his mode of expressing it. "Strange fellow! His powers gone. His spite immortal. A dead nettle."[*]

During his first session the new peer more than once had a mind to speak upon matters relating to India. In February, 1858, Lord Ellenborough gave notice of a motion for papers, with the view, as was presumed, of eliciting proofs that the Sepoy mutiny had been provoked by the proselytizing tendencies of the British Government. Macaulay, prompted by an Englishman's sense of fair play, resolved to give the eloquent and redoubtable ex-governor general a chance of paying off outstanding scores. But it all came to nothing. "*February* 19*th*.—I worked hard, to make ready for a discussion of the great question of religion and education in India. I went down to the House. Lord Ellenborough's speech merely related to a petty question about the report of a single inspector—a very silly one, I am afraid—in Bahar. Lord Granville answered well, and much more than sufficiently. Then the debate closed. Many people thought that Lord Ellenborough would have been much longer and more vehement, if he had not been taken aback by seeing me ready to reply. They say that he has less pluck than his warm and somewhat petulant manner indicates. I can only say that I was quite as much afraid of him as he could be of me. I thought of Winkle and Dowler in the 'Pickwick Papers.'"[†] On the 1st of May in the same year Macaulay says: "I meant to go to the Museum; but, seeing that Lord Shaftesbury has given notice of a petition which may produce a discussion

---

[*] Macaulay's disapprobation of Lord Brougham had been revived and intensified by a recent occurrence. "*April* 17*th*, 1856.—I had a short conversation with Lord Lansdowne about a disagreeable matter—that most cruel and calumnious attack which Brougham has made on Lord Rutherford in a paper which has been printed and circulated among the peers who form the Committee on Life Peerages. I was glad to find that there was no chance that the paper would be published. Should it be published, poor Rutherford will not want defenders."

[†] "'Mr. Winkle, sir, be calm. Don't strike me. I won't bear it. A blow! Never!' said Mr. Dowler, looking meeker than Mr. Winkle had expected from a gentleman of his ferocity."

about Christianity in India, I staid at home all day, preparing myself to speak if there should be occasion. I shall drop no hint of my intention. I can not help thinking that I shall succeed, if I have voice enough to make myself heard." But, when the day arrived, he writes: "Shaftesbury presented the petition with only a few words. Lord Ellenborough said only a few words in answer.* To make a long set speech in such circumstances would have been absurd; so I went quietly home."

In the course of the year 1858 several of those eminent Frenchmen who refused to bow the knee before the Second Empire had frequent and friendly conversations with Macaulay on the future of their unhappy country; but they failed to convince the historian of our great Revolution that the experiment of 1688 could be successfully repeated on Gallic soil. "I argued strongly," he writes on one occasion, "against the notion that much good was likely to be done by insurrection even against the bad governments of the Continent. What good have the revolutions of 1848 done? Or, rather, what harm have they not done? The only revolutions which have turned out well have been defensive revolutions — ours of 1688; the French of 1830. The American was, to a great extent, of the same kind." On the 15th of May he says: "Montalembert called. He talked long, vehemently, and with feeling about the degraded state of France. I could have said a good deal on the other side; but I refrained. I like him much." A fortnight later: "Duvergier d'Hauranne called, and brought his son. How he exclaimed against the French emperor! I do not like the emperor or his system; but I can not find that his enemies are able to hold out any reasonable hope that, if he is pulled down, a better government will be set up. I can not say to a Frenchman what I think—that the French have only themselves to thank; and that a people which violently pulls down constitutional governments, and lives quiet under despotism, must be, and ought to be, despot-

---

* Between February and May Lord Ellenborough had become Secretary of the Indian Board of Control.

ically governed. We should have reformed the government
of the House of Orleans without subverting it. We should
not have borne the yoke of *celui-ci* for one day. However,
I feel for men like Duvergier d'Hauranne and Montalembert,
who are greatly in advance of the body of their countrymen."

Macaulay had little attention to spare for the politics of the
Westminster lobbies or the Parisian boulevards; but it must
not be thought that he was growing indifferent to the wider
and more permanent interests of the British nation and the
British empire. The honor of our flag and the welfare of our
people were now, as ever, the foremost objects of his solici-
tude. "England," he writes, "seems to be profoundly quiet.
God grant that she may long continue so, and that the history
of the years which I may yet have to live may be the dullest
portion of her history! It is sad work to live in times about
which it is amusing to read." The fervor of this prayer for
public tranquillity was prompted by the recollections of 1857,
which were still fresh in Macaulay's mind. On the 29th of
June in that terrible year he notes in his diary: "To breakfast with Milnes. Horrible news from India: massacre of
Europeans at Delhi, and mutiny. I have no apprehensions for our Indian empire; but this is a frightful event.
Home; but had no heart to work. I will not try at present."
Again he says, and yet again, "I can not settle to work while
the Delhi affair is undecided." His correspondence during
the coming months overflows with allusions to India. "No
more news; that is to say, no later news than we had before
you started; but private letters are appearing daily in the
newspapers. The cruelties of the sepoys have inflamed the
nation to a degree unprecedented within my memory. Peace
Societies, and Aborigines Protection Societies, and Societies
for the Reformation of Criminals are silenced. There is one
terrible cry for revenge. The account of that dreadful military execution at Peshawur—forty men blown at once from the
mouths of cannon, their heads, legs, arms flying in all direc-
tions—was read with delight by people who three weeks ago
were against all capital punishment. Bright himself declares
for the vigorous suppression of the mutiny. The almost uni-

versal feeling is that not a single sepoy within the walls of
Delhi should be spared; and I own that it is a feeling with
which I can not help sympathizing."

When Macaulay was writing these words, the crimes of the
mutineers were still unpunished, and their power unbroken.
The belief that mercy to the sepoy was no mercy, as long as
Delhi remained in rebel hands, was sternly carried into action
in the Punjaub and the North-west provinces of India by
men who were sincerely humane both by temperament and
by religious conviction. That belief was almost universal
among people of our race on both sides of the Atlantic. The
public opinion even of philanthropic and abolitionist Boston
did not differ on this point from the public opinion of London. "The India mail," wrote Dr. Oliver Wendell Holmes,
"brings stories of women and children outraged and murdered. The royal stronghold is in the hands of the babe-killers.
England takes down the map of the world, which she has
girdled with empire, and makes a correction thus: DELHI.
Dele. The civilized world says, Amen!"

"*September* 19*th*, 1857.—The Indian business looks ill. This miserable
affair at Dinapore may produce serious inconvenience.* However, the
tide is near the turn. Within a month the flood of English will come in
fast. But it is painful to be so revengeful as I feel myself. I, who can not
bear to see a beast or bird in pain, could look on without winking while
Nana Sahib underwent all the tortures of Ravaillac. And these feelings
are not mine alone. Is it possible that a year passed under the influence
of such feelings should not have some effect on the national character?
The effect will be partly good and partly bad. The nerves of our minds
will be braced. Effeminate, mawkish philanthropy will lose all its influence. But shall we not hold human life generally cheaper than we have
done? Having brought ourselves to exult in the misery of the guilty,
shall we not feel less sympathy for the sufferings of the innocent? In one

---

* The Dinapore Brigade, a force of twenty-five hundred bayonets, muti-
nied on the 25th of July, and a few days later routed, and well-nigh destroyed, an ill-conducted expedition which had been dispatched to relieve
the European garrison at Arrah. The glorious defense of the little house,
and its equally glorious relief, have thrown into shade the memory of the
lamentable blunders which gave occasion for that display of intelligent
and heroic valor.

sense, no doubt, in exacting a tremendous retribution we are doing our
duty and performing an act of mercy. So is Calcraft when he hangs a
murderer. Yet the habit of hanging murderers is found to injure the character."

Macaulay did every thing which lay in his power to show
that at such a crisis he felt a citizen's concern in the fortunes
of the commonwealth. At the invitation of the lord mayor
he became a member of the committee for the relief of the Indian sufferers. On the day appointed for national humiliation
and prayer he writes as follows:

"*October 7th.*—Wind and rain. However, I went to church, though by
no means well. Nothing could be more solemn or earnest than the aspect
of the congregation, which was numerous. The sermon was detestable—
ignorance, stupidity, bigotry. If the maxims of this fool, and of others like
him, are followed, we shall soon have, not the mutiny of an army, but the
rebellion of a whole nation, to deal with. He would have the Government
plant missionaries everywhere, invite the sepoy to listen to Christian instruction, and turn the Government schools into Christian seminaries.
Happily there is some security against such mischievous doctrines in the
good sense of the country, and a still stronger security in its nonsense.
Christianity in teaching sounds very well; but the moment that any plan
is proposed, all the sects in the kingdom will be together by the ears. We
who are for absolute neutrality shall be supported against such fools as
this man by all the Dissenters, by the Scotch, and by the Roman Catholics."

"*October 25th,* 1857.—My birthday. Fifty-seven. I have had a not unpleasant year. My health is not good, but my head is clear and my heart
is warm. I receive numerous marks of the good opinion of the public—a
large public, including the educated men both of the old and of the new
world. I have been made a peer, with, I think, as general an approbation
as I remember in the case of any man that in my time has been made a
peer. What is much more important to my happiness than wealth, titles,
and even fame, those whom I love are well and happy, and very kind and
affectionate to me. These are great things. I have some complaints, however, to make of the past year. The Indian troubles have affected my spirits more than any public events in the whole course of my life. To be
sure, the danger which threatened the country at the beginning of April,
1848, came nearer to me. But that danger was soon over; and the Indian
Mutiny has now lasted several months, and may last months still. The
emotions which it excites, too, are of a strong kind. I may say that, till
this year, I did not know what real vindictive hatred meant. With what
horror I used to read in Livy how Fulvius put to death the whole Capuan

Senate in the Second Punic War! And with what equanimity I could hear that the whole garrison of Delhi, all the Moulavies and Mussulman doctors there, and all the rabble of the bazaar had been treated in the same way! Is this wrong? Is not the severity which springs from a great sensibility to human suffering a better thing than the lenity which springs from indifference to human suffering? The question may be argued long on both sides."

"*October 27th.*—Huzza! huzza! Thank God! Delhi is taken. A great event. Glorious to the nation, and one which will resound through all Christendom and Islam. What an exploit for that handful of Englishmen in the heart of Asia to have performed!"

"*November 11th.*—Huzza! Good news! Lucknow relieved. Delhi ours. The old dotard a prisoner. God be praised! Another letter from Longman. They have already sold 7600 more copies. This is near six thousand pounds, as I reckoned, in my pocket. But it gratified me, I am glad to be able to say with truth, far, very far, less than the Indian news. I could hardly eat my dinner for joy."

The lovers of ballad poetry may be permitted to wonder how it was that the patriotic ardor which passing events aroused in Macaulay did not find vent in strains resembling those with which he celebrated Ivry and the Armada. It is still more remarkable that (if we except the stanzas which he wrote after his defeat at Edinburgh) he never embodied in verse any of those touching expressions of personal emotion which so constantly recur in the pages of his journal. The explanation probably lies in the fact that, from the time when he became a regular contributor to the *Edinburgh Review*, he always had on hand some weighty and continuous employment which concentrated his imagination and consumed all his productive energies. There was but one short break in his labors; and that break gave us the "Lays of Ancient Rome." "If," said Goethe, "you have a great work in your head, nothing else thrives near it."* The truth of this apho-

---

* This remark was addressed to Eckermann. The whole conversation is highly interesting. "Beware," Goethe said, "of attempting a large work. It is exactly that which injures our best minds, even those distinguished by the finest talents and the most earnest efforts. I have suffered from this cause, and know how much it has injured me. What have I not let fall into the well! If I had written all that I well might, a hundred volumes would not contain it.

rism, representing, as it does, the life-long experience of the greatest master who ever consciously made an art of literature, was at first not very acceptable to Macaulay. But he soon discovered that Clio was a mistress who would be satisfied with no divided allegiance; and her sister muses thenceforward lost the homage of one who might fairly have hoped to be numbered among their favored votaries.

Long after Macaulay had abandoned all other public business, he continued to occupy himself in the administration of the British Museum. In February, 1856, he wrote to Lord Lansdowne, with the view of securing that old friend's potent influence in favor of an arrangement by which Professor Owen might be placed in a position worthy of his reputation and of his services. The circumstance which gave rise to the letter was the impending appointment of Signor Panizzi to the post of secretary and principal librarian to the Museum. " I am glad of this," writes Macaulay, " both on public and private grounds. Yet I fear that the appointment will be unpopular both within and without the walls of the Museum. There is a growing jealousy among men of science which, between ourselves, appears even at the Board of Trustees. There is a notion that the department of natural history is neglected, and that the library and the sculpture gallery are unduly favored. This feeling will certainly not be allayed by the appointment of Panizzi, whose great object, during many years, has been to make our library the best in Europe, and who would at any time give three mammoths for an Aldus."

" The Present will have its rights. The thoughts which daily press upon the poet will and should be expressed. But if you have a great work in your head, nothing else thrives near it; all other thoughts are repelled, and the pleasantness of life itself is for the time lost. What exertion and expenditure of mental force are required to arrange and round off a great whole! and then what powers, and what a tranquil, undisturbed situation in life, to express it with the proper fluency!...... But if he [the poet] daily seizes the present, and always treats with a freshness of feeling what is offered him, he always makes sure of something good, and, if he sometimes does not succeed, has, at least, lost nothing."

The English of this passage is that of Mr. Oxenford's translation.

Macaulay then went on to propose that, simultaneously with Signor Panizzi's nomination to the secretaryship, Professor Owen should be constituted superintendent of the whole department of natural history, including geology, zoölogy, botany, and mineralogy. "I can not but think," he says, "that this arrangement would be beneficial in the highest degree to the Museum. I am sure that it would be popular. I must add that I am extremely desirous that something should be done for Owen. I hardly know him to speak to. His pursuits are not mine. But his fame is spread over Europe. He is an honor to our country, and it is painful to me to think that a man of his merit should be approaching old age amidst anxieties and distresses. He told me that eight hundred a year, without a house in the Museum, would be opulence to him. He did not, he said, even wish for more. His seems to me to be a case for public patronage. Such patronage is not needed by eminent literary men or artists. A poet, a novelist, an historian, a painter, a sculptor who stood in his own line as high as Owen stands among men of science, could never be in want except by his own fault. But the greatest natural philosopher may starve, while his countrymen are boasting of his discoveries, and while foreign academies are begging for the honor of being allowed to add his name to their list."*

From the moment when, in the summer of 1854, Macaulay had definitely and deliberately braced himself to the work of completing the second great installment of the "History," he went to his daily labors without intermission and without reluctance until his allotted task had been accomplished. When that result had been attained—when his third and fourth volumes were actually in the hands of the public—it was not at first that he became aware how profoundly his already enfeebled health had been strained by the prolonged effort which the production of those volumes had cost him. At every previous epoch in his life the termination of one undertaking had

---

* On the 26th of May, 1856, Professor Owen was appointed superintendent of the department of natural history with a salary of eight hundred pounds a year.

been a signal for the immediate commencement of another; but in 1856 summer succeeded to spring, and gave place to autumn, before he again took pen in hand. For many weeks together he indulged himself in the pleasure of loitering over those agreeable occupations which follow in the train of a literary success; answering letters of congratulation; returning thanks, more or less sincere, for the suggestions and criticisms which poured in from the most opposite, and sometimes the most unexpected, quarters; preparing new editions; and reading every thing that the reviews had to say about him with the placid enjoyment of a veteran author.

"I bought the *British Quarterly Review:* an article on my book — praise and blame. Like other writers, I swallow the praise, and think the blame absurd. But in truth I do think that the fault-finding is generally unreasonable, though the book is, no doubt, faulty enough. It is well for its reputation that I do not review it, as I could review it." "*Fraser's Magazine.* Very laudatory. The author evidently John Kemble. He is quite right in saying that I have passed lightly over Continental politics. But was this wrong? I think I could defend myself. I am writing a History of England; and as to grubbing, as he recommends, in Saxon and Hessian archives for the purpose of ascertaining all the details of the Continental negotiations of that time, I should have doubled my labor, already severe enough. That I have not given a generally correct view of our Continental relations he certainly has not shown." "After breakfast to the Athenæum, and saw articles on my book in the *Dublin Review*, and the *National Review.* Very well satisfied to find that the whole skill and knowledge of Maynooth could make no impression on my account of the Irish war." "I received the *Allgemeine Zeitung*, and found in it a long article on my book, very laudatory, and to me very agreeable; for I hold the judgment of foreigners to be a more sure prognostic of what the judgment of posterity is likely to be than the judgment of my own countrymen." "I made some changes in my account of James's Declaration of 1692. If my critics had been well-informed, they might have worried me about one paragraph on that subject. But it escaped them, and now I have put every thing to rights." "To-day I got a letter from ——, pointing out what I must admit to be a gross impropriety of language in my book—an impropriety of a sort rare, I hope, with me. It shall be corrected; and I am obliged to the fellow, little as I like him."

At length, on the 1st of October, 1856, Macaulay notes in his diary: "To the Museum, and turned over the Dutch dispatches for information about the fire of Whitehall. Home, and wrote a sheet of foolscap, the first of Part III. God knows whether I shall ever finish that part. I begin it with little heart or hope." In the summer of 1857 he remarks: "How the days steal away, and nothing done! I think often of Johnson's lamentations repeated every Easter over his own idleness. But the cases differ. Often I have felt this morbid incapacity to work; but never so long and so strong as of late —the natural effect of age and ease." On the 14th of July in the same year: "I wrote a good deal to-day; Darien. The humor has returned, and I shall woo it to continue. What better amusement can I have, if it should prove no more than an amusement?" And again: "Read about the Darien affair. It will be impossible to tell the truth as to that matter without putting the Scotch into a rage. But the truth shall be told."

The intrinsic importance of the work on which Macaulay was now engaged could hardly be overrated; for the course of his "History" had brought him to a most momentous era in the political annals of our country. It was his business to tell the story, and to point the lesson, of the years from 1697 to 1701—those years when the majority in the House of Commons was already the strongest force in the State, but when the doctrine that the executive administration must be in the hands of ministers who possessed the confidence of that majority had not as yet been recognized as a constitutional axiom. Nothing which he has ever written is more valuable than his account of the grave perils which beset the kingdom during that period of transition, or than his vivid and thoughtful commentary upon our method of government by alternation of parties. No passage in all his works more clearly illustrates the union of intellectual qualities which formed the real secret of his strength — the combination in one and the same man of literary power, historical learning, and practical familiarity with the conduct of great affairs.*

Nor again, as specimens of narrative carefully planned and vigorously sustained, has he produced any thing with which his descriptions of the visit of the czar, the trial of Spencer Cowper,† and, above all, the fatal hallucination of Darien, may not fairly rank. And yet, however effective were the episodes which thickly strew the portion of his "History" that he did not live to publish, there can be no question that the alacrity with which he had once pursued his great undertaking had begun to languish. "I find it difficult," he writes in February, 1857, "to settle to my work. This is an old malady of mine. It has not prevented me from doing a good deal in the course of my life. Of late I have felt this impotence more than usual. The chief reason, I believe, is the great doubt which I feel whether I shall live long enough to finish another volume of my book." He already knew, to use the expression which he applied to the dying William of Orange, "that his time was short, and grieved, with a grief such as only noble spirits feel, to think that he must leave his work but half finished."

Gradually and unwillingly Macaulay acquiesced in the conviction that he must submit to leave untold that very portion of English history which he was competent to treat as no man again will treat it. Others may study the reign of Anne with

---

* See especially the two paragraphs in Chapter XXIV. which commence with the words, "If a minister were now to find himself thus situated—" There is little doubt that Lord Carlisle had something of this in his mind when he wrote in his diary of the 28th of March, 1861: "I finished Macaulay's fifth volume, and felt in despair to close that brilliant pictured page. I think it even surpasses in interest and animation what had gone before; and higher praise no man can give. The leading reflection is, how as a nation we have been rescued, led, and blessed; by the side of this, how much of the old faults and leaven still remains."

† The page of Macaulay's manuscript which is preserved in the British Museum is taken from his account of the trial of Spencer Cowper.

a more minute and exclusive diligence—the discovery of materials hitherto concealed can not fail from time to time to
throw fresh light upon transactions so extensive and complicated as those which took place between the rupture of the
Peace of Ryswick and the accession of the House of Bruns-
wick—but it may safely be affirmed that few or none of Macaulay's successors will be imbued like him with the enthusiasm of the period. There are phases of literary taste which
pass away, never to recur; and the early associations of future men of letters will seldom be connected with the "Rape
of the Lock" and the "Essay on Criticism"—with the *Spectator*, the *Guardian*, the *Freeholder*, the "Memoirs of Martinus
Scriblerus," and the "History of John Bull." But Macaulay's youth was nourished upon Pope, and Bolingbroke, and
Atterbury, and De Foe. Every thing which had been written
by them, or about them, was as familiar to him as "The Lady
of the Lake" and "The Bride of Abydos" were to the generation which was growing up when Lockhart's "Life of Scott"
and Moore's "Life of Byron" were making their first appearance in the circulating libraries. He had Prior's burlesque
verses and Arbuthnot's pasquinades as completely at his fingers'-ends as a clever public-school boy of fifty years ago had
the "Rejected Addresses" or the poetry of the *Anti-Jacobin*.
He knew every pamphlet which had been put forth by Swift,
or Steele, or Addison, as well as Tories of 1790 knew their
Burke, or Radicals of 1820 knew their Cobbett. There were
times when he amused himself with the hope that he might
even yet be permitted to utilize these vast stores of information, on each separate fragment of which he could so easily lay
his hand. His diary shows him to have spent more than one
summer afternoon "walking in the portico, and reading pamphlets of Queen Anne's time." But he had no real expectation that the knowledge which he thus acquired would ever be
turned to account. Others, who could not bring themselves
to believe that such raciness of phrase, and such vivacity of intellect, belonged to one whose days were already numbered,
confidently reckoned upon his making good the brave words
which form the opening sentence of the first chapter of his

"History." One old friend describes himself in a letter as looking forward to the seventh and eighth volumes in order to satisfy his curiosity about the reigns of the first two Georges ; which, he says, "are to me the dark ages." Another is sanguine enough to anticipate the pleasure of reading what Macaulay would have to say about "the great improvement of the steam-engine, and its consequences." But, by the time that he had written a few pages of his fifth volume, the author himself would have been well content to be assured that he would live to carry his "History," in a complete and connected form, down to the death of his hero, William of Orange.

During the later years of his life, Macaulay sent an occasional article to the "Encyclopædia Britannica." "He had ceased," says Mr. Adam Black, "to write for the reviews or other periodicals, though often earnestly solicited to do so. It is entirely to his friendly feeling that I am indebted for those literary gems, which could not have been purchased with money ; and it is but justice to his memory that I should record, as one of the many instances of the kindness and generosity of his heart, that he made it a stipulation of his contributing to the Encyclopædia that remuneration should not be so much as mentioned." The articles in question are those on Atterbury, Bunyan, Goldsmith, Doctor Johnson, and William Pitt. The last of these, which is little more than seventy octavo pages in length, was on hand for three quarters of a year. Early in November, 1857, Macaulay writes: "The plan of a good character of Pitt is forming in my mind ;" and, on the 9th of August, 1858: "I finished and sent off the paper which has caused me so much trouble. I began it, I see, in last November. What a time to have been dawdling over such a trifle !"

The conscientious and unsparing industry of his former days now brought Macaulay a reward of a value quite inestimable in the eyes of every true author. The habit of always working up to the highest standard within his reach was so ingrained in his nature, that, however sure and rapid might be the decline of his physical strength, the quality of his productions remained the same as ever. Instead of writing

worse, he only wrote less. Compact in form, crisp and nervous in style, these five little essays are every thing which
an article in an encyclopedia should be. The reader, as he
travels softly and swiftly along, congratulates himself on
having lighted upon what he regards as a most fascinating
literary or political memoir; but the student, on a closer examination, discovers that every fact and date and circumstance is distinctly and faithfully recorded in its due chronological sequence. Macaulay's belief about himself as a writer
was that he improved to the last; and the question of the
superiority of his later over his earlier manner may securely
be staked upon a comparison between the article on Johnson
in the *Edinburgh Review*, and the article on Johnson in the
"Encyclopædia Britannica." The latter of the two is, indeed,
a model of that which its eminent subject pronounced to be
the essential qualification of a biographer—the art of writing
trifles with dignity.*

Macaulay was under no temptation to overwrite himself;
for his time never hung heavy on his hands. He had a hundred devices for dissipating the monotony of his days. Now
that he had ceased to strain his faculties, he thought it necessary to assure himself from time to time that they were not
rusting, like an old Greek warrior who continued to exercise
in the gymnasium the vigor which he no longer expended in
the field. "I walked in the portico," he writes in October,
1857, "and learned by heart the noble fourth act of the
'Merchant of Venice.' There are four hundred lines, of
which I knew a hundred and fifty. I made myself perfect
master of the whole, the prose letter included, in two hours."
And again: "I learned the passage in which Lucretius represents Nature expostulating with men, who complain of the
general law of mortality. Very fine it is; but it strikes me
that the Epicureans exaggerated immensely the effect which

---

* A gentleman once observed to Dr. Johnson that he excelled his competitors in writing biography. "Sir," was the complacent reply, "I believe that is true. The dogs don't know how to write trifles with dignity."

religious terrors and the fear of future punishment had on
their contemporaries, for the purpose of exalting their master,
as having delivered mankind from a horrible mental slavery.
I see no trace of such feelings in any part of the literature
of those times except in these Epicurean declamations." "I
have pretty nearly learned all that I like best in Catullus.
He grows on me with intimacy. One thing he has—I do not
know whether it belongs to him or to something in myself—
but there are some chords of my mind which he touches as
nobody else does. The first lines of 'Miser Catulle;' the lines
to Cornificius, written evidently from a sick-bed;* and part
of the poem beginning 'Si qua recordanti,' affect me more
than I can explain. They always move me to tears." "I
have now gone through the first seven books of Martial, and
have learned about three hundred and sixty of the best lines.
His merit seems to me to lie, not in wit, but in the rapid succession of vivid images. I wish he were less nauseous. He
is as great a beast as Aristophanes. He certainly is a very
clever, pleasant writer. Sometimes he runs Catullus himself
hard. But, besides his indecency, his servility and his men-
dicancy disgust me. In his position, for he was a Roman
knight, something more like self-respect would have been becoming. I make large allowance for the difference of manners; but it never can have been *comme il faut* in any age or
nation for a man of note—an accomplished man—a man living
with the great—to be constantly asking for money, clothes,
and dainties, and to pursue with volleys of abuse those who
would give him nothing."

In September, 1857, Macaulay writes: "I have at odd moments been studying the 'Peerage.' I ought to be better informed about the assembly in which I am to sit." He soon
could repeat off book the entire roll of the House of Lords;
and a few days afterward comes the entry, "More exercise for
my memory—second titles." When he had done with the
"Peerage," he turned to the Cambridge, and then to the Ox-

---

* "Male est, Cornifici, tuo Catullo,
   Male est, mehercule, et laboriose."

ford, Calendar. "I have now," he says, "the whole of our university Fasti by heart; all, I mean, that is worth remembering. An idle thing, but I wished to try whether my memory is as strong as it used to be, and I perceive no decay."

"*June 1st*, 1858.—I am vexed to think I am losing my German. I resolved to win it back. No sooner said than done. I took Schiller's ' History of the War in the Netherlands' out into the garden, and read a hundred pages. I will do the same daily all the summer." Having found the want of Italian on his annual tours, Macaulay engaged a master to assist him in speaking the language. "We talked," he says, "an hour and a quarter. I got on wonderfully; much better than I at all expected." I well remember my uncle's account of the interview. As long as the lessons related to the ordinary colloquialisms of the road, the rail, and the hotel, Macaulay had little to say and much to learn; but, whenever the conversation turned upon politics or literature, his companion was fairly bewildered by the profusion of his somewhat archaic vocabulary. The preceptor could scarcely believe his ears when a pupil, who had to be taught the current expressions required for getting his luggage through the custom-house or his letters from the *poste restante*, suddenly fell to denouncing the French occupation of Rome in a torrent of phrases that might have come straight from the pen of Fra Paolo.

The zest with which Macaulay pursued the amusements that beguiled his solitary hours contributed not a little to his happiness and his equanimity. During his last two years he would often lay aside his book, and bury himself in financial calculations connected with the stock market, the revenue returns, the Civil Service estimates, and, above all, the clergy list. He would pass one evening in comparing the average duration of the lives of archbishops, prime ministers, and lord chancellors; and another in tracing the careers of the first half-dozen men in each successive mathematical tripos, in order to ascertain whether, in the race of the world, the senior wrangler generally contrived to keep ahead of his former competitors. In default of any other pastime, he would have recourse to the retrospect of old experiences and achievements, or would divert himself by giving the rein to the vagaries of his fancy. "I took up *Knight's Magazine* the other day, and, after an interval of perhaps thirty years, read a Roman novel which I wrote at Trinity. To be sure, I was a smart lad, but a sadly unripe scholar for such an undertaking."* And again : "I read my own writings during some hours, and was not ill-pleased, on the whole. Yet, alas! how short life and how long art! I feel as if I had just begun to understand how to write; and the probability is that I have very nearly done writing." "I find," he says in another place, "that I dream away a good deal of time now; not more, perhaps, than formerly; but formerly I dreamed my day-dreams chiefly while walking. Now I dream sitting or standing by my fire. I will write, if I live, a fuller disquisition than has ever yet been written on that strange habit—a good habit, in some respects. I, at least, impute to it a great part of my literary success."†

And so Macaulay dwelt at ease in his pleasant retreat, a classic in his own life-time. His critics, and still more his readers, honored him with a deferential indulgence which is seldom exhibited toward a contemporary. One or another of the magazines occasionally published an article reflecting upon his partiality as an historian; but he held his peace, and the matter, whatever it might be, soon died away. The world apparently refused to trouble itself with any misgivings that might impair the enjoyment which it derived from his pages. People were as little disposed to resent his disliking James, and admiring William, as they would have been to quarrel with Tacitus for making Tiberius a tyrant and Germanicus a hero. Macaulay, in his diary, mentions a circumstance illustrating the position which he already occupied in the popular

---

* The "Fragments of a Roman Tale" are printed in Macaulay's "Miscellaneous Writings."

† "I went yesterday to Weybridge," he says in a letter to Mr. Ellis. "We talked about the habit of building castles in the air, a habit in which Lady Trevelyan and I indulge beyond any people that I ever knew. I mentioned to George what, as far as I know, no critic has observed, that the Greeks called this habit κενὴ μακαρία (empty happiness)."

estimation. A gentleman moving in good, and even high, society—as thorough a man of the world as any in London—who had the misfortune to be a natural son, called on him in order to make a formal remonstrance on his having used the term "bastard" in his "History," and earnestly entreated him not to sanction so cruel an epithet with his immense authority.*

It may easily be supposed that Macaulay's literary celebrity attracted round him his full share of imitators and plagiarists, assailants and apologists, busybodies and mendicants. "A new number of the *Review*. There is an article which is a mocking-bird imitation of me. Somehow or other, the mimic can not catch the note, but many people would not be able to distinguish. Sometimes he borrows outright. 'Language so pure and holy that it would have become the lips of those angels—.' That is rather audacious. However, I shall not complain. A man should have enough to spare something for thieves." "I looked through ——'s two volumes. He is, I see, an imitator of me. But I am a very unsafe model. My manner is, I think, and the world thinks, on the whole, a good one; but it is very near to a very bad manner indeed, and those characteristics of my style which are most easily copied are the most questionable." "There are odd instances of folly and impertinence. A clergyman of the Scotch Episcopal Church is lecturing at Windsor. He wrote to me three weeks ago to ask the meaning of the allusion to St. Cecilia in my account of the trial of Warren Hastings. I answered him civilly, and he wrote to thank me. Now he writes again to say that he has forgotten a verse of my 'Horatius,' and begs me to write it for him; as if there were nobody in the kingdom except me to apply to. There is a fool at Wiesbaden who sent me, some days ago, a heap of execrable verses. I told him that they were bad, and advised him to take to some other pursuit. As examples illustrating my meaning, I pointed out half a dozen lines. Now he sends me twice as many verses, and

* The word in question is applied to the Duc de Maine in Macaulay's account of the siege of Namur in his twenty-first chapter.

begs me to review them. He has, he assures me, corrected the lines to which I objected. I have sent him back his second batch with a letter which he can not misunderstand." "A letter from a man in Scotland, who says that he wants to publish a novel, and that he will come up and show me the manuscript if I will send him fifty pounds. Really, I can get better novels cheaper." "What strange begging letters I receive! A fellow has written to me telling me that he is a painter, and adjuring me, as I love the fine arts, to hire or buy him a cow to paint from."

"A school-master at Cheltenham," writes Macaulay to his sister, "sent me two years and a half ago a wretched pamphlet about British India. In answering him, I pointed out two gross blunders into which he had fallen, and which, as he proposed to publish a small edition for the use of schools, I advised him to correct. My reward was that his book was advertised as 'revised and corrected by Lord Macaulay.' It is idle to be angry with people of this sort. They do after their kind. One might as well blame a fly for buzzing." "An article on me in *Blackwood.* The writer imagines that William the Third wrote his letters in English, and takes Coxe's translations for the original. A pretty fellow to set me to rights on points of history!" "I was worried by ——, who, in spite of repeated entreaties, pesters me with his officious defenses of my accuracy against all comers. Sometimes it is the *Saturday Review;* then Paget; and now it is *Blackwood.* I feel that I shall be provoked at last into saying something very sharp." "Some great fool has sent me a card printed with a distich, which he calls an impromptu on two bulky histories lately published:

> Two fabulists; how different the reward!
> One justly censured, t'other made a lord.

Whom he means by the other I have not the slightest notion. That a man should be stupid enough to take such a couplet to a printer and have it printed purely in order to give pain, which, after all, he does not give! I often think that an extensive knowledge of literary history is of inestimable value to a literary man; I mean as respects the regulating of his mind, the moderating of his hopes and of his fears, and the strengthening of his fortitude. I have had detractors enough to annoy me, if I had not known that no writer equally successful with myself has ever suffered so little from detraction; and that many writers, more deserving and less successful than myself, have excited envy which has appeared in the form of the most horrible calumnies. The proper answer to abuse is contempt, to which I am by nature sufficiently prone; and contempt does not show itself by contemptuous expressions."

Now and again, when Macaulay happened to be in a mood for criticism, he would fill a couple of pages in his journal with remarks suggested by the book which he had in reading at the time. A few of these little essays are worth preserving.

"I can not understand the mania of some people about De Foe. They think him a man of the first order of genius, and a paragon of virtue. He certainly wrote an excellent book—the first part of 'Robinson Crusoe'—one of those feats which can only be performed by the union of luck with ability. That awful solitude of a quarter of a century—that strange union of comfort, plenty, and security with the misery of loneliness — was my delight before I was five years old, and has been the delight of hundreds of thousands of boys. But what has De Foe done great except the first part of 'Robinson Crusoe?' The second part is poor in comparison. The 'History of the Plague' and the 'Memoirs of a Cavalier' are in one sense curious works of art. They are wonderfully like true histories; but, considered as novels, which they are, there is not much in them. He had undoubtedly a knack at making fiction look like truth. But is such a knack much to be admired? Is it not of the same sort with the knack of a painter who takes in the birds with his fruit? I have seen dead game painted in such a way that I thought the partridges and pheasants real; but surely such pictures do not rank high as works of art. Villemain, and before him Lord Chatham, were deceived by the 'Memoirs of a Cavalier;' but when those 'Memoirs' are known to be fictitious, what are they worth? How immeasurably inferior to 'Waverley,' or the 'Legend of Montrose,' or 'Old Mortality!' As to 'Moll Flanders,' 'Roxana,' and 'Captain Jack,' they are utterly wretched and nauseous; in no respect, that I can see, beyond the reach of Afra Behn.* As a political writer, De Foe is merely one of the crowd. He seems to have been an unprincipled hack, ready to take any side of any question. Of all writers he was the most unlucky in irony. Twice he was prosecuted for what he meant to be ironical; but he was so unskillful that every body understood him literally. Some of his tracts are worse than immoral; quite beastly. Altogether I do not like him."

"Lord Stanhope sent me the first volume of the Peel papers. I devoured them. The volume relates entirely to the Catholic question. It contains some interesting details which are new; but it leaves Peel where he was. I always noticed while he was alive, and I observe again in this his posthumous defense, an obstinate determination not to understand what the charge was which I, and others who agreed with me, brought against him. He always affected to think that we blamed him for his conduct in 1829, and he produced proofs of what we were perfectly ready to admit—that in 1829 the State would have been in great danger if the Catholic disabilities had not been removed. Now, what we blamed was his conduct in 1825, and still more in 1827. We said: 'Either you were blind not to foresee what was coming, or you acted culpably in not settling the question when it might have been settled without the disgrace of yielding to agitation and to the fear of insurrection; and you acted most culpably in deserting and persecuting

---

* "Take back your bonny Mrs. Behn," said Mrs. Keith, of Ravelstone, to her grand-nephew, Sir Walter Scott; "and, if you will take my advice, put her in the fire, for I found it impossible to get through the very first novel. But is it not a very odd thing that I, an old woman of eighty and upward, sitting alone, feel myself ashamed to read a book which, sixty years ago, I have heard read aloud for the amusement of large circles, consisting of the first and most creditable society in London?"

Canning.'   To this, which was our real point, he does not even allude.   He is a debater even in this book."*

"I walked in the garden, and read Cicero's speeches for Sextius and Cœlius, and the invective against Vatinius.   The egotism is perfectly intolerable.   I know nothing like it in literature.   The man's self-importance amounted to a monomania.   To me the speeches, tried by the standard of English forensic eloquence, seem very bad.   They have no tendency to gain a verdict.   They are fine lectures, fine declamations, excellent for Exeter Hall or the Music Room at Edinburgh; but not to be named with Scarlett's or Erskine's speeches, considered as speeches meant to convince and persuade juries. We ought to know, however, what the temper of those Roman tribunals was.   Perhaps a mere political harangue may have had an effect on the Forum which it could not have in the Court of King's Bench.   We ought also to know how far in some of these cases Hortensius and others had disposed of questions of evidence before Cicero's turn came.   The peroration seems to have been reserved for him.   But imagine a barrister now, defending a man accused of heading a riot at an election, telling the jury that he thought this an excellent opportunity of instructing the younger part of the audience in the galleries touching the distinction between Whigs and Tories; and then proceeding to give an historical dissertation of an hour on the Civil War, the Exclusion Bill, the Revolution, the Peace of Utrecht, and Heaven knows what!   Yet this is strictly analogous to what Cicero did in his defense of Sextius."

"I went to the Athenæum, and staid there two hours to read John Mill on Liberty and on Reform.   Much that is good in both.   What he says about individuality in the treatise on liberty is open, I think, to some criticism.   What is

---

* Macaulay writes elsewhere: "I read Guizot's 'Sir Robert Peel.'   Hardly quite worthy of Guizot's powers, I think; nor can it be accepted as a just estimate of Peel.   I could draw his portrait much better, but for many reasons I shall not do so."

meant by the complaint that there is no individuality now? Genius takes its own course, as it always did. Bolder invention was never known in science than in our time. The steam-ship, the steam-carriage, the electric telegraph, the gaslights, the new military engines, are instances. Geology is quite a new true science. Phrenology is quite a new false one. Whatever may be thought of the theology, the metaphysics, the political theories of our time, boldness and novelty are not what they want. Comtism, Saint-Simonianism, Fourierism, are absurd enough, but surely they are not indications of a servile respect for usage and authority. Then the clairvoyance, the spirit-rapping, the table-turning, and all those other dotages and knaveries, indicate rather a restless impatience of the beaten paths than a stupid determination to plod on in those paths. Our lighter literature, as far as I know it, is spasmodic and eccentric. Every writer seems to aim at doing something odd—at defying all rules and canons of criticism. The metre must be queer; the diction queer. So great is the taste for oddity that men who have no recommendation but oddity hold a high place in vulgar estimation. I therefore do not at all like to see a man of Mill's excellent abilities recommending eccentricity as a thing almost good in itself—as tending to prevent us from sinking into that Chinese, that Byzantine, state which I should agree with him in considering as a great calamity. He is really crying ' Fire !' in Noah's flood."

"I read the *Quarterly Reviews* of 1830, 1831, and 1832, and was astonished by the poorness and badness of the political articles. I do not think that this is either personal or political prejudice in me, though I certainly did not like Southey, and though I had a strong antipathy to Croker, who were the two chief writers. But I see the merit of many of Southey's writings with which I am far from agreeing — 'Espriella's Letters,' for example, and the 'Life of Wesley;' and I see the merit of the novels of Theodore Hook, whom I held in greater abhorrence than even Croker, stuffed as those novels are with scurrility against my political friends. Nay, I can see merit in Warren's 'Ten Thousand a Year.' I therefore believe that my estimate of these political papers in the *Quarterly Review* is a fair one; and to me they seem to be mere trash—absurd perversions of history; parallels which show no ingenuity, and from which no instruction can be derived; predictions which the event has singularly falsified; abuse substituted for argument; and not one paragraph of wit or eloquence. It is all forgotten, all gone to the dogs. The nonsense which Southey talks about political enonomy is enough to settle my opinion of his understanding. He says that no man of sense ever troubles himself about such pseudo-scientific questions as what rent is, or what wages are. Surely he could not be such a dunce as not to know that a part of the produce of a landed estate goes to the proprietor, and a part to the cultivator; and he must, unless he had a strange sort of skull, have supposed that there was some law or other which regulated the distribution of the produce between these parties. And if there be such a law, how can it be unworthy of a man of sense to try to find out what it is? Can any inquiry be more important to the welfare of society? Croker is below Southey; for Southey had a good style, and Croker had nothing but italics and capitals as substitutes for eloquence and reason."

"I read a great deal of the 'Memoirs of Southey' by his son; little more than Southey's own letters, for the most part. I do not know how it happened that I never read the book before. It has not at all altered my opinion of Southey. A good father, husband, brother, friend, but prone to hate people whom he did not know, solely on account of differences of opinion, and in his hatred singularly bitter and rancorous. Then he was arrogant beyond any man in literary history; for his self-conceit was proof against the severest admonitions. The utter failure of one of his books only confirmed him in his opinion of its excellence. Then he had none of that dissatisfaction with his own performances which I, perhaps because I have a great deal of it, am prone to believe to be a good sign. Southey says, some time after 'Madoc' had been published, and when the first ardor of composition must have abated, that the execution is perfect; that it can not be better. I have had infinitely greater success as a writer than Southey, and, though I have not written a fifth part, not a tenth part, of what he wrote, have made more thousands by literature than he made hundreds. And yet I can truly say that I never read again the most popular passages of my own works without painfully feeling how far my execution has fallen short of the standard which is in my mind. He says that 'Thalaba' is equal or superior to the 'Orlando Furioso,' and that it is the greatest poem that has appeared during ages; and this over and over again, when nobody would read it, and when the copies were heaped up in the book-sellers' garrets. His 'History of Brazil' is to be immortal—to be a mine of wealth to his family under an improved system of copyright. His 'Peninsular War,' of which I never could get through the first volume, is to live forever. To do him justice, he had a fine manly spirit where money was concerned. His conduct about Chatterton and Kirke White, at a time when a guinea was an object to himself, was most honorable. I could forgive him a great deal for it."

Macaulay had a very slight acquaintance with the works of some among the best writers of his own generation. He was not fond of new lights, unless they had been kindled at the ancient beacons; and he was apt to prefer a third-rate author, who had formed himself after some recognized model, to a man of high genius whose style and method were strikingly different from any thing that had gone before. In books, as in people and places, he loved that, and that only, to which he had been accustomed from boyhood upward.* Very few

---

* The remarks in Macaulay's journal on the "History of Civilization" curiously illustrate the spirit in which he approached a new author. What he liked best in Buckle was that he had some of the faults of Warburton. "*March 24th*, 1858.—I read Buckle's book all day, and got to the end, skipping of course. A man of talent and of a good deal of reading, but paradoxical and incoherent. He is eminently an anticipator, as Bacon would have said. He wants to make a system before he has got the ma-

among the students of Macaulay will have detected the intensity, and in some cases (it must be confessed) the willfulness, of his literary conservatism; for, with the instinctive self-restraint of a great artist, he permitted no trace of it to appear in his writings. In his character of a responsible critic, he carefully abstained from giving expression to prejudices in which, as a reader, he freely indulged. Those prejudices injured nobody but himself; and the punishment which befell him, from the very nature of the case, was exactly proportioned to the offense. To be blind to the merits of a great author is a sin which brings its own penalty, and in Macaulay's instance that penalty was severe indeed. Little as he was aware of it, it was no slight privation that one who had by heart the "Battle of Marathon," as told by Herodotus, and the "Raising of the Siege of Syracuse," as told by Thucydides, should have passed through life without having felt the glow which Mr. Carlyle's story of the charge across the ravine at Dunbar could not fail to awake even in a Jacobite; that one who so keenly relished the exquisite trifling of Plato should never have tasted the description of Coleridge's talk in the "Life of John Sterling"—a passage which yields to nothing of its own class in the "Protagoras" or the "Symposium;" that one who eagerly and minutely studied all that Lessing has written on art, or Goethe on poetry, should have left unread Mr. Ruskin's comparison between the landscape of the "Odyssey" and the landscape of "The Divine Comedy," or his analysis of the effect produced on the imagination by long-continued familiarity with the aspect of the Campanile of Giotto.

Great, beyond all question, was the intellectual enjoyment that Macaulay forfeited by his unwillingness to admit the excellence of any thing which had been written in bold defiance of the old canons; but, heavy as the sacrifice was, he could readily afford to make it. With his omnivorous and insatia-

---

terials; and he has not the excuse which Aristotle had, of having an eminently systematizing mind. The book reminds me perpetually of the 'Divine Legation.' I could draw the parallel out far."

ble appetite for books there was, indeed, little danger that he would ever be at a loss for something to read. A few short extracts, taken at random from the last volume of his journals, will sufficiently indicate how extensive and diversified were the regions of literature over which he roved at will. " I turned over Philo, and compared his narrative with Josephus. It is amusing to observe with what skill those Jews, trained in Greek learning, exhibited the philosophical side of their religion to the Pagan scholars and statesmen, and kept out of sight the ceremonial part. It was just the contrary, I imagine, with the lower class of Jews, who became, in some sense, the spiritual directors of silly women at Rome." " I read a good deal of ' Fray Gerundio.' A good book. The traits of manners are often interesting. There is something remarkable in the simple plenty and joyousness of the life of the rustics of Old Castile." " I read some of a novel about sporting — a Mr. Sponge the hero. It was a new world to me, so I bore with the hasty writing, and was entertained." " I read some of Tieck—the Brothers, and the preface to the collected works. He complains that his countrymen are slow to take a joke. He should consider that the jokes which he and some of his brother writers are in the habit of producing are not laughing matters. Then Sir Walter Scott's Life. I had ' Rokeby,' out, and turned it over. Poor work; and yet there are gleams of genius few and far between. What a blunder to make the scenery the foreground, and the human actors the background, of a picture! In ' The Lay ' the human actors stand out as they should, and the Aill, and the Tweed, and Melrose Abbey are in proper subordination. Even in ' The Lady of the Lake,' Loch Katrine does not throw Fitzjames and Roderic into the shade; but ' Rokeby ' is primarily a descriptive poem like ' Grongar Hill.' There was some foundation for Moore's sarcastic remark that Scott meant to do all the gentlemen's seats from Edinburgh to London. The only good thing in the poem is the Buccaneer." " I read 'Ælian' for the first time. Odd that it should be for the first time. I dispatched the whole volume in a few hours, skimming and reading sometimes the Greek and sometimes the Latin translation, which

I thought more than usually well written. The most interesting fact which I learned from this very miscellaneous collection of information was that there were said to be translations of Homer into the Persian and Indian languages, and that those translations were sung by the barbarians. I had never heard this mentioned. The thing is really not impossible. The conquests of Alexander must have made the Greek language well known to men whose mother-tongue was the Persian or the Sanskrit. I wish to Heaven that the translations could be found."

Some of the great metaphysical philosophers, both ancient and modern, were among the authors with whom Macaulay was most familiar; but he read them for the pleasure of admiring the ingenuity of their arguments or the elegance of their literary manner, and not from any sympathy with the subject-matter of their works. He was, in fact, very much inclined toward the opinion expressed by Voltaire in "Zadig:" "Il savait de la métaphysique ce qu'on a su dans tous les âges —c'est à dire, fort peu de chose." But there was another field of inquiry and discussion in which he was never tired of ranging. He had a strong and enduring predilection for religious speculation and controversy, and was widely and profoundly read in ecclesiastical history. His partiality for studies of this nature is proved by the full and elaborate notes with which he has covered the margin of such books as Warburton's "Julian," Middleton's "Free Inquiry," Middleton's "Letters to Venn and Waterland," and all the rest of the crop of polemical treatises which the "Free Inquiry" produced.* But no-

---

* "Middleton," writes Macaulay, "does not shine in any of his strictly controversial pieces. He is too querulous and egotistical. Above all, he is not honest. He knew that what alarmed the Church was not his conclusion, but the arguments by which he arrived at that conclusion. His conclusion might be just, and yet Christianity might be of Divine origin; but his arguments seem to be quite as applicable to the miracles related by St. Luke as to those related by Jerome. He was in a deplorable predicament. He boasted of his love of truth and of his courage, and yet he was paltering and shamming through the whole controversy. He should have made up his mind from the beginning whether he had the courage to face obloquy

where are there such numerous and deeply marked traces of his passion for Church history as in the pages of Strype's biographies of the bishops who played a leading part in the English Reformation. Those grim folios of six generations back —the Lives of Cranmer, and Grindal, and Whitgift, and Parker—acquire all the interest of a contemporary narrative if read with the accompaniment of Macaulay's vivid and varied comments. When, at the commencement of the "Life of Cranmer," Strype apologizes for employing phraseology which even in his own day was obsolete and uncouth, he obtained an easy pardon from his assiduous student. " I like," says Macaulay, " his old-fashioned style. He writes like a man who lived with the people of an earlier age. He had thoroughly imbued himself with the spirit of the sixteenth century."* And again: " Strype was an honest man and a most valuable writer. Perhaps no person with so slender abilities has done so much to improve our knowledge of English history." Somewhat later in the same volume, when Gardiner first appears upon the scene, Macaulay writes: " Gardiner had very great vices. He was a dissembler and a persecutor. But he was, on the whole, the first public man of his generation in England. He had, I believe, a real love for his country. He showed a greater respect for Parliaments than any statesman of that time. He opposed the Spanish match. When forced to consent to it, he did his best to obtain such terms as might secure the independence of the realm. He was a far more estimable man than Cranmer." Of Latimer he says: " He was the Cobbett of the

---

and abuse, to give up all hopes of preferment, and to speak plainly out. If, from selfish motives (or, as I rather believe and hope, from a real conviction that by attacking the Christian religion he should do more harm than good to mankind), he determined to call himself a Christian, and to respect the sacred books, he should have kept altogether out of a controversy which inevitably brought him into the necessity of either declaring himself an infidel, or resorting to a thousand dishonest shifts, injurious to his arguments and discreditable to his character."

* Strype himself was well enough aware that his style was suited to his subject. " In truth," he writes, " he that is a lover of antiquity loves the very language and phrases of antiquity."

Reformation, with more honesty than Cobbett, and more courage; but very like him in the character of his understanding." At the foot of a fine letter addressed by Ridley from his prison in "Bocardo, in Oxenford, to his former steward who had complied with the Romish religion," Macaulay notes "A stouthearted, honest, brave man." Grindal he more than once pronounces to be "the best Archbishop of Canterbury since the Reformation, except Tillotson." Indeed, it may safely be asserted that, in one corner or another of Macaulay's library, there is in existence his estimate of every famous or notorious English prelate from the beginning of the sixteenth to the end of the eighteenth century. The most concise of these sketches of episcopal character may be found in his copy of the letters from Warburton to Hurd, the first of which is headed in pencil with the words, "Bully to Sneak."

Valuable, indeed, is the privilege of following Macaulay through his favorite volumes, where every leaf is plentifully besprinkled with the annotations of the most lively of scholiasts; but it would be an injustice toward his reputation to separate the commentary from the text, and present it to the public in a fragmentary condition. Such a process could give but a feeble idea of the animation and humor of that species of running conversation which he frequently kept up with his author for whole chapters together. Of all the memorials of himself which he has left behind him, these dialogues with the dead are the most characteristic. The energy of his remonstrances, the heartiness of his approbation, the contemptuous vehemence of his censure, the eagerness with which he urges and reiterates his own opinions, are such as to make it at times difficult to realize that his remarks are addressed to people who died centuries, or perhaps tens of centuries, ago. But the writer of a book which had lived was always alive for Macaulay. This sense of personal relation between himself and the men of the past increased as years went on—as he became less able and willing to mix with the world, and more and more thrown back upon the society which he found in his library. His way of life would have been deemed solitary by others, but it was not solitary to him. While he had a volume in his

hands he never could be without a quaint companion to laugh
with or laugh at, an adversary to stimulate his combativeness,
a counselor to suggest wise or lofty thoughts, and a friend
with whom to share them.   When he opened for the tenth or
fifteenth time some history, or memoir, or romance—every in-
cident and almost every sentence of which he had by heart—
his feeling was precisely that which we experience on meeting
an old comrade, whom we like all the better because we know
the exact lines on which his talk will run.   There was no society in London so agreeable that Macaulay would have preferred it at breakfast or at dinner to the company of Sterne,
or Fielding, or Horace Walpole, or Boswell; and there were
many less distinguished authors with whose productions he
was very well content to cheer his repasts.   "I read," he says,
"Henderson's Iceland at breakfast—a favorite breakfast book
with me.   Why?   How oddly we are made!   Some books
which I never should dream of opening at dinner please me
at breakfast, and *vice versâ.*"   In choosing what he should
take down from his shelves he was guided at least as much by
whim as by judgment.   There were certain bad writers whose
vanity and folly had a flavor of peculiarity which was irresist-
ibly attractive to Macaulay.   In August, 1859, he says to Lady
Trevelyan: "The books which I had sent to the binder are
come; and Miss Seward's letters are in a condition to bear
twenty more reperusals."   But, amidst the infinite variety of
lighter literature with which he beguiled his leisure, "Pride
and Prejudice," and the five sister novels, remained without a
rival in his affections.   He never for a moment wavered in his
allegiance to Miss Austen.   In 1858 he notes in his journal:
"If I could get materials, I really would write a short life of
that wonderful woman, and raise a little money to put up a
monument to her in Winchester Cathedral."   Some of his old
friends may remember how he prided himself on a correction
of his own in the first page of "Persuasion," which he maintained to be worthy of Bentley, and which undoubtedly fulfills
all the conditions required to establish the credit of an emendation; for, without the alteration of a word, or even of a letter, it turns into perfectly intelligible common-sense a passage

which has puzzled, or which ought to have puzzled, two generations of Miss Austen's readers.*

Of the feelings which he entertained toward the great minds of by-gone ages it is not for any one except himself to speak. He has told us how his debt to them was incalculable; how they guided him to truth; how they filled his mind with noble and graceful images; how they stood by him in all vicissitudes—comforters in sorrow, nurses in sickness, companions in solitude, "the old friends who are never seen with new faces; who are the same in wealth and in poverty, in glory and in obscurity." Great as were the honors and possessions which Macaulay acquired by his pen, all who knew him were well aware that the titles and rewards which he gained by his own works were as nothing in the balance as compared with the pleasure which he derived from the works of others. That knowledge has largely contributed to the tenderness with which he has been treated by writers whose views on books, and events, and politics past and present, differ widely from his own. It has been well said that even the most hostile of his critics can not help being "awed and touched by his wonderful devotion to literature." And, while his ardent and sincere passion for letters has thus served as a protection to his memory, it was likewise the source of much which calls for admiration in his character and conduct. The confidence with which he could rely upon intellectual pursuits for occupation and amusement assisted him not a little to preserve that dignified composure with which he met all the changes and chances of his public career, and that spirit of cheerful and patient endurance which sustained him through years of broken health and enforced seclusion. He had no pressing need to seek for excitement and applause abroad, when he had

---

* A slight change in the punctuation effects all that is required. According to Macaulay, the sentence was intended by its author to run thus: "There, any unwelcome sensations, arising from domestic affairs, changed naturally into pity and contempt as he turned over the almost endless creations of the last century; and there, if every other leaf were powerless, he could read his own history with an interest which never failed. This was the page at which the favorite volume opened—"

beneath his own roof a never-failing store of exquisite enjoyment. That "invincible love of reading," which Gibbon declared that he would not exchange for the treasures of India, was with Macaulay a main element of happiness in one of the happiest lives that it has ever fallen to the lot of a biographer to record.

CHAPTER XV.

1859.

Melancholy Anticipations.—Visit to the English Lakes and to Scotland.—
Extracts from Macaulay's Journal.—His Death and Funeral.

WHEN the year 1859 opened, it seemed little likely that any
event was at hand which would disturb the tranquil course of
Macaulay's existence. His ailments, severe as they were, did
not render him discontented on his own account, nor diminish
the warmth of his interest in the welfare of those who were
around him. Toward the close of the preceding year, his niece
Margaret Trevelyan had been married to the son of his old
friend, Sir Henry Holland; an event which her uncle regarded with heart-felt satisfaction. Mr. Holland resided in London; and consequently the marriage, so far from depriving
Macaulay of one whom he looked on as a daughter, gave him
another household where he was as much at home as in his
own. But a most unexpected circumstance now occurred
which changed in a moment the whole complexion of his life.
Early in January, 1859, the governorship of Madras was offered to my father. He accepted the post, and sailed for India in the third week of February. My mother remained in
England for a while; but she was to follow her husband
after no very long interval, and Macaulay was fully convinced
that when he and his sister parted they would part forever.
Though he derived his belief from his own sensations, and not
from any warning of physicians, he was none the less firmly
persuaded that the end was now not far off. "I took leave of
Trevelyan," he says on the 18th of February. "He said,
'You have always been a most kind brother to me.' I certainly tried to be so. Shall we ever meet again? I do not

expect it. My health is better; but another sharp winter would probably finish me." In another place he writes: "I am no better. This malady tries me severely. However, I bear up. As to my temper, it never has been soured, and, while I keep my understanding, will not, I think, be soured, by evils for which it is evident that no human being is responsible. To be angry with relations and servants because you suffer something which they did not inflict, and which they are desirous to alleviate, is unworthy, not merely of a good man, but of a rational being. Yet I see instances enough of such irritability to fear that I may be guilty of it. But I will take care. I have thought several times of late that the last scene of the play was approaching. I should wish to act it simply, but with fortitude and gentleness united."

The prospect of a separation from one with whom he had lived in close and uninterrupted companionship since her childhood and his own early manhood—a prospect darkened by the thought that his last hour would surely come when she was thousands of miles away—was a trial which weighed heavily on Macaulay's sinking health. He endured it manfully, and almost silently; but his spirits never recovered the blow. During the spring and summer of 1859 his journal contains a few brief but significant allusions to the state of his feelings; one of which, and one only, may fitly be inserted here. "*July* 11*th*, 1859.—A letter from Hannah; very sad and affectionate. I answered her. There is a pleasure even in this exceeding sorrow; for it brings out the expression of love with a tenderness which is wanting in ordinary circumstances. But the sorrow is very, very bitter. The Duke of Argyll called, and left me the sheets of a forthcoming poem of Tennyson. I like it extremely—notwithstanding some faults, extremely. The parting of Lancelot and Guinivere, her penitence, and Arthur's farewell, are all very affecting. I cried over some passages; but I am now ἀρτίδακρυς,* as Medea says."

Toward the end of July my uncle spent a week with us at Lowood Hotel, on the shore of Windermere; and thence ac-

---

* "With the tears near the eyes."

companied my mother and my younger sister on a fortnight's tour through the Western Highlands, and by Stirling to Edinburgh. Every stage of the journey brought some fresh proof of the eager interest which his presence aroused in the minds of his fellow-countrymen, to whom his face and figure were very much less familiar than is usual in the case of a man of his eminence and reputation. He now so rarely emerged from his retirement, that whenever he appeared abroad he was attended by a respect which gratified and a curiosity which did not annoy him. " I went the day before yesterday," he writes to Mr. Ellis, " to Grasmere church-yard, and saw Wordsworth's tomb. I thought of announcing my intention of going, and issuing guinea tickets to people who wished to see me there; for a Yankee who was here a few days ago, and heard that I was expected, said that he would give the world to see that most sublime of all spectacles, Macaulay standing by the grave of Wordsworth." " In Scotland," my mother writes, " his reception was everywhere most enthusiastic. He was quickly recognized on steamers and at railway stations. At Tarbet we were escorted down to the boat by the whole household; and, while they surrounded your uncle, finding a seat for him, and making him comfortable, I sat modestly in the shade next a young woman, who called a man to her, and asked who they were making such a fuss about. He replied that it was the great Lord Macaulay, who wrote the 'History.' 'Oh,' said she, 'I thought it was considered only a romance!' However, she added herself to the group of starers. When we went to Dr. Guthrie's church at Edinburgh, the congregation made a line for us through which to walk away." At the hotels, one not uncommon form of doing Macaulay honor consisted in serving up a better dinner than had been ordered—no easy matter when he was catering for others beside himself—and then refusing to accept payment for his entertainment." At Inverary he writes: " The landlord insisted on treating us to our drive of yesterday, but I was peremptory. I was half sorry afterward, and so was Hannah, who, at the time, took my part. It is good to accept as well as to give. My feeling is too much that of Calderon's hero:

Cómo sabrá pedir
Quien solo ha sabido dar ?*

I shrink too much from receiving services which I love to render."

During this visit to the North my uncle was still the same agreeable traveling companion that we had always known him; with the same readiness to please and be pleased, and the same sweet and even temper. When one of us happened to be alone with him, there sometimes was a touch of melancholy about his conversation which imparted to it a singular charm; but when the whole of our little circle was assembled, he showed himself as ready as ever to welcome any topic which promised to afford material for amusing and abundant talk. I especially remember our sitting at the window through the best part of an afternoon, looking across Windermere, and drawing up under his superintendence a list of forty names for an imaginary English academy. The result of our labors, in the shape in which it now lies before me, bears evident marks of having been a work of compromise, and can not, therefore, be presented to the world as a faithful and authentic expression of Macaulay's estimate of his literary and scientific contemporaries.

In a letter to Mr. Ellis, written on the 24th of October, 1859, Macaulay says: "I have been very well in body since we parted; but in mind I have suffered much, and the more because I have had to put a force upon myself in order to appear cheerful. It is at last settled that Hannah and Alice are to go to Madras in February. I can not deny that it is right; and my duty is to avoid whatever can add to the pain which they suffer. But I am very unhappy. However, I read, and write, and contrive to forget my sorrow for whole hours. But it recurs, and will recur."

The trial which now at no distant date awaited Macaulay was one of the heaviest that could by any possibility have been allotted to him, and he summoned all his resources in

---

* "How will he know how to ask, who has only known how to give ?"

order to meet it with firmness and resignation. He henceforward made it a duty to occupy his mind, and fortify his powers of self-control, by hard and continuous intellectual exertion. "I must drive away," he says, "these thoughts by writing;" and with diminished strength he returned to his labors, purposing not to relax them until he had completed another section of the "History." In October, he tells Mr. Longman that he is working regularly, and that he designs to publish the next volume by itself. On the 14th of December he writes: "Finished at last the session of 1699–1700. There is a good deal in what I have written that is likely to interest readers. At any rate, this employment is a good thing for myself, and will be a better soon when I shall have little else left." Influenced by the same settled determination forcibly to divert the current of his reflections from the sombre channel in which they were now prone to run, Macaulay, even during his hours of leisure, began to read on system. On the second day after he had received the unwelcome announcement of my mother's plans with regard to India, he commenced the perusal of Nichols's "Literary Anecdotes"— a ponderous row of nine volumes, each containing seven or eight hundred closely printed pages. He searched and sifted this vast repertory of eighteenth-century erudition and gossip with a minute diligence such as few men have the patience to bestow upon a book which they do not intend to re-edit; correcting blunders, supplying omissions, stigmatizing faults in taste and grammar, and enriching every blank space which invited his pencil with a profusion of valuable and entertaining comments. Progressing steadily at the rate of a volume a week, he had read and annotated the entire work between the 17th day of October and the 21st of December.

During this period of his life Macaulay certainly was least unhappy when alone in his own library;* for, in the society of those whom he was about to lose, the enjoyment of the moment could not fail to be overclouded by sad presentiments.

---

* On the 16th of October he notes in his diary: "I read, and found, as I have always found, that an interesting book acted as an anodyne."

" I could almost wish," he writes, " that what is to be were to be immediately. I dread the next four months more than even the months which will follow the separation. This prolonged parting—this slow sipping of the vinegar and the gall —is terrible." The future was indeed dark before him; but God, who had so blessed him, dealt kindly with him even to the end, and his burden was not permitted to be greater than his strength could bear.

"*Friday, December* 16*th.*—From this morning I reckon some of the least agreeable days of my life. The physic was necessary, but I believe it brought me very low. The frost was more intense than ever, and arrested my circulation.* Bating the irregularity of the pulse, I suffered all that I suffered when, in 1852, I was forced to go to Clifton. The depression, the weakness, the sinking of the heart, the incapacity to do any thing that required steady exertion, were very distressing. To write, though but a few words, is disagreeable to me. However, I read German, Latin, and English, and got through the day tolerably."

"*December* 17*th.*—Very hard frost. The weather has seldom been colder in this latitude. I sent for Martin, and told him my story.† He says that there is no organic affection of the heart, but that the heart is weak."

"*December* 19*th.*—Still intense frost. I could hardly use my razor for the palpitation of the heart. I feel as if I were twenty years older since last Thursday—as if I were dying of old age. I am perfectly ready, and shall never be readier. A month more of such days as I have been passing of late would make me impatient to get to my little narrow crib, like a weary factory child."

" *Wednesday, December* 21*st.*—Every thing changed; the frost and frozen snow all gone; heavy rain falling; clouds from the south-west driving fast through the sky. The sun came, and it was so mild that I ventured into the veranda; but I was far from well. My two doctors, Watson and Martin, came to consult. They agreed in pronouncing my complaint a heart-complaint simply. If the heart acted with force, all the plagues would vanish together. They may be right. I am certainly very poorly—weak as a child. Yet I am less nervous than usual. I have shed no tears during some days, though with me tears ask only leave to flow, as poor Cowper says. I am sensible of no intellectual decay—not the smallest."

---

* Macaulay's habitual ill health had been aggravated by a walk which he took, in a bitter east wind, from the British Museum to the Athenæum Club.

† Sir Ranald Martin had been Macaulay's physician in Calcutta.

"*Friday, December 23d.*—In the midst of life—this morning I had scarcely left my closet when down came the ceiling in large masses. I should certainly have been stunned, probably killed, if I had staid a few minutes longer. I staid by my fire, not exerting myself to write, but making Christmas calculations, and reading. An odd declaration by Dickens, that he did not mean Leigh Hunt by Harold Skimpole. Yet he owns that he took the light externals of the character from Leigh Hunt, and surely it is by those light externals that the bulk of mankind will always recognize character. Besides, it is to be observed that the vices of Harold Skimpole are vices to which Leigh Hunt had, to say the least, some little leaning, and which the world generally imputed to him most unsparingly. That he had loose notions of *meum* and *tuum*, that he had no high feeling of independence, that he had no sense of obligation, that he took money wherever he could get it, that he felt no gratitude for it, that he was just as ready to defame a person who had relieved his distress as a person who had refused him relief—these were things which, as Dickens must have known, were said, truly or falsely, about Leigh Hunt, and had made a deep impression on the public mind. Indeed, Leigh Hunt had said himself: 'I have some peculiar notions about money. They will be found to involve considerable difference of opinion with the community, particularly in a commercial country. I have not that horror of being under obligation which is thought an essential refinement in money matters.' This is Harold Skimpole all over. How, then, could D. doubt that H. S. would be supposed to be a portrait of L. H.?"

At this point Macaulay's journal comes to an abrupt close. Two days afterward he wrote to Mr. Ellis: "The physicians think me better; but there is little change in my sensations. The day before yesterday I had a regular fainting-fit, and lay quite insensible. I wish that I had continued to be so; for if death be no more—. Up I got, however; and the doctors agree that the circumstance is altogether unimportant." Nevertheless, from this time forward there was a marked change for the worse in Macaulay. "I spent Christmas-day with him," my mother writes. "He talked very little, and was constantly dropping asleep. We had our usual Christmas dinner with him, and the next day I thought him better. Never, as long as I live, can I lose the sense of misery that I ever left him after Christmas-day. But I did not feel alarmed. I thought the accident to the ceiling had caused a shock to his nerves from which he was gradually recovering; and, when we were alone together, he gave way to so much emotion, that, while he was so weak, I rather avoided being long with him." It may give occasion for surprise that Macaulay's relatives entertained no apprehension of his being in grave and immediate danger; but the truth is that his evident unhappiness (the outward manifestations of which, during the last few days of his life, he had no longer the force to suppress) was so constantly present to the minds of us all that our attention was diverted from his bodily condition. His silence and depression—due, in reality, to physical causes—were believed by us to proceed almost entirely from mental distress.

In a contemporary account of Macaulay's last illness* it is related that on the morning of Wednesday, the 28th of December, he mustered strength to dictate a letter addressed to a poor curate, inclosing twenty-five pounds; after signing which letter he never wrote his name again. Late in the afternoon of the same day I called at Holly Lodge, intending to propose myself to dinner; an intention which was abandoned as soon as I entered the library. My uncle was sitting, with his head bent forward on his chest, in a languid and drowsy reverie. The first number of the *Cornhill Magazine* lay unheeded before him, open at the first page of Thackeray's story of "Lovel the Widower." He did not utter a word, except in answer; and the only one of my observations that at this distance of time I can recall suggested to him painful and pathetic reflections which altogether destroyed his self-command.

On hearing my report of his state, my mother resolved to spend the night at Holly Lodge. She had just left the drawing-room to make her preparations for the visit (it being, I

---

* This account, which is very brief, but apparently authentic, is preserved among the Marquis of Lansdowne's papers. Macaulay writes, on the 19th of August, 1859: "I grieve to hear about my dear old friend, Lord Lansdowne. I owe more to him than to any man living; and he never seemed to be sensible that I owed him any thing. I shall look anxiously for the next accounts." Lord Lansdowne recovered from this illness, and survived Macaulay more than three years.

suppose, a little before seven in the evening), when a servant arrived with an urgent summons. As we drove up to the porch of my uncle's house, the maids ran, crying, out into the darkness to meet us, and we knew that all was over. We found him in the library, seated in his easy-chair, and dressed as usual; with his book on the table beside him, still open at the same page. He had told his butler that he should go to bed early, as he was very tired. The man proposed his lying on the sofa. He rose as if to move, sat down again, and ceased to breathe. He died as he had always wished to die— without pain; without any formal farewell; preceding to the grave all whom he loved; and leaving behind him a great and honorable name, and the memory of a life every action of which was as clear and transparent as one of his own sentences. It would be unbecoming in me to dwell upon the regretful astonishment with which the tidings of his death were received wherever the English language is read; and quite unnecessary to describe the enduring grief of those upon whom he had lavished his affection, and for whom life had been brightened by daily converse with his genius, and ennobled by familiarity with his lofty and upright example. "We have lost" (so my mother wrote) "the light of our home, the most tender, loving, generous, unselfish, devoted of friends. What he was to me for fifty years how can I tell? What a world of love he poured out upon me and mine! The blank, the void, he has left—filling, as he did, so entirely both heart and intellect—no one can understand. For who ever knew such a life as mine passed as the cherished companion of such a man?"

He was buried in Westminster Abbey, on the 9th of January, 1860. The pall was borne by the Duke of Argyll, Lord John Russell, Lord Stanhope, Lord Carlisle, Bishop Wilberforce, Sir David Dundas, Sir Henry Holland, Dean Milman, Sir George Cornewall Lewis, the Lord Chancellor, and the Speaker of the House of Commons. "A beautiful sunrise," wrote Lord Carlisle. "The pall-bearers met in the Jerusalem Chamber. The last time I had been there on a like errand was at Canning's funeral. The whole service and ceremony were in the highest degree solemn and impressive. All befitted the man and the occasion."

He rests with his peers in Poet's Corner, near the west wall of the south transept. There, amidst the tombs of Johnson, and Garrick, and Handel, and Goldsmith, and Gay, stands conspicuous the statue of Addison; and at the feet of Addison lies the stone which bears this inscription:

THOMAS BABINGTON, LORD MACAULAY.

BORN AT ROTHLEY TEMPLE, LEICESTERSHIRE,
OCTOBER 25TH, 1800.
DIED AT HOLLY LODGE, CAMPDEN HILL,
DECEMBER 28TH, 1859.

"HIS BODY IS BURIED IN PEACE,
BUT HIS NAME LIVETH FOR EVERMORE."

THE END.

153659